The Baseball Novel

The Baseball Novel

A History and Annotated Bibliography of Adult Fiction

Noel Schraufnagel

McFarland & Company, Inc., Publishers
Jefferson, North Carolina, and London

LIBRARY OF CONGRESS CATALOGUING-IN-PUBLICATION DATA

Schraufnagel, Noel.
    The baseball novel : a history and annotated bibliography of adult fiction / Noel Schraufnagel.
        p.   cm.
    Includes bibliographical references and index.

    ISBN 978-0-7864-3557-9
    softcover : 50# alkaline paper

    1. American fiction — Bibliography. 2. Baseball stories — Bibliography. 3. Baseball stories — Stories, plots, etc. I. Title.
Z1231.F4S37   2008
[PS374.B37]   2008020879

British Library cataloguing data are available

©2008 Noel Schraufnagel. All rights reserved

No part of this book may be reproduced or transmitted in any form or by any means, electronic or mechanical, including photocopying or recording, or by any information storage and retrieval system, without permission in writing from the publisher.

Front cover background image ©2008 Shutterstock

Manufactured in the United States of America

McFarland & Company, Inc., Publishers
  Box 611, Jefferson, North Carolina 28640
    www.mcfarlandpub.com

Again to Darlene, Darcy, and Dana
(plus Shane, Noelle, and Hailee)

Table of Contents

Preface 1

I — The History of the Baseball Novel 3
II — The Novels, Year by Year 35

Appendix A: Mystery Novels 209
Appendix B: Science Fiction and Fantasy Novels 215
Appendix C: Novels That Explore Race, Ethnicity, Gender and Class 220
Appendix D: Best Baseball Novels by Year 225
Appendix E: Chronological List of Titles 227
Index 239

Preface

I enjoyed teaching a class called Sports in Literature. It dealt mostly with poetry and short stories devoted to football, basketball, and baseball. The literature of baseball, though, dominated in both quantity and quality, and eventually the famous novels of Ring Lardner, Bernard Malamud, and Robert Coover became part of the course. Later, during retirement, I decided to read all the adult baseball novels that I could find. The quest led to the accumulation of around 400 books, more than I expected, but I managed to work my way through all of them. I began to write a summary of each one and eventually decided to develop the project into what I hoped would be a text that would be of some interest to readers, baseball fans, literary critics and historians, and libraries. My record of the scope, variety, and merit of the genre could serve as a touchstone for further readings and studies of baseball novels.

Because of the vast number of baseball books written for juveniles and young adults, it was necessary to limit coverage to adult novels. I wanted to start from the beginning (in the nineteenth century) and cover every book in the twentieth century and beyond that featured baseball or that made a significant use of the game. At first, used bookstores, thrift stores, garage sales, and flea markets provided random selections. Then I purchased Andy McCue's *Baseball by the Books* and began to get serious about collecting the required texts. The bibliography of Tim Morris on the Internet also was a useful source, as was the baseball list produced by Amazon.com. I used Bookfinder to order books, and some of the out-of-print ones cost as much as one hundred dollars. I also sold assorted books from my library to a Barnes and Noble bookstore in Madison, Wisconsin, and used the credit to purchase baseball novels from another Barnes and Noble in Jackson, Mississippi. A few novels were available only through interlibrary loan. For one book (Trebor Swed's *Whichaway?*) I had to make a trip to the Jimmy Carter Library in Atlanta. After being interviewed and questioned about my motives, I was allowed one hour in which to view the text. Luckily it was only 153 pages. The project was not as simple as I thought it would be.

A manuscript finally materialized in the form of an annotated bibliography of relevant books dating from 1838 to the present. Although some of the works by major mainstream authors, such as James Fenimore Cooper, Mark Twain, F. Scott Fitzgerald, William Faulkner, James T. Farrell, Ernest Hemingway, and Thomas Wolfe, are not traditionally regarded as baseball novels, they indicate the pervasiveness of the cultural impact of the game. Often the baseball aspects of American classics, such as *The Great Gatsby, The Sound and the Fury*, and *The Old Man and the Sea*, contribute to the development of major themes. The plan, then, was to produce summaries and analyses of all adult novels (plus a few juvenile or young adult novels that transcended formulaic trends) that in some way dealt with baseball.

McFarland expressed an interest in the manuscript, and at their suggestion an historical introduction was added. The comprehensive annotated bibliography now stands as Part II and includes approximately 400 novels dating from 1838 through 2007. Appendices cover books in the subgenres of mystery and sci-fi and fantasy; offer lists of books that explore issues of race, ethnicity, and gender; present a selection of the best baseball novels; and provide a chronological list of titles. Author and title indexes conclude the book.

Thanks are due to my wife, Darlene, for her help. Errors in fact and judgment are due to my shortcomings and prejudices. I regret any omissions. I remember a book, probably from around 1960, that I read many years ago, but the author and title remain unknown to me. It was a paperback western in which the protagonist formed a baseball team while he was in prison. An escape was attempted during the course of a game. If anyone can identify this book, I would appreciate the information. In the meantime, new baseball novels keep appearing.

I

The History of the Baseball Novel

The adult baseball novel did not appear until the early twentieth century. The nineteenth century offered some fictional renderings of the game, but most of the early texts are categorized as kid lit, or they make only brief references to baseball. Books aimed at children and young adults were popular by the 1890s—a phenomenon that has continued into the twenty-first century. The emphasis here is on adult novels that deal primarily with baseball, but some books that only marginally touch on the sport and others that are usually categorized as Young Adult are included due to their historical or literary values.

As early as 1838, James Fenimore Cooper, author of *The Leatherstocking Tales*, described a ballgame in *Home as Found*. The resident of Cooperstown, New York, gives a short account of apprentice boys playing in the yard of an aristocrat. The wealthy man's lawyer is assigned the task of removing them, and he persuades the youths to play ball in the streets. Though covering only about two pages, the action predicted the future conflict between the social classes that emerged in baseball fiction, and anteceded the mythical invention of baseball in 1839.

The first novel to describe an actual baseball game was *Changing Base*, written by William Everett in 1868. It began a popular trend in sports fiction for boys, including more production from Everett. *Our Baseball Club and How It Won the Pennant* (1884) by Noah Brooks was the first novel to concentrate entirely on baseball. Although classified as kid lit, it introduced an important theme in baseball fiction: the influence of economics. In this case, a community with a semipro team hires ballplayers in order to be more competitive— to win the pennant.

In 1888, "Casey at the Bat" appeared, and Mudville's Mighty Casey became part of the nation's folklore. The poem by Ernest Thayer was popularized by actor DeWolf Hopper in his dramatic readings about the slugger who fans in the clutch. Many alternate versions follow, including those with heroic conclusions, and Casey is also the subject of two twentieth century novellas.

A year later, Mark Twain presented a short segment on baseball in *A Connecticut Yankee in King Arthur's Court*. The American protagonist, finding himself at Camelot in the year 528, introduces nineteenth-century concepts to King Arthur. One of the projects is an attempt to teach medieval knights the game of baseball. The knights, though, refuse to remove their armor, and the lesson turns into a farce.

Another negative side of baseball was exposed in Bliss Perry's *The Plated City* (1895). Along with the commercialism illustrated by Everett, racism was a factor in the nineteenth century. In real life, Cap Anson led a rebellion against black player Fleet Walker in the 1880s which led to a color barrier that existed until 1947. Perry depicts the plight of a player of questionable ethnicity who is eventually labeled as black and banned from pro baseball. Despite this early fictional account of racial prejudice, the subject was not brought up again until 1950 and did not become a literary staple until the 1970s.

More typical of nineteenth century baseball fiction is the Young Adult series of Burt L. Standish which features Frank Merriwell as a moral role model. Involved in an assortment of sporting adventures, the young hero is a pitcher for Yale in *Frank Merriwell's Danger* (1897). Frank invents the famous "double shoot," a pitch that breaks in two directions. In a sequel of 1899, he turns down offers to sell the magical pitch or to become a pro. The author stressed integrity rather than personal fame or economic gain.

Kid lit continued to dominate in the early twentieth century, although Robert Rudd Whiting's *The Fat Mascot* (1902), a collection of tall tales that skillfully blends humor and folklore, transcends the classification. Popular western novelist Zane Grey wrote primarily for juveniles in *The Shortstop* (1909) and in *The Young Pitcher* (1911), but Grey's *The Red Headed Outfield and Other Baseball Stories* (1915) can pass as adult fare. Meanwhile, the Edward Stratemeyer Syndicate produced a kids' series that deals exclusively with baseball. It started in 1912 with *Baseball Joe on the School Nine* and *Baseball Joe of the Silver Stars*. Joe Matson begins as a pitcher, but with the emergence of the long ball in the majors, thanks to Babe Ruth, Joe turns into a slugger in *Baseball Joe, Homerun King*. Another trend was the ghost-written books that capitalized on the fame of real-life heroes. Christy Mathewson's name appears on the "Matty Books," starting with *Won in the Ninth* in 1910. Ghosted by John Wheeler, they feature thinly disguised major leaguers performing heroic deeds. *Home-Run King* (1920) is credited to Babe Ruth, and Frank Chance supposedly penned *The Bride and the Pennant* (1910). These books adhere to the Horatio Alger formula in which virtue and hard work are rewarded with success.

The adult baseball novel finally emerged in 1915 with *The Ladder: The Story of a Casual Man*. Philip Curtiss records the corruption of college ball through the practice of enrolling mercenaries. Frank Connor, an accomplished semi-pro, attends several colleges and wins the "program privilege" at a major university. The deal allows him to sell his name to an advertising company for $1200 while remaining a college athlete. W.B.M. Ferguson's *A Man's Code*, also of 1915, is about an attempt to fix the World Series. A shortstop for the Boston Badgers commits a throwing error that allows the New York Manatees to win the Series, and a journalist says that a bribe is involved. Richard Steele, the Fighting Runt, cannot prove his innocence, so he is banned from baseball. However, by clinging to his code of honor, Steele is able to reveal that the journalist is the real villain and thus wins the right to return to the game. Despite the happy ending, the book shows the influence of gambling before the Black Sox scandal of 1919. From the beginning, then, the baseball novel, in the tradition of mainstream American literature, exposed the hypocrisy and immorality of society.

By this time the Ring Lardner stories, "Letters from a Busher," were appearing in *The Saturday Evening Post*. When a selection was published as *You Know Me Al* in 1916, the baseball novel had its first big hit. The semi-literate protagonist-narrator, Jack Keefe, is an uneducated, selfish man who is incapable of learning from mistakes—the opposite of Baseball Joe and Frank Merriwell of the kid books. He records his failures, on and off the field, in an epistolary format that features a dialect reminiscent of Huck Finn but without Huck's moral vision. Two more Jack Keefe books followed, but they were much less successful as they concentrated more on his war experiences than on baseball. In *Lose with a Smile* (1933), Lardner created a new ballplayer, Danny Warner, who struggles with language while also telling his story in letters. Unsuccessful on the diamond, Warner tries his luck as a singer, with the help of roommate Casey Stengel. Although Lardner's effectiveness was declining at this stage, the success of *You Know Me Al* led to a trilogy by H.C. Witwer that featured a Jack Keefe imitation in the person of Ed Harmon. First appearing in *From Baseball to Boches* in 1919, Harmon's fate is superior to that of his predecessor. Like Keefe, he temporarily postpones his athletic career in order to take part in World War I, but everything works in his favor. In his third book, *There's No Base Like Home* (1920), Harmon returns from combat to help win a World Series and is then persuaded by his wife, an actress, to follow her into the profession. Ed Harmon surpasses Jack Keefe as a ballplayer, a husband, and a businessman, but the books are decidedly inferior in literary quality to those of Lardner.

The adult baseball novel was still a rarity in the twenties and thirties, however, and Heywood Broun's *The Sun Field* (1923) is the only other quality publication of the era, and it is more about romance than baseball. A sportswriter pursues a socialite, but she is in love with a Yankee rightfielder who resembles Babe Ruth. In 1926, *The New Klondike* appeared with Peggy Griffith as author. Subtitled "A Story of a Southern Baseball Training Camp," the novella is in the

Horatio Alger mode. An interesting aspect of the publication, though, is that it is apparently based on a movie script which gives writing credits to J. Geraghty, Ben Hecht, and Ring Lardner.

By this time baseball was embedded in the national consciousness and was reflected in mainstream American literature. It plays minor roles in such classics as Fitzgerald's *The Great Gatsby* (1925) and Faulkner's *The Sound and the Fury* (1929), as well as in the fiction of James T. Farrell and Thomas Wolfe during the thirties. The 1919 Black Sox provided material for novelists, as illustrated in Fitzgerald's book in which Jay Gatsby's partner, Meyer Wolfsheim, is the man who fixed the Series. The renewed interest in the game during the Babe Ruth era was also a cultural phenomenon that attracted interest. Faulkner's Jason Compson, heir to a nearly depleted Mississippi plantation, vents his anger on those New York Jews, damn Yankees, and that nigger Ruth — the successful people whose economic security mocks his own struggle to survive financially. Babe Ruth's ethnic background is one part of the legend that makes him the most visible of all the real-life players who appear in fiction.

The first baseball mystery was published in 1934. Cortland Fitzsimmons' *Death on the Diamond* presents an unlikely plot in which gamblers murder the players that jeopardize their betting trends. The book did not start a fad as the next mystery did not arrive until 1947. George Bagby (writing as Aaron Mark Stein) produced another mediocre work of detection with *The Twin Killing*, and the subgenre languished until attaining popularity in the 1990s.

Baseball kid lit remained in vogue in the forties with John R. Tunis and Jackson Scholz leading the way. In 1948, A.S. Barnes and Company tried to capitalize on this interest by publishing novels with a similar format (the Horatio Alger motif) that were aimed at an adult audience. Ed Fitzgerald's *Turning Point* and Frank O'Rourke's *Flashing Spikes* feature admirable men who overcome adversity to win the Big Games. Jack Weeks and Arnold Hano joined the Barnes crew in producing sub-literate texts in the forties and fifties. The best of them are the O'Rourke Quaker City books with fictionalized versions of Philadelphia Phillies players. His *Bonus Rookie* of 1950 depicts a pennant for the fictional team before the actual Whiz Kids of that year accomplish the task.

Baseball science fiction and fantasy were also born in the forties. *Rhubarb* (1946) is about a cat named Rhubarb that inherits the major league New York Loons. The manager convinces the reluctant players that the yellow feline is good luck. The cat becomes a national celebrity, and the Loons win the World Series. The book is shocking in its report of the sexual antics of Rhubarb and some humans. *It Happens Every Spring* (1949) is a screenplay by Valentine Davies that he adapts as a novel. A chemistry teacher accidentally invents a magical solution that repels wood. When applied to baseballs, it causes them to swerve away from bats. The teacher, under the pseudonym King Kelly, becomes a star for St. Louis and wins all four World Series games before opting for the obscurity of his old college job. Although both of these novels are mediocre as literature, their popularity brought interest to new areas of baseball fiction.

Holmes Alexander's *Dust in the Afternoon* (1940) also achieved some status when it was serialized in the *Saturday Evening Post*. The protagonist, a player-manager of the New York Hawks, is an obvious fictional portrait of Leo Durocher. One other notable novel of the forties is Albert E. Idell's *The Great Blizzard*. Set in New York City in the 1880s, it shows the upper class prejudice against baseball and its rowdy participants. A Brooklyn pitcher, however, marries into a prominent family and converts them into baseball fans. The overall state of baseball fiction was still unimpressive at this point, but that was about to change.

In the 1950s, adult novels began to appear on a more regular basis. One of the new trends was an emphasis on race, a taboo subject since *The Plated City* of 1895. Murrell Edmunds broke the silence with *Behold, Thy Brother* (1950). The novella features the integration of the majors by a black pitcher in 1945—two years before the actual event. John Burgan's *The Long Discovery* (1950) is a competent sociological study of race, class, and baseball in a Pennsylvania mining town in 1925. Lucy Kennedy's *The Sunlit Field*, also of 1950, is one of the best books to portray the early years of the game. In the 1850s, the Brooklyn Excelsiors challenge the more established New York Knickerbockers while interested observers include an escaped slave and a poet named Walt Whitman.

Two American classics were published in 1952. Hemingway's *The Old Man and the Sea* is not really a baseball book, but the famous conversation about the game between Santiago and the boy has resulted in a book of critical essays about the author's debt to baseball. While fishing, the old man and Manolin discuss the pennant races and the merits of players, including their Cuban countrymen Mike Gonzalez and Dolf Luque. Santiago sees Joe DiMaggio as a role model who strives for perfection in the face of adversity. Playing with an injury, the Yankee centerfielder exemplifies Hemingway's code of honor. The real gem for baseball fiction, though, is Bernard Malamud's *The Natural*. Combining mythology and diamond lore, including the Black Sox scandal, the book continues to elicit critical commentary. The protagonist, a potential hero seemingly patterned after King Arthur, defeats the Whammer (a Babe Ruth figure) in personal combat but fails his big test with the New York Knights. Like Mighty Casey, he strikes out in the clutch, and like Shoeless Joe Jackson, he is in the midst of rumors about a fix.

Eliot Asinof's *Man on Spikes* (1955) is a minor classic of the era. A naturalistic depiction of minor league players, it stresses the absolute power of ruthless owners. The protagonist, along with a black teammate, spends a career in the lower levels of baseball at the mercy of manipulative management. World War II then robs outfielder Mike Kutner of a chance at the big time. In 1953, Mark Harris presented an opposing view as he began the successful career of Henry Wiggen in *The Southpaw*. The superstar narrates his story in the manner of Lardner's Jack Keefe, but the southpaw pitcher wins fame on the mound and has luck with women. Luckily, he marries one who induces a moral growth that matches his baseball heroics. The pitcher appears in three other novels — the best being *Bang the Drum Slowly* (1956).

In 1954, *The Year the Yankees Lost the Pennant*, a modern version of the Faust legend, became famous as *Damn Yankees* from the Broadway musical. The Douglas Wallop novel tells how a middle-aged businessman makes a deal with Applegate, a Mephistopheles figure, that enables him to become a star for the Washington Senators. Joe Boyd is transformed into Joe Hardy and leads the Senators to a pennant over the New York team. Although not great as literature, the musical has made it immortal, and recent editions of the book are titled *Damn Yankees*.

Although realism is represented by Charles Einstein's *Win — Or Else!* (1954) and *The Only Game in Town* (1955), plus Howard Breslin's *Autumn Comes Early* (1956), the popular books in the fifties are on the bizarre side. In Burgess Fitzpatrick's *Casey's Redemption* (1958), the slugger of "Casey at the Bat" emerges as a hero for the Mudville Hens, as well as a model of decorum, and is destined for success in life. Bud Nye's *Stay Loose* (1959) features a female administrator who uses a computer to determine that Nukiti islanders should theoretically make the best ballplayers due to their unique physical qualities. Although new to the game, they quickly upset the balance of power in the National League. Their innocence, however, clashes with physical and economic competition, and they soon return to their island paradise. Besides illustrating the basic theme of sport versus business, the novel introduced the inclusion of a woman in the front office and her use of a computer as a decision-making device in the game.

Fabulous fiction remained a common trait in the sixties. Paul Molloy's *A Pennant for the Kremlin* (1964) is a comedy in which the Soviet Union inherits the Chicago White Sox during the Cold War. The government stocks the team with Cuban players, but they defect to the United States. Martin Quigley's *Today's Game* (1965) depicts a manager who adheres to a suspect theory of aerodynamics. *Baseball's Darkest Days*, a 1965 novella, depicts an electrical engineer who plans to win a pennant for the Chicago Cubs by controlling the movement of baseballs with implanted transistors. A mad scientist controls a team with a computer in Marvin Karlins' *The Last Man Is Out* (1969). Along with a battle between man and machine, the book features a female pinch-hitter and a Faustian contract. In the same year, Felix Mendelsohn's *Superbaby* presents scientists who create a genetically-devised superior athlete. After two years of baseball heroics, though, Superbaby rejects the game and conventional society and seeks a value system worthy of his advanced intellect and morality. In baseball fiction, technology became part of the business aspect of the sport and thus increased the conflict between the idealism of pure athletic competition and the reality of economics.

I—The History of the Baseball Novel

The realistic output in the sixties was decidedly mediocre. Feldspar's *Squeeze Play* (1961) and Bradley's *Hot Curves* (1962) appeared in gaudy paperbacks that are suggestive of pornography but at most are only softcore — an indication of their lack of artistic integrity. Eliot Asinof's *The Bedfellow* (1967) deals with a black protagonist who retires after being traded, but the book is a big comedown from *Man on Spikes*. Sportswriter Mickey Herskowitz imitated Ring Lardner in *Letters from Lefty* (1966), first published in a newspaper while the author covered the Houston Colt .45s. Popular novelist Irwin Shaw illustrated the unifying effect of baseball on family life as a father watches his son play Little League ball in *Voices of a Summer Day* (1965).

A pair of thrillers set in Cuba and a mystery featuring a black detective portend future developments in subgenres. Roy Doliner's *The Orange Air* (1961) is a fictionalized version of Dodger pitcher Ralph Branca (who gave up the homer that cost the team the pennant in 1951) as he becomes engrossed in a plot to kill a Castro-like Cuban dictator. Robert Wade's *Knave of Eagles*, published in London in 1969, revolves around an attempt to smuggle a ballplayer out of Castro's Cuba. In the first baseball mystery since 1947, John Ball's *Johnny Get Your Gun* (1969) features black detective Virgil Tibbs in a case that leads to the California Angels and owner Gene Autry. (Sidney Poitier plays Tibbs in the movie version of Ball's *In the Heat of the Night*.)

The big literary event of the era, though, was the 1968 publication of Robert Coover's *The Universal Baseball Association, Inc., J. Henry Waugh, Prop*. The protagonist is an accountant who invents his own world through a game played with dice and probability charts. The fictional participants of the game come to dominate the life of the fifty-six-year-old Waugh. Unable to function effectively in reality, he begins to slip into the imaginary cosmos until, in the last chapter, he disappears, and the UBA functions on its own. A candidate for the best baseball novel, it transcends categorization and draws the critical evaluations that only *The Natural* has equaled at this point.

More than forty baseball novels came out in the seventies, eight of them in 1973. Ray Puechner's *A Grand Slam* (1973) is the first book to feature a professional female player. Ticki Denton plays second base for the major league New York Blues. She marries the team's shortstop and helps the Blues finish first in the Eastern division, but then quits the game to work on larger issues — like saving the world. Ticki, however, arranges for a female friend to have a try-out with the team. In 1976, *The Sensuous Southpaw* (by Paul B. Rothweiler) deals with a female relief pitcher for the Portland Beavers of the National League. Jeri Walker passes as a man, and when she reveals her identity the commissioner tries to ban her. Public opinion, however, changes his mind, and she goes on to pitch in the playoffs. The first-female motif of these books is notable, but the concept is treated in a farcical and melodramatic rather than an analytical manner.

One of the famous books from 1973 is *The Great American Novel* by Philip

Roth. It makes an attempt to live up to the title with the war-time story of the Rupert Mundys of the doomed Patriot League, as narrated by former sportswriter Word Smith. Now confined to a nursing home, Smith discusses the merits of the major novels of Hawthorne, Melville, Twain, and his friend Hemingway, while also relating the miraculous events of a team of homeless misfits whose records have been erased from history along with the rest of the league. An overdose of wordplay and political commentary keep the book from fulfilling its promise.

Also from 1973, Alexander Graham's *Babe Ruth Caught in a Snowstorm* attacks the economic side of the game. The Wichita Wraiths of Braintree, Massachusetts, originally compete on the amateur level for the simple joy of playing. When the team joins the National League, though, the accountants, lawyers, owners, and public relations experts take the fun away as business now rules. Babe Ruth, who appears physically in many novels, is used here as a symbol of pure baseball like that represented by the Wraiths at their inception.

Damon Rice's *Season's Past* (1976) and Lamar Herrin's *The Rio Loja Ringmaster* (1977) are also notable novels of the era. The former is a chronicle of New York City baseball from the Civil War to 1958 as reported by a fictional family. The succeeding generations relate the events of actual games and real ballplayers through the decades until the Dodgers and Giants depart for California. Herrin's novel is a precursor of the Hispanic trend that becomes popular thirty years later. It is narrated by a former star relief pitcher who flees to Mexico to find peace of mind after a ruined marriage. While living with a Mexican family and pitching for the local Rio Loja team, he realizes that contentment is within reach with the sacrifice of his competitive nature—a common theme that Herrin gives a unique treatment.

Black baseball is the subject of William Brashler's *The Bingo Long Traveling All-Stars and Motor Kings* and Jay Neugeboren's *Sam's Legacy*, both of 1973. Brashler created characters that are loosely based on Josh Gibson and Satchel Paige, famous Negro League stars. They play with the touring Louisville Ebony Aces in 1939, but the unfair practices of the owner lead to a rebellion by Long, and he forms his own team. The barnstorming era is threatened, though, by the coming of integration, and two of the young players are signed by a major league franchise. Neugeboren wemt back to the 1920s and the career of a black pitcher who has a love-hate relationship with Babe Ruth. Much of the text consists of the pitcher's manuscript called "My Life and Death in the Negro American Baseball League: A Slave Narrative." The narrator depicts himself as superior to Ruth, and the contrast between the slugger's notoriety and the black hurler's anonymity is a major theme.

The emphasis on black baseball continues with Jerome Charyn's *The Seventh Babe* (1979), John Craig's *Chappie and Me* (1979), and Martin Quigley's *The Original Colored House of David* (1981), all about barnstorming teams. Charyn's minor classic highlights the adventures of a white player, banned from

Organized Baseball, as he travels with the Cincinnati Colored Giants. Even after Kenesaw Mountain Landis lifts the ban, Babe Ragland, a lefthanded third-baseman and the seventh Babe to play for the Red Sox after Babe Ruth, persists in touring with the black team in its seven–Buick caravan. The Colored Giants are good enough to beat the Dizzy Dean All-Stars in 1934, and Ragland keeps the team alive (by using the money of his wealthy father) after World War II and perhaps into the future. A white player is also part of a black barnstorming team in Craig's novel. A young Canadian joins Chappie Johnson's Colored All-Stars in 1939. Playing in blackface, he experiences the racism that Chappie Johnson's men have learned to endure. Quigley repeats the concept as a Minnesota boy becomes a member of a black team in the summer of 1928. Known as Speedy Deefy, an albino deaf-mute, he is forced to question the pride he was taught about his Scandinavian heritage as he undergoes the same discriminatory treatment as his black teammates at the hands of the largely Viking audience.

Paul Hemphill's *Long Gone* (1979) also stresses racial prejudice in the 1956 Class D Alabama-Florida League. The star of the Graceville Oilers, black catcher Joe Louis Brown, poses as a Latino in order to escape the wrath of the KKK.

The first black author in the field was Barry Beckham. *Runner Mack* (1972) is a militant protest novel, a popular concept among African American writers of the sixties and seventies. Beckham combines baseball and fantasy as his protagonist, a black ballplayer from Mississippi, is persuaded by a rebel to join a revolutionary army that plans to overthrow the government of the United States. Realizing that his tryout with a major league team is fixed (as he is forced to hit against a batting machine that throws the ball at 150 miles per hour), the ballplayer decides to take part in the hopeless revolution.

The absence of racial references in the baseball novel lasted from 1895 to 1950, but by the 1970s interest was awakening.

Race and fantasy are also major components of *The Last Western* (1974) by Thomas Klise. A multi-ethnic ballplayer invents a magical pitch that makes him a star major leaguer and also threatens to make a mockery of baseball. The hero, though, quits the game and becomes a leader of a humanistic organization that attempts to alter the nation's value system by putting Christian concepts into action. He is elected pope but is murdered before his policies are applied. James F. Donohue also mixes ethnicity and magic in *Spitballs and Holy Water* (1977). A black nun creates her unhittable pitch and uses it to defeat the 1927 Yankees in an exhibition game. While pitching for the black Chicago American Giants, she vanquishes the famous Murderer's Row featuring Babe Ruth — and wins a million dollar wager (for the Catholic church) against the KKK. *Noonan: A Novel about Baseball, ESP, and Time Warp* (1978) by Leonard Everett Fisher is considered as kid lit, but it deals with an important theme in baseball science fiction: the conflict between ballplayers and the computers that threaten to control them.

Mysteries account for almost one-fourth of the baseball novels of the seventies, but the quality is low. *Wild Pitch* (1973) by A.B. Guthrie, author of famous historical novels, has a western setting. A teenage pitcher for a semi-pro team helps the local sheriff catch a killer by throwing a baseball that disarms the culprit. Robert B. Parker's popular Spenser series includes *Mortal Stakes* (1975). In his third appearance, the hard-boiled sleuth is hired by the Red Sox to investigate a possible gambling problem of a star pitcher. *The Rundown* (1977) by much-published novelist James Magnuson is probably the best of the group. Other titles of the period are: *A Handy Death* (1973), *The Devil to Play* (1973), *Pro #3: Strikezone* (1975), *The 7th Game* (1977), *The Cocaine Caper* (1978), *The Screwball King Murder* (1978), and *Seven Games in October* (1979). The subgenre is beginning to gain popularity at this point but has yet to hit its peak.

A conflict between tight-fisted owners and free agency emerged in the mid-seventies. Before the actual arrival of the free agent market, the owners were often revealed as unscrupulous. This was already a common theme, and it is repeated in John Craig's *All G. O. D.'s Children* (1975), Donald Honig's *The Last Great Season* (1979), and Marty Bell's *Breaking Balls* (1979). The epitome of ruthlessness, though, is seen in Gary Morgenstein's *Take Me out to the Ballgame* (1980). The owner of the Buffalo Matadors fills his stadium by promoting violence. His methods are aimed at manipulating the blue-color crowd into a frenzy of hatred against opponents — an orchestrated bedlam that results in the murder of a visiting player.

An obvious antidote to owner exploitation was the advent of free agency in 1976. The balance of power now shifted in favor of the players and their agents, and million-dollar contracts soon become the norm. The first novel to deal extensively with the new economics of the game was Jay Cronley's *Screwballs* in 1980. The manager, a martinet of the old-school, challenges the vanity and greed of his star player. When other players and agents join the fray, the manager feels that he is surrounded by a bunch of screwballs that he has to make into a pennant contender. He quits, though, before the end of the season and plans to go back to running a college team. The business of the game forces the administrators to adjust or depart.

About eighty baseball novels appeared in the 1980s as the production pace continued to increase. The roles of women in the game became more common — along with racial matters. Mysteries started to become popular, and the series detective was introduced. Hardcore science fiction, featuring future or alternate worlds and advanced technology, stayed in vogue, but fantasies made the biggest impact of the period among the subgenres.

The technology in sci-fi can lead to the creation of mad scientists, similar to those of Poe and Hawthorne, who try to control baseball through computers. *The New AToms Bombshell* (1980) is a reworking of *The Last Man Is Out* (1969), and Professor Norbert returns to manipulate the team with calculated probabilities generated by his machine. In Sal Conte's *Child's Play* (1986), scientists use computer implants in the bodies of Little League players to improve their performances. Kids who fail to cooperate disappear — permanently. A more realistic treatment of the computer in baseball occurs in Mel Knopf's *The Batting Machine* (1981). The owner of an American League team acquires technological secrets that he applies to his players with successful results. Richard Lupoff turns to space adventure, more typically associated with sci-fi, in *Countersolar* (1987). However, a subplot deals with baseball and an unlikely battery consisting of Babe Didrickson, the famed female athlete, and Josh Gibson, the great Negro League catcher. The mechanical and extraterrestrial miracles of this type of fiction, though, are often replaced by different kinds of improbabilities in the realm of fantasy.

Stressing a conscious break from reality, usually through the creation of an imaginary cosmos that operates on its own rules, fantasy is often an indirect method of analyzing the society from which it emerges. W.P. Kinsella's *Shoeless Joe* (1982) is one of the famous examples due, in part, to the movie version, *Field of Dreams*. The protagonist, Ray Kinsella, hears a voice that orders him to build a ballpark on his Iowa farm. The deed conjures forth Joe Jackson and his Black Sox teammates, long dead. With the support of reclusive author J.D. Salinger, Ray escapes from reality by enjoying ghostly baseball. The reality is represented by the syndicate that is buying farms in the area and putting pressure on the financially troubled Ray. Salinger concocts the plan for saving the farm by spreading the word of the pure baseball games being played on the Iowa diamond with the idea that the loyal fans will pay for the privilege of watching. Kinsella thus comes up with a new concept of the archetypal theme of business in conflict with sport. The point is less clear, though, in the author's *The Iowa Baseball Confederacy* (1986). Featuring a forty-day game of 2614 innings between the 1908 Chicago Cubs and the Iowa Baseball Confederacy All-Stars, the complex mythology overwhelms the plot and makes comprehension difficult.

The Faust legend appeared again in 1983. Gary Morgenstein's *The Man Who Wanted to Play Center Field for the New York Yankees* is more realistic than *Damn Yankees*, however, as the protagonist becomes a member of the Yankees as a publicity stunt. He emerges as a celebrity but dramatically walks away from the ballpark in a protest against conformity and commercialism, thus saving himself from a Mephisthophelean bargain. In the same year, *Home Game* by Paul Quarrington presents a fabulous game between a group of sideshow freaks and the House of Jonah, a fundamentalist religious sect. Dr. Sinister's circus troupe is trained by Goldenlegs Isbister, a former pro who broke his own legs in a symbolic protest against the economics of baseball. Aided by Sinister's magic, the oddities of the midway win in a triumph of pure baseball over commercial interests.

The Curious Case of Sidd Finch (1987) is George Plimpton's expansion of a magazine story in which the protagonist, through the use of lung-gom meditation, is able to throw an unhittable fastball. In his first two major league games, Finch strikes out fifty-three consecutive batters before suddenly walking off the mound — presumably to return to his role as a Buddhist monk. Gordon McAlpine's *Joy in Mudville* (1989) is set in motion by a Babe Ruth home run ball that soars across the continent. A fourteen-year-old baseball card collector, an unacknowledged son of the Babe, pursues the ball to California. He catches up to the clouted ball and is immediately assimilated into a constellation. Another expanded magazine story, Frank Deford's *Casey on the Loose* (1989), literally brings joy to Mudville. The second novella about the Casey of Ernest Thayer's famous poem, it tells of the slugger accepting a bribe to abandon the team. Casey, however, rushes back to Mudville to pinch-hit in the ninth. He fans, but the catcher misses the ball, and three runs score on a series of errors. The home team wins, and the fans are oblivious to Casey's plea that he struck out honestly. Deford, like other writers in the fantasy field, then, suggests that baseball is subject to the negative influence of economics and other problems created by off-the-field situations.

In the 1980s, women characters have major roles in fourteen novels. Unfortunately, five of them are formula romances which consist of basically the same pattern: a lady with a connection to baseball meets a man; a love affair is established; a serious altercation leads to a temporary separation; and finally, a reunion results in a happy ending.

On a somewhat higher literary level, David Ritz in *The Man Who Brought the Dodgers Back to Brooklyn* (1981) relates the story of two Brooklyn fans who rebuild Ebbets Field. They lure the Dodgers back to New York and field a team that stars Ruth Smelkinson, a female Sandy Koufax, who helps the Dodgers get to the World Series before succumbing to pregnancy.

Michael Bowen's *Can't Miss* (1987) presents another female player. Chris Tilden is the leftfielder for the Denver Marshalls, an expansion team. She contributes to the team's second-place finish and is a candidate for Rookie of the Year. Linda Sunshine, in Barbara Gregorich's *She's on First* (1987), also plays in the majors. The daughter of a former star of the All-American Girls' Professional Baseball League, Sunshine works her way up to the Chicago Eagles and overcomes the gender barrier in much the same way that Jackie Robinson broke the color line. Bowen and Gregorich are more realistic in their books than in the earlier ones by Puechner (*A Grand Slam*, 1973) and Rothweiler (*The Sensuous Southpaw*, 1976). The problems of the female characters are treated more seriously in the later novels, especially in dealing with sexism.

Women also made an impact in nonplaying roles. Ron Powers, in *Toot-Toot-Tootsie, Good-bye* (1981), introduces a beauty queen to the broadcasting booth. Veteran announcers L.C. Fanning and Turtle Teweles are devastated by the invasion. Turtle goes home to Arkansas rather than work with a female, and Fanning sees Robyn Quarrels as an enemy of the broadcasting profession and of the game. He plans revenge on the New York Nats for their betrayal—for yielding to commercialism. A victim of future shock, Fanning is a symbol of a dying era in baseball. He longs for the days before the intrusion of television, free agency, promotional gimmicks, and females.

Women sportswriters play parts in Roger Kahn's *The Seventh Game* and Michael Schiffer's *Ballpark*, both published in 1982. Johnny Longboat, an aging Native American pitcher for the New York Mohawks, praises Prissy Coe for her journalistic efforts in covering the team. Schiffer's Pauline Reese discovers the tyranny of the owner of Ballpark, an amusement park business that includes a major league franchise. Her investigation triggers the collapse of the corrupt enterprise.

Although only Ron Powers' book is a literary success, these novels of female participation show the growing significance of females, in at least, the fictional field, in a male-dominated realm.

Homosexuality, formerly a taboo topic, finally made an appearance in three novels of the 1980s. Steve Kluger's *Changing Pitches* (1984) deals with the rejuvenation of a veteran pitcher's career. A coach teaches him new pitches that prove to be effective. However, a new catcher arrives with a charisma that the pitcher finds irresistible, and he begins to question his sexuality. When the catcher admits to being in love with a football player, the pitcher sees a psychoanalyst—and then proposes to his girlfriend. John Hough's *The Conduct of the Game* (1986) stresses an umpire's situation. A gay ump commits suicide after the league president begins an investigation of his private life. The protagonist, also an umpire, refuses to testify against his gay friend and is forced to resign. In 1989, Mark Richard Zubro introduces the Tom and Scott mystery series. In *A Simple Suburban Murder*, Scott is a former major league pitcher who is involved in a gay relationship with Tom, a teacher. They work together to solve crimes, but most of the books in the series have little to do with baseball. Novelists are beginning to find that homosexuality is marketable although Organized Baseball, like other sports entities, prefers to ignore the controversial subject.

Mysteries revealed a different aspect in the eighties with the advent of the series—two or more books by an author that feature a reappearing detective. Richard D. Rosen created the first series sleuth with Harvey Blissberg. The Jewish ballplayer starts his career as an investigator in the 1984 novel *Strike Three You're Dead*, an Edgar winner for the best first mystery. Blissberg retires from baseball but continues in crime solving in *Saturday Night Dead* (1988) and *Dead Ball* (2001). Michael Geller started the Slots Resnick books in 1988 with *Major League Murder*. In the same year, Alison Gordon introduced female sportswriter Kate Henry in *Dead Pull Hitter*. The amateur detective returned in four more books in the eighties and nineties. In 1989, David Nighbert produced the first Bull Cochran story with *Strikezone*. Zubro's Tom and Scott also made their first appearance in 1989. All of these detectives are in action in the nineties or after, and they are soon joined by four more series sleuths.

The racial scene in the 1980s diversifies from the earlier emphasis on barnstorming teams and Negro League ball. *Suder* (1983) by black writer Percival Everett traces the mental decline of a Seattle Mariners player. Put on the disabled list during a prolonged slump, the black third baseman flees to the Oregon wilderness and becomes obsessed with the idea of flying. Gordon DeMarco's *Frisco Blues*, a mystery published in England in 1985, is set in 1947 — the year of Jackie Robinson's integration of major league baseball. Riley Kovach investigates the murder of a black laborer who was scheduled to play for a Satchel Paige team against the Bob Feller All-Stars. The trail leads to the Purity League, a racist group in San Francisco. Pete Gethers' *Getting Blue* (1987) deals with a racial incident that haunts the lives of a white player and his black teammate long after their playing days are over. *The Comeback Kids* (1989) by Bob Cairns also shows how a racist event of the past affects the later lives of the victims. The New Beaton Hotdogs were denied a chance to play in the Little League World Series of 1954 because the team was integrated. Thirty years later, the team's sponsor challenges the offending Poughkeepsie Pintails to play the series in an attempt to right a wrong — and to promote his business. Bill Littlefield's *Prospect* (1989) revolves around the effort of a retired scout, now in a nursing home, to return a favor to a black attendant. Pete Estey gets out of Fair Haven long enough to check out his friend's nephew and to arrange a tryout with a minor league team. Racially-oriented novels, then, are finally a mainstay in baseball fiction.

The Black Sox scandal of 1919 provides the material for several major novels. Eric Rolfe Greenberg's *The Celebrant* (1983) is in part a fictional biography of Christy Mathewson, but Jack Kapp, a Jewish jeweler, shares the spotlight with the legendary pitcher. Kapp designs rings to celebrate the feats of his hero's diamond exploits. Later, they worry about the integrity of the game during rumors of a fix during the 1919 World Series. Gassed while serving in World War I, Mathewson is dying when Kapp visits him for the last time. The ex-Giant is obsessed to the point of madness with his own heroic stature and the corruption of baseball by gamblers. *Hoopla* (1983) by Harry Stein focuses on the scandal through the opposing narrative views of Buck Weaver and Luther Pond. Weaver is one of the eight White Sox players banned by Commissioner Landis, and Pond is a journalist who exposes the alleged fix and works with Landis to condemn the suspects regardless of their guilt or innocence. Despite being acquitted in court, the so-called Black Sox, including Shoeless Joe Jackson, are turned into scapegoats by the commissioner, White Sox owner Charles Comiskey, and yellow journalism in order, presumably, to preserve the integrity of Organized Baseball. *Blue Ruin: A Novel of the 1919 World Series* (1991) by Brendan Boyd is another major treatment of the event — this time from a gambler's viewpoint. Sport Sullivan, one of the actual participants, narrates his attempt to set the fix in motion with a literary flair that elevates the book to the elite in the genre. He is a big winner in 1919, but his later attempts to bribe stars like Cobb, Speaker, and Ruth fail. When the Black Sox investigation is under way, Sullivan flees to Mexico on the advice of Arnold Rothstein, reputedly the major figure behind the scandal.

The historical baseball novel that fictionalizes actual events is becoming a major category. Another example is Gordon Weaver's *The Eight Corners of the World* (1988) which explores Moe Berg's role as a spy in the 1930s. Although only partly concerned with baseball, the book illustrates the trend of turning to history as a background for fictional material and cultural commentary. The first section of the novel takes place in Japan where, in 1934, a team of American League all-stars is on tour. Connie Mack has the honor of managing dignitaries like Ruth, Gehrig, Foxx, Gomez, and Gehringer in a series of exhibition games with Japanese teams. Journeyman catcher Moe Berg is also on the roster, but he has been recruited by the State Department to take photographs of Japan's military sites. Berg, better known for his intelligence work than as a ballplayer, befriends Yoshinori Yamaguchi, a Japanese student, with the promise that the youth will be rewarded with a college education in the United States. It becomes Yosh's story, but the fictionalized historical fragment stands out as a lasting contribution to baseball literature.

The Dixie Association (1984) by Donald Hays is a gem of cultural satire as it stresses bigotry in the South that mirrors the civil rights struggle in the fifties and sixties. Manager Lefty Marks, noted for his leftwing politics, springs slugger Hog Durham from jail to join his team of misfits, the Arkansas Reds of the Dixie Association. The minor league team, which also includes a Muslim, a woman, and an elderly Native American, is threatened by Reverend Bushrod and his gang of right-wing fanatics. With the help of a civil rights lawyer, the Reds manage to stay out of prison and contend for the pennant. The literary allusions, focusing on the great Southern writers (particularly Faulkner), are contrasted by references to the redneck prejudices that the author attacks with the gusto of Mark Twain.

Over half of the 400 or so novels annotated here appeared between 1990 and 2007. The trends already noted continued with some new twists. Troy Soos, for example, combines the historical novel with the mystery in his Mickey Rawlings series in which real and imaginary characters from the early twentieth century are involved in both factual and fictional happenings. Fictional biographies, partially presented in *The Celebrant* (1983), break out in full-fledged fashion with Moe Berg, Hal Chase, Charles Radbourn, and Ty Cobb serving as subjects. Another link to baseball history is the rejuvenation of the Hispanic novel. In the sixties, *The Orange Air* (1961) and *Knave of Eagles* (1969) explored Castro's effect on baseball. In the nineties and beyond, books set in Cuba and Mexico examine in more detail the situations of Spanish-speaking players and their American associates, including situations arising from the racial policies of the different cultures. Race is a major issue in at least twenty novels from 1990 to 2007, not all of them in the Hispanic area, and another sixteen books tackle the gender issue. Science fiction and fantasy account for over thirty novels in the nineties and beyond, but mysteries are the big gainer in subgenres with almost fifty publications. (Some of the categories, however, overlap.) Although baseball is not the national pastime it may once have been, it outdoes rival sports in literary production.

The series mysteries that began in the eighties became more popular in the nineties. Alison Gordon's Kate Henry novels are among the best. Two of them stress the homosexual motif introduced just a few years earlier. In *Safe at Home* (1990), Kate helps a black Toronto Titan write a confession when he decides to come out of the closet. The baseball world is outraged, but when the gay player helps Kate solve a crime, the anger dissipates. *Prairie Hardball* (1997) focuses on former members of the All-American Girls' Professional Baseball League. Kate's mother is being inducted into the Saskatchewan Baseball Hall of Fame. Two of her teammates on the Racine Belles during the 1940s had a lesbian affair that explodes into a mystery half a century later.

In 1990, L.L. Enger introduced Gun Pedersen in *Comeback*. The Minnesota-based sleuth, a former Detroit Tiger, is primarily concerned about protecting the environment. Journalist Carol Long helps him solve a series of ecological mysteries that are not always connected to baseball. Sportswriter Duffy House, however, is immersed in the game as he appears in the books of Crabbe Evers — three of which are published in 1991 (*Murder in Wrigley Field, Murderer's Row,* and *Bleeding Dodger Blue*). Aided by his niece, Petey, and sometimes by Red Carney (an announcer who resembles Harry Caray), House delves into baseball related problems at the request of Commissioner Chambliss. The series also includes *Fear in Fenway* and *Tigers Burning*. In most cases, the references to baseball lore are more interesting than the mysteries.

Troy Soos began the excellent Mickey Rawlings books in 1994 with *Murder at Fenway Park*. Rawlings, a utility infielder for a variety of teams, interacts with real players from the early twentieth century. In his first appearance, he suspects that Ty Cobb is the killer of the Red Sox player whose body is found at Fenway. In *Murder at Ebbets Field* (1995), Casey Stengel and John McGraw play major roles. *Murder at Wrigley Field* (1996) inculpates the owner of the Cubs who, in 1918, is responsible for displaying anti–German propaganda that leads to violence. Cobb reappears in *Hunting a Detroit Tiger* (1997) in which he supports the formation of a baseball union. Rawlings gets in the action and is wrongly accused of murdering a labor leader. In *The Cincinnati Red Stalkings* (1998), Rawlings is temporarily banned from the game for associating with alleged gamblers in the aftermath of the Black Sox scandal. The infielder plays for the St. Louis Browns in *Hanging Curve* (1999), but he moonlights in his spare time with the St. Louis Cubs, a black team in East St. Louis, Illinois. Following the race riot of 1917, the city across the river is a hotbed of the KKK, and Rawlings joins the battle against racism while investigating the death of a black player. Soos, then, explores the cultural and social history of the Ty Cobb era in novels that transcend the mystery label.

I—The History of the Baseball Novel

Donald Honig brought Joe Tinker to life in 1992 with *The Plot to Kill Jackie Robinson*. The veteran of World War II works as a sportswriter in 1947, and while covering the Dodgers in Cuba during the preseason, he uncovers a plot to kill Robinson on opening day at Ebbets Field. Tinker returns in *Last Man Out* (1993) to clear a Dodger rookie from a murder charge.

The Tom and Scott books of Zubro are usually not about baseball, but in *Rust on the Razor* (1996) major league pitcher Scott Carpenter reveals his homosexual affair. He is consequently a target for the KKK, a Neo-Nazi, and other bigots. Meanwhile, Geller's Slots Resnick and Nighbert's Bull Cochran stay busy in the nineties. Bill Granger's sleuth, not ordinarily associated with baseball, enters the field in 1994 with *Drover and the Designated Hitter*. Drover gets involved in a case in which a Cub slugger wants to be traded to the American League in order to be a DH. The ex-redneck's other desire is to marry his therapist—a black woman. The baseball mystery, then, often strays from formulaic crime solving to take on controversial issues.

Hardcore science fiction, featuring futuristic technology, remained prevalent in the nineties. Scot Moon's *Open Season* (1993) takes a horrifying look into a computerized society that threatens most of humanity. Baseball consists of players and ballparks that are programmed. The Indianapolis Leopards, the first team to perfect the mechanized system, produce a ninety-one game winning streak before national disasters, apparently caused by rampant computers, create chaos. In *The Aliens of Summer* (1995), Calvin Ross creates a planet, Ball Four, which "biofashions" players who are sent to Earth to infiltrate major league teams. One of the new breed has an "earthly" season in which he wins the Cy Young Award, breaks the homer record, and bats .435, thus proving that Ball Four has a superior civilization. James Garrett LaFemina's *They Still Play Baseball on the Moon* presents the Galactic League of Professional Baseball Clubs in the year 2278 that has turned the game into a computerized business with predetermined outcomes. An astronaut, after a 251-year solar flight, attempts to restore baseball to a legitimate status by fielding a team on the moon that rebels from the ordained scripts and plays to win in the old-fashioned way. The emphasis in these and other sci-fi baseball books is to keep technology, controlled by business interests, from dominating the sport. The time before the use of computers, steroids, and other aberrant (when applied to baseball) aspects of science is viewed as the golden age of the game.

Fantasy is also a prominent part of the era in baseball fiction. *If I Never Get Back*, by Darryl Brock, transports a late-twentieth century journalist back to 1869. Sam Fowler becomes a member of the Cincinnati Red Stockings, befriends Mark Twain and Jesse James, challenges the Fenians (a group of militant Irish nationalists), and falls in love with Cait. When Fowler is returned to the present, he finds that his wife has deserted him, and he longs for his nineteenth century life. He realizes his dream in *Two in the Field*, a sequel published in 2002.

In *The Year I Owned the Yankees* (1990), Sparky Lyle (the ex–Yankee relief pitcher and co-author with David Fisher) projects himself into a novel in which he concocts a plan to control his former team for one year. Supported by coaches Lou Piniella, Yogi Berra, and Reggie Jackson, the team makes it to the World Series. Duke Schneider, a female secretary and computer analyst, hires a man named Applegate in an effort to bribe Lyle to lose. The Yanks, however, prevail over the Dodgers with the help of Tommy John's bionic arm that is repaired by a computer. The references to *Stay Loose* and *The Year the Yankees Lost the Pennant*, earlier fantasies, are obvious, but the humor of the book helps to make it at least a mild success.

In 1994, Michael Bishop's *Brittle Innings* depicts the unusual events surrounding the 1943 Highbridge Hellbenders of the Class C Chatahoochee Valley League. Danny Boles, a seventeen-year-old shortstop, suffers from a trauma that leaves him speechless. His roommate is Jumbo Clerval, a giant first baseman with a horrifying past. The best athlete associated with the team, although he is not allowed to play, is the black bus driver, Darius Satterfield, who may be the son of the Hellbender owner. All are victims of discrimination. The mixture of fantasy and social commentary comes close to the best work of Kinsella, whose *If Wishes Were Horses* (1996) is a big step down from *Shoeless Joe*.

A new version of the Faust legend is deployed in Michael Tomkin's *The 30-Hit Season* (1995). A forty-three-year-old attorney dreams that he gets thirty consecutive hits in the big leagues. Despite objections by the Seattle Mariners' manager Lou Piniella and Commissioner George Will, the owner of the Mariners takes a chance by signing the lawyer to a contract. The dream becomes a reality. Pete Hamill's *Snow in August* (1997) is an apparent contrast as it gives the impression of being a naturalistic example of ethnic prejudice during the 1947 baseball season. As Jackie Robinson debuts with the Dodgers, the veteran Tiger slugger Hank Greenberg plays his final season as a member of the Pirates. A Catholic boy teaches Rabbi Hirsch about baseball, and they cheer for their beleaguered heroes. When anti–Semitism flares up in the neighborhood, though, the realism turns into magical realism as the boy performs the rituals that produce a golem, a superman of Jewish folklore who performs miracles—like producing snow in August, gaining revenge on the local terrorists, and animating the rabbi's dead wife. Like in most of the better fantasies, social and ethical issues are prominent.

Novels by and about women continued to flourish in the nineties. Three of them feature female teams. In 1992, Sarah Gilbert novelizes the screenplay of *A League of Their Own*, a story of the All-American Girls' Professional Baseball League in 1944. Celia Cohen's *Smokey O: A Romance* (1994) creates a new Women's Baseball League, but the emphasis is on a lesbian relationship. The best of the trio is Karen Jay Fowler's *The Sweetheart Season* (1996). In 1947, Henry Collins sponsors a female team, the Sweetwheat Sweethearts, to promote his breakfast cereal. Irini Doyle's tenure with the touring team is narrated by her equally feminist daughter, as both of them actively engage in combating sexism.

Female managers are more unusual than female players in fiction, but *The Woman in the Dugout* (1992), by Gary Lovisi and Terry Arnone, tells of the managerial qualities of Arlene Craig. The co-owner of the Brooklyn Kings takes on-the-field control when the manager dies. Despite dealing with discrimination, she leads the Kings to a pennant.

The fifth novel to feature a female player in the big leagues (as a protagonist) is *Balls* (1995) by Gorman Bechard. Louise "Balls" Gehrig plays firstbase for the Manhattan Meteorites of the National League. Battling the predictable sexist reactions, she prevails to win the Rookie of the Year award and helps the team make it to the World Series.

An amateur woman player appears in Kent Cowgill's *The Cranberry Trail: Misfits, Dreamers, Drifters on the Heartland Road*. The 1995 farcical rendition of *The Canterbury Tales* depicts the reunion of the Tabelard Honey Bees, thirty years after the college team lost seventy-six consecutive games. The former teammates travel to South Fork, Nebraska, to rebuild an old church into living quarters for their old college coach. During their pilgrimage, the out-of-shape Bees are challenged to a game by the residents of a small town. They are rescued from humiliation when the team trainer arrives on a motorcycle — with her lesbian partner — to aid on the field and to serve as a unifying and healing force.

A lady sportswriter is the protagonist of Jane Leavy's *Squeeze Play* (1990). A.B. Berkowitz reports on the Washington Senators, an expansion team in 1989. When the televangelist owner bans her from the locker room, she retaliates with exposures of the team's incompetence and the preacher's hypocrisy. Berkowitz's diary, meanwhile, is replete with entries that vent her feelings against religious-oriented sexism with the vulgarity of jock-speech — the language of athletes.

Female protagonists of baseball novels have other non-playing roles, as in Stephen King's *The Girl Who Loved Tom Gordon* (1999). The young girl who is lost in the wilderness for several days maintains her courage by her devotion to the Boston Red Sox. She listens to the games on her radio and cheers for her hero, the relief pitcher of the title. *Isabelle's Inning* (1997) by Donna Winters is a Great Lakes romance in which the heroine suffers from word blindness, or illiteracy. A ballplayer from Erskine College, however, falls in love with her, and they presumably live happily ever after. On a lighter and more entertaining note, Garrison Allen's *Baseball Cat* (1997) traces the exploits of Penelope Warren, owner of a mystery bookstore, and her cat, Big Mike. They solve the murder case associated with the Empty Creek Coyotes of the Arizona-New Mexico League. Similarly, black writer Lisa Saxon in *Caught in a Rundown* (1997) produces an amusing caper involving the wives of two D.C. Diamonds players as they pursue a baseball glove once owned by Cool Papa Bell of Negro

League fame. Females are by this time a part of baseball fiction in a variety of capacities.

Homosexuality is the subject of two of the Kate Henry mysteries plus *Smokey O, Changing Pitches,* and *Rust on the Razor.* Probably the best known of the gay novels, though, is Peter Lefcourt's *The Dreyfus Affair.* Published in 1992, it presents the double play combination of the Los Angeles Valley Vikings—a couple on and off the field. The white shortstop and the black second baseman confront fan resentment that reaches to the White House. The president puts pressure on the commissioner of baseball to ban the players for life. In a parody of history, however, sportswriter Milt Zola comes to the defense of the pair in a scathing journalistic editorial. In 1995, Bernie Bookbinder takes the topic into the realm of absurdity by featuring an all-gay team in *Out at the Old Ballgame.* When the star of the New York Gents comes out of the closet, the owner gets the idea of fielding an entire team of homosexuals. The Gents are supported by sportscaster Olivia Jacob Cobb, whose cousin Natalie hopes to make the team in the near future. Despite the protests of the Baseball Establishment and fans, the Gents make it to the seventh game of the World Series before losing to a gay pitcher of the Yankees. Another book, *Hardball: An Erotic Novel* (1999), is gay pornography. As long as the subject is controversial, then, it is likely to be depicted in fiction.

Historical baseball fiction usually consists of a mixture of actual and imaginary characters and events, as in the Troy Soos and G.S. Rowe mysteries. Novels about the Black Sox of 1919 and the Jackie Robinson integration of 1947 are standard offerings, as are the stories of black barnstorming teams and Negro League ball. Some, like *No Fun on Sunday* (1990), present situations associated with a particular aspect of the past. Frederick Manfred, for example, relates the prejudice against Sunday baseball in the Upper Midwest during the 1920s. Prospect Sherm Engelking insists on playing semipro ball despite the protest of his mother who thinks that baseball is a waste of valuable time—and a sin on the Sabbath. Swede Risberg, one of the Black Sox Eight, insists that the kid has the talent to be a pro, and a scout for the Cubs invites him to spring training. *Early Dreams* (1998) by David Nemec focuses on historical events of the 1884 season in pro baseball as experienced by a fictional character. The player signs a contract with the Cincinnati Red Stockings but is released and joins the Outlaw Reds of the rival Union Association. At the end of the season, he switches to the New York Metropolitans and participates in a championship match against the Providence Grays and star pitcher Old Hoss Radbourn. An important incident of the 1884 season that is included in the book is the move, led by Cap Anson, to keep Fleetwood Walker and other blacks out of Organized Baseball. More typical of entries in this broad category, though, are books that deal with major historical events such as war.

The Civil War is the background for Thomas Dyja's *Play for a Kingdom* (1997). During a break in the fighting in Virginia in 1864, Company L of Brooklyn is challenged to a series of games by Alabama soldiers. At the risk of a court-martial if they're discovered, the teams of the North and South indulge in baseball as a welcome relief from the war. The improvised field becomes a symbol of peace, and many of the participants from opposing sides learn to tolerate each other. Jeff Hutton's *Perfect Silence* (2000) begins in Virginia in 1864 as a Confederate soldier is captured. He is sent as a prisoner to Elmira, New York, and after the war he joins the Terryville Nines—making a name in the North as Rebel Joe Tyler. He quits the game, however, when it gets too commercial, and returns to his farm in Virginia. Both Civil War novels glorify the pastoral concept of the game that is part of baseball mythology. However, the economics of the game is the predictable contrasting factor.

World War II is central to Rick Norman's *Fielder's Choice* (1991). Gooseball Fielder wins fame with an underhanded pitch for the St. Louis Browns in 1941, but the relief specialist is called to the war and is captured by the Japanese. While a prisoner, he teaches a Japanese officer's son how to throw the gooseball. The deed is discovered, and after the war Fielder is banned from baseball. *Last Days of Summer* (1998) by Steve Kluger is a World War II story in which a New York Giants star exchanges letters with young Joey Margolis. The war intrudes in Joey's life when his friend, Craig Nakamura, is placed in a concentration camp and Charlie Banks of the Giants becomes a Marine. Joey nevertheless has a grand adventure in the war years until he is informed of the death of his hero. Although the protagonists of both books recover from the trauma of the war, they learn that the game and their lives are affected by forces that are far beyond the boundaries of ballparks.

The Vietnam War determines some of the action in the 645-page family chronicle *The Brothers K* (1992) by David James Duncan. Narrated by one of the four Chance brothers of Cames, Washington, the book relates the division in the family caused by the father's obsession with baseball and the mother's religious-based fervor that includes a disdain for the game. The domestic tension increases during the Vietnam era as the brothers disagree on the proper course of war-time action. Their attitudes toward baseball are reflected in their ethical positions on the larger problems of war and peace.

The influence of gambling in the early years of the twentieth century remains a viable topic. Despite the uproar caused by the Black Sox scandal of 1919, conditions were still conducive for illegal betting and the fixing of games, as depicted in novels of the 1990s. In Allen Hoffman's *Big League Dreams* (1997), Sirdy Sternweiss, catcher for the 1920 St. Louis Browns, is bribed to take part in a fix in a game against the Tigers of Ty Cobb. He feels that the money to be made by cheating is the only way that he can afford to get married. A rabbi, though, convinces the catcher to play it straight. In Peter Levine's *The Rabbi of Swat* (1999), pitcher Morrie Ginsberg joins John McGraw's 1927 Giants and helps the team get into the World Series. However, when Ginsberg is due to start the deciding game, he is pressured to purposely lose. It takes the intervention of famed gambler Arnold Rothstein (in a reversal of his normal role) to thwart the attempted fix. Novelists continue to stress the usual economic patterns, featuring ruthless ownership, that create vulnerability among underpaid and unorganized players.

The fictional biography, an offshoot of the historical novel, often mixes factual information of a real player's life with authorial interpretation and invention. *The Celebrant* (1983) is a forerunner in the field. In *The Cleveland Indian: The Legend of King Saturday* (1992), Luke Salisbury takes the liberty of basing the novel loosely on the career of Louis Sockalexis (under a fictional name) and taking considerable leeway in presenting his subject's later years. Sockalexis is the Native American who played for Cleveland in the 1890s and is thought to be responsible for the team being known as the Indians. As King Saturday of the novel, he stars briefly in his tenure with the team before disappearing. Narrator Henry Harrison, a friend of the athlete, realizes that Saturday had been throwing games in order to get the money to buy his own team. The lawyer tries to follow the nomadic career of the ballplayer as he appears in places such as Cuba and Mexico and builds the legend of El Indio. Not much is known about the later life of Sockalexis, so the author creatively fills in the blanks—depicting a fictional character with a strong resemblance to "the" Cleveland Indian.

There is less doubt about the protagonist of Kurt Willinger's *The Spy in a Catcher's Mask* (1995). As in the first part of *The Eight Corners of the World* (1988), Moe Berg is the baseball-playing spy who begins his work for the State Department in 1934 as a member of Connie Mack's all-star team in Japan. A Princeton scholar, Morris Berg was a shortstop for Brooklyn before becoming a catcher for the White Sox in 1927. After retiring from a mediocre major league career, the Jewish intellectual is shown resuming his espionage work for the Office of Strategic Services. In the process of spying in Germany, he makes an escape from the Nazis while playing ball on a military team. The earlier entries are of interest, but it is in the early twenty-first century that the fictional bios rise to prominence.

There were also numerous miscellaneous novels of the nineties. The Jewish participation in baseball fiction is further established in a pair of 1991 books. Philip Goldberg's *This Is Next Year* presents the Stone family, with eleven-year-old Roger narrating, as passionate Dodger fans in the championship year of 1955. Roger tries to overcome the curse on the team by delivering a lucky bat to the home of Jackie Robinson. Eric Goodman's *In Days of Awe*, Jewish Joe Singer, suspended for gambling, finds redemption through good works. He is thus reinstated by the commissioner.

The free agent market creates a problem in *Season's End* (1992) by Tom Grimes. The protagonist realizes that he is being exploited as a media product, which conflicts with his Zen principles. Suffering from a psychosomatic injury and moral ambiguity, he quits the game. Teddy Moon is another player with psychological problems. Ron Faust's *Fugitive Moon* (1995) shows that a relief pitcher known as the Moonman has difficulty coping with the pressures of conformist society. Like his literary antecedents, Huck Finn and Holden Caulfield, Moon is a morally concerned outsider who is supremely independent. The influence of Thoreau and Emerson is also evident in Colin Hester's *Diamond Sutra* (1997) in which an ex-college player searches for a significant purpose in life. One of his practices is to write letters to Bill Mazeroski, 1960 Pirate hero, who serves as a moral role model.

Novels of Little League ball steadily increased in the nineties. Bruce Brook's *What Hearts* is a Newberry Honor Book for 1992, but it surpasses the usual fare for young adult fiction as it avoids a formula plot and adds picturesque baseball action. Other ostensibly juvenile works that transcend the label include Chris Lynch's *Gold Dust* (2000) and Michael Chabon's *Sumerland* (2002). Lynch readily handles a mixture of peer pressure, racial attitudes, and sports obsession. Chabon's fantasy is an allegory that reaches far beyond typical kid lit.

On the more obviously adult level, Joe Coomer's *Flatland Fable* (1986) introduced the concept of gaining redemption through coaching Little League players that was repeated in Christopher A. Bohjalian's *Past the Bleachers* (1992) and Matthew F. Jones' *The Elements of Hitting* (1994). Gene Cartwright in *I Never Played Catch with My Father* (1995) relates how a Wall Street success returns to his hometown in Texas to revive the Little League that had died due to racism. He builds a park, revives the game, and watches an integrated team play — with a girl pitcher. A major factor in these books is the process of healing the broken lives of adults through interaction with kids and baseball. Although oversimplified to some degree, the idea is the teaching of tolerance and respect through commitment to a worthwhile cause.

A baseball card is featured in *Diminished Capacity* (1995). Sherwood Kiraly's caper focuses on an eccentric character of La Porte, Missouri, who has a 1909 tobacco card of Wildfire Schulte of the Chicago Cubs, which eventually sells for $105,000. Lawrence Block's *The Burglar Who Traded Ted Williams* (1994) first introduced baseball cards as a topic. Buro's *Bite of the Shark* and Andre's *Cards: The Best and Only Novel about Baseball Card Collectors* appear in 2002. Later card novels include *The Perfect Pafko* (2005) and *The Marinolli Treasure* (2007). A famous ball is a main attraction in Don DeLillo's *Underworld* (1997). The long and complicated novel deals in part with the home run ball that won the pennant for the Giants in 1951. Historical and fictional events surrounding the "miracle of Coogan's Bluff" are the subjects of the prologue, which also is published separately as *Pafko at the Wall*. Although the book branches into other topics, the celebrated baseball, with its diverse owners, is traced over a forty-year period. Baseball memorabilia, including cards and balls, are often as important to fans as the events on the playing fields — as these novels indicate.

Minor league ball has been depicted at its best in *The Dixie Association* and *Brittle Innings*. Other earlier examples are Paul Hemphill's *Long Gone* (1979), Morry Frank's *Every Young Man's Dream* (1984), and Jerry Klinkowitz's *Short Season* (1988). *Basepaths* (1995) is a sequel to the latter in which three members of the Mason City Royals return for the next season under a new manager. Marshall J. Cook's *The Year of the Buffalo* (1997) tells how a Class A independent team in a small Wisconsin town stays in business. *Taking Lottie Home* (1999) by Terry Kay begins with the release of two players from the Augusta Hornets in 1904. One of them maintains a correspondence with his ex-teammate (apparently modeled after Ty Cobb) who goes on to become a major league star.

Amateur adult baseball is a rarer topic, but it is the subject in *The Man Who Once Played Catch with Nellie Fox* (1998) by John Manderino. A forty-year-old failure as a ballplayer, businessman, and husband plays for the Shopalot Sharks in Chicago. He reminisces about the day his father took him to a White Sox game and arranged for a meeting with the second baseman, the diminutive Fox. The lesson from that moment gives the protagonist the incentive to strive for a better life despite his setbacks. In Scott Lasser's *Battle Creek* (1999), the manager of a semipro team is plagued by moral corruption and personal problems, but the memory, at his father's funeral, of his boyhood lessons in Judaism enable him to change his priorities.

In the continuing emphasis on racial matters, C.C. Risenhoover's *White Heat* (1992) presents another white player, as in books by Charyn, Craig, and Quigley, who joins a black touring team. In the summer of 1954, a high school pitcher from Texas goes against the prevailing custom of segregation in order to hone his skills against the tough competition that the barnstormers provide. Vicki Covington's *The Last Hotel for Women* (1996) depicts the traumatic events of 1961 in Birmingham, Alabama, as Bull Connor, a symbol of segregation, observes the arrival of the freedom riders and the integration of a local baseball field. Nineteen forty-seven is a big year in baseball that is often reflected in fiction. Christopher Renino's *The Way Home Is Longer* (1997) is a batboy's view of Robinson's first season with Brooklyn. Resentment turns to respect as the youth sees how the new Dodger handles the bigotry that emanates from his teammates. A post–Robinson racial episode is the subject of *In the Fall* (1999) by Roy Minor. A St. Louis Cardinal shortstop rebels against the manager's racist policies so that the black players can get into the lineup — at which point the team begins to win. Robert David Jaffee's *Strikeout at Hell Gate* (1998) deals with racial strife in New York City in the 1990s and the effect it has on baseball. Most of the ethnic-centered novels, like those in this group, are products of the late twentieth century and beyond.

The Hispanic novel is a related subgenre that also grows in the nineties and after. Two minor novels of the sixties are set in Cuba, but the Cuban connection to American baseball takes another thirty years to become popular. Bill Granger conjures up the Hispanic influence by stressing the clash between free agency and frustrated ownership in *The New York Yanquis* (1995). Tired of paying fortunes to players who are not producing championships, the Yankee owner persuades the State Department and Fidel Castro to allow him to hire Cubans. He signs twenty-four of them and retains a relief pitcher as player-manager because he speaks Spanish. The plan is successful, and the Cuban Yanquis are later sold to the first black owner in the majors.

The scene shifts to the island nation in *Castro's Curveball* (1999) by Tim Wendell. A retired American teacher returns to the site of his 1947–1948 winter season when he was a catcher for the Washington Senators. The young Castro, a student political leader, possessed a wicked curve but gave up baseball for revolutionary activities. The catcher also temporarily joined the revolution due to the influence of a charismatic female photographer. On his trip back to Cuba forty years later, he puts the exciting events of that winter into perspective.

Darryl Brock's *Havana Heat* (2000) depicts real pitcher Dummy Taylor's attempt to make a comeback with John McGraw's Giants who are touring in Cuba during the off-season of 1911. The deaf player, a former competent big leaguer, fails to impress the Giants manager, but he discovers a pitching prospect while working with kids from the School of Ears. The deaf youth pitches successfully against the Giants in an exhibition game, and McGraw is interested—until the kid's black grandfather shows up after the game.

Jose Latour's *Havana World Series* (2003) is a crime novel set in Cuba while the 1958 World Series between the Yankees and Milwaukee Braves is being played, which is the incentive for high-stake gambling and robbery. Probably the best of the lot, though, is Brian Shawver's *The Cuban Prospect* (2003). A scout is asked to smuggle a pitcher out of Castro's domain, but complications develop as the police and the pitcher's girlfriend interfere with the plan. An escape to Florida is finally made, but the scout stays behind to work out his moral dilemma.

The Veracruz Blues (1996) by Mark Winegardner is a story of Jorge Pasqual's Mexican League of 1946 and the raid on American baseball that lured Sal Maglie, Max Lanier, Vern Stephens, Danny Gardella, and others south of the border. Gardella, one of the narrators, relates the ill-fated attempt to create a third major league. Another narrator, black pitcher Fireball Smith, laments that he will never get a chance to play in the United States. The classic fictional history of the 1946 Mexican League also contains an interlude in Cuba at the home of Ernest Hemingway whose guests include Babe Ruth, Gene Tunney, and Pasqual.

A player from the Dominican Republic is a victim of American racism in Ben J. Martin's *Caught Stealing* (1998), but the overall result dwindles to ineffective propaganda. April Smith's *Be the One* (2000) features a female scout who discovers a Dominican player who becomes a star in the majors. Minor Hispanic characters appear in several other novels, but so far the representative fictional output has failed to keep pace with the large influx of players to big league teams.

Fictional biographies, meanwhile, hit a peak in 2002 with the publication of three good novels. Ed Dinger's *A Prince at First* traces the ambivalent career of Hal Chase. A first sacker for the New York Highlanders in the early twentieth century, Prince Hal is better known for his gambling activities. He becomes convinced that baseball is in the hands of unscrupulous owners who try to maintain the positive image of the game at the expense of ballplayers. His concept of revenge, then, is throwing games for his own profit. *Old Hoss: A Fictional Baseball Biography of Charles Radbourn* by Bennett and Raycraft concentrates on the famous nineteenth century Hall of Fame pitcher. A journalist visits Bloomington, Illinois, in 1914 for a ceremony honoring Clark Griffith and the deceased Radbourn and hears stories about Old Hoss that inspire an investigation. The journalist finds that the man who won sixty games for the Providence Grays in 1884 had a hectic life primarily due to his problems with alcohol and the belief that owners were exploiting him—common adversities for players of the era. Radbourn's inability to transcend his problems led to an early death. Ty Cobb's equally traumatic experiences are featured in Patrick Creavy's *Tyrus: An American Legend*. The teenaged Cobb joins the Detroit Tigers near the end of the 1905 season shortly after the death of his father—shot while apparently spying on his wife and her suspected lover. With the startling event on his mind, Cobb refuses to accept the harassment typically allotted to rookies of the time and consequently makes enemies of most of his teammates. In the off-season, he attends the trial of his thirty-three-year-old mother. Although she is acquitted, the tension in the Cobb family is exposed to the public and does much to reveal the story behind the madness of a legendary player.

Another novel of 2002 gives the best fictional view of Babe Ruth up to this point. *Gift of the Bambino* by Jerry Amernic shows the Babe at his highest and lowest levels. Although he remains in the background, Ruth is revealed through the eyes of the narrator's grandfather who saw Ruth hit his first pro homer while a pitcher for the Providence Grays in 1914. The grandfather also happens to be in the ballpark in 1935 when the Bambino hits his last three homers while a member of the Boston Braves. The interim reveals portraits of Ruth as a complex character who is part hero and part buffoon.

E. Dee Meeriken's *Dream Season* (2004), on the other hand, deals with the life of a real minor league pitcher from California in the 1890s. Walter Settle attracts the attention of Ned Hanlon of the major league Baltimore Orioles, but the pitcher's mother and grandfather are morally opposed to baseball. Settle thus turns down a chance for the big time and reaches his zenith in an exhibition game in which he defeats the young Walter Johnson.

The combination of depicting historical events and contriving imaginative interpretations of the lives of real players is an interesting format. The Troy

Soos historical mysteries are a variation of the concept with the use of a fictional protagonist. In a similar vein, Van Reid's *Mollie Peer: Or the Underground Adventures of the Moosepath League* (2000) turns the time back to 1896 in Portland, Maine, in which journalist Mollie Peer, aided by members of a gentleman's club and ballist Wycford O'Hearn, solves a mystery. O'Hearn, known as the Hibernian Titan, plays for the amateur Portland Bantams but later fills in on the Penobscot team of Louis Sockalexis (of Cleveland Indians fame). Mollie, the female reporter, relates the story of the case under the pseudonym of Peter Mall to avoid the prejudice against women writers.

G.S. Rowe introduced his Beantown mysteries in 2003 with *Best Bet in Beantown*. Will Beaman is hired in public relations by the Boston Beaneaters in 1897 but expands his role to detecting when shortstop Germany Long is assaulted and a bookkeeper is murdered. The resulting disclosure of foul play by both gamblers and unscrupulous owners is standard fare for fiction set in the early years of pro baseball. Beaman returns in *Squeeze Play in Beantown* (2004) which is also set in Boston during the 1897 season. While searching for Beaneater Jimmy Collins' stolen gold watch, the amateur sleuth is engrossed in Boston labor disputes fueled by the speeches of Emma Goldman. The adventure includes a quest for the missing manuscript of William Bradford's "Of Plymouth Plantation." In *Double Play in Beantown* (2005), Maud Gonne shows up in the city in 1901 to spark the drive for Irish independence. Beaman, meanwhile, accepts a job with the Boston Americans of a new league while also working on the case of a missing girl. *Foul Ball in Beantown* (2006) takes place in the war year of 1918 and focuses on the problems that threaten to cause the cancellation of the World Series.

Robert B. Parker's first baseball mystery is *Mortal Stakes* (1976). *Double Play* (2004) presents Joe Burke, a World War II vet who accepts Branch Rickey's offer to serve as a bodyguard for Jackie Robinson in 1947. The tough-guy hero makes a friend of the famous Dodger and displays his code of honor by also helping a female member of a crime family. Like Honig's Joe Tinker in *The Plot to Kill Jackie Robinson*, Burke changes from an indifferent hired gun into a compassionate humanist by his fight against bigotry.

7,000 Clams (2004) by Lee Irby is a crime novel in which a young bootlegger discovers an IOU owed to a gambler—and signed by Babe Ruth. The bootlegger tracks Ruth to Florida during spring training in hopes of collecting on the note, but problems arise. The Yankee legend is depicted as the usual profligate who offsets the supposed conditioning period by carousing and drinking.

Early baseball is given farcical treatments in Randall Beth Platt's *The 1898 Baseball Fe-As-Co* (2000) and Howard Frank Mosher's *The True Account: A Novel of the Lewis & Clark & Kinneson Expeditions* (2003). Platt writes of the floundering Bowery Bulldogs of Portland, Oregon, and their subsequent relocation to the Four Arrows Ranch. The refinanced team becomes a power in the area and entices the Boston Beaneaters into coming to the Northwest for an exhibition game — an event that has a large commercial impact, especially for gamblers. The ranch soon reverts to its normal business, which is seen as easier than producing a competitive ballclub. Mosher goes farther back in time to a westward trek led by Vermont schoolteacher True Teague Kinneson. He races Lewis and Clark in the exploration of the Louisiana Purchase, and in a comically exaggerated episode devises a ballgame between his team of Nez Perce and the members of the legitimate expedition. True pitches and bats the Native American side to a lopsided victory. It seems that the teacher had invented the American game, or Kinneson-ball, to entertain his students in the year 1800, if the account is true.

A more realistic version of what early baseball history might have been is presented in *Shadow Ball: A Novel of Baseball and Chicago* (2001) by Peter M. Rutkoff. In hopes of winning the pennant for the ill-fated White Sox of 1919, owner Charles Comiskey recruits Pop Lloyd, the legendary Negro League shortstop, to replace Swede Risberg and, at the same time, convinces other owners that integration will be good for business. However, the August race riot in Chicago, and possibly Risberg's mobilization of racist teammates, convinces Lloyd that the time is not right, and he rejects the contract. Comiskey's attempt to break the color line may not have happened, but the author makes the situation plausible in a major baseball novel.

Alternative history is also the issue in *All the Stars Came Out That Night* (2005) by Kevin King. As reported posthumously by Walter Winchell, an all-star game between black and white players took place in Fenway Park — at night in 1934. Clarence Darrow blackmails Commissioner Landis into approving the secret contest that is held in October under improvised lights. Henry Ford sponsors the game, featuring major league stars against a team led by Satchel Paige and Josh Gibson, with the idea of teaching blacks that they are inferior to their white counterparts. After a series of sensational occurrences that precede the big event, the game itself, witnessed by only a few people in on the secret, is anticlimactic and the ending ambiguous. The book is, however, entertaining as a speculative view of American culture.

Race is a main factor in the third Harvey Blissberg mystery in 2001. Rosen's *Dead Ball* exposes the bigotry directed at a black outfielder who is approaching DiMaggio's fifty-six game hit streak. The Jewish sleuth, now an ex-major leaguer, traces death threats to a man with a history of racist crimes. Bill Chastain's *The Streak* (2002) presents another player with a shot at the record. Tutored by a former Negro League player, later his business partner, a white kid goes directly from high school to the majors. He ends a season with the streak at fifty-five games — and the future looks promising.

An attribute of the racially-oriented books is the attempt to heal the wounds of the past. In *Off-Season* (2000), Eliot Asinof shows how a spoiled jock changes into a moral champion as a result of a trip to his hometown. The

Dodger pitcher discovers that his black high school batterymate has been murdered, and with the help of a female journalist, he works to expose the killer. Sabbath *Creek* (2004) by Judson Mitcham brings together a teenage white kid and an old black man. The former pitcher (and a friend of Satchel Paige) serves as a surrogate father for the troubled youth. In *Suitcase Sefton and the American Dream* (2006) by Jay Feldman, the scene shifts to a Japanese internment camp of World War II. A Yankee scout discovers a pitching prospect and tries to sign him to a contract by suggesting that he could "pass" as an Apache. Jerry Yamada rejects the plan, but the scout eventually befriends the Japanese family and falls in love with the pitcher's sister. After the war, he marries Annie, becomes a partner in a Yamada family farm, and coaches an amateur baseball team that includes the former pitching prospect. Although the corrections of past mistakes are sometimes too easily achieved, the attention to ethnic prejudice is understandable given the long period in which the issue was ignored.

Science fiction continues to flourish in the twenty-first century. Polidoro's *Project Samuel* (2002) is about the cloning of Ted Williams by a group of scientists. In Wilson's *Protocol 9* (2002), a third major league produces computer-generated scripts, or protocols, that determine the outcomes of games. Cabral's *The Pitch* (2004) tells of a planet called Spalding that performs tests on players from Earth which may have led to the early deaths of Ruth and Gehrig. Strachan's *King of Diamonds* (2004) features a team from a parallel universe and an eco-parable subplot about the preservation of a rare type of frog. Advanced technology is usually the enemy in sci-fi as it tends to become a tool of business to the detriment of the idealized concept of baseball.

In 2001, W.P. Kinsella returns to prominence in fantasy with *Magic Time*. A team based in an Iowa community recruits the protagonist to supposedly compete in the Iowa Cornbelt League. Homes and jobs are provided in town by the Boosters Committee. The protagonist's epiphany is that there is no league — that the townsmen have developed a plot to keep the young men available in order to marry the local girls and to help the community survive. The team lures players of questionable ability and mental toughness who are not likely to make it to the big leagues. The idea is that many of them will opt to remain victims of the tender trap rather than to test themselves in the competitive outside world.

On a lower literary level, Les Standiford's *Opening Day* (2001) depicts an eighty-year-old batboy of a Double A Florida League who turns into a starting pitcher for the Vero Beach Groupers. The former Negro League player finds magic in his arm and Satchel Paige in his mind as he stars on the mound. Darryl Brock's *Two in the Field* (2002) is a sequel to the time-travel fantasy *If I Never Get Back*. Michael Chabon's *Summerland* (2002) transcends the label of kid lit in its tale of Coyote's plan to destroy life. The plan is thwarted by a boy and a girl, Little League teammates, who challenge the super villain to a baseball showdown. Troon McAllister's *The Kid Who Batted 1.000* (2002) is about a kid just out of high school who has the uncanny ability to foul off every pitch in the strike zone — even on a big league level. As a designated hitter, he draws a walk every time except for one at-bat in a crucial game when he homers against the Yankees. In John A. Miller's *Coyote Moon* (2003), a catcher who may be the reincarnation of a mathematician is able to read the spin of the ball and predict its speed and direction. By thus overcoming the uncertainty principle, he can hit with great results. A super pitch is the key to success in Craig J. Weincek's *The Perfect Game* (2003). A teacher develops a butterfly floater that proves to be so effective, again in the majors, that it destroys the balance of the game as in *It Happens Every Spring* and *The Curious Case of Sidd Finch*.

Radical change must be eliminated (according to fiction) if it poses threats to the traditional game. The evolving nature of baseball, though, is seen by the actual changes that have happened: the lively ball, the lowered pitching mound, free agency, the designated hitter, specialist relief pitchers, and steroid use. The invasion of women is another traumatic event — especially on the playing field.

Females continue to play the game in the novel. The first woman player in fiction may be from the 1933 short story "Miss Gulp" by Nunnally Johnson. Puechner's *A Grand Slam* introduced in 1973 the female pro (on a male team) in longer fiction. An unrecognized girl pitcher is central to Pete Fromm's *How All This Started* (2000). Abilene can throw a baseball as hard as any boy on the high school team, but she is not allowed to play. Instead she teaches her brother to be a pitcher as a means of revenge against gender discrimination — an obsession which leads to manic depression.

Arelo C. Sederberg's *The Girl Who Saved Baseball* (2004) is the sixth novel in which a lady protagonist invades the majors. Pat Carrington, masquerading as a man, joins a minor league team managed by her unwitting dad. She works her way up to the Boston Red Sox and, late in the season, reveals her identity. Patricia is an immediate sensation as a player and a gender buster, but she retires at the end of the year and embarks on a publicity campaign to make positive changes in baseball. Her battle against sexism is modified by a concern for the humanistic goal of service to society, as well as to the game.

The Red Sox are also featured in two books in which they win the World Series — before the fact of the amazing 2004 season. In David Ferrell's *Screwball* (2003), a scout discovers a Texan who can hit and pitch like Babe Ruth. The kid signs with the Sox for $186 million and immediately leads them to the Series. Unfortunately, the star is also the chief suspect in a series of murders that coincide with the team's itinerary. However, the suspicion does not keep him from heroism in Game Seven. In Howard Frank Mosher's *Waiting for Teddy Williams* (2004), a teenager from Vermont is given advice about the game by a drifter, identified as an ex-con and former local athlete named Teddy Williams. The youth apparently follows the lessons as he becomes a Sox pitcher — and hurls them to a victory in the World Series. His other mission is to find the identity of his father, and of course Mr. Williams is a prime suspect. As sensational as these novels are, the real Red Sox matched them in the 2004 post-season play.

Miscellaneous books of the early twenty-first century that deserve mention include John Grisham's *A Painted House* (2001). In the summer of 1952, seven-year-old Luke Watson listens to Harry Caray broadcast the St. Louis Cardinal games from his rural Arkansas cotton patch. He cheers for Stan Musial and longs to be a Cardinal some day. Meanwhile, on his father's rented eighty acres, the cotton pickers are divided into the hillbillies and the Mexicans as they engage in a ballgame. Cowboy of the Mexican team teaches Luke how to throw a curve. A different type of book from the popular legal thrillers of Grisham, it stresses the idea of baseball as an escape from lower-class life.

Crooked River Burning (2001) by Winegardner, author of *The Veracruz Blues*, is another mainstream novel that includes baseball as a vital element. The protagonist, a local politician, watches the decline of Cleveland and its Indians in the years 1948 to 1969. The '48 season is highlighted by Bill Veeck's hiring of Satchel Paige, who helps the team win the World Series. The '54 Series sweep by the Giants and the trade of Rocky Colavito in 1960, however, mirror the regression of the city, which is climaxed by the burning of the Cuyahoga River in 1969.

Howard Owen's *The Rail* (2002) depicts the aftermath of a great career posted by a player known as the Virginia Rail. His retirement is not as satisfactory, however, as he serves a prison term and upon release comes home to an alienated son and unforgiving townspeople. *Breaking Balls* (2001) by Paul Lebowitz is about a Jewish pitcher from Brooklyn with mediocre talent. His only desire is to make an appearance in a big league game so that his name will be recorded in *The Baseball Encyclopedia*.

Eugena Pilek's *Cooperstown* (2005) revolves around a secret held by four residents of Cooperstown, New York, home of the Baseball Hall of Fame (as well as of the nineteenth century author James Fenimore Cooper). When a theme park is proposed for the town in 1979, some of the citizens view it as a threat to the historical ambience. Cooperstown claims to be the birthplace of baseball, but ironically the secret refers to a newspaper story that seems to discredit that claim — an article from the nineteenth century that is (wrongly) interpreted as a ban against the game within the city limits. The dilemma affects many of the local population, including a newly arrived psychiatrist who tries to resolve the issue.

The diversity of baseball fiction is one of the keys to its survival. About 400 books are considered here, with well over 300 appearing since 1973. There are about seventy-five mysteries. The following sleuths appear in the ten series that have been produced to this point: Rosen's Harvey Blissberg, Geller's Slots Resnick, Gordon's Kate Henry, Nighbert's Bull Cochran, Zubro's team of Tom and Scott, Evers' Duffy House, Enger's Gun Pedersen, Soos' Mickey Rawlings, Honig's Joe Tinker, and Rowe's Will Beaman.

About sixty-five novels are in the science fiction and fantasy field, although a further breakdown reveals that fantasy yields the best literary results with such entries as *The Natural, Shoeless Joe,* and *Brittle Innings.* Hardcore sci-fi that features advanced technology and future worlds (or parallel universes), like in *Open Season* and *They Still Play Baseball on the Moon,* tends to rate lower on the literary level.

Despite the long dormant period in the first half of the twentieth century, sixty books deal with racial matters. The female entry into the baseball realm is the subject of about thirty-five novels. Among actual big leaguers, Babe Ruth makes the most novelistic appearances, followed by Ty Cobb, Jackie Robinson, and Satchel Paige. Other real ballplayers with multiple references include Lou Gehrig, Joe DiMaggio, John McGraw, Moe Berg, Casey Stengel, Ted Williams, Josh Gibson, Cy Young, Leo Durocher, and Roger Maris.

In the difficult task of selecting the best baseball novels, the list, which is arranged chronologically, begins with Lardner's *You Know Me Al* (1916), the only entry from the early period. Five books from the 1950s are noteworthy, headed by Malamud's *The Natural.* Harris' *The Southpaw* and Wallop's *The Year the Yankees Lost the Pennant* are the commercial successes of the era, but *The Sunlit Field* by Kennedy and *Man on Spikes* by Asinof are probably superior works.

The first rival to *The Natural* as a literary masterpiece is Coover's *The Universal Baseball Association*. The best of the seventies are Roth's *The Great American Novel*, Herrin's *The Rio Loja Ringmaster*, and Charyn's *The Seventh Babe.*

In 1981, Powers' *Toot-Toot-Tootsie, Good-bye* is the best book on the breakthrough of women in the game — in this case, a beauty queen turned announcer. Kinsella's *Shoeless Joe* is a fantasy that rivals the work of Malamud and Coover. *The Celebrant* (1983) by Greenberg is sometimes mentioned as belonging at the top of the list. Hays' *The Dixie Association* (1984) is a satirical treatment of minor league ball and southern culture that is presented with a literary flair.

The Black Sox scandal is the subject of a couple of contenders: Stein's *Hoopla* (1983) and Boyd's *Blue Ruin* (1991). In the nineties, *The Brothers K* by Duncan is a monumental family saga, and Bishop's *Brittle Innings* cleverly intertwines the lives of a mute, a monster, and a mulatto during the 1943 season in the Chatahoochee Valley League. Dyja's *Play for a Kingdom* (1997), Hutton's *Perfect Silence* (2000), and Boggs' *Camp Ford* (2005) are quality Civil War novels that also feature baseball.

The best of the Hispanic novels appear between 1996 and 2003: Winegardner's *The Veracruz Blues,* Wendell's *Castro's Curveball,* Brock's *Havana Heat,* and Shawver's *The Cuban Prospect.* Creavy's *Tyrus* is the outstanding fictional biography. Finally, Rutkoff's *Shadow Ball* is an example of alternate history at its best.

A tentative top ten: *The Natural; The Universal Baseball Association; The Cuban Prospect; The Veracruz Blues; The Celebrant; Shoeless Joe; Shadow Ball; Tyrus; Toot-Toot-Tootsie, Good-bye; You Know Me Al.*

II

The Novels, Year by Year

1838

Cooper, James Fenimore. Home as Found: Sequel to Homeward Bound. London: R. Bentley, 1838. (Amsterdam, NL: Fredonia Books, 2004).

Perhaps the first mention of baseball in American fiction occurs in the novel of a resident of Cooperstown, New York. Famous for the Leatherstocking Tales, Cooper depicts what is apparently a baseball game in a short scene (in a book published a year before the mythical invention of the game) which reveals several apprentice-boys playing ball on the lawn of a wealthy man. Angered by this encroachment of aristocratic premises, he instructs his lawyer, Aristabulus Bragg, to remove the interlopers. Bragg convinces the ballplayers that it is more daring to play ball in the street than on property adorned with roses and dahlias. Although it is against the local law to play ball in the street, the rowdy apprentices gladly move the game there. The battle between social classes is prominent in the novel, and a similar conflict between working-class and educated ballplayers occurs in later fiction.

1868

Everett, William. Changing Base. Boston: Lee & Shepard, 1868.

Although classified as a young adult novel, *Changing Base* is credited with presenting the first description of a baseball game. The Royal Base Ball Club, displaying Harvard discipline, goes against the Clintons, a working class team from a neighboring town. The Royals lead by a score of 24–22 when the game is suspended due to snow — it is the third of December. Henry Clayton, the umpire and former Harvard player, warns the Clintons that teams will refuse to play them in the future unless there is some assurance that they conduct themselves like men instead of blackguards. The fear that baseball will be dominated by lower-class ruffians is evident in the description of the game action. However, most of the book deals with the schoolboy adventures of the protagonist, Edward (Ned) Rice.

1884

Brooks, Noah. *Our Baseball Club and How It Won the Championship.* New York: E.P. Dutton, 1884.

This is another novel referred to as young adult, but it is the first to deal entirely with baseball. The town of Catalpa, Illinois, has two semipro baseball teams. The Dean County Nine consists of lower- and middle-class working men. The Catalpa Nine includes professional men, students, and the sons of aristocrats. The animosity between the teams is overshadowed by a common enemy — the Jonesvilleans from eighteen miles down the Stone River. In a championship game with the Catalpa Nine, the rough and uncouth players from Jonesville win. The defeat rallies the leading citizens of Catalpa to sponsor a team that they can be proud of — even if it means inviting some of the Dean County players to participate. Money is used to lure the players that will produce a state title. The plan works as winning becomes more important than making class distinctions. The apparent positive concept of meritocracy, however, leads to a new problem for the Catalpas. The economic burden of creating a championship team now comes into play — and that is a situation that has haunted the game and is a major theme of baseball fiction.

1888

Thayer, Ernest L. "Casey at the Bat." 1888. Gardner, Martin. *The Annotated Casey at the Bat: A Collection of Ballads About the Mighty Casey.* Chicago: The University of Chicago Press, 1967.

Although a fifty-two line poem, the popular stage rendition of it by actor William deWolf Hopper spotlights the first baseball hero in literature who fails. The five minute and forty second dramatic reading by Hopper depicts an ironic folk hero. In the poem, Casey, who is idolized by doting fans, is outdone in the Big Game by a virtually anonymous opponent. "There is no joy in Mudville" becomes one of the most recognized passages in literature, and Casey's fall is an event that signifies the realistic reaction to the heroics prevalent in pulp fiction.

1889

Twain, Mark. *A Connecticut Yankee in King Arthur's Court.* New York: Charles L. Webster, 1889. (New York: Pocket Books, 2000.)

Mark Twain's Connecticut Yankee attempts to introduce baseball to the knights and rulers of sixth century England in order to channel the excesses of chivalry and tournaments into a more civilized direction. Unfortunately, the knights refuse to remove their armor, and the game becomes farcical. The sport is soon abandoned (after a page or two) for warfare, the usual pastime of the era.

1895

Perry, Bliss. *The Plated City.* New York: C. Scribner's Sons, 1895.

Although dealing briefly with baseball, the novel portrays the banning of a black player shortly after the historical fact. In the 1880s, Organized Baseball began its segregated policy by unofficially ousting Fleet Walker and other African Americans. In the book, Tom Beaulieu, an orphan raised in a black community, plays for the Buccaneers against New York at the Polo Grounds, but he is recognized by fans from Bartonvale, Connecticut (the Plated City), as the man who played second base for their team the season before. He led the State League in hitting as Beaulieu, but now he is playing as Mendoza. Newspapers pick up the story that the Spaniard of the Bucs is of questionable ethnic origin, and his teammates refuse to play with him. Mendoza/Beaulieu is released and no other pro (white) team will offer him a contract. He considers playing for the Cuban Giants and resigning to a life on the black side of the color line, but he decides to stay among friends in North Boston where race is not an issue. It took the major leagues until 1947 to integrate, and the next baseball novel to confront the problem did not appear until 1950 (*Behold, Thy Brother*).

1897

Standish, Burt L. *Frank Merriwell's Danger.* New York: Street & Smith, 1897.

The moral icon of boys' fiction plays baseball at Yale and invents a pitch, the double shoot, that breaks two ways. In the 1899 sequel, *Frank Merriwell's Double Shot*, he refuses to sell the secret of the pitch to pro players—and decides not to turn pro himself.

1902

Whiting, Robert Rudd. *The Fat Mascot.* New York: J.S. Ogilvie, 1902. (Springfield, Il: Lincoln Herndon Press, 1988.)

By the turn of the century, baseball novels are becoming popular and are primarily for kids. They tend to use the Horatio Alger formula: good boys become successful (by winning the Big Game) through hard work and good luck. Along with Noah Brooks and William Everett, writers like Wallace Peck, Tom Teaser, Bill Boxer, and Carolyn Davis are working in the genre. In the 1890s, The Burt L. Standish (Gilbert Patten) books of Frank Merriwell begin to appear, many of them dealing with baseball, and their immense popularity helps establish the formula of pulp fiction—a form of subliterature that the public devours and the publishers love. Whiting, however, strays from the popular format of heroic kid lit by presenting tall tales of baseball. Originally a collection of nineteen related stories (making it a novel by some definitions) in 123 pages, the book relates the feats of the Lightfoot Lilies and the Ringtail Roarers, baseball teams of the 1880s. In the tradition of the tall tale established by Longstreet, Ward, Billings, Harte, and Twain, which humorously exaggerates remarkable exploits, the former mascot of the Lilies narrates the adventures of some singular "ballists." Pitcher Dean Braley, for instance, invents automoroller skates so that he will not have to waste energy by running the bases. Another pitcher, Jim Timpson, throws curves that break so much that a catcher is not needed: after crossing the plate, the balls bend around to either the first or third basemen. Stump Greenwood plays with a wooden arm, and cowboy

Tanglefoot Tom wears his pistols on the field. The narrator himself, now retired, was used as a pinch-hitter because his stomach protruded so much that he would virtually always get hit by a pitch. In 1907, another Whiting book is published—*A Ball of Yarn, Its Unwinding*—which contains three more baseball stories. The two books are combined in a 1988 publication of *The Fat Mascot*.

1909–1915

Grey, Zane. *The Short-stop.* Chicago: A.C. McClurg, 1909. (New York: William Morrow, 1992.)
_____. *The Young Pitcher.* New York: Harper & Bros., 1911. (New York: Kessinger, 2004.)
_____. *The Redheaded Outfield and Other Baseball Stories.* New York: McClure Newspaper Syndicate, 1915. (New York: Kessinger, 2005.)

Juvenile dime novels are in vogue, and in 1898 Frank Tousey introduces the Fred Fearnot Series to rival the Merriwell popularity. In 1912, Edward Stratemeyer (writing as Lester Chadwick) brings Baseball Joe to life. At first, he is a high school and college player like the protagonists of Heyliger, Barbour, Dudley, and Fullerton, but Joe Matson eventually becomes a pro in a 1914 book. The same year, Gilbert Patton, the Merriwell creator, produces the first five of the Big League Series (as Burt L. Standish) featuring Lefty Locke. Baseball immortal Christy Mathewson is named as author of *Pitcher Pollock* in 1914 and several other books that are attributed to John Wheeler. In 1920, Babe Ruth is apparently supplied with a ghost writer for *The Home-Run King*.

Grey, former college baseball player and eventually popular western novelist, enters the field with two novels and a story collection usually categorized as young adult. In *The Short-stop*, Chase Alloway leaves home at eighteen to make a living at the game. He begins as a pitcher, but his curve ball is so unique that he is labeled as a crooked-eye hoodoo, and he is forced to flee. After weeks of riding the rails, he gets a chance to play with Findley. He converts the team into a winner by his Ty Cobb attitude, and he eventually signs with Detroit. The promising start of the novel deteriorates into a formula of heroic action, however, as Alloway provides a home for his mother, his crippled brother, and a hunchbacked boy. His altruism wins him the right to court an upper-class girl. Alloway also rejects an offer from a gambler to throw a game—an indication of the rampant gambling influence in the early years of pro baseball.

The Young Pitcher follows the formula from the beginning. Ken Ward overcomes a difficult first semester at Wayne University to lead the team to a championship as a freshman. Ward is another Frank Merrriwell or any of the other heroic protagonists of the genre. In the short story book, however, Grey escapes from the norm. He presents the characters as individuals with humorous traits that are welcome variations from the pattern. The redheaded outfielders and their cohorts are more like the Whiting players of *The Fat Mascot*. The Rochester Stars outfielders are patterned after the actual Buffalo Bisons of 1897, which included Grey's brother, Romer.

1910

Mathewson, Christy. *Won in the Ninth.* New York: R.J. Bodner, 1910.

The first of the "Matty Books" for Young Adults, it begins a trend in which famous players are provided with ghost writers. Frank Chance and Babe Ruth (*The Home-Run King*) also sell their names to the publishing industry in the 1910 to 1920 era.

1912

Chadwick, Lester. (Edward Stratemeyer). *Baseball Joe of the Silver Stars.* New York: Cupples & Leon, 1912.

_____. *Baseball Joe on the School Nine.* New York: Cupples & Leon, 1912.

Part of the Stratemeyer syndicate, the Baseball Joe Series for Young Adults was the first among the boys' sports series to deal exclusively with baseball.

1914

Hopper, James. *Coming Back with the Spitball: A Pitcher's Romance.* New York: Harper & Bros., 1914. (Bedford, MA: Applewood Books, 1996.)

In a marginally adult novella, Tom Carsey, a former star pitcher of the New York Giants is demoted to the Pacific Coast League. Alcohol abuse leads to his drop to the Prune City Prunepickers of the Class C Interior League. Freckles, a boy with a wooden leg, helps to restore Carsey's pride. While playing catch with Freckles, the former big-leaguer discovers the spitball, a legal pitch of the time, and works his way back to the Giants in time to help win the World Series. He signs a two-year contract and plans to get married and adopt Freckles. This is no improvement over the typical juvenile book.

1915

Curtis, Philip. *The Ladder: The Story of a Casual Man.* New York: Harper & Bros., 1915.

Frank O'Connor, an orphan, runs away from the farm of his aunt and uncle in 1897. He gets a factory job in Plummer's Falls and plays secondbase for the company team. The Spanish-American War interrupts his career, but he picks up, on his return, with a team sponsored by the Brookfield Insurance Company that plays semipro clubs from Boston. O'Connor is accomplished enough to enter Leicester University as a baseball mercenary. He attends several schools and is awarded "the program privilege" at a major university, which amounts to selling his name to an advertising company for $1200. After eventually graduating, Connor becomes a success as a reporter, dramatist, and politician.

Written in a Victorian style, with some humor, the novel is too melodramatic to claim honors. However, the disclosure of corruption in college sports at the turn of the century is noteworthy. The business aspect of the game is stressed rather than the character building associated with athletic competition in the popular kid lit of the time. The problem of economics in baseball, introduced in *Our Baseball Club and How It Won the Championship*, becomes a major theme in baseball fiction in the future.

Ferguson, William Blair Morton. *A Man's Code.* New York: G.W. Dillingham, 1915.

Richard Steele, shortstop of the Boston Badgers, commits a throwing error that allows the New York Manhattans to win the World Series. Reporter Bob Somerville accuses him of throwing the game for a $10,000 bribe. Steele admits to league authorities that the money was left in his hotel room, and that he considered accepting it to help his sick brother, but he says that he returned it. Since the money is not accounted for, Steele, known as Scrappy or the Fighting Runt, is given two weeks to prove his innocence before being banned from baseball. His time expires, and he works at a factory in Claypole, Virginia. He plays semipro ball as Smith. When Somerville arrives in Claypole, his hometown, the two become rivals for the affection of Peggy Overton. Somerville, who had framed Scrappy Steele and caused his banishment, tries it again. This time it backfires. Somerville is exposed as a villain. Steele is reinstated by major league baseball and has the option of returning to the Badgers. His code of honor, in not revealing Bob Somerville's duplicity without proof, is considered foolish by Peggy Overton, but she proclaims her love for the shortstop. Despite the predictability of the plot, the intimation of a fixed World Series before 1919 Black Sox is prophetic.

Needham, Henry B. *The Double Squeeze.* Garden City, NY: Doubleday, Page, 1915.

A young adult collection of four stories, it features Manager Tris Ford, who is based on the author's friend, Connie Mack.

1916

Lardner, Ring. *You Know Me Al.* New York: George H. Doran Co., 1916. (New York: Kessinger Publishing, 2004.)

Lardner brings national attention to baseball fiction with the Jack Keefe "Letters from a Busher" series in *The Saturday Evening Post*. The first story appears in 1914, and it becomes part of the 1916 novel which is the first classic in the field. Keefe's problem of striving for economic security in an owner-dominated game mirrors the situation of major league baseball that led to the 1919 Black Sox scandal. The players of Keefe's era are exploited by owners, which makes them vulnerable to gamblers. Jack Keefe's ignorance, however, aggravates his condition. His letters to Al Blanchard of Bedford, Indiana, Jack's hometown, reveal his inability to learn from experiences. After signing as a pitcher with owner Charles Comiskey of the Chicago White Sox, for $1500, he fails in his first major league tenure and is sent to the West Coast League. Meanwhile, he has affairs with Violet and Hazel— before marrying Florence. They move to an expensive apartment in Chicago in the off-season, but Comiskey refuses to grant an increase in salary or a loan. Florence leaves her husband, but they are reunited when a son is born. Despite continuing marital and economic problems, Keefe completes the season with the White Sox and joins the world tour of the Sox and Giant players during the winter.

Much of the charm of the book comes from the language with which Jack Keefe exposes his defects. His Huck Finn–like semi literacy tends to emphasize his misunderstanding of himself and the society. His ego always demands that someone else causes his problems, and the humor of his excuses and contradictions dominates the action. He is a static character who is doomed to repeat his errors. Jack Keefe is an archetype of baseball fiction that Lardner uses to debunk the Horatio Alger–Frank Merriwell stereotype associated with kid lit.

1918

Lardner, Ring. *Treat 'em Rough.* Indianapolis: Bobbs-Merrill, 1918. (New York: Kessinger Publishing, 2005.)

Jack Keefe gets a deferment from the draft in 1918 because of his two dependents. However, when the draft board discovers that Florrie (Florence) has a beauty shop, Jack is soon in the army at Camp Grant. He boasts of becoming a Kaiser Killer but lives in fear of the man in the next bunk. The unchanging traits of the pitcher are continued without the baseball aspect. The quality of the earlier book is not present here.

Witwer, H.C. *From Baseball to Boches.* Boston: Small, Maynard, 1918.

Much like Jack Keefe, Witwer's Ed Harmon is a pitcher who is drafted when America enters World War I. He writes to his friend Joe about his exploits in France. Harmon is much more successful than Keefe, though, or a much bigger liar. According to his reports, he marries a beautiful French woman, fights on the frontline, serves on missions to Paris and London, shoots down a German plane, and is honored by General Pershing. In London, he pitches in a game between the army and the navy. Harmon hits a game winning homer just as the Germans (Boches) commence bombing. Witwer's epistolary style is an imitation of Ring Lardner but displays less talent.

1919

Lardner, Ring. *The Real Dope.* Indianapolis: Bobbs-Merrill, 1919. (New York: Kessinger Publishing, 2005.)

Jack Keefe's wartime adventures continue. He writes an article for a regimental paper, "War and Baseball 2 Games where Brains Wins," but later rationalizes his opinion when events contradict the analogy. In action, Jack gets wounded. While recovering, he attempts to woo a nurse even though his wife Florrie has just given birth to a daughter. He is eventually sent home, but he remains the static character of *You Know Me Al*, which should have been his only novelistic appearance. Lardner did produce other stories of Keefe ("The Busher Abroad" and "The Busher Re-enlists" groups) that have not been "novelized." The portrait of the pitcher stays consistent, but some of the stories display the quality of the famous novel.

Witwer, H.C. *A Smile a Minute.* Boston: Small, Maynard, 1919.

Ed Harmon resumes his letter to Joe. The war in France is providing the second lieutenant with a "smile a minute." Though he is wounded during the capture of a German machine-gun crew, he is visited by his French wife, Jeanne, who is pregnant. He goes home as a first lieutenant and prepares to continue his baseball career. The pitcher signs with the Reds and writes to Joe about giving up nine runs to the Cubs in one inning. Ed gets mad at his friend for publishing his earlier letters as the book *From Baseball to Boches.*

1920

Witwer, H.C. *There's No Base Like Home.* Garden City, NY: Doubleday, Page, 1920.

In the conclusion of the Ed Harmon trilogy, the protagonist sells sporting goods to augment his income from baseball. He also writes articles (in his Keefe-like semiliterate style) for a newspaper. Jeanne, his wife, tries to get him into following her into the acting profession. After helping the Reds win the World Series, Ed quits baseball and becomes an actor, much to Jeanne's delight. Witwer is sometimes amusing, but his imitation of Lardner is obvious and the quality inferior.

1921

Beaumont, Gerald. *Hearts and the Diamond.* New York: Dodd, Mead, 1921.

A collection of eleven stories of Pacific Coast League baseball, it stresses wacky players (in the vogue of Whiting, Grey, Lardner and Witwer) who are involved in bizarre romances.

1923

Broun, Heywood. *The Sun Field.* New York: G.P. Putnam's Sons, 1923.

Sports writer George Wallace narrates the story of his quest for Judith Wigglesworth Winthrop who, however, is enamored with Yankee rightfielder Tiny Tyler—a slugger in the mode of Babe Ruth. Wallace accuses her of being a Puritan, as her name suggests, when she does not respond ardently to his courtship. Judith's concept of ideal male beauty in action does not apply to the diminutive writer. Tyler comes much closer to what she wants, and he eventually marries her. When an injury ends his career, he becomes a politician. Judith pursues her vocation as a novelist. Wallace rationalizes his failure by insisting that her lust for the ballplayer revealed her shallowness. Broun, a sportswriter himself (like Ring Lardner) and a member of the Algonquin Round Table (a famous literary group) knew many major leaguers, and some of them serve as models for characters in the book. Baseball, though, is of less concern in the novel than the reaction of society to feminist principles.

1925

Fitzgerald, F. Scott. *The Great Gatsby.* New York: Scribner, 2004.

While not a baseball novel, this classic uses sports, including baseball, as a means of commenting on moral corruption. Fitzgerald, a friend and neighbor of Ring Lardner, depicts the unscrupulous Tom Buchanan as an ex-college football player who never adjusts to life after his athletic career is over — an exemplary victim of the ex-jock syndrome. Jordan Baker, Nick Carraway's summer girlfriend, cheats in a golf tournament. Meyer Wolfsheim, Gatsby's business partner, is the man who fixed the 1919 World Series and is apparently a fictional version of Arnold Rothstein, the gambler associated with the Black Sox scandal. Carraway, narrator and moral arbiter of the novel, is appalled at Gatsby's link to Wolfsheim — a symbol of the corruption of the American Dream and the antithesis of Ben Franklin, Gatsby's boyhood role model. The moral and economic exploitation of baseball is testimony to the declining American value system that is the essence of the novel.

1926

Griffith, Peggy. *The New Klondike.* New York: Jacobson-Hodgkinson, 1926.

Subtitled "A Story of a Southern Baseball Training Camp," it is based on a motion picture directed by Lewis Milestone and written by Thomas J. Geraghty, Ben Hecht and Ring Lardner. The 155-page novella tells the story of Tom Kelly, a pitcher, who leaves Westbury, New Jersey, to report for spring training in Fairhaven, Florida. Traveling by ship, Kelly meets Evelyn Lana and her lawyer, Morgan West. At the baseball camp, Kelly is released from the team because he is a threat to reveal the incompetent coaching to owner Colonel Dwyer. A shady real estate deal with West gets the pitcher in financial trouble, but Dwyer comes to the rescue. He makes Kelly the manager of his team, which is moved to a park in Miami, so West loses money in his Fairhaven scheme. Kelly realizes that Evelyn Lana is not involved with the lawyer's plot, and the ballplayer and the lady declare their mutual love. The movie/book is an early form of a baseball romance, which typically features a subliterate text and sparse baseball action.

1929

Faulkner, William. *The Sound and the Fury.* New York: Vintage, 1991.

Another major American novel that is not usually included in a baseball bibliography, it does have a subtext that alludes to the game. The villainous Jason Compson, the last of a once prominent Mississippi family, tries to make money on the Commodities Market. His losses in cotton provoke a verbal assault on the New York Jews and the 1928 New York Yankees — representatives of the hated North. Compson associates the fame of Babe Ruth with the forces that deprive Southerners of economic success. Spurred by the rumors of Ruth's questionable ethnic background, the Mississippian sees the Babe as a threat to the Southern way of life — including racial superiority and the necessity of segregation. Faulkner exposes racism in much of his Yoknapatawpha County fiction, and here the baseball aspect is used effectively to mirror the social bias of the Old South.

1933

Lardner, Ring. *Lose with a Smile.* New York: Charles Scribner's Sons, 1933.

Danny Warner is the narrator/protagonist now, but he tells his story in letters like Jack Keefe. The recipient is Jessie Graham, the girl Warner wants to marry, from Centralia, Illinois. He has the same colloquial style and many of the same problems as Keefe, but Warner is favored with the advice of his roommate, Casey Stengel, who is described as a "kind of Asst mgr and coach" of the Dodgers. When Warner gets demoted to Jersey City, he invites Jessie there for a marriage proposal. However, he feels unworthy because of his demotion. He plans to give up baseball and perhaps try his luck as a singer ("grooner") on the radio. Stengel has helped with the lyrics of Warner's songs, and he hopes to emerge as Rudy, a pop singer. Jessie promises to arrive in Jersey City on Saturday — and it is leap year.

Danny Warner is a marginal baseball player, and his future in music is not too promising either. He has Jack Keefe's problem of not learning from mistakes, so he will have to learn to lose with a smile. The book has its humorous moments and Casey Stengel, but it is a weaker effort than *You Know Me Al*.

1934

Fitzsimmons, Cortland. *Death on the Diamond.* New York: Frederick A. Stokes, 1934.

Subtitled "A Baseball Mystery Story," it features mass murders of players. Rookie Larry Doyle of the New York Royal Blues is a suspect since the first victim is a rival for Frances, daughter of Blues manager Pop Clark. Other players are killed, however, and reporter Terry Burke is threatened by hoods for getting too close to the truth in his investigation. Meanwhile panic sets in and some games are cancelled. A Detroit pitcher retires because of fear. Burke discovers that the Reynold brothers, one a reporter and the other a player, are the culprits. They are betting on the Blues to win and are thus eliminating major opponents. Bill Kelly of the Homicide Squad concocts a plan to nab the gamblers by having Pop Clark purposely lose a game. He and Pop's daughter Frances convince the manager that fixing one game is justifiable if it will expose the corrupting presence of crime in baseball. Larry Doyle, now playing for the Washington Feds after being unloaded by Pop, hopes to get back to the Blues and to Frances in the near future. The first baseball mystery makes an attempt to deal with the threat of gambling, but the plot is too sensational to be taken seriously.

1932–1940

Farrell, James T. *Studs Lonigan: A Trilogy Comprising Young Lonigan, The Young Manhood of Studs Lonigan, and Judgment Day.* Urbana-Champaign: University of Illinois Press, 1993.

_____. *No Star Is Lost.* New York: Vanguard, 1938.

_____. *Father and Son.* New York: Vanguard, 1940.

Wolfe, Thomas. *Of Time and the River.* New York: Scribners, 1999.
_____. *You Can't Go Home Again.* New York: Harper Perennial, 1998.

In a bleak period for the adult baseball novel, two mainstream authors incorporated the game into their literature. Farrell, in *The Studs Lonigan Trilogy* and in the first three of the *Danny O'Neill Tetralogy*, depicts the influence of baseball on Irish Catholics of Chicago. Studs Lonigan's father follows the White Sox of Comiskey before the Black Sox scandal. Studs is not as interested as his dad or young Danny O'Neill, but he listens animatedly as Old Man O'Brien talks about the exploits of Rube Waddell, eccentric left-handed pitcher. Studs plays sandlot ball, but he does not have the talent of the younger O'Neill. As a young man, in the third volume, Studs returns to the playground as a rightfielder in a practice game, but fails both in the field and at bat. He decides to retire from active play and to perform as a star in his imagination. His lack of success in baseball mirrors his physical and social deterioration. Studs dies young — a bitter and bigoted product of the environment.

Danny O'Neill, however, with his skill and passion for the game, is able to transcend the fate of Studs. Throughout his adolescence, Danny attends White Sox games. He witnesses Ed Walsh's no-hitter and admires the skill and integrity of Eddie Collins. He writes a letter to Connie Mack in hopes of being scouted. Danny does not become a pro, but in the final novel of the series, *My Days of Anger* (1943), he evolves into a Marxist activist — a representative of his creator's philosophy. His love of baseball indicates his virile approach to life in contrast to the waning interest of Studs, which is suggestive of his early demise.

In Thomas Wolfe's *Of Time and the River*, Ben Gant, brother of protagonist Eugene, posts the scores of the 1912 World Series between the Giants and Red Sox in the newspaper office window of the small southern town of Catawba. The description of the final game illustrates the importance of baseball to American life in the early twentieth century. The poetic language intensifies the game as an event that draws the nation together (as much as segregation allows) in a fantasy of mythical proportion. The story of Nebraska Crane, however, in *You Can't Go Home Again*, is a more realistic view of the hard life of a pro at a time when owners ruled — long before free agency and high salaries. Crane, part Cherokee major leaguer, tells George (Monk) Webber, the protagonist, about the problems of making a living in baseball. He now has 300 acres of his own, and if he can no longer survive as a player, he can go home to his rural roots and farm the land. He tries to convince Webber that baseball is not the embodiment of the American Dream. It is a job, like farming.

The contradictory views of the game that Wolfe presents are indicative of the change from the early concept of a pastoral idyll into a big business. The innocence associated with the rural myth is offset by the professional teams, starting with the 1869 Cincinnati Red Stockings. The difference between the ideal of friendly competition and the reality of economic profit becomes a major literary topic.

Alexander, Holmes. *Dust in the Afternoon.* New York: Harper & Bros., 1940.

Serialized in *The Saturday Evening Post* in four parts during August of 1940, it depicts the difficult romance of Steve Grady, pitcher of the Hawks, and Julie Forbes, aspiring actress. They elope after he is released from a Georgia prison. He served six months for manslaughter—taking the blame for Julie who had been driving a car involved in a fatal accident. Grady resumes his major league career with the New York Hawks managed by shortstop Joe Duval. Worried about Julie's relationship with actor Stan Caples, the pitcher slumps and is sold to the Phillies. Julie, after an argument with her husband, gets into another car accident. She accuses Grady of driving, but during the trial, she confesses. When the Phillies release him, she persuades the Hawks to take him back. Grady becomes a star relief pitcher for the team, but Julie is tired of being a baseball widow and leaves him. In a game at the end of the season in New York, Grady pitches and bats the Hawks to a win over the Cardinals. Julie appears after the game, and she and her husband are reunited.

Alexander portrays a protagonist who is the opposite of Jack Keefe. Grady is smart and heroic. He is capable of learning and changing. He develops a new pitching style, featuring a change-up, and also accommodates his wife's desire to have her own career. However, the book is a long way from the artistic success of *You Know Me Al*. An interesting footnote is that it is listed in a Leo Durocher bibliography because Joe Duval, player-manager of the Hawks, is supposedly a fictional portrait of him.

1940–1958 John R. Tunis

The most popular writer of kid's baseball novels around mid century, Tunis persists in the Horatio Alger motif in which virtue is rewarded. *The Kid from Tomkinsville* (1940), World Series (1941), and *The Kid Comes Back* (1946) feature Roy Tucker as a courageous and determined ballplayer who changes from pitcher (after an arm injury) to outfielder and from World War I soldier to veteran Dodger star. Other novels include *Keystone Kids* (1943), *Rookie of the Year* (1944), *Highpockets* (1948), *Young Razzle* (1949), *Buddy and the Old Pro* (1955), and *Schoolboy Johnson* (1958), Tunis makes an attempt at social realism, as his characters struggle against their anti–Semitism, selfishness, and insensitivity, but the justice and sentiment of the pulp-fiction formula prevail. More authors of boys' books of the time are Clair Bee, Wilfred McCormick, Duane Decker, Jackson Scholz, Joe Archibald, Robert Sidney Bowen, Curtis K Bishop, John R. Cooper, and others. The first to deal with integration is Florence Hayes with *Skid* in 1948, a year after Jackie Robinson's arrival in Brooklyn.

1942–1970 Jackson Scholz

A major rival of Tunis in the field of Young Adult baseball fiction, Scholz follows the formula in which the hero overcomes adversity on the way to accomplishing heroic feats. Starting with *Soldiers at Bat* in 1942 and concluding with *Hot-Corner Hank* in 1970, he produced fifteen baseball novels as well as books in other sports. His books are similar (like those of Tunis) to the so-called adult productions of the A. S. Barnes Company from 1948 to 1959 (written by Frank O'Rourke, Ed Fitzgerald, Jack Weeks, and Arnold Hano) which adhere to the Horatio Alger success story.

1946

Smith, H. Allen. *Rhubarb.* Garden City, NY: Doubleday, 1946. (New York: Pocket Books, 1977.)

The title character is a cat who inherits the New York Loons. Thaddeus Banner dies and leaves the baseball team to his pet. Former sportswriter and current public relations counselor for Banner, Eric Yaeger is appointed as Rhubarb's guardian. Loons' slugger, Hannibal Tatlock, refuses to play for a cat, and he becomes the companion of Banner's daughter in her legal challenge to the will. The Loons' manager, Leonard Sickles, convinces the rest of the team that a yellow cat is good luck, and the Loons go on to win the World Series as Rhubarb emerges as a national celebrity. The illustrated book is rather shocking for the time in its depiction of the amorous exploits of Rhubarb and some of the humans, but the humor is not very well sustained, and the overall quality is mediocre.

1947

Bagby, George. *The Twin Killing.* Garden City, NY: Doubleday, 1947.

Writing as Aaron Marc Stein, the author produces an unlikely mystery with Inspector Schmidt investigating the murder of a gambler. Narrated by Baggy Schmidt's partner, the search for the killer of Vince Shane involves rookie New York stars Whitey Roos and Blackie Crawford. Schmidt discovers that a henchman of Shane is guilty of the murder and of the attempt to frame Blackie Crawford. Once in the clear, the two rookies break out of their slumps, get married, and become fathers—presumably to live happily ever after. There is not much literary merit in this second baseball mystery either (following *Death on the Diamond*, 1934).

1948

Fitzgerald, Ed. *The Turning Point.* New York: A. S. Barnes, 1948.

A. S. Barnes and Company apparently decides to capitalize on the continual popularity of juvenile baseball fiction by publishing novels in the adult field. Over the next few years, Fitzgerald, Frank O'Rourke, Arnold Hano, and Jack Weeks write books that basically follow the success formula of kid lit with a bit more sophistication but little regard for literary competency.

The first of Fitzgerald's three Marty Ferris books for A. S. Barnes, *The Turning Point*, focuses on the senior year of high school at White Plains, New York, and the following summer. Ferris helps the school team win the championship and is scouted by Lazarus Dedrick of the Yankees. As the MVP of an all-star game, he wins the right to accompany the Yanks on a road trip. Ferris makes friends with reserve outfielder Taffy Lewis, who advises him to go to college before turning pro. Albert Ferris, Marty's father, and Jean, Marty's girlfriend, support the decision to get an education first. The author, a sportswriter, has little talent as a novelist.

Idell, Albert E. *The Great Blizzard.* New York: Henry Holt, 1948.

In 1884, Zenie Rogers of New York City loves Clinton Weatherby, a pitcher for the Brooklyns. Her brother and her mother are distrustful of rowdy ballists, so Weatherby hides his identity from them. Zenie's father, however, becomes a fan of the game, and he helps the pitcher get a job of reporting on baseball for a newspaper. Clinton and Zenie get married, but he never feels like part of the family. Finally, during the blizzard of 1888, when their daughter is born, he is accepted in good standing. Meanwhile, Mr. Rogers is stranded on Wall Street by the storm, and he writes a humorous article about a mock baseball game played by wealthy stockholders who are snowed in. The book captures the ambiance of the era, including the ambiguous reactions to baseball and ballists.

O'Rourke, Frank. *Flashing Spikes.* New York: A.S. Barnes, 1948.
The first baseball novel for A. S. Barnes by the prolific writer, it tells of shortstop Bill Riley's rise from semipro ball to the big leagues. At the end of the 1947 season, he makes the majors with the Mound City Red Wings and he becomes a regular the next season. A complication develops when a reporter accuses Riley of associating with Dane Bjorland, a fictional version of Swede Risberg of the Black Sox scandal. However, the charge is dropped in the commissioner's office, and Riley signs a $15,000 contract for the next year — plus a $5.000 gift from the owner. Realistic in its depiction of baseball, the book is otherwise mediocre.

1949

Davies, Valentine. *It Happens Every Spring.* New York: Farrar, Straus, 1949. (New York: Avon, 1949.)
Also a 1949 movie, the screenplay is adapted to the novel about a chemistry teacher who invents a solution that is repellent to wood. Vernon Kelly Simpson makes the discovery by accident when a baseball breaks a window of the chemistry lab. Simpson tries out his product on college players. When they have trouble hitting the doctored balls, Simpson reports to the St. Louis team with the hopes of becoming a major league pitcher. Manager Dolan gives him a chance, and he becomes a sensation as King Kelly. As a star player, he attempts to hide his identity from the president of the college and the president's daughter, Debbie Greenleaf. However, they find out who King Kelly is and watch the games as he pitches St. Louis into the World Series against New York. Finally in the seventh game, the magical solution runs out, and he staggers to a 6–5 win, his fourth victory of the Series. Simpson has had enough of the heroic life, though, and he is glad to be reinstated in his college job by President Greenleaf, who elevates him to associate professor. A wedding is Debbie's reward for the returned teacher.
Davies, also author of the Christmas classic, *Miracle on 34th Street,* may have borrowed the plot for his fantasy from a story by Ralph Henry Barbour, prolific "prep school" writer of the early twentieth century. The novel, with help from the movie starring Ray Milland and Jean Peters, introduces sci-fi into the realm of baseball fiction, which eventually becomes a popular subgenre. The book itself is of little merit, and its premise is farcical.

O'Rourke, Frank. *The Team.* New York: A.S. Barnes, 1949.

Coach Benny Benson narrates the story of the 1949 Quaker City team managed by Billy Lawson. Real National League players are on the opposing teams while fictional characters resembling the '49 Phillies play for Quaker City. Robbie Ashton (based on Richie Asburn) sparks the team to a twenty-three game winning streak at the end of the season that boosts it to a third-place finish. After the season, Benson, Lawson, and Ashton visit a kid who is troubled by the bad things he has heard about the recently dead Baron (Babe Ruth). The manager rationalizes the outrageous behavior of the legendary figure and apparently restores the boy's faith in the glory of the game. The positive aspects of baseball are stressed, but the apology for Ruth's off-field deportment and the portrait of a non-championship team make the book unusual for an A. S. Barnes product.

1950

Burgan, John. *The Long Discovery.* New York: Farrar, Straus, 1950.

Baseball is an important factor in this sociological study of a mining town, Beautysburg, Pennsylvania, in 1925. Almost everyone in B-Burg is conditioned by the economic influence of the mines. Rose Derevnia, daughter of a coalminer, realizes that life is preordained for people like her: the men work in the mines; the women become housewives and raise more miners. However, Rose helps her brother Mike escape through baseball. When he comes home after failing, she convinces him to try again, and he eventually becomes a major leaguer. In B-Burg, though, the KKK is at work, and one of its members is on the local semipro team run by mine superintendent Daniel Riddell, who is shot while investigating Klan activity. Rose and her friends persuade Riddell to continue to work against the Klan, starting with the baseball team. The humanitarian group also helps to send a teenager to school so that he will not have to spend his life in the mines.

The book, along with two other novels published in 1950, is the start of a new trend in baseball literature. Although the A. S. Barnes writers are still in vogue, authors with more widespread interests and skills begin to enter the field.

Edmunds, Murrell. *Behold, Thy Brother.* New York: Beechhurst Press, 1950.

In an eighty-page novella, major league baseball is integrated in the 1945 season — two years before the arrival of Jackie Robinson. Manager of the Eagles, Jimmy Wharton, is running short of pitchers. Washington Hurt, just released from the army, reports to the team with a Purple Heart and a black skin. Although he has great stuff, Wharton is afraid to use the pitcher because of the Southerners on the Eagles. On the last day of the regular season, the team needs a win to clinch the pennant. Hurt gets the start and shuts out the opponents for seven innings, but when the catcher gets hurt, racist Carter Whipple takes his place. Hurt, however, completes the shutout, and the Eagles celebrate the victory. Bubber, an assistant trainer and the only other black associated with the team, cries during the postgame festivities.

The book has the formulaic victorious Big Game ending, but it is the first to deal with integration in the major leagues since the pre–Robinson era depicted in

The Plated City (1895). The performance of Washington Hurt in *Behold, Thy Brother* is too understated, though, to represent a realistic social impact. The actual story of the 1947 season more dramatically reveals the deep seated racism that existed at the time.

Fitzgerald, Ed. *College Slugger.* New York: A.S. Barnes, 1950.

In the second Marty Ferris book, he attends Fordham on a scholarship with "the blessing" of the New York Yankees which includes a verbal agreement to report to them after his college career. As a sophomore, he becomes the starting centerfielder. Besides corresponding with girlfriend Jean Turner at Wellesley, the big issues for Ferris are the avoidance of fraternities and minor league summer ball. He rejects offers from both areas. Several fraternity members leave the team during Ferris' junior year, and a couple other players are declared ineligible for playing professionally. However, the Fordham Rams win the conference title and make it to the second round of the College World Series the next season. Scout Lazarus Dedrick then signs the centerfielder to a Yankee contract. Marty Ferris will obviously stay clean and be a success as a Yankee according to the standards of the Barnes Sports Books.

Kennedy, Lucy. *The Sunlit Field.* New York: Crown, 1950.

In 1857, three people escape from the Red Tanager, a ship bound for Brooklyn. Two stowaways and a slave jump into the harbor at New York City. Pocahontas (Po) O'Reilly is a sixteen-year-old orphan who, after her father's death in Ireland, is heading for a cousin's place in Brooklyn. Larry Wainwright is leaving his mother's home in New Bedford to become a baseball player. The third person, Juba, is an escaped slave. Their lives become intertwined in the city — starting with a ballgame involving the Brooklyn Excelsiors. Larry soon becomes a member of the team. Po lives with her cousin and his wife, but the latter's social pretensions soon drive the Irish girl out. She becomes a singer-actress in Manhattan. Po also becomes friends with a baseball fan and poet named Walt who offers Whitmanesque advice. Meanwhile the Excelsiors challenge the prestigious New York Knickerbockers to a game by threatening to expose William Hymes, owner of the team, who also runs slave ships. Hymes retaliates by loading up his team and hiring ruffians to beat up some of the Excelsiors, including Larry Wainwright and The Bull, a slugger who dies from the injuries received in the beating. The Knickerbockers win two out of three games, but their unfair methods produce enemies. Po and her new friends, Dave Posen, printer and baseball reporter, and Coventry Van Leyn, son of a business partner of Hymes, along with standbys Larry, Walt, and Juba, collaborate to try to destroy Hymes. He has too much economic power to be stopped completely, however.

The moral opinions of Walt tend to affect Po and Larry. Po puts more emphasis on fighting injustice than on her career. Larry becomes manager of the Excelsiors, makes peace with his mother (who does not care for his career choice), and prepares to pursue his love interest in Po. She realizes that he has become an independent man of honor — and is ready to accept him.

This is an overlooked novel of quality. The inclusion of Walt Whitman adds zest to the baseball motif as the Good Gray Poet was a fan of the game. The social background, though, indicates the problems associated with baseball in its infancy. The pastoral concept of the sunlit field is a brief illusion as money becomes a factor. At the end, Larry and Po long for the time when an admission fee was not required for the team to survive. The game, though, was never free from profiteers like Hymes. Larry Wainwright, as manager of the Excelsiors and owner of the new Grand Union Ball Park, is acquiring an economic burden. He and Po will have to balance their Whitmanesque views with the harsh realism of running a business.

O'Rourke, Frank. *Bonus Rookie.* New York: A.S. Barnes, 1950.

Quaker City wins the 1950 pennant as the fictional Phillies battle the real-life Dodgers. Rookie pitcher Jim Ramsay is a bonus baby who is retained on the roster but is seldom used. He develops a baseball phobia after hitting a batter and gets into a fight with a reserve catcher. However, Manager Billy Lawson puts them both in the Big Game. Quaker City defeats Don Newcombe to win the pennant as Ramsay strikes out Gil Hodges with the bases loaded. Fans of the Barnes Sports Books and the 1950 Philadelphia Phillies Whiz Kids probably enjoy the book as it stops short of the World Series. It was nevertheless prophetic of the 1950 season. Some of the fictional Phillies, of course, are based on the real ones.

1951

Hano, Arnold. *The Big Out.* New York: A.S. Barnes, 1951.

Hano joins the Barnes fold with the story of a maligned superhero, Brick Palmer, a catcher who is banned from pro baseball as a result of taking the blame for his brother's gambling. Brick and his wife attempt to settle down to a life without baseball in Wisconsin until an offer comes from Osage, Quebec, to play for the Outlaws. In Canada, he fights off injuries and reputation to win the respect he formerly had as a major leaguer. His trials include a beating by the henchman of gamblers for refusing to throw a game. However, with heroics from Brick, the Outlaws win the championship. To complete the happy ending, his brother confesses, and the ban on Brick is removed.

1952

Fitzgerald, Ed. *Yankee Rookie.* New York: A.S. Barnes, 1952.

The third and final Marty Ferris book from Barnes tells of the rise to glory of the former Fordham star with the New York Yankees. He has a brief minor league stint, and when he is called by the parent team, he soon wins respect. His acceptance as a Yankee is solidified when slugger Mike Schulz, who was benched to make room for Ferris in the outfield, comes to the defense when an opponent attacks the rookie. Also, the girlfriend of the earlier novels, Jean Turner, remains loyal to the emerging hero. The most significant act of Ferris, though, takes place off the field. He rejects the offers of an agent to make paid public appearances and to endorse products. To complete the fairy tale, Marty Ferris decides that his role as a Yankee is more important than making money.

Hemingway, Ernest. *The Old Man and the Sea.* New York: Simon & Schuster, 1981.

The famous novella contains a baseball dialogue that inspired the book *Hemingway's Debt to Baseball in The Old Man and the Sea: A Collection of Critical Essays.* While fishing, Santiago, the old Cuban, and Manolin, the boy, discuss the pennant races and past and present players. Santiago mentions the father-son duo of George and Dick Sisler. The old man points out the superiority of the Hall-of-Fame father (who held the record for most hits in a season until 2004) even though the son was bigger and stronger. The Cubans talk about John McGraw and Leo Durocher, who spent time in Cuba, and compare them to Mike Gonzales and Dolf Luque, Cubans who played in America and managed at home. Santiago and Manolin express their interest in striving for perfection like the great ballplayers. The old man refers to Joe DiMaggio, who has returned to a starring role with the Yankees after an injury, as an example of the ideal code of honor. Santiago believes in grace under pressure — Hemingway's concept of heroism — when faced with adversity. The baseball conversation, then, mirrors the theme of the book.

Malamud, Bernard. *The Natural.* New York: Harcourt Brace, 1952. (New York: Dell, 1969; New York: Avon Books, 1980.)

Probably the most famous baseball novel, due partly to the altered movie version, it is also the subject of a lot of critical interpretation. On the surface, it is the story of Roy Hobbs whose promising baseball career is halted by a gunshot wound. Fifteen years later, he appears out of nowhere to ask Pop Fisher, manager of the New York Knights of the major leagues, for a spot on the team. When Bump Baily dies after running into an outfield wall, Hobbs takes his place in the line-up and becomes an instant star by wielding Wonder Boy, his bat, with authority. He also courts Memo Paris, former girlfriend of Baily. Another woman, Iris Lemon, enters Hobbs' life and tries, unsuccessfully, to teach him moral values. The Knights, meanwhile, turn their season around and make a run for the pennant. When Hobbs gets sick, the owner, Judge Banner, visits him in the hospital and offers him $25,000 to throw the Big Game. The fix is on after Hobbs demands $35,000. The pregnant Iris Lemon's entreaty to him "to win for our boy" is unheeded. The Pirates claim the pennant as Hobbs strikes out to end the game. Newspaper headlines declare a suspicion of dishonesty, and the Commissioner hints that Hobbs may be permanently suspended. In distress, he buries Wonder Boy and returns Judge Banner's bribe money, but when a kid asks him to deny the charge of throwing the game, Roy Hobbs can only weep.

According to some critics, regeneration myths and Jungian archetypes abound, but the popular approach seems to be a loose application of the Arthurian legend to baseball lore. On his way to Chicago for a baseball tryout, the future Knight engages in a duel with the Whammer, a Babe Ruth figure, and strikes him out. (Like the Babe, Hobbs is a pitcher and a slugger.) Harriet Bird witnesses the event and apparently realizes that Hobbs is not worthy of a knightly quest, and she shoots him. After suffering in the bush leagues for fifteen years, his ego demands the gratification of big league stardom. He rejects the wisdom of Iris Lemon and opts for the temptation of Memo Paris, who in revenge of Bump Baily, sets up Hobbs for the bribe and, like Harriet Bird, takes a shot at him in the end. The youthful innocence of Hobbs, symbolically wounded by Harriet Bird's gunshot and killed by the moonlight drive with Memo Paris (when she "runs over something"), yields to his selfishness. The Excalibur-like bat is held in check because of the bribe (or the resulting guilt) and the transgression on the field of battle is mirrored by Hobbs' failure to acknowledge Iris Lemon's plea to win for their "future" son. Thus Otto Zipp, the dwarf who castigates Roy Hobbs from the bleachers, speaks for the fans who demand integrity from their heroes, like the boy who demands the denial that the Knight cannot deliver. "Say it ain't so, Roy" is the newspaper declaration that equates Hobbs to Shoeless Joe Jackson of Black Sox infamy. In the Arthurian tradition, he is the thwarted and unworthy knight who is no longer welcome at the Round Table.

The Natural is probably too cryptic for many readers, but the literati keep the interest alive — and justifiably so.

O'Rourke, Frank. *Never Come Back.* New York: A.S. Barnes, 1952.

Hub Maloski, thirty-two-year-old former star, is released by the Grays and descends to minor league and semipro ball. While working for a lumberyard in Des Moines, he gets alcoholism under control and starts playing ball like he used to. Maloski is called up by Quaker City and resumes his career as a major leaguer. His ex-wife offers him $50,000 to throw a game, but he rejects the bribe and helps the team win the pennant and defeat the Yankees in the World Series. In the off-season, Lena Jensen, who helped him turn his life around in Des Moines, joins him, and they plan a future together. This is another unremarkable book from A. S. Barnes.

O'Rourke, Frank. *Nine Good Men.* New York: A.S. Barnes, 1952.

Manager Don Shelby of the Blues faces the problem of trying to repeat as a pennant winner. When local sportswriters attack the manager in print, he starts a rumor that his job is in jeopardy. Shelby knows that owner Brick Henderson supports him, but he hopes to inspire the team by his ploy. Although the Blues fail to capture the championship, Shelby is retained for the next season. He feels that the Blues will regain their former glory and that he will have his revenge on the malicious press.

Although a mediocre A. S. Barnes book, it includes an interesting footnote. A Blues pitcher named Herb Score is disabled by being struck by a batted ball. About five years later, the real Herb Score suffered a similar fate.

1953

Harris, Mark. *The Southpaw.* Indianapolis: Bobbs-Merrill, 1953. (Lincoln: University of Nebraska Press, 1984); Lincoln: Bison Books, 2003.)

The first of the four popular Henry Wiggen books is narrated in the protagonist's Huck Finn-like dialect and begins with his early years in Perkinsville, New York. The boy is tutored by Pop and a neighbor, Aaron Webster, and by Webster's niece, Holly. He grows into a big, handsome left-handed pitcher who eventually becomes a member of the New York Mammoths. Henry's success as a big leaguer is countered, however, by personal problems. Besides having an affair with Patricia Moors, owner of the team, he is labeled as "Henry the Whiner" by sportswriter Krazy Kress for comments about not being appreciated, for disagreeing with Manager Dutch Schnell's strategy, and for an anti-war statement (regarding Korea). Henry adds to the controversy by rooming with Perry Simpson, the Mammoths version of Jackie Robinson. Finally, Henry complains about what Kress calls a non-existent backache. Nevertheless, the Mammoths win the World Series with Henry as the pitching ace.

More important than Henry Wiggen's baseball stardom, though, is his marriage to Holly, the hometown girl whose moral advice becomes the heart of the book. Unlike Jack Keefe, Henry is capable of learning from his experiences. He discovers that his boyhood idol, Sam Yale, is not the hero portrayed in the book Henry read as a boy. With Holly's guidance, he wrestles with his conscience and makes moral decisions—becoming an adult version of Huck Finn. Though some critics claim that social realism is overplayed by moral romanticism, *The Southpaw* is still one of the biggies in the genre.

O'Rourke, Frank. *The Catcher and the Manager.* New York: A.S. Barnes, 1953.

The last of the author's Barnes baseball books consists of two novellas. "The Catcher" is a typical heroic success story featuring Billy Malloy. He spends six years as a minor league catcher before joining the Blues in the majors. Even though Malloy leads the team to its first pennant in thirty years, the owner, Walter Jones, dumps him when he breaks an ankle. Traded to the Eagles, the catcher hits a walk-off homer in his first game against the Blues. Strong character triumphs over greedy management.

In "The Manager," the conflict between ownership and the men of the field is again stressed. When Art Cassidy is hired to manage the Blues, he changes from being a martinet into an accommodationist in order to please the front office. In the minors, he had been compared to Leo Durocher (who appears in the story) for his hardnosed managerial tactics. However, the philosophy of the Blues under the present ownership is to treat the new brand of educated players with kid gloves. Cassidy consequently loses control of the team. He knows that he will be fired at the end of the season and has no faith that the Blues will allow him to return to their minor league system. Art and Ida Cassidy accept the predicament stoically. Their many years of baseball life have taught them that the administrative view of progress is stronger than loyalty to an organization or knowledge of the game. "The Manager," devoid of the usual diamond heroics, is probably the best baseball production of O'Rourke.

Weeks, Jack. *The Hard Way.* New York: A.S. Barnes, 1953.

The first of two Mario Canto novels for A. S. Barnes, it traces the rise of the lower-class New York City kid through his baseball success. Mario's father is killed by gangsters, and his brother, Angelo, gets in trouble for stealing baseball bats. Mario, though, takes the blame and is sent to reform school. Father Montana eventually finds him a job on the farm of Spider Moriarty who refines Mario's talents as a ballplayer. He is signed as a shortstop by Greenville of the Cotton State League and works his way up to Buffalo in Triple A when World War II intervenes. Mario saves sportswriter Bill Piper's nephew from a burning plane and is depicted as a war hero. After the war, he makes the jump to the major league Lions in the typical heroic mode.

1954

Michaels, D. J. (Charles Einstein). *Win — Or Else!* New York: Lurton Blassingame, 1954.

The novella deals with the problems of Roy McIlvaine, manager of the Ocean City Stars, as the team begins the season with a nine-game losing streak. Henry Gibbons, owner, is badgered by politicians, and he delivers the ultimatum that the Stars must win the next game or McIlvaine will by fired. Rookie Darrell Blakely hits a game-winning homer to beat the Yankees and save the manager's job — temporarily. The off-field activity focuses on the greed and corruption of upper-class society and the vulnerability of the athletes and ordinary citizens. The interaction of the characters against the backdrop of the game produces an interesting sociological study.

Wallop, Douglas. *The Year the Yankees Lost the Pennant.* New York: W.W. Norton, 1954. (New York: W.W. Norton, 2004).

Also known as *Damn Yankees* from the famous musical version, the fantasy is patterned after the Faust Legend. Applegate, the devil incarnate, makes a deal with Joe Boyd, a fifty-year-old salesman and Washington Senators fan. After signing a contract, Boyd is transformed into Joe Hardy, a twenty-one-year-old superstar. With forty-eight homers and a .545 batting average over the last half of the season, Hardy leads the Senators into a pennant chase with the Yankees. Despite his success in baseball and with the beautiful Lola (formerly a middle-aged teacher who also made a Faustian bargain) Hardy begins to have doubts about his status. He worries about Bess, his abandoned wife, and about the morality of the deal. He tries to rebel, but Applegate holds him to the contract. When Hardy scores the run that beats the Yankees and wins the pennant for Washington, he is changed back to Joe Boyd. He is happy to be an ordinary Joe again as he returns to Bess and the comforts of home. He discovers that his freedom has been won by Lola who sacrificed herself for Joe Hardy by extracting a promise from Applegate (as a result of hiding his shoes so that the cloven feet appeared) to grant the desired transformation. She becomes an unattractive spinster again but retains the memory of the glorious love affair.

Wallop's story, while not one of the better adaptations of the legend, has earned immortality through its conversion to the musical stage. Recent editions of the novel are now entitled *Damn Yankees.*

1955

Asinof, Eliot. *Man on Spikes.* New York: McGraw-Hill, 1955. (Carbondale: Southern Illinois University Press, 1998).

One of the best realistic portrayals of baseball life, it follows the career of outfielder Mike Kutner as he works his way from a Class D team to the majors. In fourteen chapters, each with a different narrator, aspects of Kutner's quest are documented, starting with high school days in a coal-mining town with a father who dislikes baseball. As a pro, he is the victim of bad luck and the greed of Jim Mellon, owner of the Chicago Lions, who thinks the outfielder is more valuable in the minors than with the parent club. With more determination than talent, Kutner represents a commitment to the game beyond the realm of the financial rewards and glory attained by major league stars. His chances of reaching the top are interrupted by service in World War II. Finally at the age of thirty-five, Kutner is given a chance with the Lions, but he fails his big league test, laughing bitterly as he realizes his career is over.

The naturalistic novel reveals the exploitation of players by owners—long before the time of free agency. The practice of "indentured servitude" is epitomized in the career of Mike Kutner, the man on spikes, the property of an unscrupulous organization.

In one chapter ("The Negro") which deals with Kutner's minor league odyssey, he and Ben Franks, a black player, discuss the impact on baseball made by Jackie Robinson. Kutner and Franks learn to respect each other, but as in *The Southpaw*, the racial concern is only a minor aspect of the book. The novella *Behold, Thy Brother* is the only other book that deals with the integration of pro baseball instigated by Robinson at this point.

Einstein, Charles. *The Only Game in Town.* New York: Dell, 1955.

Stat Hunter, former major league centerfielder, manages the Class C Conway Bears. His troubles begin when Walt Corio, a new player, encourages the star second baseman, Joe Whittier, to gamble. Stat gets Corio fired when he discovers that he had previously been banned from baseball under the name of Carsi. Stat then gets promoted to being the manager of the Phillies, but he has to take time off to help find his lost daughter. He succeeds and wins his wife back in the process. He also has time to guide the Phillies to a surprising third-place finish. This is in the same category as the A. S. Barnes books and is a big drop from *Win — Or Else!*

Weeks, Jack. *The Take-Charge Guy.* New York: A. S. Barnes, 1955.

In a sequel to *The Hard Way*, Mario Canto's successful major league career with the Lake City Lions is complicated by the gambling of his older brother, Angelo. After being the Most Valuable Player in his third year, Mario helps the Lions win the pennant two years later. He discovers, though, that Angelo has bribed pitcher Clay Fletcher to throw games. In a fight with Fletcher, Mario injures his foot and is forced to shift from shortstop to leftfield. Mario's heroism, in stopping the gambling and starring in a new position, is a bonus for the team and gets him promoted to manager for the next season. This is typical of the A. S. Barnes novels of the era.

1956

Breslin, Howard. *Autumn Comes Early.* New York: Thomas Y. Crowell, 1956.

Johnny Leo, a second baseman for the Acronville Beavers, gets involved with Deborah Clifford, local librarian and the product of her conservative Connecticut community. Her affair with a baseball player, an outsider, is a scandal. Vince Petowski, Leo's roommate, is the epitome of the town's idea of a minor leaguer — a drinker and carouser who leaves Acronville as soon as the season is over. Leo, however, is different. A native of New York City with an Italian/Catholic background, he attends Fordham and reads good books for pleasure. He is willing to marry the librarian and live in Acronville if necessary. The romance is interrupted by a devastating flood which leads to the cancellation of the rest of the baseball season. Deborah then comes to the conclusion that she is not the right woman for Johnny Leo. She is too much a part of the community value system to adjust to a change. The book is a competent sociological presentation of the impact of baseball on small-town lives.

Harris, Mark. *Bang the Drum Slowly.* New York: Alfred A. Knopf, 1956. (Lincoln: University of Nebraska Press, 1984.)

Henry Wiggen continues to narrate his career with the New York Mammoths that he began in *The Southpaw* Once again he leads the team to a World Series win, but the season is marred by the illness of Bruce Pearson, catcher and roommate. A rural Georgian who is often the butt of crude jokes by teammates, Pearson confides in Wiggen about the diagnosis of Hodgkins Disease. The pitcher decides to help his roomie by demanding a contract that will guarantee a job for both of them. At Pearson's death, Wiggen promises to give up verbal attacks on others ("from here on I rag nobody").

The novel was made into a movie in 1973 with Robert DeNiro starring as Bruce Pearson. Both book and film have been applauded as serious realistic renderings of baseball. Henry Wiggen is overbearing as a hero at times, but his vernacular narration of ballplayers' lives with off-and-on-field conflicts makes him one of the most recognizable fictional protagonists in the genre.

Harris, Mark. *A Ticket for a Seamstitch.* New York: Alfred A. Knopf, 1956. (Lincoln: University of Nebraska Press, 1984). (Lincoln: Bison Books, 2003.)

Part three of Henry Wiggen's moral education involves the story of a female fan from the West Coast who appears in New York on the Fourth of July. She came to see Henry pitch, so he feels responsible for her. He takes her to the automat for dinner and then loses the second game of a doubleheader to break his winning streak. Piney Woods, Henry's new roomie, does not like her because she is not a "looker," and Henry lectures him on the proper treatment of a loyal fan. It is doubtful if Piney learns from the experience, but Henry responds admirably to the plight of the naïve girl while being alerted to the vulnerability of his own fame and fortune. Only devout Henry Wiggen fans will appreciate this one.

Heuman, William. *Strictly from Brooklyn.* New York: William Morrow, 1956.

A writer of juvenile baseball novels (from 1951 to 1972), Heuman marginally reaches the adult level here. Manny Keefe of Brooklyn roots for the Dodgers in the fifties. He occasionally gets to Ebbets Field, but mostly he and Grandpa Keefe listen to radio broadcasts. Manny, the narrator, thinks that Grandpa has it easy in just worrying about the Dodgers while he has to patch up his daughter's love affair and help his wife in her matchmaking efforts. It is a lighthearted, but easily forgettable, romp through a Flatbush summer.

1957

Fitzgerald, Ed. *The Ball Player.* New York: A. S. Barnes, 1957.

In the last of the A. S. Barnes baseball novels, Vinnie Burns is a star of the Sox. As a youngster, he has to overcome a bad family situation. His mother hates baseball, and his alcoholic father deserts the family while Vinnie is in high school. Vinnie, however, gets married and plays for State University, until his mother and stepfather reveal that he was a pro in the Northern League in the summer. Vinnie, then, loses his scholarship and becomes a full-time professional. In 1939 the Sox call him up to the majors as a centerfielder, and he goes on to win a batting title and eventually become a playing manager. Sportswriter Joe Pepperdine, however, attacks Vinnie's managerial tactics and also exposes the prison career of his father. World War II intervenes, and on his return Vinnie leads the Sox to a pennant as a player-manager. His wife Caroline has become a successful author by this time, and the future looks bright.

A variation from the Barnes' formula is that Vinnie Burns has a sexual liaison with a temptress—until his conscience causes him to end the affair. He also makes the mistake of endorsing cigarettes, but when Pepperdine criticizes him, Vinnie admits his error. Virtue does triumph after all.

1958

Fitzpatrick, Burgess. *Casey's Redemption.* New York: Greenwich Book Publishers, 1958.

In a forty-page prose sequel to "Casey at the Bat," Johnny Casey, outfielder for the Mudville Hens, gains redemption for his "mighty" ancestor. A model of decorum, Johnny homers to win the championship game against the Centerville Hawks. He gets the attention of New York Yankee scouts as well as the love of Shirley Brady, daughter of a band leader who has a television show. Since Johnny is also an aspiring singer, he seems destined for success. This little book is not.

1959

Nye, Bud. *Stay Loose.* Garden City, NY: Doubleday, 1959. (New York: Bantam Books, 1961.)

In this fantasy, a computer is used to help create the perfect baseball team. C. K. Dick, owner of the new St. Paul Imperials, hires Dr. Evangeline Leirfallom to find the physical specimens most likely to excel at the game. The female psychologist and the computer choose the natives of the island of Nukiti for the experiment. Manager Max Gallivan teaches them the fundamentals and turns them loose to raise havoc in the National League. The physically superior islanders soon outdistance their opponents. Owners of the teams panic and try to make a deal with Gallivan to throw games—or at least make them closer. The manager refuses to tamper with baseball, but he gets sick and has to leave the team. The Nukitians cannot play without their "chief," and they start losing games. Ferris Bracken of Public Relations is appointed by Dick to persuade Gallivan to return to his job under the condition that the games are made closer. The owner's daughter, Barbara Dick, promises herself to Bracken if he succeeds in his mission. Gallivan comes back, but with the support of Bracken and Dr. Leirfallom, he produces honest baseball. The team wins the World Series, and when Barbara drops Bracken, he and Evangeline Leirfallom look for new jobs and perhaps a life together. Max Gallivan retires, and the Nukitians go back to their island with apparently no plan to play baseball in America in the future.

The pastoral innocence of the native players, then, triumphs over the evil of business. The noble savages are not corrupted by the economics of baseball. Gallivan, Bracken, and Leirfallom opt to rebel against the stereotypical greedy owner. The use of the computer, the employment of a woman, and the attempt to "scientize" baseball are omens of the future of much baseball fiction.

1961

Doliner, Roy. *The Orange Air.* New York: Charles Scribner's Sons, 1961.

Hank Easter, a fictional version of Ralph Branca, yields one of the most famous homers in history in the 1951 playoff game between the Giants and the Dodgers. Shortly after the catastrophe, the Dodger pitcher retires. Some years later, he is a television producer on his way to Cuba to promote tourist trade for the new government. By accident, he gets involved in a plot to kill the Castro-like El Commandant. Relying on the splendid coordination of mind and body that had served him at times in his baseball career, Easter foils the plot. Relinquishing the chance to profit from the assassination attempt, he does "the right thing," and is rewarded by the love of a good woman. It is a typical thriller with a baseball connection.

Feldspar, Walter. *Squeeze Play.* Manhasset, NY: Kozy Books, 1961.

Suggestive of pornography in its Kozy Book publication, the novel fails at that level and does little better in its depiction of minor league baseball. Merle Keith, whose husband owns the Class B Hurley Miners, has an affair with Lew Walls, thirty-four-year-old manager of the team. Walls tries to end the romance, but the wealthy woman wants to keep her boytoy. She arranges a deal to make the team a major league farm club and finds a job for Walls in the Pacific Coast League. The Miners manager refuses the offer and quits the team in an effort to gain his independence. He discovers his former integrity and reunites with his wife, as morality triumphs over debauchery.

1962

Bradley, Matt. *Hot Curves.* Hollywood: Imperial, 1962.

Promoted as a sexy "Boudoir Original" paperback, the sex yields (as in *Squeeze Play*), to conventional morality in the end. Chappy Chapman, shortstop for the Birds, is trying to set a major league record for stolen bases. He plays for himself instead of the team, and fans turn against him. When he is injured, he is sent to coach in Obispa, Georgia, at the lowest minor league level. The shortstop recovers physically and mentally and is called back to the Birds in September. Manager Ben Bolt is convinced that Chappy is a new man who is willing to sacrifice personal glory for the good of the team. Chappy also gets married — when he discovers that his girlfriend is not a lesbian.

1962-1963 "All-Star Baseball Series"

Argonaut Books presents juvenile novels supposedly written by Yogi Berra (*Behind the Plate*), Whitey Ford (*The Fighting Southpaw*), Roger Maris (*Slugger in Right*), and Willie Mays (*Danger in Center Field*). The books include the names of "helping" authors and tips on how to play the position.

Molloy, Paul. *A Pennant for the Kremlin.* Garden City, NY: Doubleday, 1964. (New York: Avon Books, 1966.)

In a comedy that looks back to *Rhubarb* and ahead to *The New York Yanquis*, Armistead E. Childers wills the Chicago White Sox to the Soviet Union in an attempt to promote goodwill during the Cold War Era. While angry Americans complain, the Russians appoint Mikhail Deborin to oversee the team. Cuban players are selected to be new White Sox, but they defect to the United States along with Deborin and his daughter Tasia. The Sox lose in the World Series to the Dodgers, and the Soviet Union relinquishes the team in hopes of getting the defectors back. The prospect of détente fails, however, and America comes out on top. The humor of the novel, mostly at the expense of the Soviet officials, is secondary to the propaganda — which promotes baseball as an example of democracy and the superiority of American life.

1965

Grantham, Kenneth L. *Baseball's Darkest Days.* New York: Exposition Press, 1965.

With an idea similar to that in *It Happens Every Spring*, Grantham's novella deals with a method of controlling baseballs. Red Jackson tries to exploit his scientific discovery in order to get rich. With the help of Merle Potts, an electrical engineer and former colleague in bootlegging, Jackson plants transistors in baseballs that can control flight. Doctored baseballs are used in the games of the Chicago Cubs as Luke Kimberly, equipment manager, is paid to smuggle them in. Jackson and Potts make money by betting on the Cubs — who win the World Series. However, an electronic ball is discovered, and the Commissioner investigates. Meanwhile gamblers are upset at the unusual Cub success, and Jackson, Potts, and Kimberly flee to rural Florida to escape the mob. Newspapers print articles on "baseball's darkest days," and the Commissioner demands that the third game of the Series must be replayed. The three Florida refugees, along with journalist Tim Worley, are killed while trying to escape from gamblers. Worley's article on the controlled baseballs appears posthumously. The 103-page book is far-fetched and badly written — and the Cubs' wins are tainted by foul play.

Quigley, Martin. *Today's Game.* New York: Viking Press, 1965.
Barney Mann, manager of the Blue Jays, is concerned about breaking a losing streak when international social scientists visit his office in an attempt to discover why baseball is essential to the free world during the Cold War. Mann stresses the importance of competition, of applying physical and mental attributes to the single goal of winning. He then turns his attention to the game of the day in which the Blue Jays contend with the Warriors. In order to beat Jerry Adams, ace pitcher and good friend that he has nevertheless traded to the opponents, Mann concocts a radical line-up that features left-handed power hitters at the top of the order — an application of what he considers aerodynamics to the game. The unorthodox strategy results in an 8-7 win when Bill Wellington, black outfielder traded for Adams, makes a game-saving catch. The book consists primarily of the narration of game action, and the pace is slow and detailed. The importance of baseball to the free world is not established here.

Shaw, Irwin. *Voices of a Summer Day.* New York: Delacorte Press, 1965. (New York: Dell, 1985.)
Baseball is a unifying agent in the life of Benjamin Federov, a fifty-year-old former athlete. As he watches his son in Little League games, he reflects on the past when his father took him to the Polo Grounds. The Jewish family has tried to adjust to American life, and baseball has aided in the assimilation. Descriptions of the son's game are interspersed with Federov's musing on major events in Jewish-American history. Written by a popular novelist, this is one of his lesser known works — but the baseball element makes it memorable.

1966

Herskowitz, Mickey. *Letters from Lefty.* Houston: The Houston Press Co., 1966.
"With apologies to Ring Lardner," the "letters" first appeared in a Houston newspaper when the sportswriter/author was covering the Houston Colt 45s. The fictional Lefty, a pitcher, is inserted into the team with real players. He writes to Alice about his adventures with the team, including the switch to the Astros in 1965 and his trade to the New York Mets. [In the 1980 edition, expanded to 126 pages, the Mets trade him back to the Astros, and his career continues there until 1971.] Unlike Lardner's Jack Keefe, Lefty writes in Standard English, but he has Keefe's problems in accepting responsibilities and shortcomings. He also has battles over salary and feels that he does not get the proper respect from coaches and managers.

Lefty never makes a commitment to Alice (You Know Me, Alice) and thus avoids the domestic problems of Keefe. While not the quality of *You Know Me Al*, the humorous accounts of a player on a struggling expansion team make good reading — and many of the incidents stem from early team history.

1967

Asinof, Eliot. *The Bedfellow.* New York: Simon & Schuster, 1967.

Black baseball player Mike Sorrell retires from the game when he is traded from New York to Atlanta. He takes a job on Madison Avenue rather than to submit his white wife, Janice, to the racism of the South. However he slips into the role of Othello when his boss flirts with her. The psychological pressure of his new life almost destroys him. He reflects on his baseball days and concludes that the nation is not ready to accept Brotherhood. Sorrell decides, however, to stick to his advertising job and the hypocritical world of upper-class New York. Living the good life seems more reasonable than fighting a losing battle against the indifferent world. This is the second modern adult baseball novel with a black protagonist (after *Behold, Thy Brother*), but it suffers in comparison with the author's *Man on Spikes*.

Green, Gerald. *To Brooklyn with Love.* New York: Simon & Schuster, 1967. (New York: Pocket Books, 1969.)

Potok, Chaim. *The Chosen.* New York: Simon & Schuster, 1967. (New York: Ballantine Books, 1996.)

These two novels make some baseball bibliographies although the baseball content is minimal. Potok's book presents two Jewish boys, Reuven Malter and Danny Saunders, who meet after a ballgame in which a liner off the bat of Saunders hits Malter in the eye. They become friends, even though one is Orthodox and the other Hasidic, and attend the same college as they grow to maturity in the 1940s.

Green's novel deals with a day in the life of Albert Abrams, a twelve-year-old son of a doctor, in the summer of 1934. Dr Abrams refuses to leave the poor neighborhood and Albert, smart, small, and skinny, wants to be accepted as one of the boys. One of his attempts is through participation in a street version of baseball.

1968

Coover, Robert. *The Universal Baseball Association, Inc., J. Henry Waugh, Prop.* New York: Random House, 1968. (New York: Signet Books, 1969; New York: Plume, 1971.)

A candidate for the best baseball novel, it features players who exist only in the mind of the protagonist, a fifty-six-year-old accountant who invents a game that he plays with dice and probability charts. The members of the Universal Baseball Association become more important to J. Henry Waugh than the real people he associates with. At odds with the business world, symbolized by his boss Zifferblatt, Waugh retreats into the imaginary world of the UBA. When he attempts to explain the game to Hattie, a prostitute, and Lou Engel, a friend, they do not take it seriously, and the result is further alienation from the outside world and deeper immersion into the imaginative.

Disaster occurs when pitcher Damon Rutherford of the Pioneers becomes the victim of an unfortunate dice roll which, according to the Extraordinary Occurrence Chart, rules that he is killed by a pitch from Knickerbocker Jock Casey. The Pioneer hero, son of Waugh's revered Brock Rutherford, had been pitching on only one day's rest—a violation of baseball ethics. The proprietor of the UBA continues to interfere with the integrity of the game by arranging to have Casey killed by a batted ball and by rigging games so that the Knickerbockers lose.

In the last chapter, J. Henry Waugh has disappeared and the UBA is depicted as having a life of its own in a distant future in which rituals dominate. The Damonsday Parable of the Duel presents scapegoat players who are killed in the recreation of the deaths of Rutherford and Casey. The teams consist of Damonites, who cling to tradition, and Caseyites, who prefer change. It is deadly conformity that rules, however.

There are many interpretations of this multi-leveled novel, but Coover seems to be indirectly promoting the transformation of society's value system through direct involvement with life's problems as opposed to the negative withdrawal of Waugh. His reaction to a hostile environment is to retreat from the social into the personal. Then he cheats in an attempt to control his secret universe. He turns from an impotent Walter Mitty comic character into a gothic mad scientist who creates a private chaos. Society, or the UBA, is left to the conformists and their traditions unless challenged by the rebels—the Caseyites who may represent the civil rights activists and anti-war protesters of the era. The author's attempt to bypass the conventions of narrative construction may result in ambiguity, but the book is provocative and entertaining.

1969

Ball, John. *Johnny Get Your Gun.* Boston: Little, Brown and Co., 1969.

Virgil Tibbs, black detective (played by Sidney Poitier in the movie version of *In the Heat of the Night*), investigates a case that leads to the California Angels and owner Gene Autry. Johnny McGuire, nine years old, is accosted by a gang and fires his father's gun in panic. When the black gang member dies, Johnny absconds to Anaheim. He plans to see the Angels play and to meet Tom Satriano, his hero. When refused admission to the clubhouse, Johnny fires the gun and then hides in the scoreboard. Tibbs, who has been pressured by militant blacks who demand justice for the murder, persuades Autry to don his cowboy regalia and to appear on the diamond while singing "Back in the Saddle Again" on horseback. Johnny empties his gun by firing into the air in imitation of Autry and is then apprehended. Tibbs, however, arrests Sport Dempsey, black gang member for the murder that was blamed on Johnny. The racial and baseball aspects add luster to the mystery.

Karlins, Marvin. *The Last Man Is Out.* Englewood Cliffs, NJ: Prentice-Hall, 1969.

The computer becomes a major factor for the Chicago AToms in the 2002 season. When Dr. Michael Paradise inherits the team from Thomas Samuels, he turns to Professor Norbert for help. The scientist invents Leviathan, a machine that is used in practice to improve the basic skills of the players. The professor's computers are then used to calculate probabilities and to dictate decisions off the field. Paradise himself is transformed into a pitcher (playing as Michael Alexander) whose actions are controlled by Professor Norbert.

The AToms play at Manhattan Stadium, which was built on the bottom of Lake Michigan and elevated so that it became a domed park on an island. Norbert planned the stadium as part of his takeover of the team. He recruits players that can be manipulated, and the AToms become contenders, especially after the Phoenix Flyers, the first-place team, are the victims of a mysterious plane crash (that may be attributed to Norbert). The scientist also introduces a female to major league baseball. Judy Norris is used as a pinch-hitter, and her sex appeal tends to distract pitchers—often leading to walks. Paradise falls in love with her, but he discovers that her other job with the team is as a reinforcement mechanism in the Norbert system of credit points: she sexually rewards players who perform well on the field. At this point, Paradise rebels by revealing his identity and pitching independently of computer edicts. Norbert dies, possibly by suicide, after losing control of the team.

The battle of humanity versus the machine ends when the protagonist breaks the Faustian pact with Norbert, the mad scientist who commits Hawthorne's version of the Unpardonable Sin by caring more for his experiments than for people. Just as Joe Hardy changes back to Joe Boyd (in *The Year the Yankees Lost the Pennant*), Alexander becomes Paradise again and opts to take his chances as an impotent factor in an indifferent universe. Norbert, then, is a larger version of J. Henry Waugh. Both fail in their attempts to control the worlds they inhabit, but the scientist's materialistic obsession makes him a major villain. Although the conflict between good and evil is oversimplified, the fantasy is significant in its treatment of the negative impact of technology on the game, somewhat similar to the situation in *Stay Loose* (1959), and a topic of many future novels.

Mendelsohn, Felix Jr. *Superbaby.* Los Angeles: Nash, 1969. (New York: Paperback Library, 1970.)

In the twenty-first century, Alan Corvallis, Superbaby, is created in the Laboratory of the Subatomic Sciences through gene manipulation. Delivered from a surrogate mother, he is adopted by a corporation director (Corvallis) and trained to be superior, physically and mentally. He becomes the world chess champion at twelve, a golf pro at fifteen, and heavyweight boxing champ at eighteen. At the age of twenty, he plays baseball for the New York Swingers, a major league team. He breaks batting and pitching records while leading the Swingers as a player-manager. Corvallis, or Superbaby, who also solves a centuries-old mathematical problem, uses computers to test the reaction of players. After two years of baseball, however, he gives up the game. With his superior intellect, he rejects conventional values and seeks independence from the restraints of society. He has a love affair with moviestar Fleur Duelos, but she rejects him because he lacks compassion. At the age of twenty-two, Superbaby commits suicide.

Science was successful in creating a super being with a mind and a body. However, like the mad scientists of Poe or Hawthorne, it had forgotten "the heart." Made in a laboratory and schooled by a corporation, Superbaby never connected with humanity—as the book laboriously emphasizes. As in *The Last Man Is Out*, technology fails in an attempt to manipulate humanity.

Wade, Robert. *Knave of Eagles.* New York: Random House, 1969.

Published in London, this thriller is concerned with smuggling a baseball player out of Castro's Cuba. Chombo Herrera, star pitcher of the New Orleans Pelicans of the American League, returns to his homeland to visit his family. When Castro tries to detain him, Gil Rolfe is hired to bring the pitcher back to America. He arranges to abscond with Herrera and his family, along with his girlfriend and her mother, but during the escape, Rolfe is accosted by a policeman. Herrera frees him by downing the cop with a thrown baseball, and the flight succeeds. Afterwards, Rolfe becomes disillusioned with the CIA's betrayal of Cuban rebels. He decides to return to Cuba and to help in the battle against the communist regime. Rolfe has learned that freedom and justice are more important than business—including the business aspect of baseball. The didactic message is too obvious.

1972

Ball, John. *Death of a Playmate.* Boston: Little Brown and Co., 1972.
[A re-issue of *Johnny Get Your Gun* (1969)].

Beckham, Barry. *Runner Mack.* New York: William Morrow, 1972. (Washington, D.C.: Howard University Press, 1983.)

Henry and Beatrice Adams, black Mississippians who have been conditioned in the Booker T. Washington concept of accepting the social system, go North when Henry has an opportunity for a tryout with a baseball team. Though he hit .415 with sixty-three homers for the Crowns in the minors, the Stars fix his tryout so that he has to bat against a machine that throws a ball 150 miles per hour. Unsigned by the team, Adams is manipulated at work and then sent to a surreal war in Alaska. He is willing to fight for his country against an unspecified enemy until meeting Runner Mack, a black revolutionary who plans to bomb the White House and take control of the country. Adams joins Runner Mack's rebellion and, like his leader, is destroyed.

Henry Adams is politically awakened, but the point of the fantasy is that there is no hope for African Americans in the United States, where dreams of equality are still deferred. This is a common theme in militant protest novels of the sixties (including *Many Thousands Gone, Black Jacob, The Man Who Cried I Am, The Spook Who Sat by the Door*) by black writers but the only one of the era to use baseball as a metaphor for racism.

1973

Brashler, William. *The Bingo Long Traveling All-Stars and Motor Kings.* New York: Harper & Row, 1973. (New York: New American Library, 1975; Urbana–Champaign: University of Illinois, 1993.)

Sallie Potter's Louisville Ebony Aces tour the Midwest in the summer of 1939. Featuring catcher Bingo Long and pitcher Leon Carter, the barnstorming team often has trouble with racial prejudice, including an altercation with the KKK. There is not much to be done about racism, but the team rebels against the unscrupulous tactics of Potter. Long creates his own Traveling All-Stars and Motor Kings and continues to tour despite the threat of Potter to blackball his former players and his attempts to get fans to boycott the team. Then Carter's arm goes dead, and he decides to quit baseball. Finally, two of the younger players are signed by the Canton Reds, a minor league team. With the arrival of integration, Bingo Long has the dilemma of trying to keep the All-Stars solvent, rejoining the dying Negro Leagues, or playing in Mexico or Cuba.

The first novel to deal entirely with black baseball in the pre-Robinson era, it is a realistic portrait of barnstorming life. The black dialect and comic tone help to balance the story of the semi-tragic careers of the major characters. Based loosely on the lives of Josh Gibson and Satchel Paige, Long and Carter are too old to make the major leagues, but there is hope for the younger players. Integrated baseball, however, marks the eventual demise of the Negro Leagues and barnstorming teams. Leon Carter's dead arm, then, represents the end of an era. The popular success of the book has been augmented by the 1976 movie version starring Billie Dee Williams and James Earl Jones.

Dawson, Fielding. *A Great Day for a Ballgame: A Conscious Love Story.* Indianapolis: Bobbs-Merrill, 1973.

The protagonist (Fielding Dawson) is a service manager for a furniture store. In his spare time, he plays amateur baseball. Dawson, who also tries to make a living as a writer, has an affair with his editor, Amelia, that is complicated by the pressure of her eight-year-old son. While she and the boy are in England, Dawson has an epiphany during a baseball game. As he plays, he experiences a feeling of the pastoral innocence of the game that makes life meaningful, a solace for the corruption of life associated with business—whether in baseball or in everyday events. The novella is too obviously an attempt to be literary without much success.

Fish, Robert L. and Henry Rothblatt. *A Handy Death.* New York: Simon & Schuster, 1973. New York: Pocket Book, 1976.)

Billy Depaul, former Mets bonus baby, is serving a prison term for shooting a man. Charley Quirt, vice-president of the Mets, hires attorney Hank Ross to prove the pitcher's innocence. With the help of private eye Mike Gunnerson, Ross proves that Depaul acted in self-defense. Depaul is released and is offered a chance at returning to the Mets. He also discovers that Quirt is his father. Appearing before baseball mysteries become popular, this is one of the lesser examples.

Graham, Alexander. *Babe Ruth Caught in a Snowstorm.* Boston: Houghton Mifflin, 1973.

Slezak creates the Wichita Wraiths of Braintree, Massachusetts, a baseball team that consists of players who love the game. They respond to newspaper ads that stress the creation of a club that will compete for the pure joy of the game. In the first year, pastoral innocence dominates with a democratic system in which the players run the team. However, the next year the Wraiths join the National League, and accountants, lawyers, and public relations experts move in. The previous joy and harmony are destroyed as the emphasis is now on winning and making money. Slezak, the businessman who founded the team, defends the decision to commercialize the enterprise as he narrates alternate chapters. Petashne, a catcher for the Wraiths, is the other narrator, and he bemoans the psychological destruction of the players. The season ends in chaos, and the participants, deprived of the joy of the first season, return to their prior lives of quiet desperation.

The business end of the game, then, overrules the idealistic aspect. Babe Ruth appears only in the form of a symbol — a glass paperweight on Slezak's desk. It is in the form of a ball that simulates snow when shaken, and the figurine of the immortal slugger is enclosed. Ruth, who helped to bring baseball back to popularity after the Black Sox scandal, is here displayed by the businessman to represent the control of the game by commercial interests. The heroic image of the Babe is perverted to support the economic deals enacted on the owners' fields of play. The book, closer to fantasy than realism, ably stresses the archetypical theme of baseball fiction: the domination of business.

Guthrie, A. B. *Wild Pitch.* Boston: Houghton Mifflin, 1973. (New York: Bantam Books, 1987.)

The author of *The Big Sky* and *The Way West* offers a mystery featuring Jason Beard, a seventeen-year-old pitcher for the amateur Midbury team. In the small western town, Beard assists Sheriff Chick Charleston in investigating the murders of Buster Hogue and Ben Day. The youth's interviews with townspeople lead to the arrest of Dr. Ulysses Pierpont, a psychiatrist. When Pierpont threatens Sheriff Charleston with a gun, Beard knocks it out of his hand with a thrown baseball. During the course of the investigation, Beard also finds time to pitch his team to a 5-3 win. He plans to impress Geet Hawthorne, but she marries the sheriff. The young pitcher aspires to find consolation in becoming a big league pitcher (The readers find out that the dream did not materialize — he becomes a writer instead.) Guthrie will be remembered for his earlier historical fiction, such as *The Big Sky*.

Hegner, William E. *The Idolaters.* New York: Trident Press, 1973. (New York: Pocket Books, 1973.)

Tommy Amazon is the pitching and hitting star of the New York Empires in his rookie season — the biggest drawing card since Babe Ruth. Shirley Ann Gosling is a movie star and sex goddess. She marries Amazon after his divorce from actress Jennifer Black. Under the name of Danielle Drew, Shirley Ann achieves fame but becomes a victim of drugs and alcohol. She divorces Amazon and marries dramatist Lyle Sermon. Shortly before her death, she divorces Sermon and has an affair with "a mystery man." Based on the life of Marilyn Monroe, obviously, and her marriages to Joe DiMaggio and Arthur Miller, the book is more pornographic than literary.

Neugeboren, Jay. *Sam's Legacy.* New York: Holt, Rinehart and Winston, 1973.

Negro League baseball and the Babe Ruth legend combine to dominate this novel that begins as the story of Sam Berman, a gambler living in Brooklyn in the 1970s. Sam's father Ben is leaving for a retirement home in California and his legacy to Sam, in a sense, is his relationship to Mason Tidewater, a janitor in their apartment building. Tidewater, a childhood companion of Ben, presents Sam with the manuscript of his autobiography, "My Life and Death in the Negro American Baseball League: A Slave Narrative." Sam, trying to survive in his own world, ponders the document throughout the book.

Tidewater relates that he was known as the Black Babe Ruth while starring as a pitcher and hitter for the Brooklyn Royal Dodgers in the twenties. Playing against each other in exhibition games, he and Babe Ruth form a relationship that evolves into homosexuality and that is complicated by racial ambiguity. Tidewater can pass for white, and Ruth is rumored to be black, but the arbitrary social distinctions of the time segregate them into different worlds. Although Tidewater masters Ruth when he pitches against him, he does not have the opportunity to share the glory that the Babe enjoys as an American hero. Refusing to pass the color line out of pride in his own heritage, Tidewater eventually resorts to violence. He slugs Ruth, the man he loves and idolizes, in an attempt to break free of society's restraints. He then murders Brick Johnson, his teammate and nemesis, and goes on the lam. After years of hiding from the law, Tidewater now lives and writes in the basement of the apartment building. In giving the manuscript to Sam Berman, he apparently hopes to establish his identity before death. He also presents Sam with an antique doll, made by a slave, but Sam rejects the offering—suggesting perhaps that the Jewish heritage of Berman and the African American heritage of Tidewater, though similar in their rejection by mainstream American culture, are still incompatible. Berman is not willing to accept the janitor as a surrogate father

The book is well-written and engrossing, but the counter-history of the Ruth legend from the view of super-star Mason Tidewater strains the credibility of the embedded narrative. Much of what the Negro League player relates about society's racial practices, however, is a part of baseball and cultural history.

Puechner, Ray. *A Grand Slam.* New York: Warner Books, 1973.

Manager Murry Smallworth allows Ticki Denton to audition for the New York Blues, and the twenty-year-old becomes the first woman in major league baseball. The second baseman wins a regular job, as well as the heart of shortstop Johnny Kaminski—the roommate of narrator Bill Thompson. Reporter George Swingle attacks the Blues and Ticki in print, but the team rallies and makes a run for the pennant. She and Kaminski have an affair, but the liberated woman is not ready to settle down. In fact, she seduces both Bill Thompson and his wife. Finally, Ticki marries Johnny, and the Blues win the Eastern Division (but lose in the playoffs). Ticki then decides to quit baseball (she has the world to save) but arranges a tryout for her friend Yolanda Yovarian, who she feels will make the Blues for next season.

This is the first novel to deal exclusively with a female big leaguer. Judy Norris had appeared in *The Last Man Is Out* (1969), but Ticki Denton is the real thing. Unfortunately, sensationalism takes precedence over literary quality.

Roth, Phillip. *The Great American Novel.* New York: Holt, Rinehart and Winston, 1973. (New York: Vintage Press, 1995.)

Former sportswriter Word Smith, now confined to a nursing home, relates the history of the Rupert Mundys of the ill-fated Patriot League. In 1943, the Mundys are forced to play all of their games on the road when the War Department takes over their park in Port Rupert, New Jersey. The team of misfits (with players from the age of fourteen to fifty-two, including a one-armed outfielder and a one-legged catcher) loses 120 games. At the end of the next season, the House Un-American Activities Commission begins hearings on communist infiltration of the Patriot League. As a result, the records are expunged from history, and even the host cities change their names. It is Smith's quest to tell the truth about the league that has been "erased from the national memory" and to write the great American novel as a means of achieving immortality through art.

Smith (call me Smitty) discusses literature with Hemingway and critiques the major novels of Hawthorne, Melville, and Twain. In his dual role of narrator and protagonist, he portrays the alienated artist who exposes the hypocrisies of the conservative capitalists who preach patriotism and religious fundamentalism but whose real god is commercialism. The author "helps" Smith make his point by creating villainous baseball "lords" like General Oakhart, Ulysses Fairsmith, and Angela Whittling Trust — the right-wing fanatic whose obsessions with out-moded tradition dominate the Patriot League.

Allegorical characters like Gil Gamesh and Roland Agni add to the literary emphasis. Gamesh, the pitcher who is banished from baseball, becomes a Communist agent but eventually aids Mrs. Trust (former lover of baseball greats Ty Cobb and Babe Ruth) in charging the Patriot League with communist dealings. The resulting investigation parodies the Senator McCarthy witch-hunt — a black mark in American history. But Gamesh is also used as a mock-heroic version of the "Epic of Gilgamesh," an ancient legend about a King's search for immortality. Roland Agni, on the other hand, suggests ironic comparison to the hero of "Song of Roland," a medieval chivalric romance. Agni is the one true athlete of the Mundys, but his parents punish him for his arrogance by forcing him to play with the homeless team. Agni retaliates by eating "doctored" Wheaties made in an underground laboratory and leads the Mundys into a brief but miraculous winning streak. He is mistakenly killed (by an umpire gunning for Gil Gamesh) but becomes a posthumous hero — a status aided by his reputed stance against communism. Through literary and historical allusion, usually parodic, Roth promotes the concept of the novelist as a critic of society.

Word Smith's task of telling the story of the demise of the Patriot League parallels Roth's attempt to write the novel that, like *Huck Finn* or *Moby Dick,* represents the essence of America and its value system. Like Malamud and Coover, Roth employs literary methods that distinguish his book from most baseball fiction. The verbal play (word-smithing), the farcical tone, and the attack on McCarthyism tend to be overwhelming eventually, and the book has not gained the status of a major classic or reached the level of *The Natural* or *The Universal Baseball Association.*

1974

Holton, Leonard. *The Devil to Play.* New York: Dodd, Mead, 1974.

Father Joseph Bredder attends a Los Angeles Miner baseball game and witnesses a crime. Tio Manuel is shot in the leg while rounding thirdbase. Bredder and Lieutenant Minardi of the LAPD investigate. The trail leads to Stookey Harris, manager of the Miners. When Harris is murdered, the sleuths discover that he was in debt to gamblers and got in the drug business to bail himself out. The bullet that hit Manuel could have been intended for Harris who was coaching third at the time, or it could have been an attempt to eliminate key Miner players to keep them out of the World Series. Several of the drug dealers are arrested. The wounded Manuel gives tickets for the Series to Bredder, who in turn gives them to friends—as justice and harmony reign in a mediocre mystery.

Klise, Thomas. *The Last Western.* Niles, IL: Argus Communications, 1974. (Allen, TX: Argus Communications, 1974.)

Born in New Mexico of Irish, Chinese, African, Mexican, and Native American extraction, Willie grows up in Houston. He invents a super pitch and becomes a major star for the New York Hawks. The magical pitch produces perfect games and makes a mockery of baseball. Officials ask him to compromise, but Willie and Clio Russell, a black catcher, quit playing ball and join the Silent Servants of the Used, Abused and Utterly Screwed Up. The organization puts LOVE into action and disrupts society's value system. Willie becomes famous as a peace-maker and is eventually made the pope. However, he is murdered shortly before Herman Felder, western movie director, carries out his celebration for Willie at the Arizona site where many of the movies had been filmed.

By trying to put Christian tenets into action, Willie is a gadfly to the Establishment. Representatives of Big Business are suspected of the murder. Willie is on his way to visit the owner of the Hawks, the symbol of the military-industrial complex, when he is gunned down — and his white heart is torn out. While Willie is a crucified Christ figure, his friend and former catcher, Clio, becomes the leader of a rebel army. Both the active Christian and the outlaw soldier are doomed to failure against the prevailing economic-based power structure. Capitalism is the villain in the fantasy, and baseball is part of the corrupt business world that is under attack. Faulkner's "The Bear" is a prime example of the chaos that occurs when Christianity is applied to the business world, but *The Last Western* falls more than a little short of being a literary equivalent.

Sorrentino, Gilbert. *Flawless Play Restored: The Masque of the Fungo.* Los Angeles: Black Sparrow Press, 1974.

Eventually incorporated into the novel *Mulligan Stew* (1979), this closet drama tells of the miraculous transformation of Foots Fungo, shortstop of the Amarillo Centipedes. Surrealistic masquers, representing nine elements of Ugliness, sing of Fungo's incompetence, including an .002 batting average. Characters named James Joyce, Susan B. Anthony, Jack Armstrong, and Alice Bluegown depict an obscene, iconoclastic vision of hypocrisy in contemporary culture. Fungo's career, meanwhile, reaches its nadir when he is sold to the Biloxi Crips for forty-five dollars. However, the minuscule figure of Ty Cobb appears and gives Fungo advice. He then becomes a star, and the masquers descend on the stage in white uniforms and representations of Beauty and Goodness. The author seems to be saying that dedication to one's craft can create the potential to overcome the negative aspects of life — maybe.

1975

Craig, John. *All G.O.D.'s Children.* New York: William Morrow, 1975. (New York: New American Library, 1975.)
 Edsel Ames narrates the season of the Hollywood B's of the American League. Gomer O. Dudley (G. O. D.) is the new owner, and the team is a division of Dudley Enterprises. Manager Luke Morton guides the B's into the World Series with the New York Dets, but just before the Series he resigns and accepts the job of managing the Dets for the next season. Dudley retaliates by hiring the Dets manager, Dooley Duoro, for the B's. Restraining orders are put on both managers, and the World Series is played without them. The players, tired of being manipulated by unscrupulous ownership, decide to stop the Series in a tie after six games. Ames considers joining the new World Baseball League. Told in a raunchy, humorous style, the emphasis is on exposing the irresponsibility of owners who approach the game only from the business angle. The book is obviously more of a comic fantasy than a realistic portrayal of baseball.

Curtis, Richard. *The Pro #3: Strike Zone.* New York: Warner Paperback, 1975.
 During a baseball strike, Willie Hesketh, promising Mets prospect, is mugged when he tries to report to spring training. Four men wielding baseball bats inflict enough damage to presumably end his career. Hesketh's agent, Dave Bolt, is asked by Commissioner Bailey to investigate. With the integrity of baseball at stake, Bolt is able to pin the crime on Mark Fioretta, head of a union that is a rival to the union that is trying to enroll baseball players. At the same time, Bolt, a former Dallas Cowboy, is able to make a deal that releases Lonnie Raintree from jail and that allows the third baseman to audition with the Omaha Honchos, a new major league franchise.
 Dave Bolt, who admits to being a "tiny part Negro," is a blond tough guy who has to fight off the women. However, he still loves his ex-wife and their daughter — attesting to his soft-hearted moral core. It adds up to a less than interesting book.

Keifitz, Norman. *The Sensation.* New York: Atheneum, 1975.
 Potter Cindy, a centerfielder compared to Mays and Mantle, has a sexual problem that shortens his career. Emerging from a New Mexico Little League and the University of Arizona, he signs with F. M. Heller's Redbirds of the majors. He marries an actress, buys a Gremlin with a "Honk! If you love Jesus" sticker, and contemplates suicide. The story of his need to expose himself to little girls is made public, and he is humiliated at the All-star Game. The owner, who had been using Cindy in commercials, trades him to the Texas Rustlers. The problem arises again, and he flees to New Mexico, eventually becoming a cowboy.
 F. M. Heller, Redbird owner, is the villain as he puts business ahead of altruism in his treatment of Potter Cindy — an archetypal literary theme that is preva-

lent in baseball fiction. The book, however, exploits the sensational aspect of the sexual perversion.

Parker, Robert B. *Mortal Stakes.* Boston: Houghton Mifflin Co., 1975. (New York: Dell, 1987; New York: Dell, 1994.)

Parker's famous Spenser, in his third appearance, is hired by Harold Erskine of the Red Sox to find out if pitcher Marty Rabb has gambling connections. Spenser discovers that Rabb's wife is a former prostitute and porn star and that Bucky Maynard, Red Sox announcer, is blackmailing Rabb. Maynard gets the pitcher to throw games in order to pay off the announcer's debt to Frank Doerr, a gangster. Spenser kills Doerr and his bodyguard in the course of the investigation, and thus convinces Maynard to eliminate the fixed games. Marty Rabb is free to pursue glory with the Red Sox. Spenser, however, feels guilty until his girlfriend, Susan Silverman, convinces him that a compromise of his code was necessary in this case — that violence was essential in order to save the Rabbs and to protect the integrity of baseball.

Spenser is a latter-day version of the hard-boiled protagonist of Raymond Chandler and Dashiell Hammett. Thus he operates by a code of honor which implies that, while disorder is permanent, the process of solving a crime is a stopgap against total chaos. Baseball is used here as a symbol of stability, and fixed games are a threat to Spenser's view of the necessity of trying to maintain an ordered social structure. The appearance of the literate, wise-cracking, and tough-guy detective in a baseball mystery is an omen of the coming popularity of the subgenre.

1976

Linthurst, Randolph. *The Journal of Leo Smith: Story of a Nineteenth Century Shortstop.* Chicago: Adams Press, 1976.

In a fifty-five page pamphlet, created or edited by Linthurst, Leo Smith's diary records the fate of the Trenton team of the Eastern League in 1884. The shortstop provides information on the games of the minor league club, but he is more concerned about the plight of the league. The Richmond, Redding, and Wilmington franchises drop out, and only five teams are left at the end of the season. Trenton is in first place despite having only ten men. With declining attendance, ownership will not pay for more players. The future of the Eastern League looks doubtful. Smith hopes to play somewhere next year even though baseball is a difficult life.

In a "Postscript," the record of the real-life good field/no-hit shortstop is presented for the rest of his pro career. He had a brief shot at the majors, appearing in thirty-five games and hitting .190 for Pat Powers, his manager at Trenton. The only player from the '84 team with a major league career was Thomas Daly, but Old Hoss Radbourn is the most famous to be mentioned in the journal. Whether fact or fiction, the manuscript is a rambling commentary on baseball and society of the era that is of some historical value.

Rice, Damon. *Seasons Past.* New York: Praeger, 1976.

A pseudonym of the authors, Damon Rice is one of the narrators of a family that chronicles New York City baseball from the Civil War to 1958. Fletcher Rice begins the story, and his sons Alex and Harry, report on the progress of the game into the 1930s. Fictional family history is interspersed with factual baseball history. Each season is summarized, and the players, managers, and owners are discussed and judged. Damon, Alex's son, carries the narration through the fifties and the departure of the Dodgers and Giants to California. The book ends with the destruction of Ebbets Field in 1960. Alex escapes from a nursing home to witness the demolition that marks the end of an era in New York. This reads better as a partial history of major league baseball than as a work of fiction.

Rothweiler, Paul B. The Sensuous Southpaw. New York: G. P. Putnam's Sons, 1976.

Jeri (Red) Walker is a female relief pitcher (for the Portland Beavers of the National League) who passes as a man. She eventually reveals her identity, and a furor results. The Commissioner tries to negate her contract, and teammates sign a petition that objects to her presence on the team. Beavers owner, King Spade, however, orders the manager to keep her on the team. The Giants forfeit a game rather than to play against her, but she perseveres and is selected for the All-Star Game. A Red Walker fan club is formed, and she appears in magazines and on television. When a gambler exposes film of her in compromising positions, the Commissioner suspends her. However, Red now has the support of her teammates, and with the help of a sportswriter, the Commissioner is persuaded to lift the suspension. Red returns to the team and pitches against the Mets in the playoffs.

The second novel to deal exclusively with a female in the majors, like its predecessor (*A Grand Slam*, 1973), it exploits sexual promiscuity. However, there is more stress here on sexual discrimination so that a comparison to Jackie Robinson's entry into a racist baseball establishment is viable. A variation from the typical view of an unscrupulous owner occurs as King Spade tries to protect Red from adverse publicity and sexism. The capricious tone undercuts the argument to some extent, and the heroics of the protagonist are melodramatic.

Winston, Peter. Luke. New York: Manor Books, 1976.

Luke Playtowski is a superhero for the major league Center City Stars, but he is also a playboy whose off-field antics create trouble. He competes with teammate Ben Franklin (the black Babe Ruth) for sexual partners, which causes havoc with Luke's marital situation. His relatively low salary (in 1963) and inability to manage money tempt Luke into betting on sporting events, which results in a temporary suspension. He returns to the Stars in time to hit a seventh game walk-off homer in the World Series (after turning down a bribe). Sensing danger after the Series is over, he rushes home to find his house on fire and his baby son dead. The inclusion of a tight-fisted owner, malicious gamblers, and vulnerable players is typical of plots that antecede the free agency era. Even more obvious here, though, is the melodrama.

1977

Dawson, Fielding. Two Penny Lane. Santa Barbara: Black Sparrow Press, 1977.

About one-fifth of a seemingly plotless 106 page novella is given to a graphic description of a Met-Giant game. Lucky, a novelist, dislikes the typical journalistic reports of baseball games, so he presents the contest from the view of a passionate fan. The Mets (featuring Seaver, Koosman, Staub, Kranepool, and Grote) are dramatically portrayed as characters of myth enacting deeds of consequence for the spectators who are trying to escape the humdrum of daily routine. After the game, the names, numbers and symbols on the scorecard represent a drama of human endeavor. The baseball section is excerpted in *Baseball Diamonds: Tales, Traces, Visions, and Voodoo from a Native American Rite* edited by Kerrane and Grossinger for Anchor Books in 1980.

Donohue, James F. *Spitballs and Holy Water.* New York: Avon Books, 1977.

Shovel Lloyd (another Black Babe Ruth) narrates the fantastic exploits of Sister Timothy Stokes, a black nun, in the summer of 1927. Playing for a barnstorming team, Shovel witnesses the miraculous pitching of the nun. He serves as a negotiator for her in arranging a meeting with Rube Foster and Babe Ruth in order to set up a seven-game series between the New York Yankees and the Chicago American Giants, which now features Sister Timothy. She bets one million dollars, sponsored by the Catholic Church, against the KKK, in expectation that her team will beat the Yankees. In order to make the series a reality, she manipulates a Boston Cardinal, a Grand Wizard of the Klan, and Al Capone. In three games, Sister Timothy pitches the black team to wins over the Yankees of Murderer's Row fame — repeatedly striking out Ruth. However, Charlie Minihan, Cardinal of New York, stops the series and puts the nun on trial for witchcraft. She uses her magical powers to escape, and then takes on Satan at Yankee Stadium, striking him out with a spitball soaked in holy water. Her bet with Satan was that a colored man playing for Atlanta would break Ruth's home run record. Although competently written, the fantasy falls far short of the quality of *The Year the Yankees Lost the Pennant.*

Herrin, Lamar. *The Rio Loja Ringmaster.* New York: Viking Press, 1977. (New York: Avon Books, 1983.)

Dick Dixon narrates his search for a meaningful life while residing at his retreat in San Lorenzo, Mexico. Once a star relief pitcher for the Cincinnati Brewmasters and the victor over the Yankees in the seventh game of a World Series, he is now haunted by the vision of his wife's infidelity. At the age of thirty, he fled to Mexico in an attempt to find peace of mind. Memories of his puritanical mother who was always at odds with his profligate father complicate the situation, but it was his wife's divorce terms that prompted the Mexican journey.

Dixon does not escape from baseball, though, as he pitches for Juan Antonio's San Lorenzo team. Playing in Rio Loja, he envisions himself as an Aztec ringmaster, the hero of an ancient sport. In the meantime, he has managed to pitch 8 2/3 innings of a perfect game. However, the federales, Mexican police who apparently want to deport the American, arrive at the diamond. Dixon throws a looper (that the batter hits out of the park) and then makes his escape and returns to his Mexican home with the help of Antonio.

As Ricardo Dixon, he lives with Juan and Carlota Antonio and marries their daughter, Consuelo. He learns to stifle his ego and to restrain his competitive nature as a member of the Mexican family. Dixon finds an inner peace that is illustrated in an imaginary game in which he, a new form of ringmaster, throws "affectionate lobs" at the plate and is indifferent to the outcome.

Using baseball as a metaphor for the American competitive way of life, the author condemns the culture and retreats to the pastoral aspect of the game in Mexico by changing his philosophy. This is a book that demands close reading, but it is worth the effort.

Johnson, Curt. *The Morning Light.* Pomeroy, OH: Carpenter Press, 1977.

Arnie (Swede) Sivardsson is a former New York Giant who has returned to Mills, Iowa, in 1954. Injuries and a loss of concentration hurt his career. Refusing to take a pay cut, he comes home to work at a feed plant and to try to fix a problematic marriage. Hoodlum Vic Westphal complicates matters by trying to blackmail him (with photos of Swede and "another" woman). The ex-Giant refuses to cooperate with Westphal and, after repairing his domestic situation and his conscience, considers the resumption of his baseball career.

In the process of coming to terms with his life, Swede Sivardsson feels that he is doing the right things in a fouled-up world. Returning to his code of honor, he can face the future. This is a competent novel that uses baseball as a symbol of redemption in a chaotic universe.

Kowett, Don. *The 7th Game.* New York: Dell, 1977.

Rookie Jim Pallafox wins thirty games for the Oakland Golds, helps defeat the Cardinals in the playoffs, and is prepared to face the New York Patriots in the World Series. However, his daughter is kidnapped and used as bait for the pitcher to lose the games he starts in the Series. Detective Hardrock Harrison discovers that the owner of the Golds, Walter O. Kelly, is responsible for the crime. He has bet against his team and assumes that he can make a fortune with Pallafox under control. The detective clears the way for the rookie superstar to compete, however, and he wins the seventh game with a no-hitter. Pallafox is reunited with his daughter and her mother, the pitcher's old girlfriend. Other than being a fast read, this thriller has no redeeming qualities.

Magnuson, James. *The Rundown.* New York: Dial Press, 1977.

When Carrie, daughter of New York Warriors owner Fred Brennan, is missing, he hires Ron Price to find her. A former third baseman of the team and now a scout, Price finds a connection between Carrie Brennan and Vic Rawlings, a Warrior star who has disappeared. Rawlings is found, murdered, and Price learns that the owner is responsible. He had committed a murder twenty years ago, and when Rawlings found out, he had to be eliminated also. Price, who had helped Brennan win his first pennant but was released, unravels the pieces that condemn his ruthless boss in a complicated mystery that escapes mediocrity by its stylistic narration.

Swed, Trebor (Robert P. Dews). *Whichaway?* New York: Rebel Books, 1977.

Bob of Albany, Georgia, receives a letter from New York City asking him to find information about an escape from a chain gang in 1935. Since the letter is verified by Governor Jimmy Carter, Bob begins an investigation. A second letter provides the background material of the request. The sender, addressing himself as Mr. New York, tells of the baseball escapade that led to an arrest and imprisonment in Georgia. In 1934, Mr. New York went to Florida to watch Joe McCarthy's Yankees in spring training. He was introduced to Babe Ruth and got a chance to work out with the team. The Yankees sent him to Albany for a tryout with its minor league team, but while there he was mistakenly arrested and sent to the Calhoun County Work Camp. He escaped with the help of Tom Vaccaro and then played as Gator, the catcher, on the Blue Moon Café, Vaccaro's amateur team. He eventually married Teresa, Vaccaro's sister, and returned to New York City.

In the present, the protagonist and his wife visit Bob in Albany. There is no longer any search for the escaped convict of 1935, and Mr. New York, now a prominent politician, is released from a long-troubling burden. Bob is now free to write the story.

The actual author is the father of Atlanta Braves coach Bobby Dews. Probably the most interesting aspect of the 153-page book is the young catcher's notice of the coolness between Babe Ruth and Lou Gehrig — and the differences between them, including the way they swing the bat. Literary merit, however, is lacking.

Zacharia, Irwin. *Grandstand Rookie.* Canoga Park, CA: Major Books, 1977.

Arnold Morton is a rookie superstar of the New York Titans. The first baseman has problems off the field, however. He is an adulterer, his marriage is in jeopardy, and his financial status is not progressing. Morton's worries deepen when his son is injured due to his wife's negligence. When the Titan is himself hit in the head by a pitch, he has time, while recuperating, to realize both his vulnerability and his need of a stable family. He reforms and creates a healthy domestic relationship. He also signs a new contract without demanding the raise he had previously asked for (it is still before free agency). Morton is now more concerned about proving himself as a husband, father, and player. While his transformation is commendable, the book is not.

1978

Clifton, Merritt. A Baseball Classic. Richford, VT: Samisdat, 1978.

Reissued as part of *A Double Play of Underground Baseball Novellas* in 1997 (with John Sandman's "Praying for Rain") it features a tryout in Portland, Oregon, in which a female is signed to a pro contract. Mac McCarver quits his job, sells his car, and rides a train to the camp in order to test his pitching skills. He discovers that Joe Schaeffer, secondbase candidate, is a girl, Jo Ann Schaeffer. Leon Klein, major league slugger of the past, coaches her on the side, and keeps her identity secret. When she signs a contract, she reveals herself — as she becomes the first woman player in Organized Baseball. Mac, meanwhile, hurts his arm and loses his chance. Most of the story is concerned with his life as a laborer, beer drinker, and semipro player who keeps alive the dream of becoming a professional. The section dealing with the tryout camp is hurried — and should probably have been developed into a full-length book. Jo Ann Schaeffer, a potential big leaguer, deserves a story of her own.

Fisher, Leonard Everett. *Noonan: A Novel About Baseball, ESP, and Time Warps.* Garden City, NY: Doubleday, 1978.

Although a novella written supposedly for juveniles, this illustrated sci-fi book is interesting enough to be considered here. Johnny Noonan of the Continental League's Brooklyn Dutchmen is playing, at the age of fifteen, against the Cincinnati Red Stockings in 1896. When he is hit in the head by a liner, he is transported a century into the future. Baseball has been computerized, and automation has dehumanized the population. In a world without oil, the American League has been eliminated in order to conserve energy. Umpires are no longer necessary, and the players are equipped with transmitter receivers for computer identification. In this brave new world, Johnny becomes a pitcher for the Mets under the guidance of Coach Jerry Koosman. With his magical pitches, Johnny hurls two perfect games as the Mets beat the Cubs in the World Series. However, he wakes up to find himself pitching against the Red Stockings back in 1896. He dazzles them with his art for a couple of innings before rain washes out the game. Subsequently, Johnny loses his magic, and there is no record that he ever existed. The frivolous plot of the book is overshadowed and almost redeemed by the dark vision of the future in which baseball has become a victim of technology, like the rest of society.

Paradis, Vincent A. *The Cocaine Caper.* New York: Manor Books, 1978.

Theodore (Tut) Claw, special agent, investigates cocaine shipments coming from Mexico. He suspects Panton Products, which sponsors an industrial league baseball team. While pitching for the team, he discovers that the manager and the catcher are the smugglers. Tut traces the problem to the ringleaders: Jim Burns of Panton Products and Pat Cage of the Caggiani crime family. In the process, Tut proves to be a master of disguises and of women — in an easily forgettable thriller.

Platt, Kin. *The Screwball King Murder.* New York: Random House, 1978.

Private detective Max Roper checks into the murder of Hondo Kenyan, left-handed Los Angeles Dodger's pitcher. Roper discovers that the popular playboy was involved in a drug smuggling and distributing operation. He kept a diary of the business, and his cohort, Patty Bone, killed him when he threatened to expose her. There is not much baseball or quality writing here.

Tennenbaum, Silvia. *Rachel, the Rabbi's Wife.* New York: William Morrow, 1978.

Rachel Sonnsheim is an artistic middle-aged woman who, during a critical year of her life, finds solace by attending the games of the New York Mets. Seymour, her husband, is having an extramarital affair. Rachel, who is attempting to get her own painting studio, runs into an old lover and renews her relationship with him. Meanwhile, the congregation fires the rabbi and sells the Sonnsheim house. Aaron, the son of Rachel and Seymour, often attends ball games with his mother.

He informs her that his new girlfriend is black. Despite the distractions, Rachel gives up her old lover and tries to keep the family intact while also pursuing her artistic career. Throughout her tribulations, baseball serves as therapy.

1979

Bell, Marty. *Breaking Balls.* New York: Signet, 1979.

Gather Morse, pitcher for the Washington Dudes, concocts a plan to free himself from the team and the villainous owner, Augie August. Tired of being treated like a piece of property, Morse makes racist comments that get him labeled as the Baseball Bigot. He hopes that August will trade him, but the plan backfires, and the owner considers Morse a promotional genius. When the pitcher is caught in bed with Melinda, who lives with August, he is traded anyway—to the last place Mets. Morse accepts his fate and changes into a responsible person by marrying Melinda. As he reports to the Mets, Manager Joe Torre reports that August has died of heart failure.

A typical parsimonious owner appears once again, but this time his death signifies the end of an era -as free agency begins. The emphasis in the book, however, is on the sexual exploits of the protagonist, along with his other ridiculous antics, which puts it in the category of *The Sensuous Southpaw* or *All G .O .D's Children.*

Brady, Charles. *Seven Games in October.* Boston: Little, Brown and Co., 1979.

In a thriller similar to Kowet's *The 7th Game* (1977), Roosevelt Chad's two kids and his mother are kidnapped. The Dodger star is pressured to lose games in the World Series against the Washington Senators as a result. He makes an error to help the Senators win the fourth game. In the seventh game, a Dodger is suspiciously picked off base with Chad at bat, and the Senators win the Series. Robert Hencill, a gambler, has embezzled $600,000 from his company to bet on the Senators. He collects his money, but, in a strange twist, is robbed by a trial lawyer and an FBI agent. The book is a fast read but has little else to recommend it.

Charyn, Jerome. *The Seventh Babe.* New York: Arbor House, 1979. (Oxford: University of Mississippi Press, 1996.)

Cedric Tennehill, son of a millionaire, plays baseball for the Red Sox in 1923 under the name of Babe Ragland. A left-handed third baseman and the seventh Babe to play for Boston since Babe Ruth, journalists help to make him a legend by comparing him to Ruth. Ragland rooms with Scarborough, a humpbacked dwarf who serves as the team's mascot and batboy. He marries Iva Cottonmouth, ward of Sox owner Hollis McKee, but leaves her after discovering her infidelity. Ragland then becomes the Bad Boy of Baseball and associates with gamblers. Commissioner Kenesaw Mountain Landis bans him from major league baseball.

Ragland starts a new career as a barnstormer with the Cincinnati Colored Giants. He continues to tour with them even after Landis clears him and after inheriting a copper company and a cattle ranch. Accompanied by Scarborough, he becomes a mythical figure as he travels with the Colored Giants in a seven-Buick caravan, which includes a magician/witch doctor and some of the best players in the country When the team gets in financial trouble, Ragland uses some of the Tennehill money and his own voodoo wizardry to keep it in business. Landis warns all-star teams to boycott the Colored Giants, but in 1934 they play the Dizzy Dean All-Stars and beat them.

After World War II, scouts start to look for black players, and Ira Sharp of the Giants signs with the Boston Braves. In 1949, Ragland briefly returns to the majors with the St. Louis Browns. The Negro National League then convinces him to play for awhile, but he soon resigns and revives the Colored Giants—now baseball dinosaurs, the last of the barnstorming teams. He rediscovers Iva, his wife, and with Scarborough (the dwarf) dead, she becomes his new roommate as he plays on into old age. As the novel ends, Ragland convinces Garland James, a former Red Sox teammate and now a seventy-nine-year-old inmate of a nursing home, to join the Colored Giants as they head for another game—somewhere.

In the tradition of Malamud, Coover, and Roth, Charyn presents a challenging literary work with baseball lore suffused in magical realism. Essentially, though, Babe Ragland is a Peter Pan, a kid who is caught in time as the pure baseball player who refuses to be corrupted by the business aspects of the game. His relationship with Scarborough indicates his child-like innocence. He finds his identity by playing with a barnstorming team for the love of the game rather than for the fame that was his as a member of the Red Sox.

Craig, John. *Chappie and Me: An Autobiographical Novel.* New York: Dodd, Mead, 1979.

Chappie Johnson's Colored All-Stars play in Trentville, Ontario, in 1933. Joe Giffen, a fifteen-year-old white kid, receives lessons from Johnson on playing firstbase. Six years later, Giffen, now a hobo, encounters the team during his travels. The barnstormers are short a man, and Giffen joins the team. He performs in black face and experiences the problems of racism in Canada and the U. S. He meets a girl in Minnesota, out of his disguise, but his attraction to her ends when she reveals her racism. Despite the hardships of living on the road and adjusting to Jim Crow rules, Giffen learns to appreciate the black ballplayers and their nomadic way of life.

News of the war erupting in Europe puts a blight on the summer of 1939, however, and Giffen decides to go home to Canada rather than to make a southern trek with the team. Passing for black in the Deep South seems frivolous now. On his way home, he thinks about visiting a girl in Detroit, Ellen Marshall, who is "part black." In contrast to *The Seventh Babe*, this is a candid, realistic account of black barnstormers that is similar to *Bingo Long*, although smaller in scope.

Harris, Mark. *It Looked Like Forever.* New York: McGraw-Hill, 1979.

In the fourth Henry Wiggen novel, the left-handed pitcher is released by the New York Mammoths at the age of forty. He hopes to be manager of the team, since Dutch Schnell has died; when the job does not go to him, he looks elsewhere. No major league team will hire him, so he goes to Japan—but refuses to play there. Holly, his wife, wants him to retire, and his troubled youngest daughter, Hilary, wants desperately to see him play. After briefly joining the Friday Night Baseball team of announcers, Wiggen returns to action as a big league pitcher. He signs with California and pitches, in scattered appearances, nine successive no-hit innings, until a liner to the head ends his baseball career.

Holly is happy that it is over—now there will be time for the family, including Hilary, who seems to have adjusted to her father's retirement. Wiggen has had a probable Hall-of-Fame career, has grown wealthy, has matured, and has become virtuous (through Holly's directions). He has accomplished nearly all the positive things that Lardner's Jack Keefe could not do—but that is part of the problem. His life is too successful, including the authorial efforts—even though his language skills never improve. A forty-year-old Huck Finn who becomes a success in his society does not seem credible, and Harris' novels fall short of the best baseball fiction.

Hemphill, Paul. *Long Gone.* New York: Viking Press, 1979.

In 1956, the Florida panhandle town of Graceville, home of the Oilers of the Class D Alabama-Florida League, is trying to hang on to the past and is aghast at what has happened since Jackie Robinson integrated baseball. The star of the team, owned by Q. Talmadge Ramey, is Joe Louis Brown, a black catcher who pretends to be from Venezuela in order to escape the wrath of the KKK. Stud Cantrell is the thirty-nine-year-old player-manager whose major league hope was ruined by an injury in World War II. The Oilers start winning with the arrival of teenage second baseman Jamie Weeks.

However, when Ramey, a preacher and owner of a funeral home, gets in financial trouble, he arranges with Cantrell to lose to the Dothan Cardinals so that the Alabama team can win the pennant. The manager, also a pitcher and a slugger for the Oilers, agrees to the fix. Meanwhile, Jamie Weeks impregnates Esther Wrenn, a Southern Belle, who escapes to an aunt's home in Mobile to have the baby without her parents' knowledge.

The hypocrisy of a dying Old South is emphasized. The major villain is the owner, Reverend Ramey, who preaches fundamentalist gospel on station WGOD but who blackmails Stud Cantrell to save his businesses. Despite the book's vivid ambience, it is formulaic in its exploitation of sex and its stereotypical characters.

Honig, Donald. *The Last Great Season.* New York: Simon & Schuster, 1979.

Young reporter Todd McNeil observes the ruthless antics of New York Lions owner Allie Brandon in 1942. When star centerfielder Buddy Lockridge is beaned, Brandon rushes onto the field and demands that Pirate pitcher Banjo Bob Clemens be arrested. The owner's motive, however, stems from business rather than altruism, as he prematurely rushes Lockridge back into action. The centerfielder keels over during a game and is temporarily paralyzed. The Lions win the pennant without their star, but succumb to the Yankees in the World Series.

McNeil attacks Brandon in print by accusing him of nailing a pennant to the staff and a man to the cross. The owner, however, is murdered by his mistress, tennis player Paula Craft. Ironically, Brandon had just announced that he planned to sell the team and participate in World War II. The point, though, is that Brandon, like so many of the owners depicted in baseball fiction, is obsessed with winning and creating a successful business. His role as a typical capitalist is balanced by

McNeil as a moral arbiter. This is the first adult baseball novel by a prolific and competent author.

Newlin, Paul. *It Had to Be a Woman.* New York: Stein and Day, 1979. (Scarborough House, 1979; New York: Day Books, 1981.)
   Darrell Morgan, ex-high school basketball coach and English teacher, considers suicide after his wife runs off with a sociologist. Also distraught by being rejected for a coaching job at Knickerbocker State College, he resorts to violence (beating his wife's boyfriend) and flees into the night. On the road, he fantasizes about pitching to real former major league catcher Willard Hershberger, who committed suicide after a doubleheader loss. The rumor is that the death must have been due to a woman. Morgan fails at a suicide attempt in Cincinnati and then decides to drive to Los Angeles to watch the Reds play the Dodgers. In his fantasy, he will be pitching the game.
   Described as a realistic men's lib novel, the baseball background is what makes it mildly interesting. The reference to Willard Hershberger, an actual backup of Ernie Lombardi for the Reds in 1940, is the most intriguing aspect of the book

O'Connor, Phillip. *Stealing Home.* New York: Alfred A. Knopf, 1979.
   Benjamin Dunne is a bookstore owner and manager of the Gray's Cleaners Pee Wee team, which includes his son Bobo. Troubled with business and domestic issues, Dunne also has a problem with the team's sponsor who will not supply uniforms—until pressure is applied. In the meantime, Dunne has an affair with the mother of one of his players. He examines the situation and concludes that he prefers winning-at-any-cost to sportsmanship. After the final game, in which his team wins the championship, Dunne wrestles with the possibility of leaving his family and heading west—but he finally opts to stay home. There is no easy answer to the protagonist's dilemma in this first adult novel to deal with Little League life.

Sorrentino, Gilbert. *Mulligan Stew.* New York: Grove Press, 1979. (Lincoln: Dalkey Archive Press, 1996.)
   It contains the baseball segment published in 1974 as *Flawless Play Restored: The Masque of Fungo.*

1980

Anderson, Richard. *Muckaluck: A Curious Episode in the Cavalry's Winning of the West.* New York: Delacorte Press, 1980.
   A farcical account of the 1873 Muckaluck Indian War in the Northwest, it stresses the government's decision to act against the Native Americans in an effort to accommodate the continual arrival of settlers. The Muckalucks refuse to be limited to reservations, though, and a showdown is inevitable. In a lull before the war, the soldiers introduce baseball to the tribe at Fort Klamath. However, during a game, they terrorize the Indians with the nails on their shoes. The shaman of the Muckalucks helps to keep the violence in check until General Canby is able to main-

tain a temporary détente. War eventually erupts, and the Indians keep the soldiers temporarily at bay by fighting from the protection of lava beds. The black humor and the baseball interlude add some interest to what is only a small contribution to baseball and/or historical fiction.

Browne, Robert. *The New AToms Bombshell.* New York: Ballantine Books, 1980.

In a reworking of Karlin's *The Last Man Is Out* (1969), the Chicago AToms win the 2002 divisional title, as opposed to the late season collapse in the earlier book. Once again, Dr. Michael Paradise (pitching as Mike Alexander) turns to Professor Norbert for help. The scientist computerizes the team and provides calculated probabilities for strategic moves on the field. He also employs the female player, Judy Norris, in a legitimate role with the team (as compared to her use as a sexual payoff to "deserving" players in the original version), and it is her pinch-hit that wins the title game. Although Paradise/Alexander rebels against the extensive use of Norbert's computers, he sticks with the team and pitches the AToms to victory in the final game. Norbert is not depicted as a mad scientist, Judy Norris is now worthy of being a love interest, Dr. Paradise is a diamond hero, and the book should not have been written.

Cohler, David Keith. *Gamemaker.* Garden City, NY: Doubleday, 1980. (New York: New American Library, 1981.)

Vietnam vet Raymond Derwinski tries to make a living by inventing games, but he evolves into the Chessboard Killer. He murders centerfielder Willie Bush in Yankee stadium during a game attended by almost 50,000 fans and then proceeds to attack a jockey, a tennis player, a boxer, and the Harlem Globetrotters. He demands that all pro sports events in New York City be cancelled, or he will strike again. The motive appears to be that pro athletes are being paid too much (in the 1970s) and that they are therefore symbols of a society that has gone wrong through the worship of economics. It turns out, though, that the personal psychological problems of Derwinski (fueled by the death of his father in a football game) are the real cause of the manic behavior. The book, then, is basically a typical crime thriller rather than a serious sociological study of the business of pro sports.

Cronley, Jay. *Screwballs.* Garden City, NY: Doubleday, 1980. (New York: Pinnacle, 1981.)

Wilbur Moss narrates his partial season as manager of a major league team of what he considers pampered and greedy ballplayers from the era of free agency. Moss is a martinet from the old school of basics and discipline, so he runs counter to the vanity of star Sammie Land and his agent. Moss perseveres and shapes the team into a contender despite the annoying fact that "the screwballs" play only for money. With ten games to go and a one-game lead in the American League, though, the manager abruptly quits the team. He goes back to Arizona to coach college baseball. When his former team wins the pennant, Moss feels that he inspired it by his resignation.

The first novel to deal in some detail with free agency, the point is that the new era of the game leads to a lack of discipline and dedication. Players and their agents help to make the business aspect more dominant — thus Moss signs off. Stereotypes and clichés are too obvious, however, and the impact of the theme is weakened.

Herskowitz, Mickey. *Letters from Lefty.* Houston: The Houston Press, 1980 (revised edition).

An updating from the 1966 edition, it records the career of the pitcher from 1967 to 1971. He continues to write to Alice in the style of Jack Keefe — except for the grammar. The book is stretched out to 126 pages — most of it amusing but not much of a novel.

Morgenstein, Gary. *Take Me Out to the Ballgame.* New York: St. Martin's Press, 1980.

The new owner of the Buffalo Matadors plans to upgrade fan enthusiasm by supplying incentives. He gets rid of high-salaried superstars, allows beer and booze in the stands, hires cheerleaders, promotes bigoted ethnicity, and caters to blind patriotism. Ned Switzer is in charge of selling the team's new look to the blue-collar fans that are most likely to support the team — a predominantly white group. Thus Homer Jefferson, black player, is traded because he is too militant. Despite the warning of journalist Eddie Olds, War Memorial Stadium turns into a battleground during a crucial series with the Indianapolis Racers that includes death threats to Virgil Kent, Racers star.

Cal Fleisher, who works at a chicken warehouse, is typical of the targeted group of fans. He and his friends form the Marauding Matador Monsters fan club. Acts of violence are encouraged by inflammatory public relations hype. Manager Cy Trattora, worried about unbridled emotions from the stands, resigns. His concern is verified when Cal Fleisher shoots Virgil Kent during a game.

The competitive nature of sports fans is exaggerated here — but maybe it is only a slight stretching of the mania that is produced by the quest to produce winning teams. Again, the major villain is the owner who creates the fan frenzy as a ploy to make money. The novel is a competently written warning about irresponsible fandom and ownership — and the economic factor behind the scenes.

Spencer, Ross H. *The Stranger City Caper.* New York: Avon Books, 1980.

Chance Purdue, Chicago private eye, is hired by Vito Chericole to check on a minor league team in Stranger City, Illinois. The all-lefthanded team plays in a two-team league with the Creepy Hollow Vampires. A fanatical religious sect, the Bobby Crackers Blitzkrieg for Christ, invades the town and, after collecting cash donations, persuades the players to retire because baseball is a "sinful game with personal gain at its root." Secret agent Brandy Alexander informs Purdue that the leader of the cult is really Boboi Krazezoff, a member of the KGB. After a semblance of order is restored, the detective returns to the Windy City and is rewarded for his report on the state of baseball in Stranger City. The humor in this parody of the hardboiled mystery is just barely able to keep the narrative interesting.

Wolff, Miles. *Season of the Owl.* New York: Stein and Day, 1980. (London: Octagon Press, 1996).

The Centerville Owls play in the Class B Carolina League in the 1950s. Teenager Tom, the narrator, lives with Uncle Will, the general manager of the team. The 1958 season is highlighted by a pennant for the Owls, but racial tension and the discovery of a body buried under the centerfield fence detract from the success of the team.

When black protesters, with the support of Uncle Will, try to integrate the stadium, the owner resists. At the end of the season, he announces that there will be no pro baseball in Centerville, North Carolina, the next year. The tradition of segregation and the threat of continued demonstrations make business too risky. The narrator returns to town years later to find Centerville Stadium a dying structure with rotted seats and a weedy field.

The murder, it turns out, was committed by Tom himself. He killed his father with an iron pipe and buried him with the help of a retarded friend and an Owls outfielder. Like Huck rebelling against the tyranny of Pap Finn, Tom chooses his own way of life.

The author, president of a minor league team, competently conveys the atmosphere of the South in the civil rights era — and relates it to baseball. The coming-of-age story, however, gets rather murky, especially about the murder, and keeps the book from achieving major status.

1981

Knopf, Mel. The Batting Machine. Great Neck, NY: Todd & Honeywell, 1981.

In the near future, John Cloud buys the Portland Jacks of the American League. He manages the team himself and trains the players on a computerized machine that is kept in seclusion on his estate near San Diego. Ben Craddock (the narrator) and Charlie Warner are hired to scout the minors for the best pitching prospects and deals are made to sign some of them. Then the coaching staff selects three weak hitters and conditions them on the batting simulator. The advanced technology turns the trio into excellent batsmen, and with the help of the young pitching talent, the Jacks win the division championship before losing to the Yankees in the playoffs. Cloud, though, is sure that he can train more hitters with his machine and win a World Series soon.

Subtitled "The Revolution in Baseball," the sci-fi aspect is the main point of interest. On the negative side, the characters are conventional and the writing is amateurish.

Powers, Ron. Toot-Toot-Tootsie, Good-bye. New York: Delacorte Press, 1981.

The world of L. C. Fanning, radio announcer for the New York Nats, is threatened by change. For over forty years, he has celebrated the beauty of baseball from his booth. He and his partner, Turtle Teweles, are the epitome of the old school — the time before the invasion of television and promotional gimmicks. Thus when beauty queen Robyn Quarrels is hired as a member of the broadcasting team, it creates chaos. Turtle, a Dizzy Dean clone, refuses to work with a woman and returns to his home in Arkansas. L. C., a victim of future shock, sees the female intruder as an agent for the enemies of radio announcing and of pure baseball. He develops a plan of revenge which he hopes to reveal on the expected Fanning Day. (He is in his last season of broadcasting and assumes that the Nats will honor him.) First, he descends to the South in an attempt to persuade Turtle to come back to the booth and share the tribute. Turtle knows that the old ways are over, however, and refuses to cooperate. When L. C. rejoins the team, his appearance has deteriorated. His paranoia produces a physical reaction that ages him, and his attire is a disaster compared to his former dapper wardrobe. What keeps him going is the anticipation of Fanning Day at Flushing Stadium.

The dismal season is down to the last day, and L. C. has been forgotten. With only 914 fans in attendance, the only honoree is Robyn Quarrels who is rewarded by being promoted to a television job with the Nats. It is the final blasphemy for L. C., a victory of commercialism over the art of the game. His revenge is to put on a recording of the Giants-Dodgers game of October 3, 1951—when Bobby Thompson's homer epitomized the last "pure season" when "life was green and good." At the climactic moment, with Pafko at the wall, L. C. interjects: "And Pafko ... makes the catch!" It is the farewell of a man who has outlived his time, who has not been able to adjust to a new era. The "got-cha" beat that Fanning hears in contemporary music takes bodily form in Robyn Quarrels and indicates the psychological destruction that has occurred. The presentation of the announcer's downfall is a classic in the genre.

Quigley, Martin. *The Original Colored House of David.* Boston: Houghton Mifflin, 1981. (revised edition, Boston: Houghton Mifflin, 1987.)

Tim Nelson, seventeen, of Indian Springs, Minnesota, takes a big step to the adult world when he encounters a black barnstorming baseball team on July 4, 1928. He joins the team as Speedy Deefy, an albino deaf-mute, and becomes part of the comic routines as they travel through the upper Midwest. Proud of his Viking heritage, Tim is distraught as he experiences the racism directed at the black players by the Scandinavians who make up the largest share of the audiences. Like Hester Prynne, he is able to step outside the society and to judge it objectively.

At the end of the summer, he comes home with his salary stowed in his tin pail. Formerly a sign of his childhood, it now represents his entrance into the realm of economics. Tim Nelson has been initiated into adulthood by living as an outsider, which has painfully altered his view of the world.

As in Charyn's *The Seventh Babe* (1979) and Craig's *Chappie and Me* (1979), the exploits of a white on a black barnstorming team stress racism in an era preceding the civil rights movement. *The Original Colored House of David* is similar to Craig's novel (although with a more pronounced moral emphasis), but falls short of the literary quality of the Jerome Charyn book.

Ritz, David. *The Man Who Brought the Dodgers Back to Brooklyn.* New York: Simon & Schuster, 1981. (New York: Pocket Books, 1982.)

Bobby Hanes and Dan Malone of Brooklyn are Dodger fans as schoolboys and are shocked when the team moves to Los Angeles. Malone, the narrator, is a catcher whose big league dreams end when he loses a leg. He settles down into the life of a jeweler until Hanes, now a wealthy playboy, requests his help in bringing the Dodgers back to Brooklyn. Oran Ellis, female sportswriter, doubts the ability of

Hanes to complete his mission, but she is impressed when he rebuilds Ebbets Field in time for the 1988 season,

Dan (Squat) Malone becomes manager of the Brooklyn Dodgers, and one of his players is Ruth Smelkinson, a female Sandy Koufax who is discovered by Oran Ellis and signed by Hanes. The owner also visits Castro in Cuba and talks him into allowing a great Cuban pitcher to play for Brooklyn. The Dodgers go on to win the pennant. However, they lose the World Series to the Yankees when Smelkinson is grounded by her doctor due to pregnancy. Malone marries her, and Hanes weds Oran Ellis. Dodger fans wait till next year.

Ruth Smelkinson joins Judy Norris, Ticki Denton and Jeri Walker (along with the magical Sister Timothy Stokes) as female pioneers in pro baseball. The semi-fantasy is amusing enough to somewhat compensate for its sentimentality.

Rubin, Louis D., Jr. *Surfaces of a Diamond.* Baton Rouge: Louisiana State University Press, (Baton Rouge: Louisiana State University Press, 2004.)

In the summer of 1939 in Charleston, South Carolina, Omar Kohn comes of age. The fifteen-year-old has an unhappy home life: his father is ill, and his mother has a nervous breakdown. While playing for the Neighborhood League baseball team, he commits an error in the final game of the season which costs the team a chance to win the championship. However, his reports on softball games are printed in a local newspaper, which is some consolation. While visiting his mother's family in Richmond, he sees the difference between a serious approach to a Jewish heritage and his own casual attitude. Like his Uncle Ben, a screenwriter in California, Omar chooses to strive for independence rather than to yield to tradition. His experience in baseball is a factor in the educational process.

1982

Carmona, Al. *Andy: The First Switch Pitcher.* Los Angeles: Self-published, 1982.

Andy Valko, rural Texas kid, is taught by his father to throw rocks with both hands. He makes rock piles (with the help of Carolyne, a neighbor girl) that a cement company buys at twelve dollars each — the major source of the family's income. A baseball scout spots Andy and, although the youth has never heard of baseball, signs him for the Los Angeles Dodgers. At eighteen, pitching from both sides, Andy becomes a sensation. He talks the manager into playing in every other game, and the Dodgers climb from the bottom to a World Series match against Oakland. However, a gambler hires a girl to distract Andy from his work, and he misses three games of the Series while indulging in his first sexual experiences. The Dodger manager finally tracks him down and gets him to the ballpark for the sixth and seventh games. Andy, of course, bats and pitches his team to wins in both. He signs a multi-year contract, marries Carolyne, and goes on to win Cy Young and Most valuable Player Awards (as well as batting championships).

The sexual escapade eliminates the book from the kid lit list — where it would otherwise seem to fit. As an adult novel, it ranks among the worst ever.

DeAndrea, William. *Five O'Clock Lightning.* New York: St. Martin's Press, 1982.

In New York City, in 1953, Congressman Rex Simmons is murdered at Yankee Stadium. Founder of the Communism-in-Sports subcommittee, Simmons had been convinced that the Red Scare had infiltrated baseball. Russ Garrett, a former Yankee minor leaguer (whose career was ended by a wound in Korea) is one off the investigators. One of the congressman's targets was Mickey Mantle whose 4-F status was seen as draft dodging. After Simmons' death, Mantle a friend of Garrett, receives a death threat. The trail leads eventually to Professor David Laird, who had been subpoenaed by Simmons' committee.

This is a mediocre mystery bolstered somewhat by the inclusion of the McCarthy-like witch hunting and the Mickey Mantle escapade.

Kahn, Roger. *The Seventh Game.* New York: New American Library, 1982. (New York: Signet, 1983.)

Johnny Longboat, forty-one-year-old Native American, is pitching the seventh game of the World Series for the New York Mohawks against the Los Angeles Mastodons of the American League. In a series of flashbacks, much of his life is revealed. A future Hall-of-Famer, the pitcher has problems that include a sore shoulder. He is also having an adulterous affair with Christina Moresby, wife of a gambler who has tried to bribe Longboat into throwing games — and who is also the brother of Commissioner Amory Moresby. The pitcher's son is in a special school that emphasizes behavior modification due to the unsavory home environment. Against this background, Longboat yields a walk-off grandslam to lose the big game 4-0.

The pitcher's heroics take place after the Series. He ends the affair with Christina Moresby, rejoins his wife, and decides to retire. He plans to return to his Oklahoma home to teach and coach — and to take his son with him. Longboat also pays homage to Prissy Coe for her work as a reporter. In contrast, Commissioner Moresby is exposed as an assistant to a gambling ring headed by his brother. The owner of the Mohawks, Gus Vermont, is another villainous character who is obsessed with the evils of free agency.

While a step above Don Kowett's *The 7th Game* (1977), Kahn's novel does not match the quality of his nonfiction such as *The Boys of Summer.*

Kinsella, W. P. *Shoeless Joe.* Boston: Houghton Mifflin, 1982. (Boston: First Mariner Books, 1999.)

Popularized by the movie version, *Field of Dreams,* the novel is the winner of a Houghton Mifflin Literary Fellowship Award. It is the story of Iowa farmer Ray Kinsella who hears a voice telling him to build a baseball diamond ("If you build it, he will come") in order to bring back Shoeless Joe Jackson and other members of the Black Sox team of 1919 — as well as Ray's father and writer J. D. Salinger. Ordered to "ease his pain," Ray finds the reclusive author of *The Catcher in the Rye* and convinces him to share the fantasy. After attending a Red Sox game, they go to Minnesota to recruit Doc (Moonlight) Graham who as a young man (Archie) had played one inning in the majors.

Back in Iowa, Ray, supported by his wife (Annie) and daughter (Karen), conjures up Shoeless Joe and his teammates. (Ray's father had convinced him that the eight banned White Sox players of 1919 were unjustly treated by Commissioner Landis.) Joining the participants at the Iowa ballpark are Richard, Ray's twin, and Johnny, their late father who was a Class B catcher. Old Eddie Scisson, former owner of Ray's farm, watches the baseball action. Claiming to have played for the Cubs from 1908 to 1910, he is exposed as a fake but nevertheless delivers a sermon on the "living word of baseball" that will set free those who accept it.

Opposing the pastoral concept of pure baseball, however, is the realistic realm of business personified by Mark (Ray's brother-in-law) and Blustein, a representative of the syndicate that is buying up the farms in the area. The Kinsella farm is in economic trouble, and pressure is being applied. Salinger, though, who has heard the voice with Ray demanding that they "go the distance," has a plan that will save the farm and the ballpark. When the word gets out, people will appear to watch the games—and will pay for the privilege. This is what happens, and the famous author is chosen to join the ghostly players who disappear through the door in the outfield fence after the games are over. He explains to the envious Ray that the players chose him perhaps so that he will break his publishing silence and write the story of the miraculous events

Baseball, then, triumphs over big business. For those who love the game, it offers a redemptive power that can replace the negativity of economics, the real world that is governed by greed. Belief in baseball is an antidote for religious fundamentalism and its repressive tendencies. Eddy Scisson's "sermon" is a parody of religious language in which salvation is offered through baseball—the heaven on earth that Ray creates on his farm. It restores the imaginative powers of the author's version of Salinger (chosen perhaps because the name of Ray Kinsella appears in a Salinger short story, and Richard Kinsella is a character in *The Catcher in the Rye*) and depicts him as a representative of the concept of the novelist as a crusader for artistic integrity. Employing the aspects of magical realism, fantasy, and metafiction, the novel is in the company of *The Natural, The Universal Baseball Association*, and other top works of the genre.

Klein, Dave. *Hit and Run.* New York: Ace Charter, 1982.

In a sci-fi thriller, mind-controlling drugs are used to produce criminal acts. Butch Lewis, sportswriter, is involved in the trouble of Yankee superstar Berto Escoban, a victim of blackmailing. The villain, Polano, has a porno film of Escoban's wife, and he uses it to force the ballplayer into smuggling heroin. When the police get into the act, Escoban is killed by a poison dart while in a batting cage. The murderer is "good guy" Butch Lewis who has been programmed by drugs to do Polano's bidding. In turn, Lewis' girlfriend is "activated" by the super bad guy and his miracle device and ordered to kill her boyfriend. The plot, at least, does not follow a formula.

Lipsyte, Robert. *Jock and Jill.* New York: Harper & Row, 1982. (New York: Scholastic, 1983.)

Listed in the "12 and up" category, it is also a candidate for a higher reading level. Jumpin' Jack Ryder, junior at Nearmont High in New Jersey, pitches his team to a Metro Championship game in Yankee Stadium. Along the way, he dumps his tennis-player girlfriend for Jillian, an activist photographer, in an attempt to make a difference in society. "Jock and Jill" make friends with a Puerto Rican gang member and confront the mayor of New York City to demand changes in the living conditions of the poor. In the championship contest, Ryder walks away from a perfect game and writes on the scoreboard: "Kids are dying."

It is arguable whether it is an unusual kids' book, a parody of the juvenile sports novel, or a work that transcends the Young Adult label. But it is different from the formula scripts that dominate much of juvenile fiction.

McCormack, Tom. *Strictly Amateur.* New York: Pinnacle, 1982.

New York centerfielder Holden Gates is kidnapped, and the case is handed to Sam Vacco, Stadium Director of Security and a former police detective. The FBI gets involved, but it is Vacco who rescues the ballplayer. However, he dies of wounds after engaging in a gunfight with the criminals, and the FBI takes the credit of solving the case. The owner of the team bribes a reporter to write a story that makes Gates and Manager Skipper Bowen the heroes. The Bureau and the ballclub are more interested in their reputation than in the truth. The parts of the story that might sully the organization are thus stifled. The analysis of business practices makes this an unusual mystery/thriller that almost escapes from mediocrity.

Schiffer, Michael. *Ballpark.* New York: Simon and Schuster, 1982. (New York: New American Library, 1983.)

Phil Raneer creates Ballpark, an Ohio amusement park complex that includes Ballclub, a major league team. He signs free agent Darryl Pardee, a future Hall-of-Fame thirdbaseman and a Vietnam War hero, in an attempt to win a pennant. The owner also hires sportswriter Pauline Reese to do television broadcasts. However, when she does not yield to his sexual requests, she is treated as an enemy. She, in turn, discovers the shaky economic basis of Raneer's enterprise and becomes a threat to him. Raneer retaliates by ordering Pardee, Pauline's boyfriend, benched. Manager Fritz Hart plays his thirdbaseman, though, until a beaning incident. When Pardee slugs the pitcher who throws at him, Commissioner O'Neill suspends the Ballpark star—and the team consequently loses its chance for a championship. Pardee and Pauline Reese declare their love for each other—and Raneer's empire collapses. Justice prevails as the evil owner is punished and the good guys live happily—at least temporarily. There is not much to recommend here.

Small, David. *Almost Famous.* New York: W.W. Norton, 1982. (New York: Avon Books, 1983; (New York: W.W. Norton, 1990.)

In 1955, Ward Sullivan is the hottest prospect in the Red Sox farm system. He is only twenty, and Ted Williams calls him a great natural hitter. Obsessed with baseball, Sullivan gets upset when his girlfriend, Blue, distracts him from the game. The night of a party in honor of his promotion to the majors, he drinks too much, argues with Blue, and has a car accident that ends his baseball career and her life.

Sullivan returns to his home in Pennsylvania and works in a factory. In his spare time, he washes the car the Red Sox gave him and plays a dice baseball game. He becomes bitter, and his condition intensifies with the insanity of his mother and the illness of his father. In the father's will, the bulk of the estate is left to the youngest son, and Ward receives $20,000 and the advice to go somewhere to make a new start. By the end of the story, Ward Sullivan has built a home and a house in Maine. It ends with a family baseball game — a sign of his rehabilitation. *Almost Famous* was nominated for the 1982 American Book Award for the best first novel.

1983

Engleman, Paul. *Dead in Centerfield.* New York: Ballantine Books, 1983.

Mark Renzler, private detective, and his black assistant, Nate Moore, are hired to investigate curious events involving the New York Gents. As Marvin Wallace approaches Babe Ruth's record of sixty homers (the current season is 1961), the manager of the Gents is receiving threatening letters ordering him to bench the slugger. Wallace's wife is also concerned about a blackmailing attempt. The detectives discover that Commissioner Ebel Chapman and eccentric millionaire William Bosworth Tidwell are obsessed with preserving Ruth's record. Chapman invents the "Wallace asterisk rule," and Tidwell hires a killer. The plot to murder Wallace is foiled, of course.

The most interesting aspect of the mediocre mystery is the portrait of Marvin Wallace as patterned after Roger Maris and his 1961 season. Down the stretch, as he nears the record sixty-one homers, the New York Gent hero suffers from psychological problems that mirror the Maris situation.

Everett, Percival. *Suder.* New York: Viking Press, 1983. (Baton Rouge: Louisiana State University Press, 1999.)

Craig Suder, black thirdbaseman of the Seattle Mariners, is in a slump that has lowered his batting average to 198. At home he is estranged from his wife Thelma and their son Peter. Manager Lou Tyler finally puts Suder on the disabled list and advises a vacation. Haunted by memories of boyhood years when his mother went insane, he departs for Tyler's cabin in the wilds of Oregon. Obsessed with the idea of flight, fueled by Charlie Parker's recording of "Ornithology," Suder hides in the woods after absconding with the money of drug dealer Sid Willis. His companions are Renoir, an elephant purchased from a carnival, and Jincy, a nine-year-old girl who has run away from an abusive mother.

While Suder builds wings in his preparation for flying, Sheriff Prager is searching for him because a hooker from the nearest town claims that he raped her. With the Sheriff and Sid Willis in pursuit, Suder jumps off Willet Rock and flies above Ezra Pond — briefly.

The black author's novel is a tragicomedy that alternates between Suder's journey to insanity and his boyhood reflections in Fayetteville, North Carolina — and his mother's similar problem. The humorous tone, highlighted by the escapades with the elephant and the girl, balance the desperate attempt of the protagonist to ward off his fate. The result is a strange but commendable work of literature.

Greenberg, Eric Rolfe. *The Celebrant.* New York: Everest House, 1983. (Lincoln: University of Nebraska Press, 1993.)

Jack Kapp (originally Yakov Kapinski) designs rings to commemorate the pitching feats of Christy Mathewson of the Giants. Jack's brother Arthur uses the Mathewson connection to enlarge the family jewelry business. The artistic temperament of Jack turns into disillusionment as his brother tends to turn art into functionalism by converting the business to time-study management. The artistry of Jack is deemed unimportant. At the same time, the career of Mathewson begins to decline. He finally turns to managing at Cincinnati, but he cannot control the gambling of Hal Chase. Then, in World War 1, the future Hall-of-Famer is gassed, and his health declines. In a final meeting with Mathewson during the 1919 World Series, Jack is warned that another Kapp brother, Eli, is in trouble with gamblers. Mathewson, near the end of his life, is depicted as being deluded to the point of madness. His obsession with the corruption of baseball and his Christ-like demeanor influence Jack, however, and he abandons his brother when Eli is unable to pay his debts after betting on the White Sox. According to sportswriter Hugh Fullerton, Jack worships Mathewson to the extent that he is partially responsible for Eli Kapp's subsequent suicide.

In a realistic historical novel, the attempt at Jewish assimilation into mainstream American life through baseball and hero worship leads to the decay of ideals and to a concession to the power of economics. Neither baseball nor art is free of commercial corruption, as the Black Sox scandal and the decline of craftsmanship in the jewelry business illustrate. Besides Fullerton, Mathewson, and Chase, the baseball people involved in the action include John McGraw, Honus Wagner, and Connie Mack. This is another candidate for the top ten list of baseball novels.

Kennedy, William. *Ironweed.* New York: Viking Press, 1983. (New York: Penguin Books, 1984.)

Winner of a Pulitzer Prize and a National Book Critic Circle Award, it features ex-thirdbaseman Francis Phelan as he returns to Albany, New York, after twenty-two years of wandering. His first flight from town occurs when he kills a scab with an accurately thrown rock during a 1901 strike. He later returns, gets married, and plays baseball. However, after a day of drinking, he drops his thirteen-day-old son. The resulting death leads to another flight. In Phelan's adventures on the road, he kills one tramp and injures two more with a baseball bat when attacked in a bum jungle. Back in Albany again, he gains a sense of redemption by digging graves, working on a junk wagon, and visiting his son Billy. The book is marginally about baseball, as the game is essentially a source of soothing memories in the difficult life of the protagonist.

Morgenstein, Gary. *The Man Who Wanted to Play Center Field for the New York Yankees.* New York: Atheneum, 1983.

Danny Neuman, at thirty-three, makes the rash decision to go into training in preparation for a tryout with the New York Yankees. His wife Sarah thinks that he is crazy; his boss fires him. Sadie and Pistol, transvestite neighbors, help him to get in shape. As a result of his performance, Public Relations Director Paul Patterson is ordered to get Neuman signed with the Greensboro Hornets, a farm team, as a "terrific humanitarian gesture." He becomes a celebrity and Jewish role model, but he jeopardizes his fame by proclaiming at a bar mitzvah that the Establishment brainwashes people. The Yankees, though, call him up at the end of the season, and he homers in his first at-bat. Aware that his promotion to the Yankees is a gimmick and that the organization is merely using him for publicity, Neuman walks away from the ballpark with a game in progress. Despite being cursed by an autograph-seeker for not being Mickey Mantle, Neuman and his reconciled wife stroll contentedly into the city.

A somewhat realistic but more rebellious version of Joe Boyd of *The Year the Yankees Lost the Pennant,* Danny Neuman is the embodiment of nonconformity. He refuses to yield to public opinion or the societal value system. He realizes that fulfilling fantasies is secondary to doing the right thing. Neuman takes a place in a long line of fictional rebels who reject the business aspect of baseball.

Munn, Vella. *Summer Season.* New York: Harlequin Books, 1983.

In a Harlequin American Romance, Dawn Morrell gives up nursing to become a trainer for a baseball team in the Northwest League. The general manager of the team is her former heartthrob Brian Riegel. He now has a son and an ex-wife. He has become a bitter man, but after some serious doubt and problems in dealing with Dawn, true love triumphs.

Paulos, Sheila. *Wild Roses.* New York: Dell, 1983.

A Candlelight Ecstasy Romance (108), it features Nickie Alexander, female sports reporter and announcer. She falls for pitching star Craig Boone of the Seattle Vikings. According to formula, they meet, copulate, separate, and reunite. Since she is a liberated woman, he agrees to let her work after they are married.

Quarrington, Paul. *Home Game.* Toronto: Doubleday Canada, 1983.

Just before World War II in Burton's Harbor in the Upper Peninsula of Michigan, a strange baseball game is played. The narrator, grandson of Dustin Doubleday (the game's umpire) relates the plight of a marooned circus sideshow, The Exhibition of Extraordinary Eccentricities, led by Dr. Sinister. A fundamentalist religious group of the area wants the freaks to leave. Featuring a noted baseball team, the House of Jonah, the group challenges Dr. Sinister, a magician, to a game — with the condition that the loser must vacate the Upper Peninsula.

Tekel Ambrose of the House of Jonah is reputed to be one of the best amateur players of all time, but Major Mite, a sideshow midget, proclaims that the freaks have two secret weapons. They turn out to be Angus McCallister, the world's strongest man, and Nathaniel Isbister, a hobo who has wandered into the camp. Goldenlegs Isbister is a former star of pro baseball, but he broke his own legs because he was tired of being treated as a commodity. Now known as Crybaby, the cripple teaches the Hisslop Sisters (Siamese twins), the Alligator Man, The Rubber Boy, The Hippopotamus Boy, Madame Tanya, two giants, a midget, and Janus (a two headed dog) the game of baseball.

The Eccentricities win the unusual game with an eight-run rally in the eighth inning, 15-14. Dr Sinister (Poindexter Wilhelm Frip) strikes out Tekel Ambrose to end the game on a pitch that may have been "unnatural," unless the Jonah star missed it on purpose. Sinister, though, allows the Fundamentalists to remain in their homes providing that they donate a horse to any member of the sideshow troupe (which is disbanding) who wants to leave. Isbister's fate is unknown after he wanders off with Janus the Wonderdog.

The comic fantasy promotes the concept of pastoral baseball (played for the pure joy of the game) primarily through the acts of Isbister, but the condition imposed by the House of Jonah and the betting by the audience indicate the impossibility of achieving that status. The novel, then, mirrors the correlation of baseball and business that has existed since the inception of the game. Canadian Paul Quarrington's book was selected as one of 1983's ten best by the *Toronto Star* and CBC's *Morningside*.

Stein, Harry. *Hoopla.* New York: Alfred A. Knopf, 1983. (New York: St. Martin's Press, 1986, New York: Dell, 1997).

Narrated, in part, by Buck Weaver, thirdbaseman of the 1919 White Sox and one of the eight players banned for life, the book contrasts his view of the Black Sox scandal with that of journalist Luther Pond, the other major narrator. Pond is a self-promoter who poses as a protector of baseball's integrity while building his own image. He reveals the names of those supposedly in on the fix and coins the term Black Sox. With Pond's help, the owners and Commissioner Landis work to restore the game's reputation. In the process, the eight players are made the scapegoats despite being acquitted in court.

Weaver tries to exonerate himself and Shoeless Joe Jackson, but the yellow journalism of Pond, the money of White Sox owner Charles Comiskey, and the self-righteousness of Kenesaw Mountain Landis overwhelm the claim of innocence. (Weaver hit .324 in the Series; Jackson hit .375.) In addition to the Sox scapegoats, the book also features the trial of Ty Cobb and Tris Speaker, two of the game's icons, who are cleared on gambling charges by Landis in 1927—although released by their teams.

The point is that the low salaries and lack of security of the players of the era make them vulnerable to gamblers and, to some extent, victims of the owners. Thus Shoeless Joe Jackson, one of the game's great hitters, is defeated by businessman Charles Comiskey. The historical characters and events are colorfully presented—making this a companion piece to Eliot Asinof's nonfiction *Eight Men Out* (1963) as prime portraits of the Black Sox scandal.

Stone, Natalie. *Double Play.* New York: Dell, 1983.

Candlelight Ecstasy Romance (198) provides another lady sportscaster. Sally Denning covers the Kansas City Royals in spring training. However, she is replaced in the job by injured star Peter Decker and is demoted to a cooking show. Sally resists his courtship, but, when he returns to the field and leads the team to a championship, she reconsiders. Ecstasy is the result.

1984

Benjamin, Paul (Paul Auster). *Squeeze Play.* New York: Avon Books, 1984. (New York: Penguin Books, 1990.)

George Chapman, thirdbaseman of the New York Americans, loses his leg in a car accident after signing a long-term contract. Five years later, he receives a threatening letter and hires Max Klein to investigate. Chapman is then murdered, and Klein confronts Professor Briles who is in love with Judy Chapman, George's wife. Briles commits suicide to apparently end the case — although it is discovered that the ballplayer had been betting on his performance on the diamond and is in debt to a gambler. Probably the best feature of the mystery is the enthusiasm for baseball expressed by Max Klein's nine-year-old son.

Carkeet, David. *The Greatest Slump of All Time.* New York: Harper & Row, 1984. (New York: Penguin, 1985.)

Grammock, an Arkansas redneck, manages a major league team of eccentrics. Most of the time, several of the key players are depressed. The tone, though, is humorous and the crazy antics of the team members do not get in the way of winning. However, in the World Series a tragedy occurs. Centerfielder Eddy commits suicide — apparently as the result of his wife's treatment of their daughter. Six members of the team decide to boycott the final game out of respect for their teammate and perhaps due to their guilt for not helping with his problem. The rebel group goes fishing, and the team wins the Series without them.

There is a disparity between the comedy and the tragedy that is not resolved. The book touches on problems but glosses over them without deeply probing into the sources. Dilemmas dealing with sexuality, marriage, race, egotism, and nationality (especially relating to language) are presented, but there is too much activity on too many levels — and the result is chaotic.

Frank, Morry. *Every Young Man's Dream: Confessions of a Southern League Shortstop.* Chicago: Silverback Books, 1984. (Chicago: Silverback Books, 2006.)

Darrel Skaits from Gary, Indiana, plays shortstop for the Nashville Vols in the sixties. Despite hitting as many as twenty-seven homers in a season, he gets no chance at the big leagues. He blames Manager Zinn Swineling for blacklisting him. Skaits finally slugs the manager and flees to Chicago. He still hopes to get back into baseball, but the dream ends when he kills a man over a gambling debt.

Much like Lardner's Jack Keefe, Skaits blames everyone else for his problems and is incapable of learning from his mistakes. There is no humor, however, as the book is in the naturalistic mode — sort of a novelistic film noir. Raised in a dysfunctional family and stymied by the competitive nature of baseball and society, he is a victim of the environment — and is too weak to overcome it.

Hays, Donald. *The Dixie Association.* New York: Simon & Schuster, 1984. (Baton Rouge: Louisiana State University Press, 1997.)

Manager Lefty Marks of the Arkansas Reds springs Hog Durham (the narrator) from prison to play for his minor league team in the Dixie Association. Lefty is a one-armed former major leaguer known for his leftwing politics. Opposing his integrated team is the Reverend G. Forest Bushrod, an "ordained vigilante," and his rightwing fanatics. When a Muslim and a woman (Susan Pankhurst) join the ex-con (Durham) as new members of the Reds, the protest of the fundamentalists is intensified. With the help of civil rights lawyer Barry Rotenberg, the Reds players manage to stay out of jail and make a run for the pennant. Behind the pitching of forty-six-year-old Jeremiah Eversole, Native American, and the hitting of Durham, whose homer wins the clincher, the Reds emerge as champs of the Dixie Association.

The league consists of the Reds, the Nashville Fugitives, the Asheville Wolves, the Milledgeville Peacocks, the Plaquemine Pirates, the Memphis Kings, the Oxford Fury, and the Selma Americans. The satire on Southern culture, then, is a key aspect, especially in the book's scathing portrait of rabid segregationists as opposed to the tolerant racial, religious, and sexual policies of Lefty Marks that work together as a championship team. The literary allusions, referring to great Southern writers like Faulkner, Wolfe, and O'Connor, are welcome additions. The book is funny and subversive, but it is too obvious in its depiction of good versus bad. The transformation of Hog Durham from egotist to humanitarian is a little slick also. Susan Pankhurst joins the growing list of female players in the men's pro game.

Jordan, Pat. *The Cheat.* New York: Villard Books, 1984. (New York: Ballantine Books, 1985.)

Journalist Bobby Giacquinto is assigned a story on Stanley Muraski, supposedly the fastest pitcher ever. Muraski dies before the reporter interviews him, however, and the details of his life have to be researched. The fireballer never made it to the majors and became an alcoholic and an itinerant worker. Giacquinto needs to find out what happened to the legendary pitcher.

In1968, Muraski, Tony Vincent, and Rodney Jones are competing for a spot on the roster of the major league Hollywood Stars. It is Jones, a born-again fundamentalist, who is promoted. He goes on to win the 1974 Cy Young Award. Giacquinto learns from Vincent and sportswriter Babe Henry that Jones encouraged Muraski to drink, knowing his weakness, and thus improved his own chances of getting a chance with the Stars. Muraski, meanwhile, never recovers from his lost opportunity and keeps on drinking.

Although Giacquinto cheats on his wife, the real cheat in the story is Rodney Jones, who hides the truth behind his evangelical pose. The author is justifiably better known for his nonfiction baseball works *A Flase Spring* and *The Suitors of Spring.*

Katz, Steve. *Wier & Pouce.* College Park, MD: Sun & Moon Press, 1984.

The first chapter (Bunt) depicts a baseball game between the Bullets and the Condors. The New York Bullets Social and Athletic Club, consisting mostly of Jewish kids, has a reputation for brains while the Condors are better known for fighting. In a close game, Dusty Wier is called on to bunt. Nobody sees the ball deflect from the bat to his eye (which should have been ruled a foul ball), and the Condors pitcher carelessly hurls the ball into centerfield to put runners on first and third. They both score on a triple, and the Bullets hang on to win. On the way home, Wier is filled with love for his Jimmy Piersall glove, the Condors, baseball, and life in general. He then decides to spend the night in a sewer.

The rest of the surreal novel, spanning the years from about 1950 to 1983, contrasts the humanistic concerns of Dusty Wier to the amoral career of E. Pouce.

Wier eventually settles in to a utopian existence at Cape Breton Island, and Pouce pursues business success. At one point, he returns from a business trip minus a face — thus revealing "the morbidity of spirit" underneath. The book ends with the First Annual Cape Breton Stoned Olympic softball extravaganza. In the game, Wier hits a ball that is carried into the ocean by an eagle. A huge Roberto Clemente mitt rises from the water to make the catch. Meanwhile, Pouce is devising a system that will allow him to monitor all the information and communication networks of the world.

A complex experimental novel, it suggests that baseball, in its mythical sense, is a positive symbol of human endeavor as opposed to unscrupulous economic action. The first part of a trilogy (including *Florry of Washington Heights* and *Swanny's Way*) emphasizes the opposing views of the title characters — Wier versus Pouce.

Kluger, Steve. *Changing Pitches: A Novel of Love and Baseball.* New York: St. Martin's Press, (Los Angeles: Alyson Publications, 1998.)

Scotty Mackay, thirty-six-year-old lefthander, goes 21-6 for the division winning Washington Senators after he develops new pitches. The former Cy Young Award winner had been going downhill until former catcher Buddy Budlong rejuvenated his career with tips on the deliveries. The problem, though, is that Mackay feels unduly attracted to new catcher Jason Cornell. Worried about being a homosexual, he sees a psychoanalyst. As a result, he proposes to his girlfriend. Cornell, meanwhile, confesses that he is in love with a football player.

Mackay, the narrator, includes letters, fantasy sequences, locker-room messages, mound conferences, and newspaper stories to portray a critical period of his life. The innovative writing makes up for the implausible plot.

Mayer, Robert. *The Grace of Shortstops.* Garden City, NY: Doubleday, 1984.

In 1947, eight-year-old Benjamin "Peewee" Brunig roots for his hometown Brooklyn Dodgers, especially shortstop Peewee Reese and his new teammate Jackie Robinson. The summer is interrupted by the kidnapping of Lisa Hirsch, Brunig's baby cousin. He and his friends play detective and discover that the Rag Lady has the baby. The case is complicated by the appearance of a diary in which Ruth, Peewee's mother, writes of her affair with her brother-in-law, Mickey Hirsch, father of the kidnapped baby. Peewee gets Lisa back from the Rag Lady, but he is distraught by his mother's adultery. Meanwhile, his father, Rabbi Louis Brunig, is obsessed with the Holocaust and joins an anti-Nazi group of militants.

As the Dodgers lose the World Series to the Yankees, Peewee agonizes over the secret of the diary, but he finally decides to burn it and keep the information to himself. He realizes that the glory of baseball, the grace of shortstops, is not always a viable balance for the harsh reality of life. This is a quality coming-of-age novel with a baseball background.

Rosen, Richard D. *Strike Three You're Dead.* New York: Walker, 1984. (New York: Onyx Books, 1989; New York: Walker, 2001.)

The first Harvey Blissberg novel presents the Jewish centerfielder, formerly of the Red Sox, playing for the Providence Jewels, an American League expansion team. He dates Mickey Slavin, female sportscaster for the team and tries to keep his batting average above .300 as his career is waning. When his roommate, relief pitcher Randy Furth, is murdered, Blissberg, searches for the killer. He finds out that Frances Shalhoub, wife of the Jewels manager, is secretly part-owner of the team and that she had been paying Furth to throw games when pitching in relief of Bobby Wagner. When Wagner found out, he killed Furth with a bat. As Blissberg closes in, Wagner attempts to kill him also, but the centerfielder escapes and takes the story to the police — who arrest Wagner and Frances Shalhoub.

The book is the winner of an Edgar Award for the best first mystery. It is the first baseball mystery to feature a series detective — as Harvey Blissberg returns to detecting in future novels.

Willard, Nancy. *Things Invisible to See.* New York: Alfred A. Knopf, 1984. (Spectra, 1988; Lincoln: iUniverse, 2000.)

Described as a metaphysical fantasy, the novel features Ben Harkissian and Clare Bishop. Their lives connect when Ben, a pitcher for the Ann Arbor highschool team in 1941 hits a baseball that paralyzes Clare. The Ancestress, a spiritwoman, comforts Clare at night. Ben meets Clare and confesses that he is the cause of her condition. After high school, Ben takes part in World War II and is "visited" by a girl while adrift on a raft in the Pacific Ocean. While still on the raft, he also wagers with Death on the result of a baseball game to be played between his boyhood team, the South Avenue Rovers, and the Dead Knights. According to the contract, Death will claim the Rovers if the Knights win.

At the end of the book, Death recruits Willie, Ben's twin brother, and then causes Ben to be injured in a bus accident so that he is unable to play in the Big Game. The South Avenue team is reduced mostly to the mothers of the Rovers—who take the field against the ghosts of Lou Gehrig, Christy Mathewson, and other baseball legends. Ben, however, is miraculously able to appear as a pinch-hitter; Clare, healed by a conjure woman, is on base with the game on the line. The result is ambiguous—just as the novel as a whole.

1985

Beardslee, Ken. *Partners.* Milford, IN: Self-published, 1985.

In a marginally adult novella, the beautiful world of Alexander Riggs is shown in all its glory. In 1928, he accepts a job at a high school in Maine. He teaches math and coaches baseball — emerging with a championship team. When Riggs gets sick before the Big Game, he appoints a woman to manage the team. Effie Corey, his landlord's housekeeper, leads the team to victory. At the celebratory banquet, Effie gives a speech and "wins the podium award." A self-published 138-page atrocity, its only point of interest is the inclusion of the female manager.

DeMarco, Gordon. *Frisco Blues.* London: Pluto Press, 1985. (Portland, OR: West Coast Crime, 1995.)

"A Riley Kovachs Detective Novel," the book explores racism in the San Francisco of 1947 — the year of Jackie Robinson's integration. Chet Jones is killed while working for Pacific Shipyard, and his wife Ruby asks Kovachs to look into what she considers a murder. The detective finds out that the black laborer was a ballplayer who was scheduled to play for the Satchel Paige team against the Bob Feller All-Stars. Kovachs attends the game at Seals Stadium and sees Paige shut out the major league team 8-0. He also realizes that the Purity League, a racist organization, may be involved in the death of Jones. After the game, Kovachs and three blacks are attacked by the League members, but they are rescued by a group of Communists. The next day, Kovachs plans to present information that will implicate the Purity League and the Assistant District Attorney in the murder of Chet Jones. He does not expect justice to prevail over the Jim Crow system, however.

The social history of the era is featured. The detective's fight against the entrenched powers of the city, plus the inclusion of historical events and people, is presented with skill and helps make this an exceptional mystery.

Guy, David. *Second Brother.* New York: New American Library, 1985. (New York: New American Trade, 1986.)

In Pittsburgh in the early 1960s, Henry Wilder is overshadowed by Bennet, his brother who is a year older. The one thing Henry is better at is baseball. In a game between the eighth and ninth grades, he fans Bennet three times (only to lose 2-0). Sam Golden, a friend, analyzes him as a perennial second brother who is doomed to disappointment. Henry finally attempts to reject the prognosis of Golden and to succeed on his own. Baseball plays at least a minor role in building his confidence.

Kinsella, W. P. *The Thrill of the Grass.* New York: Penguin, 1985.

A short story collection on baseball by the author of *Shoeless Joe*.

Marlowe, Dan J. *The Comeback.* Belmont, CA: Fearon Education, 1985.

A twenty-eight page novella written for an adult literacy program. *Double the Glory* (30 pages) and *The Hitter* (61 pages) appear in 1987.

McManus, James. *Chin Music.* New York: Crown, 1985. (New York: Random House Value Press, 1985; New York: Grove Press, 1987.)

The third game of the World Series is cancelled by a nuclear attack in World War III. White Sox pitcher Raymond Zajack escapes from a hospital to try to find the way home to his wife and son through the chaotic streets of Chicago. A Guardian Angel helps him.

Pomeranz, Guy. *Out at Home.* Boston: Houghton Mifflin, 1985. (New York: Random House Value Publishing, 1990.)

Arnie Barzov gets expelled from the University of Illinois (in the fifties) for gambling. He returns to Chicago and his mother — who dates the manager of the Cubs, Spieler LaChance. The Cubs move into first place in July, but Spieler resigns when he realizes that some of the team's games are being fixed. He explains to Arnie that ballplayers are vulnerable to gamblers because of the reserve clause and the power of greedy owners. Spieler compares the Cubs of the fifties to the Black Sox of 1919. Arnie then confronts the owner of the Cubs and threatens to expose him for his part in the fixed games. Wentworth, the owner, calls off the gamblers, raises the players' salaries, and allows Spieler to return as manager. Without the extra help, though, the Cubs lose the pennant to the Dodgers. Arnie decides to go back to school; he gives up gambling but remains a Cubs fan.

A subplot involving Kim, an illegal alien, and hoodlum Johnny Salerno's threat of blackmailing her adds to the suspense but does not save the book from mediocrity.

Tapply, William G. *Follow the Sharks.* New York: Charles Scribner's Sons, 1985. (New York: Ballantine Books, 1986.)

In "A Brady Coyne Mystery," Red Sox pitcher Eddie Donagan seems to be a victim of the Steve Blass syndrome during the 1973 season. After a great rookie year, Donagan's sudden loss of control causes him to quit the game. He leaves his family and sells shoes in a mall. Years later, his son E. J. is kidnapped, and Coyne is called into action by Jan, E. J.'s mother and Eddie's estranged wife. The lawyer uncovers the real reason the pitcher quit baseball. He was being blackmailed into throwing games by scout Stump Kelly—who is also the kidnapper. Coyne rescues E. J., but Donagan is killed by Kelly. The mystery is ordinary, but there are good descriptions of baseball.

1986

Ardizzone, Tony. *The Heart of the Order.* New York: Henry Holt, 1986.

Danny Bacigalupo tells the story of his boyhood in Chicago and his fourteen-year pro baseball career to his son Tip. As a kid, Danny hits a ball that kills Mickey Meehan. His Catholic education promotes a guilt that develops into a psychological trauma. He is convinced that the spirit of Mickey possesses his body. While working his way through the minors as a slugging thirdbaseman, Danny is schizophrenic, not knowing whether he is Mickey or Danny. At the major league level with the Denver Dynes, he repeats the "crime" by hitting Abner Double with a ball. When Double survives, Danny thinks that Mickey is transposed into the big first baseman's body.

Bacigalupo's troubles increase when Meenan's father, after nursing his grievance for years, detonates himself at Mile High Stadium. Danny is injured and becomes a spectator for the rest of the season (his only one in the majors) as the Dynes win the World Series. He then resumes his minor league career and eventually becomes a scout. In the process, he evolves into a single identity. In confessing the details to his son (who was found in a basket at a minor league park), Bacigalupo expiates his guilt and finds consolation through responsibility. A difficult psychological study, the book is the recipient of the Virginia Prize for Fiction.

Burch, Mark H. *Road Game: A Summer's Tale.* New York: Vanguard Press, 1986.

Jimmy Lee Lester, former Columbia English teacher, takes a summer job in Alexandria, Louisiana, as an assistant sports editor. While covering the Metropolitans of the Class A Gulf South League, he comes into conflict with Larry Ray Pangburn, an evangelist of the Southern Regional Director for the Blueprint Campaign. The fundamentalist group tries to woo second baseman Tommy Monroe, which leads Lester into writing a newspaper article on the errors of trying to force games to serve the public goal of narrowly perceived moral conduct — basically an attack on Pangburn. The evangelist comes under the scrutiny of the FBI, but he escapes with a stolen fortune.

The Alexandria Metropolitans, meanwhile, are led to the league championship by Dub Benson, former Cy Young Award winner for the Houston Astros. Lester, revitalized by his summer experience with baseball, prepares to interview for another academic job. Although less satirical and smaller in scope, the book is reminiscent of *The Dixie Association.*

Conte, Sal. *Child's Play.* New York: Leisure Books, 1986. (New York: Leisure Books, 1990).

Mad scientists prevail in a horror story about Little League baseball. Philip Dreiser and Fritz Warner use computer implants to make kids better players. Those who fail to cooperate with the scientists disappear. In 1982, Dana Evers moves to town (Crandall, New York) and works as an investigative reporter for Max Richter's newspaper. When the truth is discovered, Max is murdered, and Dana and her husband are turned into robot-like victims of the villains. The danger of unprincipled science is taken to the limit here.

Coomer, Joe. *A Flatland Fable.* Austin: Texas Monthly Press, 1986.

In Eckley, Texas, forty-year-old Horgan is a bored fireman who coaches a Little League team. Something finally happens, though, to end his malaise. Horgan's father Joe is dying, and in talking with him, some discoveries are made. Horgan's mother, it turns out is Miss Eckley, the eccentric owner of the grain elevator that dominates the town — the woman who poisons birds, runs her business ruthlessly, and refuses to sponsor the Little League team. She married Joe after she was raped and impregnated — but then had the marriage annulled. Joe, who raised Horgan, is not his biological father.

Horgan retreats to the solace of the baseball team and his wife, Kidder, who informs him that she is pregnant. Moments later, a homer from an unlikely source wins the game for his team. In the course of the day, Horgan realizes that he loves his life. The miracle homer and news of the baby combine with the story of his heritage to change his philosophy. Despite some melodrama, the book is well written.

Dews, Bob, Jr. *Largo.* Edison, GA: Golden Marsh Publishers, 1986.

In a marginal entry, one of the four sections of the book is a baseball novella — "Year of the Cat." It tells of the career of Tony Direlli whose father, Big Tony, plays major league ball but dies in the Korean War. Little Tony grows up as a Yankee fan and evolves into a good player. In 1964, he is promoted to the St. Louis Cardinals on the recommendation of Eddie Stanky. He plays shortstop, but the Cards replace him in '65, and he goes back to the minors until retiring in 1978.

Living in Largo, Georgia, Tony has trouble adjusting to life without baseball.

He helps with the high school team until Ted Turner persuades Bobby Cox to invite Tony to spring training with the Braves. Now known as Old Cat Direlli, he makes the team but dies at the end of the season. The Braves do a television special on him with narration by Skip Caray, Ernie Johnson, and Pete Van Wieren.

Written by an *Atlanta* Braves coach (and son of the author of *Whichaway?)* the story is weak and melodramatic. The inclusion of real baseball people adds some interest.

Hough, John. *The Conduct of the Game.* New York: Harcourt Brace Jovanovich, 1986. (New York: Warner Books, 1987.)

Lee Malcolm works his way up to the majors as an umpire. Sensitive to racial and sexual bigotry, he is often in conflict with two of his umpiring partners: Bugs and McKnight. Malcolm's tolerance is tested when Ron Chapman, a black player dates his old girlfriend. Another test occurs when Roy Van Arsdale, the fourth member of the umpiring crew, is suspected of being gay. Malcolm refuses to cooperate with the league president in trying to build a case against Van Arsdale. The gay ump, however, commits suicide, and Malcolm is pressured into resigning as the result of trying to protect him.

Malcolm has learned that the conduct of his life is more important than the policing of the game. He is content to let baseball officials think that his resignation is good for the integrity of their enterprise. The book is a gutsy enquiry into the sexual phobia of sports.

Kinsella, W. P. *The Iowa Baseball Confederacy.* Boston: Houghton Mifflin, 1986. (New York: Ballantine Books, 1987.)

In a complex fantasy, Gideon Clarke sets out on a quest to prove that his father's obsession is correct: that the 1908 Chicago Cubs played an exhibition game of 2614 innings against the Iowa Baseball Confederacy All-Stars. Gideon's father, Matthew, possesses the knowledge of the game (after being struck by lightning), but when he is killed by a baseball, there is no record of the game: the information is transposed to the son who then travels back in time from 1978 to1908 to search for proof. With his pal, Stan Rogalski, he arrives in Big Inning (now Onamata), Iowa, and observes the strange game that is played in the rain for forty days. Teddy Roosevelt and Leonardo da Vinci are among the visitors who drop in for the spectacle. In inning 2614, Drifting Away, mythical Native American, hits a ball off Three Finger Brown that eludes the grasp of rightfielder Wildfire Schulte and wins the game for the Confederacy. The town of Big Inning is then washed away by a flood that also destroys the Twelve-Hour Church of Time Immemorial and the holy tree that is worshipped by the fundamentalist congregation.

Besides trying to verify the existence of the IBC and the1908 game with the Cubs, Gideon Clarke shares his father's fatal fascination for transient women. His mother, Darlin Maudie, abandons Gideon when he is six, and Sunny, his wife, comes and goes at will. She is eventually killed by a car — the same fate that Sarah, Gideon's love-interest in 1908, succumbs to. When he returns to 1978, his mother and sister (Enola Gay — an urban terrorist of the sixties) are also dead, and he is left with Missy, a woman suffering from Down's syndrome who is expected to die soon. In Onamata of 1978, Gideon and Missy meet two Indians—the current versions of Drifting Away and the Black Angel of Death (a mythical figure and a statue) who had departed together from the ballpark in 1908.

The connection between Drifting Away and Gideon Clarke is one of the keys to the book. They both seem to be ruled by inherited obsessions. The Indian has a dream vision of baseball in which the game is a test by which he can expiate himself from the Native American gods for not killing Gideon after his attempt to take Sarah away. Gideon attempts to stop Drifting Away from pinch-hitting because he knows that he will win the game. Further, he knows that he will lose Sarah when the game ends, but he relents since the Indian's need seems to be greater than his. Both are making personal sacrifices to overcome their weaknesses of pride and obstinacy. Drifting Away explains that when an obsession overrides love and brotherhood it is a negative concept. Thus Gideon ends his protest of Drifting Away's participation and resigns himself to returning to the present without proving his father's dream. His consolation is the knowledge that he is capable of revoking his personal passions.

The magical realism is too difficult and incredulous to earn the popularity of *Shoeless Joe*. It is sort of like James Joyce creating *Finnegans Wake* after the notoriety of *Ulysses*.

Toth, Pamela. *Fever Pitch.* New York: Dell, 1986.
Marty Gibson, female fast-pitch softball star, needs a sponsor for her team, the Bower of Flowers, so that it can participate in a Seattle tournament. She persuades ex-major-league baseball player, Rick Stokes, to put up the money by striking him out in a showdown. He wants her on his terms, which she tries to resist, but her desire is at fever pitch, and after the usual problems, they become a couple—in a formulaic Candlelight Ecstasy Romance.

1987

Bowen, Michael. *Can't Miss.* New York: Harper & Row, 1987.
Chris Tilden is the first female to play for a major league team, the expansion Denver Marshalls. Coming from MacAlester College, she is a regular by midseason—hitting second and playing leftfield. The Marshalls challenge Seattle in the American League West but end up in second place. Chris hits .341 and is a candidate for Rookie of the Year. Her boyfriend, sportswriter Nathan Morris, suggests that she succeeds because of her love of the game and the ability to withstand sexism. She feels that she is accepted as part of the team and looks forward to the 1990 season.

This is a less sensational account of a female player than in *A Grand Slam* or *The Sensuous Southpaw*. The quality, however, is still in the mediocre range.

Gethers, Peter. *Getting Blue.* New York: Delacorte Press, 1987. (New York: Laurel, 1989.)
Alex Justin begins his pro career in North Carolina in the fifties. Willie Trotty, a black teammate, teaches him the concept of getting blue through jazz—a personal questing for what is important by creating obsessively. Trotty, however, is

beaten and mutilated by the KKK when the team integrates a café. Justin goes on to a mediocre major league career. He has his "Moment" with the Yankees, though, when he preserves a World Series win with a great catch.

After retiring from baseball, Justin works for a sporting goods company, but his wife divorces him and his son commits suicide. In an attempt to transfer the Moment (getting blue) to his life off the diamond, Justin becomes part-owner of a jazz bar (Getting Blue). Willie Trotty reappears and works at the bar, but Justin's quest for happiness still seems doubtful.

Easy answers to life's problems seem to elude Alex Justin. The novel has won some respect as a well-written psychological portrait of a complicated character.

Gill, Charles. *The Boozer Challenge.* New York: E. P. Dutton, 1987. (New York Penguin, 1989.)

Henry Quinn Boozer, the Mustard King and owner of the New York Mohawks, issues a challenge to his four adult children. The first to earn $100,000 will inherit Treetop, the family estate. If they fail in a specified time, the prize will go to his mistress. Boo Boozer wants to be a novelist, but he turns his immense body to baseball — becoming a member of the Boston Revolution, a major league rival of his dad's Mohawks. Boo hits .519 for the season and leads the team to a World Series date with, of course, the Mohawks. He spurs the Revolution to wins in the first two games but becomes unnerved when his father lectures him on the importance of team play and sacrifice. The New York team wins the next three games. Boo is beaned in Game Six, but his team wins to force the deciding game. Boo recovers and hits a grandslam in the ninth for a Boston victory. Henry Boozer dies after seeing all of his children meet the challenge. Boo Boozer hopes to help with the family business, but he is more concerned with becoming a great writer. The author of this book may have had the same desire — but not the talent.

Gregorich, Barbara. *She's on First.* Chicago: Contemporary Books, 1987.

Linda Sunshine prepares to break the gender line in major league baseball by playing with the Memphis Arrows in AA ball. Al Mowerinski, owner of the Chicago Eagles, plans to treat her like the Dodgers did Jackie Robinson so that she will be ready to make baseball history. Linda moves up to the Iowa Pioneers of AAA before being called to the big time with the Eagles. The team threatens to strike, but Mowerinski orders the manager to put her in at shortstop. When a teammate tries to rape her, he is traded.

Sportswriter Neal Vanderlin supports Sunshine's historic presence in newspaper articles. He also exposes her as being the daughter of Mowerinski and Amanda Quitman, former star of the All-American Girls' Baseball League. The shortstop (adopted and raised by Tom and Karen Sunshine) almost breaks under the pressure and temporarily quits. However, she declares her love of Vanderlin and his devotion to the Eagles and returns to the team.

This female view of gender breakthrough in baseball is somewhat realistic (like *Can't Miss*) as opposed to the more sensational treatment presented in *A Grand Slam* and *The Sensuous Southpaw*). Linda Sunshine joins Ticki Denton, Jeri Walker, and Chris Tilden as female protagonists playing in the majors.

Hudson, Anna (JoAnn Algernissen). *Fun and Games.* New York: Dell, 1987.

In Candlelight Ecstasy Romance (491), Joyce MacIntyre, wealthy phy-ed teacher, manages the Astros, a Texas Little League team. Ben Williams, mathematician, is the uncle and ward of Stacy, the only girl on the team. Joyce applies her plan of rotating positions, despite the objections of a sexist assistant coach, and the Astros take first place. In the meantime, the manager lusts after Ben, but she is too independent to yield easily. According to formula, they mate, fight, and reunite. At the end of the season, they are married and Joyce is prepared to give up baseball to become a mother.

Katz, Steve. *Florry of Washington Heights.* Los Angeles: Sun & Moon Press, 1987.

William Swanson (Swanny) is a member of the Jewish organization — The New Bullets Social and Athletic Club. In Washington Heights, the club is surrounded and threatened by ethnic gangs: the Fanwoods (Irish) and the Condors (Italian). The Bullets play neighborhood baseball, but trouble arises when Fred Sugarman, the team's shortstop, is seen with Florry O'Neill, allegedly the girlfriend of Jack Ryan, the warlord of the Fanwoods. Florry is murdered — a crime which is not solved.

In the spring, a baseball game is scheduled between the Bullets and the Fanwoods. Swanny starts a rally with a bunt single and his team wins. Pride infuses the Bullets, at least temporarily, and a great future is expected for them in the approaching Kiwanis League season.

From his adult perspective as a lawyer, long after the events of 1950 or thereabouts, Swanson reflects on his unrequited love for Florry O'Neill. Baseball is only a minor aspect of this nostalgic bildungsroman.

Lupoff, Richard. *Countersolar.* New York: Arbor House, 1987. (New York: Ace Books, 1989.)

In a sci-fi adventure involving a race of spaceships for Counter Earth and discussions between Albert Einstein and the President of the United States about the threat of the bomb, baseball plays a role. In 1942, Babe Didrickson is the first woman to play major league ball. The famous athlete pitches for Brooklyn, and her battery mate is Josh Gibson, star of the Negro Leagues. Gibson talks about catching for Satchel Paige and of barnstorming in Cuba with Babe Ruth. At one point in the space fantasy, Gibson uses an improvised bat to destroy forty-eight golden spheres that threaten America's capital cities — thus temporarily saving the country. The inclusion of the real-life athletes provides some interest for the science fiction novel that is otherwise less than thrilling.

Plimpton, George. *The Curious Case of Sidd Finch.* New York: Macmillan, (New York: Four Walls Eight Windows, 2004.)

From the 1985 *Sports Illustrated* story, the novel expands the career of the Buddhist monk with a 168 miles-per-hour fastball. Narrator Robert Temple, a journalist suffering from post-traumatic stress disorder after returning from Vietnam, is contacted by the New York Mets. The team has discovered Sidd Finch who has learned to throw a baseball in the mountains of Tibet through the practice of lunggom, a type of meditation. The Mets want Temple to live with Finch and to convince him to pitch for them. The story of the miraculous fastball appears in a magazine article written by a certain George Plimpton.

Commissioner Ueberroth is warned that Finch could upset the balance between pitcher and batter, if allowed to play, but Davey Johnson, Mets manager, wants to pitch him every other day. Given clearance, Finch strikes out twenty-seven in succession in his first game. The baseball world panics at the threat to the game. In his second start, the fireballer strikes out the first twenty-six — and then quits, leaving Jesse Orosco to get the last out in a 1-0 Met win. Temple thinks that Finch is trying to reach Tharpa (supreme liberation). There is a chance that he will return to the game for the 1986 season or sometime in the future.

Although a second-rate novel, the concept is stimulating and the baseball lore also adds interest. The book joins the growing list of sci-fi/fantasy baseball literature.

Snyder, Don J. *Veterans Park.* New York: Franklin Watts, 1987. (New York: Ivy Books, 1988.)

In 1969, Bobbi Ann Mullens is attracted to pitcher Brad Schaffer, a Princeton grad who plays for Waterboro, Maine — a Cleveland Indian affiliate. Bobbi Ann lives on her father's farm with her daughter Zooey, the product of an affair with an earlier Waterboro player. Abandoned by her mother, Bobbi Ann poses for pornographer Colonel Ellis to keep the farm solvent. Schaffer gets involved with her and makes friends with Page, her father. At the same time, he worries about his brother, Michael, who is in Vietnam. In order to protect Bobbi Ann, he throws one game in a deal with Ellis, but late in the season, he gets called up by the Indians.

Shaffer goes on to have a short but successful major league career. He marries Bobbi Ann, settles in a Boston suburb, and he and his wife have two children. In 1982, the family visits Washington, D.C., and pays homage to the name of Michael Schaffer inscribed on the black granite wall.

A well-written book, sprinkled with literary allusions, it may be a long-shot for inclusion in a list of the best baseball novels.

Spencer, Ross H. *Kirby's Last Circus.* New York: Donald L. Fine, 1987. (Toronto: Worldwide Library, 1989.)

A farcical mystery similar to the author's *Stranger City Caper* (1980), it depicts the plight of Birch Kirby, a middle-aged Chicago detective who is behind in the rent and has an unpaid bar bill at Lulu's Jungle Tap. He takes a job as a bullpen catcher for the Grizzly Gulch No Sox of the Southern Illinois Association. His real mission is to investigate the KGB, which has apparently infiltrated the Admiral Doldrum Circus of Grizzly Gulch. The result is mayhem — and very little baseball. Kirby's ineptitude is mistaken for astuteness as he stumbles toward a solution. Once again, the humor makes the book almost worthwhile.

Stansberry, Domenic. *The Spoiler: A Novel of Baseball and Mystery.* New York: Atlantic Monthly Press, 1987. (New York: Permanent Press, 2002.)

Frank Lofton, an itinerant journalist, takes a job covering the Holyoke Redwings, a Massachusetts minor league team operated by the big league California Blues. Regina Amanti, mistress of one of the team owners, tells Lofton enough for him to establish a connection between the Redwings, local politicians, and the fires that have been plaguing the city. The journalist discovers the body of the Holyoke shortstop and realizes that he had been murdered because he knew the story behind the arson. Lofton writes "The Holyoke Story" to expose the criminal action that is tied to local politics, but when the article appears, he is murdered also. This is more of a muckraking exposure of corruption than a typical mystery or baseball novel.

1988

Geller, Michael. *Major League Murder.* New York: St. Martin's Press, 1988.

Private-eye Slots Resnick, former NYC Chief of Detectives and minor league player, is asked by bookie-priest Harry Quinn to clear Jefferson (Nightmare) Davis, a suspended pitcher. Even though the black hurler beaned him and called him a racist (when they were both in the minors), Resnick takes the job after talking to Arthur, Davis' unacknowledged son, and Theda, Arthur's mother. They persuade the detective that Davis has been framed in the charge of doctoring baseballs—the reason for his suspension. Resnick verifies this by pinning the blame on Cynthia and Jeremy Marsh and umpire Augie Casillo. They bet on a playoff game in which Casillo ejected Davis for supposedly using vaseline on baseballs. When the umpire is murdered, the Sherlock Holmes-like detective frees the pitcher of suspicion and points to the Marsh couple as the culprits. He then advises Nightmare Davis, his old nemesis, to spend some time with his son. The racial element adds some spice to a routine mystery.

Gordon, Alison. *The Dead Pull Hitter.* Toronto: McClelland & Stewart, 1988. (New York: Onyx Press, 1991; New York: Random House Value Publishers, 1992.)

In the first Kate Henry mystery, the sportswriter, who covers the Toronto Titans of the American League East, is enmeshed in the murders of two players. Sultan Sanchez (designated hitter) and Steve Thorson (pitcher) are found dead in the Titan clubhouse. Kate finds out that Sanchez was blackmailing the pitcher who had thrown a game in college. The killer sends the blackmail file to Kate to throw suspicion on others, but she traces the clues to Moose Greer, a clubhouse employee who is smuggling drugs to offset a gambling problem. Greer is discovered with cocaine by Sanchez, so he kills the DH. He murders Thorson when the pitcher refuses to throw a game that Greer had bet on. Kate corners Greer but needs the help of Andy Munro, Toronto cop, to arrest him.

Munro becomes a fixture in Kate Henry's life in future mysteries. He is joined by Kate's cat (Elwy) and her tenants: Sally and her son T. C. The book is a nice mixture of baseball, detection, and domestic life.

King, Frank. *Southpaw.* New York: Lynx Books, 1988.

A shaman seeks revenge for a betrayed Faustian bargain in a sci-fi/horror story.

John True, a Nootkan-speaking Coast Indian, had made a pact with Walter Bunsen, owner of the Oaktown Wolves of the Pacific Coast League, which enabled the team to win the pennant in 1963. After twenty-five years in jail, True takes vengeance on Bunsen's daughter, Bunny, now the owner of the team. Her father had reneged on his end of the deal, and True turns Bunny into a werewolf-like creature that murders and mutilates the manager of the Wolves. Dominic Lombardi, manager of the '63 team, returns to the helm. A former teammate of Joe DiMaggio with the San Francisco Seals, Lombardi's Wolves are sixteen and a half games out of first place with thirty-one to play. When John True says that the Wolves can win, the new manager asks for the terms. A supernatural deal is suggested in what is, at least, a fast read.

Kinsella, W. P. *The Further Adventures of Slugger McBatt.* Boston: Houghton Mifflin, 1988.
A collection of ten baseball stories.

Klinkowitz, Jerry. *Short Season and Other Baseball Stories.* Baltimore: Johns Hopkins University Press, 1988. (Baltimore: Johns Hopkins University Press, 2000.)
In this case, the stories are related in what amounts to an episodic novel. The twenty-eight stories or chapters depict the Mason City Royals of the Class A Midcontinent League. Recurring characters include: Carl Peterson, the manager; Mack Pteszynski, pitching coach; Bill White, public address announcer; Hal Woods, baseball historian; Jolene, foulball chaser; Jane Alpert, the centerfielder's wife; Jeff, general manager; Earl Hansen, bus driver; Dick Crew, sportswriter; and others.
The Royals win the league championship and relief pitcher Freddie Guagliardo, in his fourth year of A ball, gets called up to Kansas City of the majors. Many aspects of minor league life are presented: language problems, umpire deficiencies, low pay, hard traveling, and termination (getting cut from the team — or promoted to a higher level). The humor and the inside view of the lower level of pro baseball make it an interesting addition to the genre.

Rosen, Richard D. *Saturday Night Dead.* New York: Viking Press, 1988. (New York: Onyx Press, 1989.)
Harvey Blissberg returns (from *Strike Three You're Dead*) to take the job of keeping outfielder Dave Kasick sober so that he can guest-host a television program. When Roy Ganz, the producer of the show, is murdered, Blissberg has a bigger task on his hands. The trail leads to Max Wiley who directed a program that included Ganz as a child actor. Unlike Rosen's first baseball mystery, there is little about the game here.

Weaver, Gordon. *The Eight Corners of the World.* Chelsea, VT: Chelsea Green, (Chelsea, VT: Chelsea Green, 1990.)
The first section of the novel that deals with the life of Yoshinori Yamaguchi focuses on his stint as a companion to Moe Berg during an American League All-Star team's tour of Japan in 1934. Berg, a reserve catcher for most of his major

league career, is recruited by the State Department as a spy. A graduate of Princeton and panelist on "Information Please," a radio program, the catcher is asked to photograph key military sites while touring with Connie Mack's team. The sixteen-year-old Japanese student is appointed as Berg's interpreter by the Imperial Ministry of Education. Berg is a linguist, however, and uses Yamaguchi as a guide and assistant photographer instead of an interpreter. Yosh, who narrates in a colorful American patois, knows that he is being used, but he is willing to work with the catcher on the promise that Berg will get him into an Ivy League school.

Yosh evolves into Foto Joe Yamaguchi and gets to America, but not in the way that he hoped for. He continues to relate his life's adventures that are eventually summarized by his tattoos. The early baseball part of the book includes portraits of Babe Ruth, Lou Gehrig, Jimmie Foxx, Lefty Gomez, and Charlie Gehringer. In contrast to the scholarly Morris Berg, who could speak twelve languages, the Connie Mack All-Stars (Ruth in particular) are depicted as ugly Americans who are ignorant and disrespectful of Japanese culture. (Berg, a .243 lifetime hitter, joined Wild Bill Donovan's Office of Strategic Services after his baseball career was over and served on several missions in Europe during World War II.) Baseball and Berg are a relatively small part of this highly praised novel, however.

1989

Cairns, Bob. *The Comeback Kids.* New York: St. Martin's Press, 1989.

The New Beaton Hot Dogs are a victim of racial prejudice at the Little League World Series of 1954. The racially integrated team does not get a chance to compete despite the promise that Elmer Thumma, former New York Giant pitcher, made to the players. Now, thirty years later, Elmer's Little Giants, Incorporated, is threatened by corporate takeover, so Thumma proposes a five-game series with the Poughkeepsie Pintails (The Little World Series That Shoulda Been but Never Was) to promote his hotdog products. The former little leaguers, now middle-aged, tour the country in a frankfurter-shaped van and play in famous places: Wrigley Field, Fenway Park, and Yankee Stadium. However, a reporter covering the miniseries suggests that a fix is on. Hooter Horton, catcher for the Hot Dogs, exposes two of his teammates that had accepted bribes, and they are banned. In the Big Game, Elmer Thumma does the pitching in place of one of the cheaters, and the Hot Dogs win. The business is saved, and Horton writes the story of the oldest little leaguers. The racial element and the light-hearted rendition of the book offset the sentimental heroics.

Deford, Frank. *Casey on the Loose.* New York: Viking Press, 1989.

The events surrounding Thayer's famous poem, "Casey at the Bat," are depicted in a 106-page novella. In 1888, Timothy F. X. Casey takes Florence (Flossie) Clury to Nantucket Beach with the idea of getting married. Chester Drinkwater, the Trolley King, has bribed him to abandon the Mudville team. Casey puts up the $500 he got from Drinkwater to bet on himself (at twenty-to-one odds) against John L Sullivan in a boxing match. Casey is the first man to beat the Boston Strong Boy. He rushes back to Mudville for the game with the Lynn team, but he is late.

He arrives in time to pinch-hit in the ninth with the score, of course, 4-2 in favor of the opponents (and Flynn and Blake on base). Casey strikes out, but the ball eludes the catcher and after a series of overthrows, all three runs score. There is joy in Mudville (with a 5-4 win), but Flossie is down on Casey for attempting to throw the game (based on her knowledge of Drinkwater's money and his promise to get Casey a shot with a big team in the future). Casey protests by insisting that he struck out honestly, and he talks Flossie into marrying him. However, he does not become a baseball star.

An enlargement of a *Sports Illustrated* story by Deford, the inclusion of historical figures like Sullivan, Ernest Thayer, and James Naismith (just before he invents basketball) adds color to the Casey legend. While a clever pastiche of Thayer's famous poem, it is, however, not exactly great literature.

Gorman, Ed. *Graves' Retreat.* New York: Doubleday, 1989. (New York: Leisure Books, 1999.)

In a Double D Western, Les Graves pitches for the Cedar Rapids Municipal team in 1884. He longs for marriage and respectability, but he is haunted by his outlaw brother and a failure at a big league training camp. Les now works at a bank, but his life reaches a crisis when his brother, T. Z., and his cohort, Neely, arrive in town with the idea of robbing the bank with the help of Les, who does not want to cooperate.

Further trouble occurs as Susan Edmonds, Les' intended, dumps him for someone else. As he is preparing to pitch against a big-time team, T. Z. and Neely try to rob the bank. Les foils the attempt by felling Neely with a thrown paperweight. In the process, he is shot in the arm (which ends his pitching career). However, he has learned that he can live without his dream of baseball fame. He turns to his first girlfriend, May, and hopes to gain the respect of the townsmen that usually eludes "ballists." The brief look at nineteenth century baseball is the book's redeeming feature.

Landers, Lynda Stowe. *A Season to Remember.* New York: Thomas Bouregy, 1989.

Lady sportswriter Tori Ashford (in An Avalon Career Romance) reports on the Dallas Texans. She is enthralled with new second baseman, Currie Volmer, formerly a star of the Big Red Machine. According to formula, romance blooms, falters, and reblooms during the course of the season. The injured hero leads the Texans to a World Series win and proves to be an altruist who helps children. A wedding is inevitable.

Littlefield, Bill. *Prospect.* Boston: Houghton Mifflin, 1989. (Boston: Mariner Books, 2001.)

Pete Estey is a retired scout living in Fair Haven, a Florida retirement home. Louise, a black attendant and a Dodger fan from the Jackie Robinson era, tells Estey about her grandnephew and his baseball skills. When Fair Haven is damaged by a fire, Louise invites the ex-scout to stay with her. She gets him to take a look at Jack Brown, a semipro pitcher. Estey likes what he sees but thinks that the kid's future is at shortstop. He gets Cappy Haynes to sign him for the Lions' AA team in Albany.

Louise dies of a stroke just before Brown is called up to the majors. Pete Estey, however, sees him play in a big league game. He then moves back to Fair Haven and looks forward to telling stories about baseball prospects.

Interspersed with baseball lore, including discussions of the Black Sox and Ty Cobb, the novel is well written. Alternately narrated by Pete and Louise, the humanitarian theme is augmented by the uniting aspect of baseball.

McAlpine, Gordon. *Joy in Mudville.* New York: E. P. Dutton, 1989. (Rockville, MD: Wildside Press, 2003).

In this fantasy, Babe Ruth calls his shot in the 1932 World Series, and the ball travels to California with three Chicagoans in pursuit: Buddy Easter, fourteen-year-old baseball card collector; Loren Woodville, a scientist; and Alice, a dancer and ex-waitress. Alice has jilted Al Capone, and his gang is after her as she tries to get a message to Ruth. The scientist, contemplating suicide, is dangling from a bridge when he spots a spacecraft, which turns out to be the home run ball. Buddy follows the flight of the ball from a roof top as he consorts with his invisible companion—Abner Doubleday. All three chase the ball on its trip to the Pacific Coast. Along the way, they encounter Woody Guthrie, Clark Kent, Professor Marvel, and Capone and his hoods.

The journey ends in Long Beach. While they wait for the sphere to descend, it is revealed that Buddy Easter is the son of Alice and Babe Ruth. Alice had disappeared after giving birth, and her mother gave the baby to an orphanage. Buddy (actually George Herman Ruth, Jr.) catches the ball and disappears into a constellation. Woodville goes into a forty-year coma and is attended by Alice. When he awakes, he and Alice begin a book that will explain how Buddy's baseball cards found their way into the stratosphere—occasionally falling to earth.

Similar but not quite equal to the books of W. P. Kinsella (or perhaps L. Frank Baum), it combines magical realism and baseball lore. The result, though, is too abstruse for popular consumption.

Nighbert, David F. *Strikezone.* New York: St. Martin's Press, 1989.

Bull Cochran, former pro pitcher now in the moving business, becomes an amateur detective when his partner, Juice Hanzlik, is murdered. Hanzlik, a former minor league teammate of Bull, leaves his partner with a suitcase full of cash (made from drug dealing). Both the hoods and the police search for the loot. Bull is also pursued by Hanzlik's killer—who turns out to be Jose Sanchez, brother of the player Bull had killed with a pitch (the incident that caused Bull to quit the game). Sanchez and his henchmen try to kill Bull, but he disables one by throwing a brass baseball (a gift from Hanzlik), and the police shoot the other. Detective Molly Flanagan is among the rescuers, and she and Bull become a couple.

The incident in which an ex-ballplayer injures a criminal with a thrown object has become a convention by this point. It suggests the lack of imagination that dominates this mystery.

Seaver, Tom, and Herb Rescinow. *Beanball: Murder at the World Series.* New York: William Morrow, 1989. (New York: Random House Value Publishing, 1991.)

As the Brooklyn Bandits and Jersey Boomers prepare to meet in the World Series, Slippery Sam Prager, owner of the Bandits, is murdered. Sportswriter Marcus Burr and Lieutenant Danzig track down Butch Bello, manager of the Bandits. He wants to run the team without the owner's interference. Brooklyn goes on to win the Series, but Burr accosts the manager at the conclusion. Bello attacks Burr, and the sportswriter kills him in self-defense. For his heroics, Burr requests a raise so that he can afford to get married. Seaver needed more relief help in order to save this one.

Zubro, Mark Richard. *A Simple Suburban Murder.* New York: St. Martin's Press, 1989.
This is the first of the Tom and Scott mystery series featuring a teacher and a major league pitcher as a gay couple. Tom Mason teaches remedial sophomores and honors English at Grover Cleveland High School in River's Edge, a Chicago suburb. Scott is a celebrity who pitched two no-hitters in a World Series. He decides to come out of the closet but is the victim of a backlash that costs him a big endorsement deal. The emphasis is on homophobia in all levels of society—baseball is virtually irrelevant in the series—which includes: *Why Is Becky Twitchell Dead?* (1990), *The Only Good Priest* (1992), *An* Echo *of Death (1994), Rust on the Razor* (1996), *Are You Nuts* (1998), *The Dead Drag Queen* (2000), and *Here Comes the Corpse* (2002).

1990

Brock, Darryl. *If I Never Get Back.* New York: Crown, 1990. (New York: Ballantine Books, 1991; New York: Plume, 2002.)
Sam Fowler, a San Francisco journalist, is transported back to 1869 and becomes a member of the Cincinnati Red Stockings. After attending his father's funeral in Cleveland, Sam is on his way home, but the modern-day Amtrak turns into a steam locomotive full of ballists—the 1869 Red Stockings. He makes friends with Andy Leonard, leftfielder, and his sister Cait, a widow with a connection to the Fenians -Irish militants. Her husband, Colm, was murdered in the Civil War by a rival for her affections—but now she falls in love with Sam (who may be a reincarnation of Colm).

Fowler plays and travels with the team and also finds himself in trouble with the Fenian Brotherhood by foiling a robbery and by unearthing $10,000 in gold that the group is searching for. Mark Twain (Sam's name is Samuel Clemens Fowler, and he had written a thesis on the famous author) leads him to the buried hoard.

As the Red Stockings travel west, Fowler is aided by Frank and Jessie James while he is being pursued by Fenians. In San Francisco, he has a showdown with Colm's murderer—and is the victor with the help of supernatural forces, presumably the ghost of Colm. However, he is eventually transported back to the future. Fowler sees that his divorced wife has remarried and that his daughter no longer needs him. He returns to his newspaper job, but he longs for Cait.

Sam Fowler gets his wish in a sequel (*Two in the Field,* 2002). Despite the supernatural aspect of the plot, much of the historical view of baseball and culture is realistic. Like Twain's *A Connecticut Yankee in King Arthur's Court*, social ills are stressed. Brock's book is a viable mixture of fantastic adventure, social realism, and baseball.

Cronin, Justin. *A Short History of the Long Ball.* Tulsa: Council Oaks Books, 1990.

A New York City journalist narrates his friendship with a troubled friend over a twenty-two-year period. As boys, the narrator and Donny Flannigin play baseball together. The zenith of the future reporter's athletic endeavors is a long homer he hits one summer. Donny, however, in comparison to his friend's stable home life, is from a problem family, and he eventually becomes a drug addict. Years later, he appears on a day that his old buddy and his four-year-old son are playing ball in the yard. Donny joins the activity, and as the book ends, he hits a long one into the woods.

The contrasting value systems of the boys and their families are balanced by the strength of their friendship. The ninety-pager is the winner of a National Novella Award.

Enger, L. L. *Comeback.* New York: St. Martin's Press, 1990. (New York: Pocket Books, 1990).

Gun Pedersen, former Detroit outfielder, lives in northern Minnesota and spends a lot of time regretting the past. His wife Amanda was killed in a plane wreck while on her way to question him about rumors of infidelity. Pedersen is stirred into action by Lyle Hedman's plan to turn the surrounding wilderness into Loon Country, a version of Disney Land. The ex-Tiger refuses to sell any of his land to the speculator. With the help of friends, bar owner Jack LaSalle and journalist Carol Long, Pedersen works to thwart the deal and to preserve the ecosystem. He succeeds in tough-guy fashion in the first of a series by brothers Leif and Lin Enger.

Gordon, Alison. *Safe at Home.* Toronto: McClelland & Stewart, 1990.

Kate Henry, in her second mystery, returns to Toronto, after reporting on the Titans in spring training, to find her boyfriend, Andy Munro, embroiled in the case of the Daylight Stalker, a child-killer. At her newspaper office, meanwhile, Kate gets a call from Joe Kelsey, a black Titan known as Preacher due to his religious fundamentalism. He wants Kate to write his confession as a homosexual. The article creates a sensation, and Kelsey's teammates, Stinger Swain and Goober Graboski, proclaim their outrage. Kelsey continues to play well despite the negative reaction to coming out of the closet.

The Daylight Stalker turns Kate's attention to a more important matter, though, as T. C., son of Sally (Kate's tenant and friend), is kidnapped. Kate rescues the boy and exposes the kidnapper and child-killer as Dickie Greaves, newspaper photographer. She is aided by Joe Kelsey and his lover — and consequently Preacher Joe earns the respect of his teammates.

Although Kate Henry upstages police detective Andy Munro, their relationship perseveres, and with the safe return of T. C., domestic harmony is restored. Although the homosexual motif is melodramatic, it features the second fictional big leaguer to create a public protest as the result of the disclosure.

Grimes, Tom. *A Stone of the Heart.* New York: Four Walls Eight Windows, 1990. (Dallas: Southern Methodist University Press, 1997.)

Living in Queens in the summer of 1961, the fourteen-year-old narrator is entranced by the quest of Roger Maris to top Ruth's homer record. Unhappy about his alcoholic father, the boy finds solace in baseball stats. His grandfather takes him to Yankee Stadium when Maris has sixty, but the record is not broken that day. Back at home, the boy's drunken father breaks into the house — resulting in his arrest and assignment to an institution for psychiatric care.

When Maris hits his sixty-first homer, it is anticlimactic for the narrator, who has learned that life is more complex than statistics can measure. Babe Ruth is the standard for power hitting, and when his record is surpassed, it suggests the uncertainty of the human condition. The boy tries to make peace with his father and to accept the chaos and sadness that permeates his vision of the world — in a competent coming-of-age novella.

Grosser, Morton. *The Fabulous Fifty.* New York: Atheneum, 1990.

Although labeled as a "twelve-and-up" book, the description of the eight-game 1921 World Series between the Giants and Yankees makes it unique enough to be included here. The fourteen-year-old narrator, Sol Janus of Philadelphia, tells of his baseball fanaticism. He and his friends compete in a newspaper contest to win a trip to New York and the World Series. Sol's friend Tony Ammanati is among the fabulous fifty winners, and Sol illegally accompanies him on the trip. The boys accidentally get involved with a gambler and win $200 — getting fifty in cash and the rest in trade from the clothing store hustler who had tried to take advantage of them. After the Series, they return to school in Philadelphia with an autographed ball — including Babe Ruth's signature. The account of the games between John McGraw's Giants and Miller Huggins' Yankees elevates the book from a playful young adult status to one that any baseball fan could enjoy.

Irvine, Robert. *Gone to Glory.* New York: St. Martin's Press, 1990. (New York: Pocket Books, 1991.)

Salt Lake City private eye Moroni Traveler is hired by Hap Kilgore, former manager of the Salt Lake City Bees, to clear the name of ex-shortstop Pepper Dalton. Once a boyhood hero of Traveler, Dalton is trying to buy the minor league team, now called the Saints, and to restore it to glory as the Bees of his playing days. However, he is suspected of killing his sister, Priscilla, in order to obtain the money for the deal. After Priscilla's death, he takes possession of Glory, a ghost town full of coal deposits, and sells it to the Mormons. Before he can take ownership of the team, however, Traveler, a former NFL linebacker, discovers that his old hero has been manipulating people in order to fulfill his dream. Although he has no proof that Dalton committed a crime, Traveler is morally appalled at his behavior, and he makes a deal with the unscrupulous Mormons to purchase the team. The behind-the-scene power play psychologically destroys Pepper Dalton, and the detective gains his version of justice. Baseball is just a device used to disclose greed and corruption in an unusual mystery.

Kiraly, Sherwood. *California Rush.* New York: Macmillan, 1990. (New York: Berkley Publishing Group, 1997.)

Charlie Tyke, Jay Bates, and Davy Tremayne are minor league teammates. They make it to the majors, eventually, and go their separate ways. When Bates becomes manager of the expansion California Rush, he persuades Tyke to give up announcing to become his thirdbase coach. When they quarrel, and Tyke is fired, Tremayne, manager of St. Louis, hires him there.

The final game between the teams for the divisional title is an incredible misadventure. After eight innings, St. Louis leads 3-0 even though pitcher Fabian Koonce, sporting an 8.43 ERA, has yielded twenty-six hits. The Rush apparently win on a grandslam in the ninth, but the homer is disallowed because Bates had called timeout before the pitch. The fans, when informed of the decision, start a riot, and the game is forfeited to St. Louis.

Charlie Tyke narrates the farcical events. Despite some comical moments, though, the book is not of major quality.

Leavy, Jane. *Squeeze Play.* Garden City, NY: Doubleday, 1990. (New York: Harper Perennial, 2003.)

Female sportswriter Ariadne Bloom (A. B.) Berkowitz covers the 1989 Washington Senators, a first-year expansion team owned by televangelist Tommy Boy Collins. Founder of the Christian Fellowship Entertainment Network, the fundamentalist forbids his players from talking to the woman invader of the locker room. A. B. responds with scathing stories of the team's ineptitude and sexism. A girlhood fan of the Yankees and Joe Proud (similar to Mickey Mantle), A. B. becomes a friend of a veteran catcher of the Senators and goes on to competently analyze their season as they finish within one game of matching the losing record of the 1962 Mets. She also gains revenge on Collins by catching him in a compromising position with a girl named Lola.

Written in the form of a diary, the book is rife with vulgarity and jock-speak. The stress is on the debunking of right-wing fanatics and their sexist policies.. It has been called the *Semi-Tough* of baseball, which at least means that it is funny, sexy, and popular.

Lechuk, Alan. *Brooklyn Boy.* New York: McGraw-Hill, 1990. (New York: Bassett, 1990; New York: Terrace Books, 2003.)

The early life of Aaron Schlossberg is reported as he grows to maturity in Brooklyn during the forties and fifties. Son of Jewish immigrants, the boy tries to assimilate American culture, and baseball is one of the main factors in the process. Besides playing ball in the streets and playgrounds, Aaron visits the sacred Ebbets Field and commemorates the Boys of Summer as one of the True Believers. The radio reports of Red Barber, the Voice of the Bums, fill the Schlossberg apartment, but being at the ballpark is the ultimate joy. The featured season is 1947, the year of Branch Rickey and Jackie Robinson. At school, Aaron gets into fights with those who malign the Dodgers. Later, the Cold War and the Red Scare are alleviated by the presence of baseball.

Much of the earlier juvenile book *On Home Ground* (1987) is incorporated into the novel. It is a typical bildungsroman that is enhanced by the baseball section that dominates the protagonist's youth.

Lyle, Sparky, and David Fisher. *The Year I Owned the Yankees.* New York: Bantam, 1990.

Lyle gains possession of the Yankees for one season. He hires Lou Piniella as manager and Berra, Nettles, and Stanley as coaches. Reggie Jackson, part of the broadcast team, doubles as ego adviser. The most important member of the staff, however, is traveling secretary and computer analyst, Duke Schneider — a woman. It is her computer that guides the team, which leads to a conflict with Piniella and his eventual firing.

When the Yankees make it to the World Series, a Mr. Applegate tries to make a deal with Lyle. He discovers, though, that it is not the devil-figure from *Damn Yankees* but the agent of Schnneider. She is really a die-hard Dodger fan and is trying to sabotage her own computer system so that the Dodgers will win. Lyle has to fire her, and the Yankees go on to beat the Koufax and Drysdale team without the benefit of a machine — except for Yankee Tommy John's bionic arm that is repaired by a computer.

During the course of the zany season, the first woman to play in the majors (joining a long line of fictional females) joins the Atlanta Braves. Julia Nevez has a brief career before going to the NFL as a place kicker. But the computer application of Schneider is the major impact on baseball fiction. Earlier books, including *Stay Loose, The Last Man Is Out,* and *The Batting Machine,* had also employed computers in improving skills and perfecting tactics, and it is the prime reason for the Yankee success here — even though the Series is played without one — and a statement on the growing dependency on technology in life and baseball. The flakiness of Sparky Lyle's narration, spiced with New York Yankee lore, makes this one of the funniest baseball novels.

Manfred, Frederick. *No Fun on Sunday.* Norman: University of Oklahoma Press, 1990.

Sherm Engelking, of the rural Upper Midwest (Siouxland) in the 1920s, dreams of playing shortstop for the Cubs. His mother, though, is prejudiced against baseball — especially on Sundays. As a teenager, Sherm moves to the farms of his siblings and plays for various teams until catching on with the Bonnie Boys who play formidable foes such as the Hello Homebrews, the Hazard Hoboes, and a barnstorming black team featuring a pitcher with a fastball like Satchel Paige or Smokey Joe Williams.

Swede Risberg, late of the 1919 Black Sox, plays for the Hoboes, and he suggests that Sherm is good enough for the big time. Deacon Blake, a scout for the Cubs, asks him to play a Sunday game against a top team in order to make a final judgment. Sherm stars in the contest, but his mother criticizes his Sunday participation in a frivolous sport in a godless city. The scout, though, invites the youth to spring training with the Cubs, but an off-season accident ends Sherm's hopes of being a major leaguer.

Manfred is a former semipro player, sportswriter, and author of the Buckskin Man Tales, including *Lord Grizzly.* His baseball novel, however, is less commendable.

Slattery, Marty. *Diamonds Are Trumps.* Memphis: St. Luke's Press, 1990.

"A Pitcher's First Novel" summarizes the 1981 minor league season of sore-armed, almost-forty Bill Mahoney of the Lodi Dodgers. Alienated from wife, kids, and father, he reviews his life and nurses a dream of making the majors. He pitches, rarely, in relief and spends most of his ballpark time riding the bench and reflecting. He dates Alice from the concession stand. In the last game of the season, though, Mahoney rediscovers his fastball when he is inserted into the game in the seventh inning. Pitching with a pain-free arm, he mows down the Fresno Giants and gains renewed hope for a baseball future. He also makes peace with his father and plans ahead with Alice. Despite the hokey ending, it is a provocative study of minor league life.

1991

Bowen, Michael. *Fielder's Choice.* New York: St. Martin's Press, 1991.

The body of Jerry Fielder is found in the press box at a Mets-Brewer game in 1962. Tom and Sandy Curry, of the Curry and Furst law firm, are among the murdered man's guests at the ballpark that day. With the help of their senior partners and Lt. Bernstein, they close in on Louis Kovacs, who had ruined the basketball career of Fielder's friend Rainbow Madden. When Madden retaliates by killing Kovacs, the investigators allow him to get away with it. The plot is further complicated by the discovery that Fielder had been trying to fix Met games so that they would set a record for the most losses. An unusual mystery, it is augmented by the historical background of the Kennedy era and the civil rights movement.

Boyd, Brendan. *Blue Ruin: A Novel of the 1919 World Series.* New York: W. W. Norton, 1991. (New York: Harper Perennial, 1993.)

Joseph (Sport) Sullivan, one of the real-life gamblers involved in the Black Sox scandal, presents his fictionalized story of the event. After talking to Chick Gandil of the White Sox about a possible fix, Sport turns to the notorious Arnold Rothstein for financial backing. He gets $50,000 from the big-time gambler's henchman Nat Evans, but complications arise when Abe Attell and Sleepy Bill Burns try to run their own scams. Nevertheless, Sport gives $10,000 to Gandil and bets $40,000 on Cincinnati, the eventual winner of the Series. Winning $400,000, Sport goes on to attempt other bribes of ballplayers—including Babe Ruth, Ty Cobb, and Tris Speaker. He has no luck with the superstars, however, and when the investigation of the 1919 Series becomes serious a year later, Rothstein advises him to go on the lam in Mexico. After Rose, Sport's girlfriend, absconds with half of his bankroll, he takes Rothstein's advice and seeks refuge in La Pesca.

Like Stein's *Hoopla* (1983), the novel gets into many details of the Scandal, but the emphasis is on the gamblers rather than the "eight men out" of the White Sox. Sport Sullivan is presented as a literate narrator whose commentary on the off-field action is entertaining and perceptive. Before his fall from glory, he comes in contact with the elite of the era, including General Pershing, George M. Cohan, Lon Chaney, William G. Harding, and Thomas Edison. But Sullivan is a little guy compared to Rothstein who, like the fictional Meyer Wolfsheim in *The Great Gatsby*, operates from a position of power. Along with Charles Comisky's underpaid players, Sullivan is vulnerable. When big business and the integrity of baseball are at risk, the small-time gambler, too, is taken out of the game. Sullivan's report on his downfall results in one of the elite baseball novels.

Enger, L. L. *Swing.* New York: Pocket Books, 1991.
  Ex-major leaguer Gun Pedersen, in his second mystery, leaves Minnesota to help an old friend in Florida. Moses Gates, a black ex-teammate, now manages a Senior League team. A player has been murdered, and a reporter who was a suspect in the case has turned up dead — by hanging. Pedersen traces the crimes to a pair of bigots: Rott Weiler, former big leaguer and a Senior League manager, and his uncle Casper Leavitt. The detective, a tough guy with a soft heart, thinks and fights his way to justice.

Evers, Crabbe. *Bleeding Dodger Blue.* New York: Bantam Books, 1991.
  Former sportswriter Duffy House is now about to write his memoirs. He visits Jack Remsen, manager of the Los Angeles Dodgers to collect some of his storehouse of anecdotes that refer to the Brooklyn days. However, Remsen becomes the sixth victim of the Sunset Slasher, and Commissioner Chambliss, as usual, wants Duffy to look into the murder. Niece Petey joins the quest, and they discover that Bob Ferguson, former Dodger pitcher with big debts, had talked Remsen into financing a drug deal. They tell the cops, and the deal is thwarted. Duffy and Petey also discover that Remsen was a random victim of the Slasher — who is exposed as a woman who stalks elderly men on the assumption that one of them may be her no-good husband.
  Cubs announcer Red Carney congratulates House and his niece at the end. However, the celebration is subdued because the drug dealers got away — with the money. Also, old friend Jack Remsen had been played for a sucker by Ferguson and then killed by a madwoman merely by chance. This issue of the series resembles the film noir and is an improvement, as a mystery, over the two other Evers products of the year.

Evers, Crabbe. *Murder in Wrigley Field.* New York: Bantam Books, 1991.
  One of three Duffy House mysteries published in 1991 (written by William Brashler and Reinder Van Til), it features the famous sportswriter noted for his "On the House" articles in a Chicago newspaper. He is asked by Commissioner Granville Chambliss to investigate the murder of Dream Weaver, star left-handed Cub pitcher. With the help of Petey, his niece, House obtains clues from Obie Blinstein, Weaver's friend who has letters from Weaver's female admirers. One of them turns out to be Lila Rohe, wife of the Cubs general manager, George Rohe. As House searches the security office at Wrigley Field, he is attacked by George Whiteman, Rohe's assistant. Petey (Petrinella Biggers), a red-headed beauty, and Red Carney, (an announcer who resembles Harry Caray) arrive in time to save House — who then reveals that Whiteman killed Dream Weaver on Rohe's orders. The GM thought that the pitcher, with his amorous affairs and gangster connections, was a disgrace to the Cub organization. The rumor of Lila's association with Weaver was apparently what set Rohe into action.

The baseball lore and commentary make up for the so-so mystery. Brasher, part of the writing team, is the author of *The Bingo Long Traveling All-Stars and Motor Kings.*

Evers, Crabbe. *Murderer's Row.* New York: Bantam Books, 1991.
This time Duffy House and niece Petey Biggers are involved in a murder at Yankee Stadium. Commissioner Chambliss again asks for help when Rubert Huston, owner of the Yankees, is shot by a sniper. House, Petey, and even Cub broadcaster Red Carney run through a list of suspects. In the process, Petey is infatuated with John Brush, Yankee general manager. He is a baseball traditionalist who hates what Huston had been doing with the team. Brush tells Duffy a story (that he got from Waite Hoyt) about the mystique of Babe Ruth as he virtually made baseball the national pastime after the stigma of the Black Sox. Brush wants to restore the game to its former stature as an American icon, and he reveals his distrust of Huston's lack of respect of baseball tradition. Unfortunately, the GM's obsession makes him a suspect, and the murder is eventually traced to him.
Like *Murder in Wrigley Field,* the baseball background elevates the mystery story into a competent novel.

Everson, David. *Suicide Squeeze.* New York: St. Martin's Press, 1991. (New York: Fawcett, 1995.)
The 1969 Cubs and Mets stage a fantasy game at Wrigley Field twenty years later. Dewey Farmer, suspended from baseball for gambling, is trying to make a comeback. Robert Miles, former minor leaguer, is a private eye from Springfield, Illinois. In checking out death threats made to Farmer, Miles uncovers a plot conceived by Farmer and Anna Kennedy to gain sympathy from the media, to earn clearance by the baseball commissioner, and to provide material for a book. The exposure of the plan puts the detective in a hazardous situation, but the police rescue him in the proverbial nick of time.
Baseball references add some zest to the book. There is also a subplot in which Lisa, Miles' girlfriend, is working on a biography of William Faulkner. The mystery, though, is of questionable credibility.

Goldberg. Philip. *This Is Next Year.* New York: Ballantine Books, 1992. (Booksinprint.com, 2000.)
Eleven-year-old Roger Stone narrates the story of his family and the neighborhood during the Brooklyn Dodgers' drive for the pennant in 1955. In a Jewish section of the borough (Brownsville), the hope that "this is next year" becomes an obsession as the summer progresses. The Stone family, including Roger's brothers Hubbell and Hank, root for the Bums and try to overcome the team's curse. When the Dodgers win the pennant, Roger persuades the family to work to offset The Thing (curse) by visiting the home of Jackie Robinson and presenting him with a lucky bat.
The Dodgers, of course, go on to beat the Yankees in the Series (with Podres and Snider starring) and "demented frenzy" reigns in the neighborhood. Roger feels responsible for the success of the team and the welfare of his family.
The cultural events of the era, including racial integration, play a role but are

not assimilated into the plot with much conviction. It is still a good period piece featuring the Brooklyn Dodgers.

Goodman, Eric. *In Days of Awe.* New York: Knopf, 1991. (New York: Washington Square Press, 1992.)

Jewish Joe Singer exiles himself to Hermosa Beach, California, after being suspended from baseball for gambling. His father, Handsome Jack, is responsible for getting Joe into trouble. Finding solace in womanizing, Joe begins to make a moral comeback by his association with Frannie. She involves him into her efforts to help runaway kids and to campaign for a gun control law. During the Days of Awe, the week between Rosh Hashanah and Yom Kippur, Joe seeks redemption with "the God of Jewish Athletes" and his father, Jack.

Reinstated by the commissioner, Joe's baseball comeback is thwarted by an opponent of the proposed gun control bill. Joe is shot in his pitching arm, and Jack retaliates by killing the gunman. Father and son are reunited, and Joe apologizes to baseball officials for his past conduct. He visits his former teammates in New York and asks for their forgiveness. Joe also makes a verbal commitment to girlfriend Frannie — and his redemption is apparently complete.

Although a maudlin moral tale, the humor saves it to some extent. The humanistic concerns are presented too subjectively, however, to be an effective part of the plot.

Jenkins, Jerry G. *Rookie.* Brentwood, TN: Wolgemuth & Hyatt Publishers, 1991. (Sisters, OR: Multimedia Publishers, 1997.)

Elgin Woodell and his mother move from Hattiesburg, Mississippi, to Chicago after his father is imprisoned. Neal Woodell wastes his baseball talent through alcoholism. Elgin inherits his father's athleticism and becomes a baseball star in the city. Sharpening his hitting skills on the pitching machine in the basement, he becomes so proficient that he plays with the Chicago Cubs at the age of thirteen. His twenty-seven-year career features a .382 lifetime average, 998 homers, and sixteen MVPs. Heredity and his mother's Christian devotion are responsible for creating a super hero — and a weak novel.

Kinsella, W. P. *Box Socials.* New York: Harper Collins, 1991. (New York: Ballantine Books, 1993.)

In the 1940s, Truckbox Al McClintock, rightfielder of the New Oslo Blue Devils, hit five homers in a game. Narrator Jamie O'Day reports that the last one went across the Pembina River and prompted Bear Lundquist to offer Al a spot on the Sangulo Mustangs. Although the scout for the St. Louis Cardinals (that Lundquist promised) never appears, Al plays well enough to be picked to play for the Alberta All-Stars against a group of American major leaguers. Al gets to pinch-hit against Bob Feller — and strikes out on three pitches. Next spring, he tries out for the New Edmonton Hotel Eskimos, but he fails to make the team. Truckbox Al fades away after that, but he plays occasionally at sports days and picnics and still hits a long ball now and then.

Most of Kinsella's third baseball novel consists of whimsical anecdotes of Canadian folk life. In contrast to *Shoeless Joe* and *The Iowa Baseball Confederacy*, the game is de-emphasized.

Lapin, Mark. *Pledge of Allegiance.* New York: E.P. Dutton, 1991.

Josh Rankin is a nine-year-old Dodger fan. His life in complicated by his parents' association with the Communist Party during the witch-hunting era of Joe McCarthy. Josh is the only kid from P. S. 187 in Washington Heights to attend the 1953 May Day parade, and his teacher and classmates taunt him for being a commie. Kicked off the Little League team and ostracized by his former friends, Josh becomes the target of Dale, an FBI agent who suspects him of possessing an address book of Party members. The agent takes him to a double-header at Ebbets Field (Wilhelm and Maglie pitch against Roe and Black.) After the games, the boy is taken to the Dodger clubhouse and gets Peewee Reese's autograph. Dale, however, wants the address book in return, and when Josh rebels, the agent uses force to get what he wants. A few days later, Dale appears in the neighborhood and tosses Josh an autographed baseball.

The protagonist's moral dilemma is assimilated into the historical background and the baseball motif with skill. It adds up to a competent coming-of-age novel, although also published as a Young Adult book.

Norman, Rick. *Fielder's Choice.* Little Rock: August House Publishers, 1991. (Little Rock: August House Publishers, 1993.)

Andrew Jackson (Gooseball) Fielder from Smackover, Arkansas, is a relief pitcher for the St. Louis Browns in 1941. He wins fame as a rookie with an unorthodox underhanded delivery, but he has the misfortune of balking in the run that cost the Browns the pennant in the last game of the season. After Pearl Harbor, Fielder becomes a gunner on a B-29 and is captured. While a POW, he teaches the Japanese admiral's son how to throw the gooseball. When the war is over, however, Fielder is banned from baseball for treasonous conduct. Twenty years later, he is forgiven as the Air Force and Organized Baseball co-sponsor a Fan Appreciation Day for Gooseball Fielder at a Yankee-Senators game in Washington.

Gooseball Fielder narrates his story in a Southern dialect, and like an older version of Huck Finn, is primarily concerned with doing the right thing. He concludes by asserting that choices, right or wrong, have to be done for the right reason—which is love. Fielder evolves from a Jack Keefe type of egoist to a Henry Wiggen-like moralist. This is a more complex book than the other *Fielder's Choice*, Michael Bowen's mystery that is also published in 1991—and it rates higher in critical evaluation.

Shaara, Michael. *For Love of the Game.* New York: Carroll & Graf, 1991. (New York: Ballantine Books, 1999.)

Billy Chapel, a big league pitcher for seventeen years and a future Hall-of Famer, learns that he is about to be traded. As he pitches what he assumes will be his last game for the last-place team, he reflects on his life. He realizes that his four-year relationship with Carol Gray is in jeopardy; she says that he does not need her. As he agonizes over the affair and other aspects of his existence, he just happens to hurl a perfect game. After the celebration, he calls Carol and convinces her that she is necessary to his life, and she agrees. Chapel thinks about the meaning of love and life as the book concludes

The movie version helped to make the novel popular—along with the name of a Pulitzer Prize winning author. However, this is one of the sappiest of the baseball novels—and one of the biggest disappointments.

1992

Bohjalian, Christopher A. *Past the Bleachers.* New York: Carroll & Graf, 1992.

Bill and Harper Parrish of Havington, Vermont, lose their ten-year-old son to leukemia. Bill tries to find consolation in coaching a Little League team, but his life is further complicated by the appearance of Lucky Diamond. A mute, he joins the team and becomes a star. Parrish probes into the kid's mysterious past and discovers that Lucky is the son of a Red Sox player, killed in a car crash, and a teenager who died in childbirth. Hilton Burberry, Little League Commissioner, has placed Lucky on the team in hopes of gaining the interest of the mourning couple. It works, as the Parrishes adopt Lucky. He goes on to become a college baseball player, and the Parrishes have a daughter of their own.

The novel is essentially a sentimental tale of redemption. It was made into a television movie for ABC in 1995.

Brooks, Bruce. *What Hearts.* New York: Harper Collins, 1992. (New York: Harper Trophy, 1992.)

A Newberry Honor Book and the recipient of other commendations for young adult fiction, it deserves mention here for its overall quality and its limited but graphically described baseball action.

From the first to the seventh grade, Asa moves with his twice divorced mother to a variety of homes. He antagonizes many of his peers with his intellect but finds some consolation in baseball. Asa thinks he has the talent and technique for the game. However, he is aware that his lack of size and power will probably prevent him from being a star. The big moment of his short career occurs when he saves a win by throwing out a runner at first on a liner to centerfield. When his mother gets sick, he temporarily gives up baseball. His first love affair is ended as he moves to a new home once again. There is no formula here, as psychological problems are stressed rather than athletic heroics.

Duncan, David James. *The Brothers K.* Garden City, NY: Doubleday, 1992. (New York: Bantam, 1993.)

In a 645-page family saga, Kincaid Chance reflects on the impact of his father's baseball career on the lives of his three brothers, twin sisters, and mother. Hugh's minor league pitching stint is halted by a thumb injury, and he unhappily works in a mill in Cames, Washington, during the sixties. The family is divided by the conflict between Hugh's obsession with the game and their mother's dislike of it. While the father is secular, Laura is a devout Seventh Day Adventist—creating more friction.

Hugh Chance never gives up on baseball, and he has surgery in which a toe is transplanted to his thumb. He practices pitching at home and eventually returns to the minors as a pitching coach and player for the Portland Tugs in the early seventies. He becomes known as Papa Toe and earns a reputation as a mentor of young players in the farm system of the Pittsburgh Pirates.

In the meantime, Kincaid reports on his brothers. Everett is a campus radical who flees to Canada as a draft dodger in protest over the Vietnam War. Peter is a scholar who seeks religious solace in India. Irwin follows his mother's fundamentalist tendencies and serves as a soldier in Vietnam. The family reunites, though, when Irwin is put in a mental institution after attacking an officer who ordered him to kill a Vietcong youth. Hugh leaves baseball to help the rest of the family free his son from the Army's verdict of insanity. Irwin is finally released but lingers in lethargy until Hugh is dying of cancer. Irwin returns to life with a flurry of activity: he gets married, adopts Southeast Asian kids, and starts a business. Kincaid joins his brother's enterprise by running the warehouse for Wind River Woodstoves. The other siblings graduate from college and pursue careers.

The story of the Chance family's struggle for a meaningful existence has been compared to that of the Brothers Karamazov, as the title suggests, but here the quest is tied to baseball, as various attitudes toward the game mirror different philosophies. Manager Gale Durham thinks of baseball as serving a divine purpose in its role as an inherently anti-war activity. To Hugh Chance, baseball, in the Ty Cobb tradition, is a test of character — a chance to prove oneself against a hostile, competitive world. To Hugh's mother (whose opinion is much like his wife's), it is a boy's game that ruins her son's life.

The book is interspersed with vignettes on aspects of the game's history. It includes a discussion of the Pirates and their emphasis on family in the seventies. There is an argument that Roger Maris sacrificed his career by going after Babe Ruth's home run record. Also enclosed is the interview with Ty Cobb in which he states that he could hit .320 at the age of sixty-two. Cobb is the epitome, according to Kincaid Chance, of a player who upholds the metaphor of baseball as life. *The Brothers K* is a major novel in which baseball is symbolic of ethical values.

Enger, L. L. *Strike.* New York: Pocket Books, 1992.

Gun Pedersen returns to action as the death of an Ojibwa youth leads to a Native American protest movement aimed at the prevention of the drilling for minerals on reservations in northern Minnesota. Pedersen, again with the help of Jack La Salle and Carol Long, struggles to defend the innocent and to preserve the environment. It is a way of atoning for the selfish behavior of his baseball days (when he hit over 400 homers for the Detroit Tigers before quitting in his prime after his wife's death). At one point, Gun takes batting practice in a remodeled barn which was once used by Babe Ruth for the same purpose. The mystery is rather mundane, but the ecological motif improves the overall effect of the book.

Geller, Michael. *Three Strikes, You're Dead.* New York: St. Martin's Press, 1992.

Slots Resnick, in his second mystery, is hired by the New York Mets to do a background check on Billy Joe Howlett, a college player from Norville, Colorado. The prospect turns out to be Billie Jo, a female. Unfortunately, she is a suspect in the murder of her stepmother. However, Resnick pins the blame on Gordon Wallace, Billie Jo's stepfather, who is also responsible for the murders of his wife and Billie Jo's parents. Enraged by the disclosure, she kills Wallace, but the detective convinces the sheriff that it is suicide. He then announces that Ms. Howlett (part Native American) will be the first female signed by a major league team and that she will begin her pro career with the Tidewater Tides in the minors.

The first-woman motif makes this an unusual mystery. That she is a (part) Native American who is allowed to get away with murder adds to the originality. This should not be confused with *Strike Three You're Dead* by Rosen (1984) or with Donald Bain's *Murder, She Wrote: Three Strikes and You're Dead* (2006).

Gilbert, Sarah. *A League of Their Own.* New York: Warner Books, 1992.

A novelization of a story by Kim Wilson and Kelly Candaele and a screenplay by Lowell Ganz and Babaloo Mandel, it focuses on the 1944 season of the All American Girls' Professional Baseball League. Jimmy Dugan reluctantly manages the Rockford Peaches. The heavy drinking former big leaguer (perhaps based on Jimmie Foxx) eventually gets interested in the job as he sees that the women can play the game, The emphasis, though, is on sisters Kit and Dottie who have trouble getting along. Kit is traded to Racine, and when South Bend and Kenosha are eliminated, she gets to play against her sister in a seven-game championship series. Kit runs over Dottie, the catcher, to score the winning run as Racine wins the title. Dottie goes back home to Oregon, and Kit stays on to play in the league, which existed until 1954.

The movie, with Tom Hanks, Geena Davis, and Madonna, is a disappointment as it stresses melodrama rather than the essence of women's pro baseball. Although this is the first fictional account of the subject, it fails artistically as it is too similar to the screenplay.

Gordon, Alison. *Night Game.* Toronto: McClelland & Stewart, 1992. (New York: St. Martin's Press, 1993.)

Kate Henry's third mystery takes place in Florida while she is reporting on the Toronto Titans during spring training. On the night of Kate's forty-second birthday, the body of Lucy Cartwright is found on the beach. Domingo Avilo, one of Lucy's many ballplayer friends, is arrested as a suspect. Some of his Titan teammates ask Kate to find the murderer. Andy Munro, Toronto cop and Kate's boyfriend, comes down to help out. In Nero Wolfe fashion, Kate assembles the witnesses and suspects and solves the crime. Tracy Swain, wife of a Titan, killed Lucy when she saw her in a compromising position with her husband. As usual, it is a pleasing mixture of murder, humor, and baseball.

Grimes, Tom. *Season's End.* Boston: Little, Brown & Company, 1992. (Lincoln: University of Nebraska Press, 1996.)

Mike Williams is propelled into a cultural power by his agent, Alvin Hammer, following a Rookie of the Year season. Due to the free agent market, Williams' financial status soars, but he is bothered by the moral dilemma it creates. He feels like a media product that is being exploited by Hammer and team owner Edmond

P. Percy. The Zen concepts that he had learned from minor league teammate, George O'Kane, are being compromised by his descent into the greedy capitalism that he once despised.

In 1981, Williams develops a sore shoulder that threatens his career, but there is no medical evidence of physical damage. The malady, perhaps indicative of his psychological condition, leads to alienation from the game and his family. He turns for solace to black teammate Otis Armstrong, and they drive off into the night together.

The ambiguous ending, in which two players escape from the commercial world that contrasts to the "sweet illusions' of baseball, suggests the difficulty of providing answers to major moral problems. Mike Williams, who majored in American literature, is in the tradition of the alienated, sensitive rebel who has trouble adjusting to a value system based on economics. Like Huck Finn or Holden Caulfield, he sets out for some version of pastoral innocence that baseball can no longer provide. The book, though, self-consciously and laboriously struggles to present its message.

Homel, David. *Rat Palms.* New York: Harper Collins, 1992. (New York: Harper Collins, 1993.)

Tim (Toadfish) Justice is suspended from a Catholic school. His incompatible parents have a house on the Isle of Hope near Savannah, Georgia. When Tim's father Zeke returns from his two-week major league stint, he is put into a mental institution. Tim's mother Evangeline is upset at the declining social status of the once aristocratic family. She flees to Los Angeles with her son, but Tim's mission is to return to his father and free the legendary minor league pitcher (of the Savannah Indians) from the hospital. He succeeds, but Zeke is murdered by Evangeline's father who never liked his Yankee son-in-law and his career as a ballplayer. Tim feels that life is too complicated. Deciding not to return to school, he sets out on his own to face an uncertain future.

This is a good coming-of-age story with no easy solutions to moral and cultural conflicts.

Honig, Donald. *The Plot to Kill Jackie Robinson.* New York: Dutton, 1992. (New York: Signet, 1993.)

Joe Tinker returns from World War II and is assigned by a New York paper to cover the Dodgers who are at spring training in Cuba. Tinker, who was once called a hell of a drinker by Babe Ruth, hears a rumor that Jackie Robinson will be killed at Ebbets Field on Opening Day, 1947. Branch Rickey warns Robinson about the danger, but the project of integration is continued. Tinker observes that Don Newcombe and Roy Campanella are also working out with the Dodgers in Havana. The journalist eventually traces the threat to Quentin Wilson, a racist from Queens. He is the brother of Harry, a cop who was killed in Harlem while visiting his daughter and her mother, Etta Peerson, a black dancer. Quentin Wilson is crazed by Harry's racial transgression, and he focuses on Robinson as a symbol of his frustration and animosity. On Opening Day, he plans to shoot him from the sanctuary of the scoreboard, but Tinker foils the plan. The newspaper and the law want the story suppressed, but Tinker's girlfriend convinces him that he has an obligation to write the story and expose the truth.

This is an effective presentation of the racist furor caused by baseball's "noble experiment." More than an ordinary mystery, it rivals the quality of the author's *The Last Great Season* (1979).

Hullinger, David P. *Ball Park Numbers: The Year They Did Not Play Ball.* New York: Vantage Press, 1992.

Consisting mostly of computer-generated statistics, the sixty-nine page novella tells of the 1999 season that occurs without the employment of players. With a baseball strike on, George Orason invents a plan to have a season in which computers determine the outcomes of games—using numbers rather than humans. Since the strike is not resolved, a third major league is created, and games are played on a technological level. Fans presumably follow the standings and the stats just as if people were involved.

The ballplayers, meanwhile, barnstorm to try to make a living—and to stay in shape in case they are ever needed. The sportswriters are forced to find worthwhile careers in other areas.

Cincinnati wins the three-way World Series. In the numbers game, it is discovered that a team is more likely to win a championship than to finish at .500. The fact means little—and the book follows suit.

Lefcourt, Peter. *The Dreyfus Affair.* New York: Random House, 1992. (New York: Harper Perennial, 1993.)

Susie Dreyfus, former Rose Bowl queen, is suspicious of her husband Randy, star shortstop for the Los Angles Valley Vikings, and hires a private eye. The detective thinks Randy is having an affair with a dog, but when the shortstop is discovered kissing D. J. Pickett, black second baseman of the Vikings in a department store, homophobia invades the world of major league baseball. The ball club tries to cover up the situation, but fan resentment is too great to let it die. Even a shopping mall named after Dreyfus is renamed (for Arnold Schwarzenegger). Finally the President of the United States puts pressure on the Commissioner of Baseball to protect the purity of the game. Thus, the two players are banned for life. However, in a parody of the historical Dreyfus Affair (in which Emile Zola helped to rescue Colonel Alfred Dreyfus from French anti-Semites with his essay "J'accuse"), sportswriter Milt Zola comes to the aid of the condemned players with a newspaper article. It results in the reinstatement of Dreyfus and Pickett. They join the team during the World Series, but the shortstop is shot while circling the bases on a homer. The Reds win the Series, Dreyfus recovers, and he and Pickett go fishing together.

In the 1980s, *A Simple Suburban Murder, Out at Home,* and *Changing Pitches* deal with homophobia. *The Dreyfus Affair* gives the topic a farcical facet, but in this case the social commentary is partially undermined by the humorous and melodramatic extremes.

Lovisi, Gary, and Terry Arnone. *The Woman in the Dugout: The Story of the Brooklyn Kings.* Brooklyn: Gryphon, 1992.

The Brooklyn Kings are a minor league team owned by Oscar and Arlene Craig. When Tom Colby is fired, Arlene talks her husband into letting her take his place as first base coach. (Her father had been a coach for the Dodgers in their last year at Ebbets Field.) Joey Gardenia, an ex–major leaguer, leads a sexist faction against her, but Arlene eventually persuades Joey that she can handle the job. When the manager dies, she takes over the helm and manages the Kings to the pennant. In an experimental minor league World Series, Arlene suspends Gardenia and several teammates for public brawling, but when she discovers that the players were fighting in defense of her reputation, she reinstates them in time to win the championship. She is then offered the job of managing the New York Yankees.

The seventy-six-page novella is equally ineffective as a feminist tract and a work of art.

Nighbert, David F. *Squeezeplay.* New York: St. Martin's Press, 1992.

Bull Cochran, in his second mystery, is asked by Peg Ahern to investigate the death of her husband. A former teammate of Bull and a star pitcher of the Astros, Holy Joe Ahern supposedly committed suicide after murdering a prostitute. Bull suspects foul play and questions Jerry Lamp, Joe's business partner. Bull finds out that Bubba Lusby committed both murders in a scheme to fleece Lamp Enterprises. With help from girlfriend Molly, a cop, he gets to the solution in typical tough-guy fashion

The unofficial partnership with a woman, though, is the only unique aspect of the book. Paul Benjamin and Jane Leavy wrote novels titled *Squeeze Play*, not to be confused with this one-word title.

Risenhoover, C. C. *White Heat.* Dallas: Baskerville, 1992.

Randy Joe Keegan, high school pitcher in Jason, Texas, plays on a black barnstorming team in the summer of 1954. The only white player, he gets heat from the town and the school, but his father, R. M., stands up for him despite being labeled a communist and threatened with violence. Randy Joe climaxes the summer by pitching sensationally in a tournament. He goes on to play at the University of Oklahoma. In 1959, he signs with the Yankees, but arm trouble ends his career after two seasons. Randy Joe becomes a marine and is killed in Vietnam in 1967.

Most of the townspeople never understand why he chose to play with the black team, but Randy Joe did more than play ball: he taught some of his teammates to read. The problem is, though, that Keegan is a virtual Superhero, which detracts from the book and makes it inferior to *Bingo Long, Chappie and Me*, and *The Original Colored House of David*, which also feature black barnstorming teams.

Russell, Randy. *Caught Looking.* New York: Doubleday, 1992.

Rooster Franklin, ex-con, is asked to recover pitcher Randy Monroe's lucky glove which was lost when his car was stolen. A teenager, Bird, has the glove and an X-rated videotape of Monroe and a woman in compromising positions. Bird's game is blackmail, and Rooster has to restore order in the life of the Kansas City rookie. George Brett, Bo Jackson, and other real Royal players make appearances.

Salisbury, Luke. *The Cleveland Indian: The Legend of King Saturday.* Brooklyn: The Smith, 1992. (Brooklyn: The Smith, 1995.)

Lawyer Henry Harrison narrates the story of King Saturday, the Native American who plays for the Cleveland Indians in the 1890s. A fictional version of Louis M. Sockalexis, who may have been the reason for the Cleveland team to be known as the Indians, Saturday becomes a star, briefly, before his disappearance. Saturday's dream is to own a team, and Harrison becomes his partner—banking the money the ballplayer makes from gambling. Harrison finally realizes that Saturday is throwing games in order to make a fortune.

King Saturday disappears at the time that the notorious tavern, the Gin Palace, burns down and two Cleveland gamblers are murdered. Harrison traces the outfielder to Cuba and finds him playing with a black team (during the Spanish-American War). He is next reported as performing as the legendary El Indio in Mexico. Then in 1899, the lawyer gets word to bring Saturday's money to Leadville, Colorado. Following the robbing of a Standard Oil magnate, the ballplayer vanishes permanently, and Harrison returns to the East to marry Saturday's old girlfriend and to become president of the Rochester team.

The brief but calamitous career of King Saturday is dramatized, and he is presented as a larger-than-life hero/outlaw, like Robin Hood, who is seen as a victim of injustice in a society that exploits laborers just as the team owners exploit ballplayers. Although Saturday is romanticized in this role, the baseball and cultural scenes of the end of the nineteenth century are rendered with gusto. The real Chief Sockalexis hit .313 in ninety-four big league games before his heavy drinking reputedly ended his career. While inspiring tall tales as a result of his charisma and athletic prowess, the ballplayer's life does not quite match the fictional sensationalism of King Saturday.

Wilcox, Stephen. *All the Dead Heroes.* New York: St. Martin's Press, 1992.

"A T. S. Sheridan Mystery," it features the freelance reporter as he works on a story of Frank Wooley, the second black player of the Yankees. The Bronx Black Sheep was a second baseman from 1958 to 1966 and was then traded to the Phillies. He became a controversial figure due to his marriage to a white woman, a strong voice for civil rights, and a protest against the Vietnam War. He also was banned from baseball for gambling but was cleared in 1985 and eventually elected to the Hall of Fame.

Tim Heridan interviews Wooley, but the ex-second baseman is found dead a short time later—along with sportswriter Mike Delfey—in what the police call a murder-suicide. Sheridan, though, discovers that the two were murdered by Louis Garci, sponsor of poker scams at baseball memorabilia shows. Wooley, it turns out, had been blackmailing Garci. Since he played before free agency, the ex-Yankee did not make big money, which he thought he deserved.

Sheridan writes the story of Wooley, one of his childhood heroes, and reveals him as a victim of the old-fashioned system—both economically and racially. The social commentary tends to make the book better than most mysteries.

1993

Baker, Kevin. *Sometimes You See It Coming.* New York: Crown, 1993. (New York: Harper Perennial, 2003.)

Ellsworth Pippin, owner of the New York Mets, uses a computer to put the team on advanced management, which tends to reduce the players to statistics. The greatest of the Mets, John Barr, goes into a major slump midway in the season, as reported by his black teammate Ricky Falls (Old Swizzlehead). Falls and sportswriter Ellie Jay trace Barr's malaise to a letter sent by his mother, recently dead. The amateur sleuths find out that Barr's mother, years earlier, shot her husband and that consequently Barr gave up sports during his senior year in high school. With the help of the two friends, the Mets superstar recovers in time to lead the team to victory in the World Series. In the off-season, he is killed in a plane wreck while delivering medical supplies.

References to the trauma in the early baseball life of Ty Cobb and to the death of Roberto Clemente merely add to the melodrama here. The commendable acts of John Barr, Ricky Falls, and Ellie Jay are too obviously contrasted to the inhumane business deeds of Ellsworth Pippin and thus contribute to the book's didacticism.

Bennett, Richard. *Yankee Belle.* New York: Carlton, 1993.

Pitcher Ralph Dawson has a dream of buying a ranch and settling down with his wife Belle when his baseball days are over. His plan is to draw two salaries. He dons a disguise and pitches from the left as Reggie Duquesne. He then invents a dispute between the two so that there is an excuse for never appearing together. Lady sportswriter Lisa Storm wonders why Bella Dawson is so often seen in the company of Duquesne, but Manager Maxie Dugan is willing to accept the strange behavior as long as the Yankees keep winning.

The bizarre plot works until the seventh game of the World Series when Duquesne is felled by a line drive that injures his left arm. He removes the wig and mask and continues to pitch as the righthanded Dawson — and wins. The book is a prime candidate for one of the worst.

Dee, Jonathan. *The Liberty Campaign.* New York: Doubleday, 1993. (New York: Pocket Books, 1995.)

Gene Trowbridge is an advertising executive with a home in an exclusive neighborhood of Long Island. His son Jack is a pro baseball player in the Atlanta Braves system. Gene is caught in a moral dilemma when he discovers that his friend (and neighbor) is suspected of being a former Brazilian soldier responsible for torturing prisoners. Gene agonizes over making the right decision and decides to abandon the friend. In his analysis of the act and in an attempt to justify his career, Gene becomes obsessed with guilt and the corruptive influence of capricious power.

In contrast, Jack comes home after being released by the Braves and indulges in the glorification of his body and his ego. Even though he failed as a big leaguer, he is accepted as a hero in the neighborhood. Jack works out, drinks, copulates, and basks in luxury — before signing a contract with an AA team in the Eastern League. His father, meanwhile, tries to figure out how to adjust to what he considers an ambiguous value system.

The game of baseball is embedded in the morally suspect business world, and Gene Trowbridge wrestles with the question of proper behavior that his son is unaware of or ignores. Jack, unfortunately, is revealed to be more typical of American citizens. Although a marginal baseball novel, it is a commendable literary endeavor.

Enger, L. L. *Sacrifice.* New York: Pocket Books, 1993.
    The fourth installment of Gun Pedersen's exploits starts with the Minnesota recluse postponing his wedding and returning to his hometown in Michigan for the funeral of Harry Summers, former boyhood baseball star. Summers had disappeared in 1969, twenty years ago, but his skeleton has been found and identified. Unfortunately, a hammer belonging to Gun's father is found with the bones— making him a suspect. Gun, however, traces the murder to Summer's cousin. The killer's father had covered up the deed not only to protect his son but because he was ashamed of the decision of his nephew (Summers) to defect to Canada rather than to serve in Vietnam.
    Pedersen returns to his refuge in Minnesota, patches up his romance, and pursues his hobby of hitting baseballs into Stony Lake. The fast-paced action helps to make up for the predictable heroics of the stereotypical tough-guy detective.

Evers, Crabbe. *Fear in Fenway.* New York: William Morrow, 1993. (New York: Avon, 1994.)
    In the fourth Duffy House mystery, former Red Sox players are being murdered. Commissioner Chambliss puts Duffy on the job, and niece Petey joins in the investigation, which relates to the sale of the team by Patsy Dougherty. The victims turn out to be prospective buyers. Duffy and Petey find that Jake Stahl, who has an obsession with the Boston Red Sox, is the killer.
    After the case is closed, Duffy confesses to his niece and their friend Red Carney that he has lost his incentive to write Patsy Dougherty's memoirs— his one time goal. He feels that there is too much dirt in the business end of baseball. The former sportswriter prefers to talk about baseball, love, and nostalgia — including references to the Curse of the Bambino, a Sox nemesis until 2004.

Graham, Heather. *Spirit of the Season.* New York: Delacorte Press, 1993. (New York: Random House Value Publishing, 1995.)
    Becky Wexham, a single mother with three kids and no steady job, is further burdened when nine-year-old Davey, her nephew is orphaned and becomes part of her family. Davey is a Babe Ruth fan and prays to his hero nightly for help in making the Little League team, the Sharks, coached by Tim Yaegher, former big leaguer and a suitor of Becky. The ghost of Ruth appears and offers advice that makes Davey a star in the final game of the season. Becky and Tim wed, and the "reborn" Ruth gets to manage the Sharks -managing being a job that eluded the Babe in real life.
    Written by one of the queens of Romance, the book easily makes it near the bottom of the baseball novel list.

Honig, Donald. *Last Man Out.* New York: E.P. Dutton, 1993. (New York: Signet, 1994.)
    In his second appearance, ex-marine Joe Tinker is suffering from battle fatigue

(post-traumatic stress syndrome). It is 1946, and the New York sportswriter is languishing in his job. However, he is brought to life by the dilemma of Dodger rookie Harvey Tippen who is accused of murdering socialite Gloria Manley and her maid Maria Espardo. Tippen, a "playmate" of Manley, confesses to the crimes, but Tinker delves into the case and finds that Bobby Pilleter, a guest in Manley's house, is the murderer. A former Fascist in the Spanish Civil War, he had been recognized by the Spanish maid, and he killed her to keep his identity a secret. Gloria Manley, who appeared on the scene, was an inadvertent victim. The Dodger rookie had confessed because he had seduced the owner's wife and was afraid that his fanatical father would kill him if the indiscretion were discovered.

This is a step down from the first mystery of Tinker—*The Plot to Kill Jackie Robinson*. It should not be confused with Karlin's *The Last Man Out* (1969).

Moon, Scot. *Open Season.* Pittsburgh: Dorrance, 1993. (Xlibris Corporation, 2003.)

The year is 2007, and computer technology threatens humanity—a classic sci-fi theme. Ivan Ullery, owner of the new Indianapolis Leopards, plans to revolutionize baseball by computerizing the players and the stadium. He starts the project by drafting a career-minor-leaguer without the currently required college degree, to be the team leader—knowing that his program can convert mediocre players to winners. The scientific method of conditioning, including hypnotism and drugs, is initiated in spring training and results in a ninety-one game winning streak for the Leopards in the regular season.

When Ullery dies, the team is under the control of the general manager, Arthur Barron—the epitome of evil. Computers appear to be the cause of national disasters. Brad Sensor and Claudia Ullery, Ivan's daughter, suspect Barron as the evil force that haunts the country, and they fight to return stability to society—and to baseball. Somehow they succeed, and their mission serves as a warning of technological obsession and the abuses of power.

Similar to *The Last Man Out*, the plot here is also a formulaic good against evil. In its frightening vision of the future, this is a baseball version of *1984* (although of a much lesser quality).

Standiford, Les. *Done Deal.* New York: Harper Collins, 1993. (Brooklyn: Poisoned Pen Press, 2002.)

Jack Deal, former college baseball player and now a Miami building contractor, is threatened when he refuses to sell land to speculators who want to build a baseball stadium. His wife is kidnapped, but Deal enlists his secretary and a dwarf to help track down the criminals. Jack and Janice Deal survive and enjoy the new baseball franchise in Miami—in a typical thriller with baseball as a minor factor.

Valenza, Mark Allen. *Baseball and Benevolence.* Sarasota, NY: Bark Publishers, 1994.

Little George is an angel who habituates Tommy's Bar in New York City. He relates the story of his mission to preserve the faith of John Greco, star of the New York Highlanders. Greco is approached about throwing a game in order to cover his brother Natt's gambling debt. He refuses to cooperate, though, and wins the game with a grandslam after writing L-O-V-E in the dirt at homeplate.

Greco eventually becomes a scout for the Highlanders. He attends the last game to be played at Ruth Memorial Stadium, the team's home, and inspires his nephew (Natt's son) to hit a game-winning homer. John Greco himself had been inspired by the ghost of Babe Ruth who talked to him of baseball and benevolence. Greco then converts fans into believing in the redemptive power of baseball.

A 389 page fantasy, it is like a long version of *Spirit of the Season* — not a flattering kind of comparison.

Wade, Bob. *Line Drive.* Renfrew, Ontario: General Store Publishing House, 1993.

The Capital City Cataracts, a struggling National League team in Canada, are in danger of losing the franchise. Owner Jean La Sarre talks the general manager into making a trade for two aging veterans and a young pitcher. The deal is made, and Donnie Desmond, the pitcher, becomes a key in the team's drive for the pennant, which it wins. After losing the first two games of the World Series, the two veterans rise to the occasion and propel the Cataracts to a third-game win. As the book ends, the team seems to be on the threshold of success. The end is welcome.

1994

Bishop, Michael. *Brittle Innings.* New York: Bantam, 1994. (New York: Bantam, 1995.)

Danny Boles is a seventeen-year-old shortstop for the 1943 Highbridge Hellbenders of the Class C Chatahoochee Valley League. He is rendered temporarily mute as the result of being raped on the train taking him to Georgia (from Tenkiller, Oklahoma). Boles settles in on Jordan McKissick's team and rooms with Jumbo Hank Clerval, giant first baseman. In the course of the season, Danny discovers Jumbo's secret: he is Frankenstein. He has learned to play baseball in an attempt to pass as human, but he still has to recharge with lightning bolts encountered from the stadium roof. The Hellbenders win the pennant, but Boles' career is ended by an injury. Jumbo Clerval punishes the player who hurt his roommate — and then disappears.

Another friend of Danny Boles is Darius Satterfield, the black bus driver who is rumored to be the son of McKissick, team owner. Reputedly a great pitcher, segregation keeps Satterfiled off the team. However, when Boles, still crippled, watches the Hellbenders play an exhibition game against a black barnstorming team the next year, he discovers that the former bus driver is a star for the touring team.

In 1947, Boles gets a letter from Jumbo Clerval and later joins the giant on Attu, where he has discovered the grave of Dick Boles, Danny's father who was killed in World War II. Jumbo then decides to stay in exile in order to attempt to re-create himself — to become a real person. Danny Boles becomes a scout for the Phillies and the Braves; his story is told in *The Good Scout*, a biography by sportswriter Gabriel Stewart (who is interviewing the aged Boles as the novel begins).

A mixture of fantasy and social realism, the novel is surprisingly good. The ordeals of the three outsiders (the mute, the monster, and the mulatto) are rendered realistically — even when it comes to the dilemma of Frankenstein. The lives of minor league players in the segregated Deep South are reminiscent of those portrayed in *The Dixie Association,* but the tone here is more serious. The inclusion of the Frankenstein legend stresses the theme of discrimination against those who are different, and it is handled well enough to be a viable part of the plot.

Block, Lawrence. *The Burglar Who Traded Ted Williams.* New York: Dutton, 1994.

Bookseller Bernie Rhodenbarr is angry when his landlord raises the rent on the New York City apartment. Barely making a profit from Barnegat, a used bookstore in Greenwich Village, Rhodenbarr resorts to his former profession — burglary. In stealing a large sum of cash, he is also falsely accused of taking a valuable baseball card collection which includes a prize T-206 Honus Wagner and a Topps 1952 set. Along with Mickey Mantle, Babe Ruth, and Joe DiMaggio rarities, the collection includes a set of forty Ted Williams cards by Chalmers Mustard. By the time Rhodenbarr finds the real thief, many of the cards have been sold. He salvages the Chalmers Mustard set, however, and sells it at an extravagant price to his former landlord (who is unaware that Rhodenbarr has also bought the apartment building).

From a series of Bernie Rhodenbarr mysteries by the Edgar Award winning author, the book is enhanced by the mystique of the cards and the talks about books at Barnegat. Later novels that feature baseball cards are: *A Diminished Capacity, Cards, Bite of the Shark,* and *The Marinolli Treasure.*

Bouton, Jim, and Eliot Asinof. *Strike Zone.* New York: Viking, 1994. (New York: Signet, 1995.)

In 1993, the Chicago Cubs win ten straight games to tie the Phillies on the last day of the season. Due to a depleted pitching staff, the manager calls on Sam Ward, a thirty-two-year-old rookie, to get his first big league start in the decisive game — against the Phillies. Ward pitches well, but the calls of umpire Ernie Kolacka seem to be going against him. The reason is that the ump's friend, who had saved his life in Korea, has asked Kolacka to throw the game in order to get him out of a tight spot (presumably with gamblers). However, the Cubs go ahead, 5-4, on Sammy Sosa's eighth-inning homer, and in the ninth, Kolacka calls a third strike on the Phillies batter to end the game and give the Cubs the win, as his honesty triumphs. As Ward and his teammates celebrate, the umpire worries about his friend. He discovers, though, that the friend lied — all he really wanted was a fixed game that he could make a bundle on. Kolacka then has a private celebration.

The quality is far from Asinof's *Man on Spikes,* so the blame probably goes to the former pitcher.

Cohen, Celia. *Smokey O: A Romance.* Tallahassee: Naiad Press, 1994.

Smokey O'Neill plays firstbase for the Boston Colonials of the new Woman's Baseball League. She makes a scathing remark about Jill MacDonnell, star of the Delaware Blue Diamonds, and is then traded to Delaware. The war between the young first baseman and the older outfielder ensues. Before long, though, they become lovers, and the Blue Diamonds win the championship.

Smokey O has the honor of being the first lesbian baseball novel, but the credit ends there.

Enger, L. L. *The Sinner's League.* New York: Otto Penzler Books, 1994.

Gun Pedersen, in his fifth mystery, is married to journalist Carol Long and still residing in northern Minnesota. He tries to stay in shape by taking batting practice with the use of a home-made pitching machine. However, when his old friend Dianne Apple is murdered, he feels obligated, despite Carol's objection, to find the killer. The trail leads to a prominent lawyer, Harper Lamont. Assuming that Lamont will never be prosecuted for the crime, Pedersen kills him. He returns to the woods, now alienated from Carol, and does penance for his actions. The moral dilemma of Gun Pedersen elevates this book from the rest of the series.

Evers, Crabbe. *Tigers Burning.* New York: William Morrow, 1994. (New York: Avon Books, 1995.)

Former sportswriter Duffy House and his niece Petey appear for the fifth time as they investigate the burning of Tiger Stadium. The body of Kit Gleason, head of a stadium preservation organization, is found in the ruins. She was last seen with Tiger star Al Shaw, a black ex-con, which produces rumors and racial tension in Detroit. Black detective Holmes helps Duffy and Petey to track down Georgia Stallings—who is in love with Kit's husband. She shot Kit and hired an arsonist to burn the ballpark. As usual, Red Carney joins his friends for the celebratory conclusion. Typically, the book is spiced with baseball commentary—this time focusing on the history of the Detroit Tigers.

Granger, Bill. *Drover and the Designated Hitter.* New York: William Morrow, 1994. (New York: Avon Books, 1995.)

Jimmy Drover, a former sportswriter who currently works for a Las Vegas oddsmaker, is asked to check on the status of Homer White, a slugger for the Cubs who wants to be traded to the American League as a designated hitter. The former redneck carouser has apparently changed his life style. He acts like a gentleman and plans to marry his therapist, Helen Brown, who is black. The change in Homer worries his ex-wife, Mae, who is concerned about her financial future. She hopes to murder the couple before the wedding. Drover and his friend Kelly foil the proposed crime, though, and Homer White gets traded to Kansas City and begs Helen Brown to marry him.

The interracial affair is the only distinguishing feature of the mystery.

Jones, Matthew F. *The Elements of Hitting.* New York: Hyperion Books, 1994. (New York: Bloomsbury USA, 2000.)

Walter Innis is haunted by the past and alienated from the present. The former minor league pitcher (whose career was ended by arm trouble), has lost his wife and his job and is considering a blackmail project. Then he meets Jeannie Weatherrup and her son Billy, and his life begins to change. Innis becomes a Little

League coach and devises a list of the elements of hitting—which is a guide to life as well as baseball. He envisions a future in a love-filled home.

The redemptive powers of love and baseball serve as antidotes for the fragmentation and alienation often produced by a competitive society. The protagonist wrestles with morality while his best friend, a lawyer, functions in the amoral business world. The contrast, though, between virtue and immorality is too obvious.

LaFemina, James Garrett. *They Still Play Baseball on the Moon.* N.p.: Cosmo Publishing Company, 1994.

The Galactic League of Professional Baseball Clubs in the year 2287 is run by Commissioner Felton Malgammis. The game has been reduced to a mechanized business with preordained results. Players are ordered to follow scripts that determine the outcomes of the events—in other words, baseball games are routinely fixed.

Captain Harry Wright, awakened by a computer after circling the Solar System for 291 years, decides to restore baseball to its glory days. Since Earth is dead, the work begins on the moon. Wright joins forces with Gordy Mathewson on a new franchise. Wright and the descendant of the immortal Christy Mathewson help to make the Pioneers a team that plays to win. On Opening Day, the Pioneers rebel from the ordained script and produce a victory. A courageous reporter announces the news: "They still play baseball on the moon."

The sci-fi/fantasy novel is a playful but amateurish attack on the business aspect of baseball. It yearns for the pastoral game that never really existed—a utopian concept in which owners are not greedy and players have no need of a union or agents—an apt subject for fantasy.

Newman, Christopher. *Dead End Game.* New York: Putnam, 1994. (New York: Berkley Publishing Group, 1995.)

Willie Cintron, twenty-one-year-old star pitcher of the Kansas City Royals, is found dead from a heroin overdose during the playoff series with the Yankees. Lieutenant Joe Dante and his partner Jumbo Richardson of the NYPD encounter a variety of unsavory characters and dangerous situations in their investigation. They discover that Cintron's death is actually a murder. Anticlimactically, the Yankees best the Royals but lose a five-game World Series to the Giants—in an easily forgettable book.

Roemer, William F., Jr. *Mob Power Plays.* New York: S.P.I. Books, 1993.

FBI agent Bill Richards stalks the Chicago Mob, led by Rocko Robustelli. The children of the adversaries, however, are friends. Richards coaches a Little League team that includes his sons (Bill and Bob) and Robustelli's son (Ricky). Richards finally gets enough evidence on the hood to arrest him, but Robustelli is allowed his freedom in exchange for inside information. Ricky Robustelli eventually becomes a pitcher for the Cubs.

Written by a former member of the FBI, the book reads more like a report of a case study than a novel.

Soos, Troy. *Murder at Fenway Park.* New York: Kensington, 1994. (New York: Zebra Books, 1995.)

Mickey Rawlings, new Red Sox utility player, discovers the body of Red Corriden at Fenway. The apparent murder of the thirdbaseman draws Rawlings into a private investigation. He gets help from girlfriend Peggy Shaw and journalist Karl Landfors.

Ty Cobb is a suspect because two years earlier, in 1910, Corriden had played a deep thirdbase against Nap Lajoie so that he could beat out bunts and consequently win a batting title contested by the Detroit star. Rawlings finds out that his roommate, Billy Neal, along with notorious gambler/player Hal Chase, had bet against Cobb in the 1910 race for the best batting average. They bribed Corriden, but when they tried to get the thirdbaseman to fix games later, he rebelled, and Neal killed him with a bat.

Billy Neal then turns up dead in what is described as a hunting accident at the lodge of infamous gambler Arnold Rothstein. Rawlings thinks that Neal was murdered on the order of Bob Tyler, one of the Red Sox owners, who is also a gambler and may have been trying to cover his role in the Red Corriden affair. The utility man, after completing his investigation, is cut from the team shortly before it wins the pennant.

Rawlings tells his story years later as a guest of an exhibition game between the Red Sox and the Cubs; he is the oldest living members of both teams.

This is the first of the series in which the much-traded player appears. The Mickey Rawlings mysteries are steeped in baseball history from the early twentieth century. The inclusion of real people and events of the game as vital parts of the plot helps to place the book (and its sequels) into the elite of baseball mysteries.

1995

Abrahams, Peter. *The Fan.* New York: Warner Books, 1995. (New York: Fawcett, 2002.)

The life of Gil Renard, knife salesman, is in decline, but his love for the Sox and the team's acquisition of Bobby Rayburn give him some hope. He loses his job, though, and turns to burglary and murder. One of his victims is Primo, the Sox shortstop, who would not yield his number to Rayburn. When the Sox outfielder goes into a slump, however, Renard assumes that it is due to a loss of interest in baseball. He kidnaps Sean, Rayburn's son, and uses him in order to challenge the slugger to a pitcher-batter duel. It takes place, and Renard, the former Little League pitcher, is no match for Rayburn, the current big leaguer. Renard's murder attempt is then foiled by a policeman and reporter Jewel Stern.

Renard escapes and later attempts to kill Rayburn during a game. The police stop the act and kill the criminal in the process. The Sox, led by a rejuvenated Rayburn, go on to a World Series victory.

The movie version, with Robert DeNiro excelling as the crazed killer, is more impressive than the novel. The book, however, presents a credible portrait of a psychopathic baseball fan.

Bechard, Gorman. *Balls.* New York: Plume, 1995.

Louise "Balls" Gehrig is the first baseman of the Manhattan Meteorites of the National League in 2000. Dan Quayle is now commissioner of baseball, the Yankees have moved to New Jersey, and the Supreme Court has ruled that females can play in the majors. An English major at Yale, Louise encourages her teammates to read. Her education helps her to handle the pressure of being the first to break the gender barrier. Her private life, though, is complicated by her mother's romance with Meteorite catcher Bob Dixon who is pursuing the single season homer record, and her own love for Cole Robinson, pitcher for the New Jersey Yankees.

Louise Gehrig is a victim of bigotry and a target of tabloids through the season, but she perseveres and helps the team win the pennant while winning the Rookie of the Year Award. Bob Dixon, however, is out of the World Series when he takes a bullet from a ballpark sniper that he thought was meant for Gehrig. He discovers later that it was fired at him by a Roger Maris fan in an attempt to protect his idol's record. Manhattan beats New Jersey in the World Series anyway, and Gehrig, now pregnant, donates her winner's share to Planned Parenthood. In the off season, she moves into a Victorian house with Cole Robinson.

Essentially a farce, the book attacks sexists and fundamentalists while promoting the feminism of the protagonist. It is less sensational than *The Sensuous Southpaw* (1977), *She's on First* (1987), and *A Grand Slam* (1973). *Balls* is closer to the quasi-realism of *Can't Miss* (1987) but with a tongue-in-check tone that the latter book does not possess. To this point, though, there has not been a quality novel featuring the first-female-in-the-majors.

Bookbinder, Bernie. *Out at the Old Ballgame.* Bridgehampton, NY: n.p., 1995.

Scrappy Schwrtznbgr, owner-manager of the New York Gents, is appalled when star Dick "Rootie" Toote comes out of the closet. He tries to sell the first baseman to the Yankees, but when other gay players are identified, an idea is born. Despite the protests of the Baseball Establishment, Scrappy proceeds to put together an all-gay team — and goes on to win the 1996 pennant.

Olivia Jacob (O. J.) Cobb is the sportscaster for the Gents, and she promotes the homosexual theme. Journalist Stan Mann, on the other hand, leads the homophobia crusade against the team. The season comes down to the seventh game of the World Series— and the Gents lose to a gay pitcher of the Yankees. Olivia looks forward to seeing her cousin Natalie play for the team next year.

Like the "first female" books, the "all gay" novel stresses the problem of overcoming bigotry in the baseball world — which is a mirror of society. Humor is the key ingredient in the attack on prejudice, but the satire hardly matches that of Jane Austen or Jonathan Swift.

Cartwright, Gene. *I Never Played Catch with My Father.* Los Angeles: Falcon Creek, 1995.

James Phalen of Rosedale, Texas, is a success on Wall Street, but he regrets that he did not become a pro baseball player and that he never experienced a playful moment with his father. In an attempt to find inner peace, he returns to Rosedale. He learns that Little League Baseball has died — rather than integrate. He decides to finance the building of John Q. Phalen Park (named for his father) and to bring back the game. At the opening of the ballpark, Phalen watches the integrated Rosedale Dodgers, with a girl pitcher, beat the Waco Giants. The redemptive ingredients of love and baseball bring him the happiness that money could not. A preachy, sentimental book, it is marginal both as a baseball novel and a work of quality.

Cowgill, Kent. *The Cranberry Trail: Misfits, Dreamers, and Drifters on the Heartland Road.* Rochester, MN: Lone Oak Press, 1996.

Thirty years after the Tabelard Honey Bees lost seventy-six college baseball games in succession, the team captain calls a teammate (the narrator) with a proposition. Curt Knight asks Jeffrey "Shoeoff" Shoemaker to make a trip to South Fork, Nebraska, as a favor to their old coach, Harold Heddes, who supposedly intends to rebuild an old church into living quarters. Most of the oddball team assembles and, while riding in Heddes' van, each one tells his story in an imitation of Chaucer's *Canterbury Tales.*

In a town along the way, they are challenged to a game by the local rednecks. The Bees, suffering from physical decay, are in trouble until the team trainer appears on a motorcycle — with her lesbian partner. Allison Bathgate takes over at third-base and homers to put the Bees in contention. However, she is beaned and is taken to the nearest hospital. From her bed, Allison works her healing magic on Coach Heddes (suffering from the ex-jock syndrome) and also gives a boost to the life of Shoeoff with her positive philosophy.

Once again, the healing or redemptive aspects of love and baseball are stressed. Feminism is also a major theme. The humor and the classical format help to produce at least a moderate success.

Faust, Ron. *Fugitive Moon.* New York: Forge, 1995. (New York: Tor Books, 1996).

Teddy Moon, a relief pitcher and mental patient known as the Moonman, flees to the West after slugging the manager. Treated temporarily at the Alamo Ranch Sanitorium in New Mexico, he tracks down ex-wives and current girlfriends, but he cannot escape from the pressure he feels from rightwing society that is punishing him for being a nonconformist. Moon eventually rejoins the team but is shot while on the mound. He recovers from his wound and, donning a blanket cape, returns to the ballpark as Baseballman. He gets a standing ovation when appearing on the field and then retreats to the dugout — which proves to be a hostile environment.

The madcap adventures of the Moonman are frowned upon in a commercialized and standardized America of the 1980s. As a unique individual, Moon puts himself in jeopardy and expects to be punished. He confronts conformity in the tradition of the transcendentalists (like Emerson and Thoreau) and vies for a place among legendary fictional characters like Huck Finn and Holden Caulfield -and although he falls short, the authorial attempt is commendable.

Ford, Richard. *Independence Day.* New York: Knopf, 1995. (New York: Vintage, 1996.)

Frank Bascombe, ex-sportswriter, is a real estate salesman in New Jersey who is languishing in an "Existence Period." His ex-wife has remarried and taken their two children to Connecticut, and he is content to merely exist without commitment and with no ties to his former life. On a July Fourth vacation with his troubled teenage son, though, Bascombe has an epiphany in Cooperstown, New York, home of the Hall of Fame. While trying to help his son in a batting cage, he realizes that a new phase of life is possible. Bascombe resolves to resume a search for a meaningful existence that includes an involvement in human relationships.

Although dealing with the familiar redemptive theme (and arbitrarily classified as a baseball novel), the book does no harm to Ford's reputation as a respected mainstream author.

Glading, Gregory T. *64 Intruder.* Huntington, WV: University Editions, 1995.

Bill Waldron teaches English at Filbert High School in Philadelphia. Estranged from his wife, Laura, and son, Randy, he drinks a lot and follows the Phillies in the 1990s. It is the 1964 season that he experienced with his father that haunts him, however. He recalls the glory of Shibe Park and the heroics of Stan Lopata, his father's favorite player. But it is also the year his father died in a bar fight as he was defending the reputation of the Phillies, who blew a big late-season lead and lost the pennant to the Cardinals.

As an adult, Bill is hurt in an accident and spends seventeen days in a coma. During this period, he replays the 1964 season. Later, while searching for his son, Bill falls off a cliff and awakes in a limousine with Drago, a Mephistopheles-like figure, who proclaims that Bill is the man who changed history by winning the '64 pennant for the Phillies. He takes Bill to Yankee Stadium, but in the fantasy World Series the Phillies lose to the Yankees, and Drago releases Bill to the Hell of his own making — the modern Philadelphia.

The ending is happy, though, as the family is reunited. The attempt to create psychological realism clashes with the Faustian fantasy to produce a muddled result. The book is almost saved by the clever use of references to real players and baseball events in imaginary situations.

Gordon, Alison. *Striking Out.* Toronto: McClelland & Stewart, 1995. (Toronto: McClelland & Stewart, 1996.)

The fourth Kate Henry mystery finds the Toronto sportswriter on a break from baseball during the strike of 1994. When a homeless woman from the neighborhood disappears, Kate starts a search. In the process, she battles the Reverend Ken MacKenzie, leader of an anti-abortion group. She also gets involved in a racially tense situation as her boyfriend, Andy Munro, is shot by a black kid — and Andy's police partner retaliates by killing the kid. Kate prevails and finds the missing woman, the victim of an abusive husband.

While solving crimes, practicing feminism, and nursing the wounded, Kate keeps up with the baseball news through her friend Joe Kelsey, the only acknowledged homosexual in the game. A typical Kate Henry book, it was short listed for the Arthur Ellis Award for Best Crime Novel.

Granger, Bill. *The New York Yanquis.* New York: Arcade Press, 1995.

Yankee owner George Bremerhaven is disgusted about paying a fortune to players who do not produce championships. He fires twenty-four of them and makes a deal with the State Department and Fidel Castro to hire Cubans as replacements. Veteran relief pitcher Ryan Shawn is retained because he speaks Spanish. Shawn, also the narrator, manages the New Yanquis (sometime in the near future) and contends for first place despite the added pressures of keeping the American government and Castro happy. The government prefers that the Cubans do not win, and the chief Cuban is concerned about the welfare of his countrymen — and perhaps their defection. Shawn also has to train the ballplayers into tolerating the American way of life while getting their best performances on the field.

The team wins the American League Championship as the pitcher-manager stars in the clinching game. Before the World Series, though, the Yanquis are bought by Deke Williams, Shawn's friend who also becomes the first black owner in the majors. Shawn does not report on the outcome of the Series, but he does say that Bremerhaven, who he considers a rightwing money-grubbing bastard, has taken the job of ambassador to Guatemala.

Known for his November Man spy series and the Grover mysteries, Granger here emphasizes the owner-player conflict in a satirical fable. The melodramatic heroism is the major flaw.

Grant, Robert. *The December Rose.* Carmel, IN: Islands End Publishers, 1995.

Luke Hanlon, star of the Cincinnati Reds in the fifties and sixties, returns to the team at the age of sixty-five. He has been rejuvenated by a miracle drug and performs heroics once again. Commissioner Vossler suspends him when the drug is declared illegal, but the FDA approves it. Hanlon is reinstated and leads the Red to the World Series.

A parallel story deals with Ty Hartman, a representative of the modern player. He has an agent and is signed by the highest bidder, but he develops a drug problem and is put in rehab.

The fantasy, then, contrasts the Hero of the Good Old Days with the contemporary Spoiled Athlete of post-free-agency. Hanlon contributes to charities anonymously and works on a ranch in the off-season to stress the old-fashioned concepts of morality and innocence that are associated with the pastoral image of the game. However, the case is grossly overstated.

Hoyt, Richard. *Japanese Game.* New York: Forge, 1995.

James Burlane, ex–CIA employee, is hired by the Vice President of the United States to find his kidnapped daughter. Barlane finds Linda Shive in Japan where she is the sex slave of Kobayashi, owner of the Yokohama Stars. Burlane rescues her and kills the villain. He also judges that Japanese baseball, with its concept of Wa, the spirit of harmony (which makes tie games respectable) is inferior to the American game. The United States, then, triumphs over Japan and its culture. The pace is fast and the propaganda obvious.

Kiraly, Sherwood. *A Diminished Capacity.* New York: Berkley, 1995. (New York: Berkley Publishing Group, 1997.)

Roland Zerbs (Uncle Rollie to narrator Cooper Zerbs, journalist) is considered eccentric in La Porte, Missouri. He edits fish poetry, for instance, that is created by hooking lines to typewriter keys. However, Rollie owns a 1909 tobacco baseball card of Wildfire Schulte of the Chicago Cubs. Cooper and his uncle take the card to Chicago to see what price it will bring. At a card show, people try to take advantage of Rollie, who is described as having a diminished capacity. The Schulte card eventually sells for $105,000. Rollie's luck continues when they return to La Porte, as the Purple Cow Press prints the fish poetry, citing it as experimental and multicultural verse.

The amusing capers of Uncle Rollie and friends are an improvement over the author's *California Rush* (1990). Block's *The Burglar Who Traded Ted Williams* (1994) is the only other entry in the subgenre of baseball card novels at this point (with more to come, however).

Klinkowitz, Jerry. *Basepaths.* Baltimore: The Johns Hopkins University Press, 1995.

Three of the players from *Short Season and Other Baseball Stories* (1988) return to the Mason City Royals under new manager Ken Boyenga, a former major league catcher. However, farcical events begin when his estranged wife, Lois, decides to move to the Iowa town. At the same time, two of Boyenga's ex-teammates show up for a baseball card show. On the day of the show, the rowdy friends get in a mess with a New-Nazi. At the ballpark, the game is forfeited when the president of the team incites the crowd against the umpires. To top it off, Boyenga loses his job.

The author's first book is a humorous portrait of minor league life. *Basepaths* is less effective as the zany off-field events that dominate are too far-fetched.

Nighbert, David. *Shutout.* New York: St. Martin's Press, 1995.

Bull Cochran, in his third mystery, accompanies girlfriend Molly (Detective Sergeant Emily Louise Flanagan of the Galveston Police Department) to Knoxville to help her with a family problem. The former minor league pitcher foils the plot of an illegitimate Flanagan who murders Molly's Uncle Dewey and plans to steal a fortune. The typical hardboiled mystery does not directly deal with baseball.

Ross, Calvin. *The Aliens of Summer.* Napa, CA: Distant Star, 1995.

On an advanced technological planet, Ball Four, baseball Commissioner Tern discloses that the Cleveland Indians of Earth have been infiltrated with Ball-Fourian players. Belteron, the brightest star on Ball Four, decides to be bio- fashioned as Lou Gehrig and to invade American baseball on his own. Playing as Billy Icarus for the San Francisco Giants, he introduces "the mind game" of his planet and makes the Giants contenders. He explains to his teammates, after revealing his identity, that the Earth's ruling class suppresses technical knowledge through the use of religion. As both pitcher and catcher, he leads the Giants to a win over the Indians in the World Series.

It turns out, though, that Tern and Dr. Avion of Ball Four are controlling the action behind the scenes. They had planned to let Belteron/Icarus join the Giants and to teach the Ball-Fourian baseball techniques to Americans as a lesson to the citizens of Ball Four to strive for perfection. It is an attempt to change the complacency and devolution on the planet into progressive evolution. Belteron continues to play ball at home, but as Icarus he also plays on Earth, and one season he wins the Cy Young Award, breaks the home run record, and bats .435 — to prove that the combination of baseball and technology used on Ball Four is superior (once again).

Applying advanced technology to the game is a standard sci-fi concept, but the book also stresses the necessity for continuous education in which knowledge must be a factor in moving society toward a humanitarian goal. Rather than being the conventional mad scientists, Tern and Avion are benevolent educators who try to improve universal conditions through baseball. The typical dystopian technocracy is avoided here — a unique view in baseball sci-fi.

Shoemaker, Rob. *The Final Game.* Sudbury, MI: Featherland Press, 1995.

Walter Johnson and Cy Young each pitch an inning of an exhibition game in 1933 at a county fair in Ohio. Willis Hudlin, a Cleveland pitcher, saves a ball signed by both, which is eventually inherited by his grandson, Tim Pope, a Red Sox pitcher in the nineties.

In the last game to be played at Fenway Park (due to structural damage caused by an earthquake), Pope pitches and bats the Red Sox to a World Series win over the Marlins. Pope, who goes 26-6 during the season despite being diagnosed with multiple sclerosis, wins the sixth game of the Series and then enters the seventh game in extra innings and shuts down the Marlins. The pitch that records the last out is made with the 1933 ball (signed by Johnson and Young) that has been smuggled into the game. Looking at the ball (that took a magical hop), Pope discovers that his own signature has joined those of the Hall-of-Famers and includes the date "October 31, The Final Game."

Years later, Pope appears at the Fenway Park Museum. He is in a wheel chair but is accompanied by a wife and two children. The conclusion summarizes the message of the inspirational fantasy, which is burdened by unlikely heroics and patronizing preaching.

Soos, Troy. *Murder at Ebbets Field.* New York: Kensington Publishing Corporation, 1995.

Mickey Rawlings is a utility infielder for John McGraw's Giants in 1914, but he does some acting on the side. He appears in *Florence at the Ballpark,* a movie starring Florence Hampton and Tom Kelly — along with Casey Stengel of the Dodgers. When Rawlings discovers the body of Hampton, the sister of friend Karl Landfors, he searches for the killer with the help of Margie Turner and Landfors, a muckraking journalist. They eventually find that actor Arthur Carlyle is guilty — and that he also poisoned William Daley, the owner of the Dodgers and husband of Florence Hampton.

Meanwhile, the pennant race is on, and unfortunately for the Giants, 1914 is the year of the Miracle Boston Braves who rally to win the pennant and sweep the Philadelphia Athletics in the World Series. The Federal League is also trying to establish itself, and Rawlings has a contract with the Brooklyn Tip-Tops, but he destroys it rather than to gamble on the future. McGraw offers him a spot with the

Giants for 1915, and the infielder, whose dream is to hit .250 and play in a World Series, hopes for the rebirth that comes with the spring.

The second Mickey Rawlings book is only mediocre as a mystery. However, as a novel that deals with baseball, it is an entertaining and informative look at the 1914 season. Real players and events are embedded in the plot to help bring the book to life.

Tomkins, D. Michael. *The 30 Hit Season.* Seattle: Peanut Butter Publishing, 1995. (Seattle: Peanut Butter Publishing, 2001.)

Despite hitting only .268 in a slowpitch softball league, David Pasteur dreams of getting thirty consecutive hits in major league baseball. The forty-three-year-old attorney is inspired by the signing of Bly Levin, a forty-four-year-old pitcher, to a Mariners contract. Pasteur convinces the owner of the Seattle team to give him a chance to play. The objections of the lawyer's wife, Manager Lou Piniella, and Commissioner George Will are offset by Cyrus Andvik's determination to inspire the slumping Mariners by signing Pasteur to a contract. He is used as a pinch-hitter and proceeds to make the dream a reality by "bleeding cheap hits" that manage to elude opposing fielders and to win games for the Mariners. In the World Series against the Dodgers, the thirtieth consecutive hit occurs in the fifth game. In the seventh game, though, Pasteur is sent into bat with the score tied in the ninth — and the bases loaded. He swings feebly at the third strike — but the catcher interferes, and the winning run scores.

Somewhat reminiscent of *It Happens Every Spring* and *The Year the Yankees Lost the Pennant,* this fantasy does not have the charm of the earlier books. The humor, however, keeps it interesting.

Willington, Kurt. *The Spy in a Catcher's Mask.* Troy, MI: Momentum Books Limited, 1995.

The life of Morris (Moe) Berg, catcher, spy, and panelist on "Information Please," is fictionalized here. He attends the Temple Beth-El Hebrew School, Barrington High School, and Princeton. He is a scholar but is a good enough shortstop to play for the Brooklyn Dodgers—labeled as good field-no hit. In 1927, Berg becomes a catcher for the White Sox. His best year in the majors is 1929, when he hits .289 in 109 games. In 1932, Berg joins the Senators of Manager Walter Johnson, and in 1934 he is traded to the Indians.

It is in the '34 off-season that Moe Berg's career as a spy commences. He is recruited for a team of major league all-stars that tours Japan (as fictionally described in *Eight Corners of the World*). Berg's secret job is to take photos of Japanese military sites for the U.S. State Department. The pictures are later used by General Doolittle. After retiring from baseball in 1939, he becomes part of Wild Bill Donovan's Office of Strategic Services and helps to determine Germany's nuclear potential. When the Germans try to arrest him while he is playing baseball on a military team in Switzerland, Berg and his crew make an adventurous escape. After the war, Berg is offered a job of deterring Fascism in South America.

His work for the State Department, his proficiency in twelve languages, and the knowledge that he demonstrated on the radio program, "Information Please," made Moe Berg a legendary American. His .243 lifetime batting average, however, does not qualify him for baseball fame. The novel is more interesting as biography or history than as creative literature.

1996

Covington, Vicki. *The Last Hotel for Women.* New York: Simon & Schuster, 1996. (Tuscaloosa: University of Alabama Press, 1999.)

In 1961, Birmingham's Commissioner of Public Safety, Bull Connor, observes freedom riders being attacked by the KKK. The civil rights movement is threatening Connor's world of orderly segregation, and he seeks consolation at the hotel run by Dinah Fraley. Her dead mother was Connor's true love, and he assumes that Dinah is his daughter. However, when she offers protection to a female freedom rider, his haven is disturbed. Further trouble comes when Dinah's husband, a foundry worker who pitches for a company team, invites black catcher Nathan Stamps and his teammates to practice with the white team. Now his surrogate family is instigating integration, and it drives the legendary racist, a symbol of the Old South, to the brink of madness.

The socially relevant novel pictures Dixie on its deathbed as "outside agitators" and moral forces from within are changing the times. Bull Connor is a victim of future shock, and integrated baseball is a sign of a new day.

Daniel, David, and Chris Carpenter. *Murder at the Baseball Hall of Fame.* New York: St Martin's Press, 1996.

While visiting the Hall of Fame in Cooperstown, New York, private eye Frank Branco witnesses the death of Herb Frawley in a car crash. The local police take no interest in an investigation, so Frawley's ex-wife hires Branco to check out the alleged accident. He finds that Frawley was an ex-big leaguer whose career declined after the death of Raylynn Hazlitt, who was in love with Frawley's roommate Jack Livingstone, a long-time major league star. Branco and his black friend, Ty Gilchrist, a wheelchair-bound ex-football player, trace Raylynn's connection with a pornographer to Livingstone. Stan Nordgren killed Raylynn, and Livingstone covered it up. Frawley knew about the crime, and it bothered him to the point that his hitting was affected. After Frawley quit baseball, he blackmailed Livingstone and Nordgren — and his death was arranged to look like an accident.

Although a run-of-the-mill mystery, the book is enhanced by the inclusion of real players and by making the fictional ones (compete with stats) seem credible.

Fisher, Nancy. *Special Treatment.* New York: Signet Books, 1996. (Backinprint.com, 2000.)

When three superheroes suddenly emerge for the New York Comets, something unusual is suspected by Dr. Adam Salt and female reporter Robin Kennedy. They discover that the players are products of an experiment by team owner, Morgan Hudson, who has been pumping a compressed gas containing a special hormone into the training room of the Pro Club. When the three players workout together, they imbibe the hormone that enhances their performance, but Dr. Salt suspects that it may be lethal.

Kenny Reese, a member of the trio, hits a homer that wins the World Series for the Comets, but he drops dead at homeplate. The owner commits suicide, and Commissioner Locke and Inspector Lorenzo decide to cover up the story to protect the integrity of the game. Salt and Kennedy agree to keep the hormone a secret.

The book is presumably a warning against the use of performance-enhancing drugs. The decision to stifle the truth is a questionable conclusion, however, that seems to make the protection of cultural icons more important than morality and the physical threat to athletes.

Fowler, Karen Jay. *The Sweetheart Season.* New York: Henry Holt, 1996. (New York: Ballantine Books, 1998).

Irini Doyle is nineteen in 1947 when she becomes a member of the Sweetwheat Sweethearts, a woman's baseball team founded by Henry Collins to promote his breakfast cereal. He also creates Maggie Collins—a fictional advisor on cooking, etiquette, and household hints. The team tours the area and plays against men. The '47 season ends early, though, when Ruby Redd, the star pitcher disappears. (She emerges years later on a male team.)

An offshoot of the promotion of Sweetwheat cereal by the touring team is the search for husbands. The men of Magrit, Minnesota, did not return after World War II. Irini is interested in Thomas Holcrow, until he turns out to be an FBI agent searching for communists. She eventually marries Walter Collins, Henry's grandson, but Irini is more liberated than most women of her era. Her rebellious side is revealed in her daughter, who narrates the story during the sixties. As part of a rebellious decade, she is an advocate of civil rights and a protestor of the Vietnam War.

Over the years, the advice in the Maggie Collins columns becomes militant. Taking on a feminist tone, they urge females to break away from religion, reputation, and romance — the three Rs that suppress them. Although the author of more recent articles is not revealed, the philosophy of Irini and her daughter is evident. The emphasis of the novel, then, is the struggle to overcome sexism. Irini and her daughter are iconoclastic in their attempts to battle against conformity—and the restrictions of traditions that are meant to keep them in bondage to males. Playing baseball is a rebellious act that sets the tone of the book—which is superior to *A League of Their Own.*

Hester, M. L. *Another Jackie Robinson.* Greensboro, NC: Tudor, 1996.

Sam Bean owns the Behemoths, a Class D team in Alma, North Carolina, in 1953. In order to boost attendance, he sends a trio of scouts to search for a Darker Person who will attract a black audience. Fourteen-year-old E. Z. Poole narrates the quest he undertakes to find another Jackie Robinson. Accompanying the young second baseman are Doc Stevens, an unlicensed team doctor, and Pop, the geriatric manager of the Behemoths.

In Cleo, Florida, the three misfits stumble across Josh Loganberry, who can hit and pitch like Babe Ruth. Unfortunately, he is not black, but with the application of 30-1 oil, they turn him into a Patagonian in hope that he will pass for a black or a foreigner. Reverend Elihu Johnson owns the town, however, and he becomes Loganberry's agent when he realizes that big money may be available. The dimwitted pig farmer signs with the Alma team and leads it to a 60-3 record as a pitcher and slugger. Sam Bean manages to persuade the major league Zephyrs to play the Behemoths in an exhibition game so that his product can be exposed. Loganberry holds the big leaguers in check for seven innings, but then he gets hit in the head and loses his stuff. The Zephyrs win the game 7-2 when Poole, consumed by guilt for his part in the exploitation of Loganberry (who just wants to go home to his pigs and to be a volunteer fireman) commits an error that leads to a big rally.

Though Reverend Johnson still hopes to capitalize on his role as an agent, Bean and the alcoholic Doc Stevens, who realize that Loganberry really dislikes baseball, blackmail the preacher with photos of his sexual exploits. Then they arrange a fake death for the country bumpkin so that he can go home to feed his pigs and to fight fires with no fear of being bothered by baseball agents or scouts.

E. Z. Poole is an imitation of Huck Finn as he narrates in dialect. He also has the moral concerns of Huck, and they are transferred to the adults who opt for altruism rather than profiteering. The imitation, though, is too obvious, and the moral victory is melodramatic.

Kinsella, W. P. *If Wishes Were Horses.* New York: Harper Collins, 1996.

Joe (Kid) McCoy, a former unsuccessful major league pitcher, gets fired from a newspaper for writing an article on UFOs. Then he is charged with kidnapping an ambassador's baby and while on the run makes the FBI's Ten Most Wanted List. He flees to his home state of Iowa and relates his predicament to Ray Kinsella (of *Shoeless Joe*) and Gideon Clarke (of *The Iowa Baseball Confederacy*). He also talks about his dream of an alternate life with Maureen, a high school girlfriend.

Still a fugitive, McCoy visits Maureen and discovers that, after a loveless and childless marriage, she is dying of cancer. The tag on her wrist identifies her as Maureen McCoy. He locks the authorities out of her hospital room, but as the police close in, his alternate life seems to take over, and freedom seems possible.

Kid McCoy's existence in parallel worlds, whether real or imaginary, is a comedown from the magical realism of Kinsella's best books. The lack of baseball action also tends to be disappointing.

McDonald, Sheri. *Diamonds.* Sisters, OR: Palisades, 1996.

In a Palisades Contemporary Romance, a lady sportscaster, Casey Foster, inherits an AA baseball team, The Bend Bachelors of Oregon. She works to earn the respect of her coaches and players, but she gives special attention to Tucker (Big Time) Boyd, former major league pitcher who is trying to make a comeback from a shoulder injury. Casey, though, believes that God is more important than baseball, and she transmits her tenet to Boyd. Thus when he is called up to the big league Phoenix Stars, he decides to return to Casey's team even after a successful stint at the top. This is, apparently, the kind of sacrifice expected in a Christian Romance.

Shilstone, Steve. *Chance.* New York: Breakaway Books, 1996.

Chance Caine spends twenty-two years as the shortstop of the Lions in the National League. Although the Lions never win a World Series in this period, Caine's hitting records make him a sure Hall-of-Famer. At his retirement, Chance Caine Day, crazed sportswriter Ben Blessee attempts to kill him. Caine survives the bullet wounds, however, and twenty years later has a wife and teenage kids. One of them is an illegitimate nineteen-year-old shortstop in the Lion's farm system.

The story is told in diary entries, interviews, and journal "personalisms," but the attempts to spice up the life of a boring superhero do not work. The literary format, perhaps an attempt at metafiction (a book about the creative process), fails to bring the protagonist to life.

Soos, Troy. *Murder at Wrigley Field.* New York: Kensington Publishing Group, 1996.

Because many players are in the military in 1918, Mickey Rawlings is playing secondbase for the Cubs. He accepts the proposal of Cub owner Charles Weegham to look into the source of the anti-German propaganda that is keeping attendance down. Then Willie Kaiser, Cub shortstop and brother of Rawlings' current girlfriend, Edna Chapman, is murdered. The suspicion falls on Bennett Harrington, another Cub owner, who wants to move the team to Terrapin Park in Baltimore. Rawlings discovers that Harrington, feeling the pressure of his investigation, had hired a man to kill him — and that Willie Kaiser was shot by mistake - Rawlings was the intended target.

When Edna Chapman kills Harrington to avenge her bother's death, Rawlings protects her by hiding the murder weapon. He then joins the army — even though the Cubs have cinched the pennant. Playing in the World Series is one of his main ambitions, but Mickey Rawlings feels that there are values more important than personal goals.

The usual baseball action, featuring real players and events from 1918, is present, but the main focus here is on Rawlings as moral arbiter who covers up a justified murder and bypasses his dream of participating in a World Series. He reports that the Cubs lost to the Red Sox (due to the pitching of Carl Mays and Babe Ruth) and that Weegham sold a controlling interest of the Chicago team to Wrigley, but those events are secondary to those of World War I and to the conscience of a man who is more than just a baseball player. Again, Soos proves to be the best of the baseball mystery writers.

Winegardner, Mark. *The Veracruz Blues.* New York: Viking Press, 1996. (New York: Penguin, 1997.)

The Mexican League's raid of American baseball in 1946 is told in part by Frank Bullinger, journalist and would-be novelist. Contributing to the narration are three participants in the League: Fireball Smith, Roberto Ortiz, and Danny Gardella. Another part-time narrator is Maria Felix, an actress and girlfriend of Jorge Pasqual, the man behind the raid and the commissioner of the Mexican League.

Angered by the reserve clause and overwhelmed by the return of the players who participated in World War II, twenty-seven Americans jump to Mexico in 1946, including Sal Maglie, Max Lanier, Mickey Owen, Vern Stephens, and Danny

Gardella. African Americans also opt to play there as Jackie Robinson has not yet integrated the majors. Fireball Smith, for one, is angered that Robinson is the player to be considered for the noble experiment.

Bullinger, while visiting Ernest Hemingway in Cuba, presents the manuscript of his novel to the famous writer (which he never reads). Among Hemingway's guests are Babe Ruth, Gene Tunney, Dolph Luque, Maria Felix, and Jorge and Alfonso Pasqual. In the revelry, the manuscript gets lost, and Bullinger instead recreates the story of the Veracruz Blues as they compete in the 1946 Mexican League.

With the integrated assemblage of players, the League approaches the level of the majors, but Pasqual's dream of a third major league does not work out. After the 1948 season, the new commissioner puts a quota on foreign players. Though Happy Chandler, American commissioner, banned Mexican participants for five years, Gardella sued, and the players won amnesty in 1949. Older black players like Fireball Smith and Ray Dandridge never did get a shot at the majors, though, and of the league jumpers from 1946, only Maglie and Stephens went on to stardom.

The novel is memorable for its dramatization of the 1946 season with the players and personalities, most of them real, who are involved in the action. It could use a stronger focal point, but is good enough to be a New York Times Book Review Notable Book of the Year and to be nominated for the 1997 Los Angeles Times Book Prize.

Zubro, Mark. *Rust on the Razor.* New York: St. Martin's, 1996.

The sixth Tom and Scott mystery in a long series, this is the one in which Scott Carpenter comes out of the closet. The major league pitcher announces his homosexuality and becomes the victim of a backlash — including the loss of a big endorsement deal. He then gets injured and goes on the disabled list. Along with his partner, teacher Tom Mason, he visits the Carpenter family in Georgia when his father has a heart attack. The gay couple has to ward off the KKK and a Neo-Nazi, but they find time to free Scott's sister from a murder charge.

The series uses a baseball player as a means of stressing homophobia in society. Baseball is essentially nonexistent — although Scott Carpenter is portrayed as a famous pitcher who incredibly threw two no-hitters in a World Series.

1997

Allen, Garrison. *Baseball Cat.* New York: Kensington Publishing Corporation, 1997. (New York: Kensington Publishing Corporation, 1998.)

Penelope Warren, owner of Mycroft and Company (a mystery bookstore), looks for the killer of Peter Adcock, co-owner of the Empty Creek Coyotes of the Arizona-New Mexico League. Assisting her is Big Mike (Mycroft), a twenty-five pound cat. Kendall McCoffey is the first suspect. The other co-owner of the Coyotes, his wife was having an affair with Adcock. However, former big leaguer Eddie Stiles helps to point the way to Angelique Lamont, owner of the Dynamite Lounge. Involved in a drug deal with Adcock, she killed him with a baseball bat when he sexually accosted her while she was in the process of delivering the contraband to the Eagles dugout.

After the case is solved, Penelope enjoys herself as the Eagles go on a winning streak, and Eddie Stiles returns to the majors. Part of the Big Mike mystery series, the book does not do much with baseball. It is, though, replete with oddball characters and humorous action.

Cook, Marshall J. *The Year of the Buffalo.* Superior, WI: Savage Press, 1997.

Subtitled "A Novel of Love and Minor League Baseball," it focuses on one season of the Beymer Buffalo, a Class A independent team in a Wisconsin town of 2000 people. Tommy Lee Smith arrives in a last ditch effort to save his pitching career. New manager Dutch Brannigan, meanwhile, is informed of the ultimatum that the team must draw 95,000 fans for the season in order to remain in Beymer, the smallest town in the country to have a pro franchise. Further, Maas, one of the owners, states that he will give the orders. One of them is that the townspeople prefer to keep White Eagle on the bench due to the recent local controversy with Native Americans

Brannigan and Smith, who doubles a pitching coach, run the team their way and make it a winner. Journalist Bruce Kelly and restauranteur Billie Jo support the Buffalo and help to boost the attendance. With Smith and White Eagle starring, the team wins the pennant. The major owner, Glendennon, arrives in Beymer and offers Smith a contract to manage the team next year — with Brannigan moving up to Yuma in Double A ball. Smith and Billie Jo become a couple, and Brannigan makes contact with his son after years of estrangement.

Despite the melodrama and sentiment, the struggles to keep the small-town team alive—as well as some baseball careers—are effectively presented as a communal activity. The result is a book that appeals to the popular taste but probably not to the critics.

Delillo, Don. *Pafko at the Wall.* New York: Scribner, 1997.

The ninety-page novella first appeared in the October 1992 issue of *Harpers's* in a somewhat different form. It is the Prologue ("The Triumph of Death") in the novel *Underworld.* The scene is the famous game between the Dodgers and the Giants on October 3, 1951, The Miracle of Coogan's Bluff. Cotter Martin sneaks into the Polo Grounds that day and is the lucky kid who grabs the Bobby Thomson home run ball. He escapes to his Harlem apartment with the magical ball that is a part of the Shot Heard Round the World.

In contrast, the celebrities at the game indulge their fantasies, egos, and appetites as the action unfolds. J. Edgar Hoover, Toots Shor, Frank Sinatra, and Jackie Gleason see Ralph Branca's pitch (hit by Thomson) sail over Andy Pafko's head as the winning runs cross the plate—causing Russ Hodges to shout repeatedly on the radio: "The Giants win the pennant."

Standing alone, the novella presents a unique view of one of the great games in baseball history. Besides capturing the ambience of the Polo Grounds, it stresses the social discrepancy between the black kid and the American elite as they are brought together by baseball.

Delillo, Don. *Underworld.* New York: Scribner, 1997. (New York: Scribner, 1998.)

The Prologue (printed separately as *Pafko at the Wall*) tells of Cotter Martin's capture of the Bobby Thomson home run ball at the Miracle of Coogan's Bluff (the Polo Grounds) in 1951. The book then expands (to 825 pages) in various directions. One strand follows the history of the baseball which eventually ends up with Nick Shay forty years later. A former hood, Shay is in the waste management industry; he reunites with Kara Sax, an artist who works on de-commissioned B-52s in a Nevada desert that also contains radioactive waste material.

While baseball is a factor, the emphasis gradually shifts to the Cold War and the threat of nuclear destruction, including the Soviet Union's experiment with bombs in 1951. The book has been described as a black comedy about the technological victimization of humanity dating from the inception of the bombs to the computerization of the world in the 1990s. Baseball is symbolic of a pastoral age in contrast to the era that produces radioactive trash. One of the owners of the home run ball collects baseball memorabilia as a means of warding off the terror of the nuclear age — a main concern of the novel, which was a finalist for the National Book Award.

Dyja, Thomas. *Play for a Kingdom.* New York: Harcourt. 1997. (New York: Harvest, 1998.)

Company L, the Brooklyn 14th, finds a clearing in the Virginia woods in May of 1864 during the Battle of Spotsylvania. Lyman Alder and Newt Fry throw a baseball around, as observed by Alabama Confederates. They challenge the Yankees to a baseball game. The teams from New York and Alabama play a five-game series, then, in a respite from the Civil War, even though the players are risking court-martial.

To most of the participants, the games are a welcome relief from warfare, but Lt. Barridge of the Union army uses the encounters to obtain information from a spy — Sidney Mink, a plantation-owner and Harvard-educated Rebel officer. While there are racists among the Northerners and abolitionists in the Alabama group, most of the men learn a semblance of tolerance and respect for each other. The field designated as a baseball diamond becomes a symbol of peace, as the pastoral aspect of the game is contrasted to the horror and business of warfare.

It is the business of war that dominates, though, as the spying episode suggests. Another example is provided by Newt Fry, one of the Brooklyn ballplayers. While recovering from a wound, he is assigned to serve as a surgeon's assistant. As he witnesses the carnage of the clinic, he becomes resolved to return to the battlefield and to dedicate himself to the emancipation of the slaves. The war will go on.

The first Civil War baseball novel, it deserves to be recognized as a quality work of literature. *Play for a Kingdom* is the winner of the Casey Award for the best baseball book of the year.

Gordon, Alison. *Prairie Hardball.* Toronto: McClelland & Stewart, 1997.

Kate Henry, Toronto sportswriter, attends the induction ceremony of her mother into the Saskatchewan Baseball Hall of Fame. Kate is accompanied by Andy Munro, homicide detective. She wants to show him the beauty of her homeland in Indian Head, still the home of Mrs. Henry who played with the Racine Belles of the All-American Girls' Professional Baseball League in the forties.

At the Hall of Fame Museum, though, Kate discovers the body of Virna Wilton, the biggest star of the league. Although she tries to stay out of the investigation, Kate realizes that the murderer is Garth Elshaw, husband of the woman that Virna was romantically involved with.

The shock, however, comes when Kate's mother confesses that Virna Wilton's adopted son is actually her illegitimate offspring. Kate is astonished to learn about her half-brother and is glad to head back to Toronto—even though she has been informed that her cat, Elwy, has died. The lesbian affair is the clue in the fifth Kate Henry mystery. Like the other books in the series, it is well written — although a bit more melodramatic than usual.

Hamill, Pete. *Snow in August.* Boston: Little, Brown & Co., 1997. (New York: Warner Books, 1999).

Michael Devlin, an eleven-year-old Irish-Catholic in Brooklyn, makes friends with Rabbi Judah Hirsch in 1947, the year Jackie Robinson debuts with the Dodgers. Mike teaches the rabbi about baseball, and they go to Ebbets Field to cheer for Robinson and Hank Greenberg, who plays firstbase for the Pirates in '47. In turn, Hirsch tells of his life in Prague and of the imprisonment of his wife by the Nazis. He entertains Mike with tales of the Golem, an enforcer of justice, much like the boy's hero — Captain Marvel.

The racism that haunts the Dodgers during the season is compared to the anti-Semitism that exists in the neighborhood. Mike witnesses the beating of a Jewish merchant by the Falcons—a gang that also attacks Mike. The boy decides to take action by conjuring up a Golem of his own from mud and magical rites. The Golem appears as a black man who produces snow in August — and then punishes the Falcons. The superhero completes his work by enabling thousands of Jews to appear, including the rabbi's dead wife.

Most of the novel is naturalistic so that the switch to fantasy or magical realism at the end is unexpected — and disappointing. However, the exposition of ethnic prejudice in the coming-of-age story of Michael Devlin tends to compensate for the questionable conclusion.

Hester, Colin. *Diamond Sutra.* Washington, D.C.: Counterpoint, 1997.

Rudyard Gillette, ex-college baseball player, is a forty-year-old textbook salesman. After his father's suicide, he searches for a meaningful life. He is obsessed with the memory of his mother, who died when he was a boy. He remembers asking her about the 1960 World Series when her favorites, the Yankees, were beaten by the Pirates and Bill Mazeroski's seventh-game homer. As an adult, Gillette writes letters to Mazeroski in which he inquires about the science of life. He then turns to Zen for a possible solution.

In a complex psychological study, baseball is an important element in the mind of the protagonist. The game's uncertainties parallel the mutability of his existence.

Hoffman, Allen. *Big League Dreams.* New York: Abbeville Press, 1997.

Matti (Sirdy) Sternweiss is a catcher for the St. Louis Browns in 1920. One of the Krimsk Jews who migrated to America in 1903, Sirdy decides that the only way he can afford to marry Penny Pinkham is to place a bet on a fixed game (despite the rumors of the Black Sox scandal of the year before).He contacts Barasch, a gambler, to bet on Saturday's game against the Tigers of the Ty Cobb era, but the word gets out. Inspector Doheen takes action to negate the bet, and Rebbe Yeckov Finebaum convinces Sirdy that he has the opportunity for holiness by beating the Tigers. The catcher does the job by tagging Cobb out on a collision at home plate and then hitting a homer to win the game.

Mobsters retaliate by killing Sirdy Sternweiss for failing to cooperate with them. Finebaum, though, eulogizes him as one who served holiness and is therefore not in need of mourning. Inspector Doheen, who had confiscated the money bet by Sirdy and Rarasch (and then bet it on the Browns) turns over $26,000 to the Sternweiss family. (Browns player Dufer Rawlings gets engaged to Penny Pinkham.)

The baseball and gambling aspects of the story are melodramatic. The presentation of Jewish life in a hostile environment, however, is handled skillfully and realistically.

Renino, Christopher. *The Way Home Is Longer.* New York: St. Martin's Press, 1997.

Subtitled "A Novel of the Historic 1947 Dodgers through the Eyes of Their Batboy," it features Vince Stigiano, nineteen, whose personal problems mirror the dissension on the team. He observes the trials of Jackie Robinson (who replaces Stigiano's hero, Howie Schultz, at first base) as he faces bigotry from opponents and the racists among the Dodgers: Dixie Walker, Eddie Stanky, Kirby Higbe, Hugh Casey, and Bobby Bragan. The batboy sides with Robinson as the season progresses, and the team, under Burt Shotton, adjusts to the tension and wins the pennant (before losing to the Yankees in the World Series.)

On the home front, the big event for the summer is the return of Sam LaVista, a World War II pilot. Stigiano and Sam's sister, Alma, try to help him adjust to civilian life, but he seems to be in shock from his war experiences. LaVista dies in a car crash that may have been a suicide. The batboy gets infatuated with Alma, but the affair is in jeopardy when she makes plans to attend college. Stigiano refuses the offer to return to the Dodgers for the next season, as he decides to start life anew.

Stigiano feels that he has learned from his experience with the 1947 Dodgers and can now find his own way. The novel is a typical bildungsroman in which the protagonist develops to maturity.

Sandman, John. *Praying for Rain* (in *A Double Play of Underground Baseball Novellas*). Delhi, NY: Birch Book Press, 1997.

The seventy-six page novella takes place at the end of the season in the Class A Tri-State Florida League. Pitcher Carlton Hubbs and catcher Joe Sperma are marginal players for the Lake Worth Worthies; both are concerned about their doubtful futures in baseball. They are also worried about the approaching hurricane. The storm spares the building which houses their new baseball card business, but when their partner is arrested for tax evasion, the desperate dreams of economic success are destroyed.

In the off-season, Sperma accepts a promising job with NASA, but Hubbs returns to his wife and two kids in a trailer park and a job at K-Mart. He feels that he is a loser, like his father, and reflects on his brief major league career. When an offer to play winter ball in the Dominican Republic is made, Hubbs goes for it — even though his wife says that she and the kids will be gone when he returns.

A probable victim of the ex-jock syndrome, referring to an athlete who does not prepare for a future beyond his athletic career, Carlton Hubbs clings to thoughts of big league glory. His predicament is realistically and unsentimentally presented by Sandman.

Saxon, Lisa. *Caught in a Rundown.* New York: Scribner, 1997.

Jewel Averick is mad at her husband, the D.C. Diamonds centerfielder, and sells his prized possession: a baseball glove used by Cool Papa Bell of the Negro Leagues. She replaces the glove with a cheaper one that belonged to someone called Two-Mile McLemore. Jewel finds a clue in the glove, and she and her friend Dee White, wife of the second baseman of the Diamonds, set out to discover the identity of McLemore.

Duke Crammer and his gang of hoods are also in the search. The brother of Two-Mile, Robert McLemore, has stolen a valuable gem from Crammer, and he plans to get it back by following the clues left in the glove. The women discover the Star Diamond first, however, and also learn from Robert that his brother was killed by Crammer while both were trying to gain possession of the diamond.

The African American author features interracial friends: Jewel is black and Dee is white. Their humorous escapades help to offset an unlikely mystery.

Soos, Troy. *Hunting a Detroit Tiger.* New York: Kensington Publishing Corporation, 1997.

Mickey Rawlings is a reserve infielder with the Tigers in 1920. Falsely credited with being a war hero, he is also wrongly accused of killing labor leader Emmett Siever, a former big leaguer. The Industrial Workers of the World is trying to unionize baseball, and American League President Ban Johnson is against it: both sides declare the neutral Rawlings an enemy. Karl Landfors, socialist writer, and Margie Turner, actress, help Rawlings try to clear himself.

Teammates Dutch Leonard and Ty Cobb, who favor the union, make Rawlings' tenure as a Tiger difficult, but he prevails and eventually discovers that Siever was killed by a government agent. The utility infielder makes a deal with the authorities to stifle the truth in exchange for the release of his friend, Karl Landfors, who had been in custody for defending Sacco and Vanzetti, the alleged anarchists. Rawlings gladly returns to Navin Field, home of the Tigers, despite the animosity of Ty Cobb and company. His romance with Margie Turner gives him hope for the future.

The fourth book in the series combines baseball and history to create a good novel that transcends the typical mystery.

Winters, Donna. *Isabelle's Inning.* N.p.: Bigwater Publishing, 1997.

A Great Lakes Romance set in 1903, it deals with the plight of Isabelle Dorlon and her connection to the Erskine College baseball team. Her brother Tracey is a member of the team, and another player, Jack Weatherby, rooms at her mother's boarding house. Isabelle, nineteen, sells brooms, but her secret is that she cannot read; she is diagnosed with word blindness. Weatherby, a hero on and off the field, still feels empty — until he woos Isabelle and follows her in "the Lord's path."

The book promises that it will contain "no explicit sex, offensive language, or gratuitous violence." It also has virtually no literary quality.

1998

Constantine, K. C. *Brushback.* New York: Mysterious Press, 1998.

Detective Sergeant Rugs Carlucci of Rocksburg, Pennsylvania, investigates the murder of Bobby Blasco, once known as the Brushback Kid when he pitched briefly with the Boston Red Sox. In 1959, he purposely decked Ted Williams in a spring training game. His career floundered, however, and he returned to Rocksburg to run an illegal gambling club. Carlucci finds that Blasco had abused several of his wives and that the father of one of them killed the ex-pitcher for revenge.

The book, only touching on baseball, displays the protagonist, however, with compassion and humor. The acting police chief (after Balzac, the hero of other Constantine mysteries, retires) tries to balance the demands of the job with the tribulations of the domestic scene — which features his demanding mother.

Jaffee, Robert David. *Strikeout at Hell Gate.* Bloomington, IN: 1st Books Library, 1998.

Set in New York City during racial strife of the early 1990s, the plot focuses in part on Jim Keough's development of the Baseball Ferry, a hovercraft for transporting fans to the ballpark. An urban planner, Keough sees his plan become a reality, but politicians claim the credit for inaugurating the project.

In the meantime, the New York Titans are slumping. The manager blames sportswriter Marty Goldin for the problem, and Goldin is fired. The slump is partially due to the injury of black rightfielder Devin (Roto) Magruder. He gets hurt during the pennant drive after earlier missing three months with a brain virus. Hell Gate, a dangerous passage in the East River, appears in Magruder's dreams and suggests complications and failures.

The book stresses the contrast between the surface glory of the city and its baseball and the degradation of racism and political corruption. References to the Negro Leagues and Jewish ballplayers suggest that the idealized concept of the game, like the concept of an equitable society, has not been completely attained. The author of the complex (but ultimately disappointing) novel actually created a Baseball Ferry for the Mets in the eighties.

Kluger, Steve. *Last Days of Summer.* New York: William Morrow, 1998. (New York: Avon, 2005.)

Joe Margolis, Jewish kid who lives with his mother and aunt in Brooklyn, is ready to turn to crime in 1940. His divorced father does not take him to Coney Island as promised, he is tired of being mugged by neighborhood Italians, and Hitler is starting to worry him. At the age of twelve, he begins to write to Charlie Banks, the Racine Rocket, who plays thirdbase for the New York Giants. Joey claims to be blind and dying of an incurable disease, and after developing a relationship by mail, Banks agrees to meet the kid.

Despite Joey's lies, the boy and the ballplayer become friends, and Charlie takes him on a road trip with the Giants. World War II intervenes, however, and the thirdbaseman becomes a marine. Craig Nakamura, Joey's friend, is put in a concentration camp — although they continue to communicate in the roles of the Green Hornet and The Shadow. While Craig is imprisoned and Banks is in the war, Joey reaps the benefit of fame with trips to the White House and visits with movie stars — until the telegram arrives stating that the Giant player was killed in action. Charlie's wife sends Joey the letter that Charlie meant for him in case of the soldier's death. It is filled with fatherly advice and love.

In the Epilogue, Joey appears at a Charlie Banks Day in Racine, Wisconsin. He is now a sportswriter (and his friend, Craig Nakamura, is a civil liberties attorney) who is asked to speak at the event which takes place twenty-five years after the death of the big league star.

Mostly an epistolary novel, it also includes postcards, telegrams, newspaper articles, and interviews. There is an overly emphasized contrast between the humorous episodes and the horror of the war, and the sentiment tends to be maudlin, but the book is entertaining.

Manderino, John. *The Man Who Once Played Catch with Nellie Fox.* Chicago: Academy Press, 1998.

Forty-year-old Hank Lingerman, ex-minor leaguer, plays with a Chicago semi-pro team, the Shopalot Sharks. He works at Whitey's Sunoco, a garage once owned by his dad but now in the hands of George Turner, a black man who once worked for Whitey. Lingerman loses the business, his wife, and his pro baseball career; he feels that he has failed as a son and as a man. He dates Karen, but her ten-year-old son hates him. Hank then develops the Oblomov Syndrome — he refuses to leave his bed.

Years earlier, his father took Hank to see the go-go White Sox play. Whitey arranged a game of catch with his son and Nellie Fox, the Sox second baseman. Now as a middle-aged failure, Hank Lingerman dwells on the past and is afraid to confront the present. However, his friends from Jerry and Larry's Sport Palace take turns visiting him, and one of them wins a bet by getting Hank to return to the world of the living

Back with the Sharks, Hank participates in a championship game with the Haines Insurance Hounds from Hell, but he strikes out in the ninth to seal a loss. After the game, he forces Brian to play catch with him — remembering his boyhood day with Nellie Fox, a little guy who never gave up despite the odds against him. Hank decides that there is still a chance for him to succeed in life.

The idealized concept of baseball's redemptive power is stressed here — a common theme in the fiction of the game. The psychological portrait of the protagonist, along with the humor and whimsy, helps to make this more than a mediocre book about baseball.

Martin, Ben J. *Caught Stealing: A Love Story with a Baseball Background.* Chicago: Adams Press, 1998.

Manny Hernandez, winner of the Cy Young Award as a relief pitcher, helps the Cardinals win the World Series. However, his wife and her lawyer trick him into giving up the children and most of his wealth. The Dominican player prevails, though, and gets everything back—and adds a good woman: Keri Robinson, a sportswriter. In the meantime, the wife and lawyer get into trouble for drug dealing.

The book illustrates that Hispanic baseball players are victimized by women, lawyers, and American prejudice. However, the justice of god will eventually reward virtue and punish evil, according to the author's narrow viewpoint.

Nemec, David. *Early Dreams.* Baseball Press Books, 1998. (Clifton, VA: Pocol Press, 2004.)

Earl Draves signs a contract with the Cincinnati Red Stockings in 1884. He plays with the reserve team until it disbands in June and then is injured while with the Red Stockings—and released. Draves, however, joins the Cincinnati team of the Union Association, the Outlaw Reds, and plays thirdbase for the contending team. At the end of the season, he is released again, but fortunately gets the chance to play secondbase for the New York Metropolitans in a championship series against the Providence Grays. The Grays win the pre-World Series match behind the pitching of Old Hoss Radbourn.

The 172-page book by a baseball historian is told in a diary and the letters of the protagonist, a fictional creation who is involved with real people and events of the 1884 season. One of the historical incidents is the plan, headed by Cap Anson, to keep Fleet Walker, first black major leaguer, out of the game. The novel is thoroughly researched, but it is not of a high literary quality.

Soos, Troy. *The Cincinnati Red Stalkings.* Kensington Publishing Corporation, 1998.

Mickey Rawlings is a utility infielder with Cincinnati in 1921 until, like the Black Sox Eight, he is banned by Commissioner Landis for consorting with gamblers. In Rawlings' case the ban is only temporary, though, while Landis checks on the murder of Rufus Yates, an associate of Arnold Rothstein; Yates and Rawlings have appeared in photos together. Oliver Perriman, an exhibitor of 1869 Red Stockings memorabilia, is also murdered, and he has a connection with Rawlings as well. When threatened by someone who wanted items from the collection, Perriman gave some of the material to the infielder.

Actress Margie Turner and journalist Karl Landfors once again help Rawlings solve the mystery. They trace the crimes to Nathaniel Bonner who was searching for evidence to use in blackmailing a former assistant treasurer of the team. Commissioner Landis clears the utility player so that he can rejoin the Reds. The fifth mystery in the series continues the tradition of mixing detection with baseball history.

1999

Clarke, Mike. *The Migration of Willie* Mackerels. San Francisco: Robert D. Reed, 1999.

Listed as both and adult and young adult novel, it contrasts the humorous adventures of Bill Michaels (Willie Mackerels) in high school with the grim experiences of his cousin Harvey in the Korean War. The Michaels family moves from Seattle to Happy Valley in the Olympic Peninsula of Washington, and Willie plays baseball for the hopeless Milk Maids. He foolishly thinks that a scout from the St Louis Cardinals is watching his high school career, even though he cannot throw hard; he is in what he calls his Eddie Lopat phase of pitching. Ironically, it is Harvey, who sends letters from Korea, who is the real pitching prospect. Willie's unremarkable career is highlighted by a victory of his nemesis, Teddy Snodgrass, a rival for the attention of Trudy Trammel. The ecstasy is cut short, though, by a letter from Korea stating the Harvey has lost his pitching arm in the war. Willie finally realizes that his future is not in baseball.

Narrated by Willie Mackerels in the style of Holden Caulfield, the bildungsroman falls far short of *The Catcher in the Rye*. It is similar, though, to *Last Days of Summer* (1998), particularly in the treatment of boyhood escapades that are juxtaposed with an older person's experience in war.

Coben, Harlan. *The Final Detail.* New York: Delacorte Press, 1999. (New York: Dell, 2000.)

Sports agent Myron Bolitar is on vacation, but his friend, Windsor Horne Lockwood III, informs him that Esperanza Diaz, Myron's partner, has been arrested for killing a client: Clu Haid, Yankee pitcher. The crime is traced to Yankee owner, Sophie Mayor, who framed Diaz after the pitcher committed suicide. She wanted revenge on Haid for driving a car that was involved in an accident that killed her daughter. Bolitar had bribed the police to get the drunk Yankee off the hook after the car crash, so Sophie Mayor retaliated by arranging a fixed drug test for Haid—which led to his death. Sophie confesses to Bolitar but rationalizes her behavior as a proper revenge and compares it to the action of the sports agent in protecting Haid. The truth hurts as Bolitar is uncomfortable with compromised morality. His friend Win Lockwood, though, says that adjusting to injustice is the proper method of survival.

The Edgar Award winning author presents witty dialogue and colorful characters— although baseball is of little significance in the novel.

Craig, David. *Our Lady of the Outfield.* Oak Lawn, IL: CMJ Marian Publishers, 1999.

Keith (Beto) Wells grows up in California and plays shortstop in high school. Drafted by Cleveland, he works his way up to the majors, but is unhappy. Then, after Beto becomes a Catholic, the Queen of Heaven begins to appear in the outfield. Mass healings occur, and games have to be played in front of hysterical crowds waiting for miracles. One of them is a World Championship for the Cleveland Indians.

Money, a sportswriter, takes over the narration from Joseph, an angel, and reiterates the season from his viewpoint. In what he calls the Year of the Holy Championship, virtuous action is rewarded as Beto Wells leads the Indians to a "real" World Series win over the Yokahoma Giants. In the process, Wells had to ask the

Queen of Heaven to desist from her public appearances to keep the fans from disrupting the games. After the miracle season, Wells retires and spends time with his family, fixes car, plays music, and prays.

What starts as a less than mediocre baseball novella (120 pages) deteriorates into religious propaganda, with little attention to artistic integrity.

Hitman, T. *Hardball: An Erotic Novel.* Los Angeles: Alyson Books, 1999.

The Seaside Toy Socks have an incredible season on the way to the World Series. Teamwork is the key as Tommy Bruno, aging centerfielder, recovers from a divorce by his attraction to rookie roommate, Tim Weare. For 260 pages, then, gay pornography dominates as the rest of the team joins the action — which is mostly off the field. This is another candidate for "the worst ever."

Kay, Terry. *Taking Lottie Home.* New York: William Morrow, 2000. (New York: Harper Perennial, 2001.)

Outfielder Ben Phelps and infielder Foster Lanier are released from the Augusta Hornets, a minor league time, in 1904. On the way back to Jericho, Georgia, Phelps meets the captivating Lottie Barton on the train. Several years later, a carnival arrives in Jericho, and Lottie and Lanier are part of the show. Phelps, a clerk at Arthur Ledford's Dry Goods Store, becomes a local legend by getting a hit off a giant one-armed pitcher that no other batter can touch. Lanier, though, had manipulated his carnival act so that his former teammate could look good to the hometown crowd. Phelps is again attracted to the alluring Lottie, a carnival girl.

Years later, the Jericho native courts hometown girl Sally Ledford. He also corresponds with Milo Wade, a homeboy who makes it to the big leagues (and is apparently modeled after Ty Cobb). One day, Phelps gets a letter from Lottie asking him to visit her and Lanier, her dying husband, in Kentucky. He agrees to make the journey, and he promises Lanier that he will take Lottie (and her son Ben) home to Augusta, Georgia. When Little Ben gets sick on the train, they go to Jericho instead. Lottie becomes a fixture at Ledford's Dry Goods Store, and the boy is "adopted" by Phelps' mother.

Eventually, Ben Phelps escorts Lottie and Ben Lanier to Augusta. Some time later, he marries Sally Ledford, and Little Ben appears at the wedding without his mother. An Epilogue reveals that Arthur Ledford, owner of the Dry Goods Store, had been having an affair with Lottie until her death in Charleston, South Carolina, in 1933. Ledford arranges to have her buried in Jericho, claiming that she is a cousin.

Although baseball is a minor factor, the novel is extremely well written. The sexual tension between Ben Phelps and Lottie is comparable to the Ethan Frome and Mattie Silver relationship in the Edith Wharton classic.

Kelly, Robert J. *Gifts of the Gods.* Bloomington, IN: 1st Books Library, 1999.

Mike Grange becomes the centerfielder of the Philadelphia Phillies at the age of sixteen. The superhero breaks every major record and wins the MVP Award and the Triple Crown twenty times each. He is named the Greatest Player of All-Time while still active. With the help of his sister Carol, a lawyer, Grange gets fabulously wealthy and also becomes a noted philanthropist. When he retires from baseball, he is elected as the President of the United States.

Mike Grange is superior to Mendelsohn's Superbaby as he is not created by genetic manipulation, and he is able to adjust to society and improve it rather than to self-destruct. As a novel, however, even *Superbaby* is much better — as this is another candidate for "the ten worst list."

King, Stephen. *The Girl Who Loved Tom Gordon.* New York: Scribners, 1999. (New York: Pocket Books, 2000.)

Trisha McFarland, nine, gets lost on the Maine-New Hampshire branch of the Appalachian Trail. Wearing a Red Sox jersey with "36 Gordon" on the back, she listens to the Boston games on her radio as a means of warding off panic. Trisha is elated when Tom (Flash) Gordon subdues the Yankees on his way to recording forty-three straight saves. When a bear appears, she plays the role of a pitcher as she faces the enemy with the Walkman substituting for a baseball. She understands how Tom Gordon must feel in the silence of the cyclone's core as she goes into her windup. Just then a hunter scares the bear away with a rifle shot, but Trisha delivers her pitch — strike three called.

Atypical of King's popular horror fiction, this in only mildly scary as a child's love of baseball saves her from the darkness. Although well-written, and fast-paced, the book is sentimental and conventional.

Lasser, Scott. *Battle Creek.* New York: Bob Weisbach Books, 1999.

Gil Davison is the manager of the semipro Koch & Sons Dodgers, a team that has the annual habit of losing in the championship tournament at Battle Creek, Michigan. He is plagued by personal problems: he is estranged from his son, and his father is dying of cancer. Further, his coach is dying of emphysema, and the team's ace pitcher is throwing illegal spitballs. The Dodgers are also in financial trouble, and Davison is secretly diverting funds from his father's account to keep the team solvent.

A break comes when slugger Luke James, a twenty-two-year-old ex-convict, joins the team and supplies a big lift. In the championship game, though, James is killed by a beanball. The Dodgers win, but Davison has to hustle to his father's funeral. The officiating rabbi reminds the grieving Davison of his forsaken boyhood lessons in Judaism. He realizes that the price of winning may have been too high — that his morally suspect acts have been misdirected.

The moral awakening of Gil Davison, the main subject of the book, is attained melodramatically. The contrived ending offsets the quality of the writing displayed in the major portion of the text. It is still a good study of amateur baseball.

Levine, Peter. *The Rabbi of Swat.* East Lansing: Michigan State University Press, 1999.

Morrie Ginsberg emerges from a Jewish family in Brooklyn to join John McGraw's 1927 Giants as a pitcher. Catcher Zack Taylor reveals to Ginsberg that he is also Jewish (having changed his name from Schwartz). The Giants win the pennant and play the Yankees in the World Series. Before the seventh game, though, Ginsberg's father is kidnapped, and a message is sent which advises the pitcher to lose the contest. Notorious gambler Arnold Rothstein foils the crime and gets

Jake Ginsberg to the game in time to see his son lose legitimately to Babe Ruth's homer.

In a 1934 aftermath, Ginsberg is still pitching for the Giants, but the manager is Babe Ruth, a position which eluded him in real life. His intertextual comments are the most entertaining aspect of the book. Rothstein also gets a reprieve as he is treated as a semi-hero despite references to the Black Sox scandal.

The emphasis, however, is on the Jewish experience as Morrie Ginsberg, unlike his conservative father, tries to assimilate into the American culture. The father-son conflict is also applied to the Babe as it is suggested that his flamboyant lifestyle may have been a result of his mishandled childhood experiences.

The mixture of real players with imaginary ones is a standard part of baseball fiction, but it is strained here. Historical facts are also altered, especially those of the World Series. Finally, the melodrama distracts from the portrait of Jewish assimilation and the interesting presentation of Babe Ruth as a co-narrator.

Minor, Roy. *In the Fall.* Pittsburgh: Sterling House, 1999.

Max Murphy is sixteen when he runs away from home because of his stepfather's cruel treatment. He gets a job on the O'Brien farm, courts Carol Simmons, and plays shortstop for a semipro team. At LaSalle High School, Murphy assists his black friend in integrating athletic events. In 1959, he is the shortstop for the St. Louis Cardinals, but he gets in trouble with the manager for defending his black teammates. A reporter exposes the racial strife on the team, and the manager is fired. Bill Kline takes over, and with the best players in the line-up, the Cardinals go on a winning streak.

After the season, Murphy returns to LaSalle, Missouri, and marries Carol. His long-lost father appears and explains why he had abandoned the family. As a minor leaguer, Mike Murphy refused to accept bribes to throw games, and was subsequently forced to go into hiding to escape the Mafia. Max, then, feels that baseball is tainted, and he decides to quit the game.

The double sins of racism and gambling drive the young star out of baseball, an unlikely situation. Literature here is secondary to moral preaching.

Orzula, Ed. *One More Time.* Harvard, IL: Chris Mystery Publisher, 1999.

As Pete Fletcher is on his deathbed, he theorizes that life is not what he thinks it to be. Thus he decides on a "do-over," a version of what his existence could have been. Instead of his career as a hard-drinking laborer, he envisions a scene in the trophy room of a mansion as he reflects on his past as a Cubs superstar who was voted into the Hall of Fame in 1980. In this alternate life, he won MVP Awards and led the Cubs to World Series wins during the sixties and seventies. However, the dream is interrupted by the intrusion of Will Turner, a high school friend who was killed in a car accident. Turner is jealous and tries to ruin Fletcher's life by baiting him with alcohol and adultery. The protagonist prevails, though, and since it is his dream, it is Turner who dies, and Fletcher leaves the hospital with a beautiful woman. Unfortunately, the writing is as suspect as the protagonist's fantasy.

Phillips, Donald T. *A Diamond in Spring.* Arlington: Summit Publishing Group, 1999.

A star thirdbaseman for the Texas Rangers, Jeff Delling makes plans to form the Joy Cancer Foundation after the death of his wife. In the meantime, he is in rehab for a knee injury. As he returns to the team, he is welcomed by the Rangers and their opponents. The organist plays "God Bless America" when he gets a hit, and he is carried on the shoulders of fans and players as a celebration of love. Hope, a girlfriend of his youth, promises a happy future for the hero and spiritual leader of the nation. Delling is only a slightly reduced version of Mike Grange (*Gifts of the Gods*), and the book is at the same low level.

Sharpe, Jon. *The Bush League.* (The Trailsman No 210). New York: Signet, 1999.

Skye Fargo accepts the job of guiding Jack Arnold's baseball players from Kansas City to San Francisco by wagon train. Along the way, he shows an aptitude for the game, but he turns down the manager's offer to join the team. He also discovers and foils a plot to rob the procession — a plan conceived by Arnold's daughter. Once in San Francisco, Fargo makes his own plan to steal the owner's girlfriend.

Sex, deceit, and violence are staples of the Trailsman Series of westerns. The inclusion of baseball makes this one unique, but it does not improve the substandard literary quality.

Soos, Troy. *Hanging Curve.* New York: Kensington Publishing Corporation, 1999.

In 1922 Mickey Rawlings, now thirty, is traded to the St Louis Browns. George Sisler, Ken Williams, and Urban Shocker are the stars, and the infield is set with Gedeon, Gerber, and Smith, so Rawlings does not play much. He accepts an invitation to make some extra money with the semi-pro Enoch's Elcars in a game against the St. Louis Cubs, a black team, in East St. Louis, Illinois— a hotbed for the KKK since the race riot of 1917. The Cubs win, but their pitcher, Slip Crawford, is lynched. Rawlings teams up with Margie Turner, Karl Landfors, and Franklin Aubury, a black attorney, to try to prevent further violence and to find the killers. They expose an Elcars player as the ringleader of the lynching mob, but the Klan murders him as a means of protecting itself.

As usual in the Rawlings series, real players appear, including Cool Papa Bell and other black stars, and historical events are in the background. There is less baseball here than in the five previous mysteries as the emphasis is on the battle for racial justice.

Wendell, Tim. *Castro's Curveball.* New York: Ballantine Books, 1999.

Billy Bryan's daughter, Cassy, discovers a scrapbook that documents a 1947-48 winter league baseball season in Cuba. Bryan, a widower and retired teacher, remembers his Cuban adventure with nostalgia and agrees to visit there with Cassy. Forty-six years ago, he was a minor league catcher in the Washington Senators organization. While playing for the Habana Lions in Cuba, he witnessed a student protest led by a young Fidel Castro. Bryan discovered that the political leader was also a pitcher with a wicked curveball, and he tried to recruit him for the Senators.

Bryan was captivated by Malena Fonseca as well. The photographer and political activist persuaded him to join the revolution in Cuba. In love with Malena, he agreed even though he saw Castro as a charismatic fraud. Bryan returned to America after the winter season, but Malena was too enmeshed in politics to accompany him.

In the present, Bryan meets Malena's daughter in Cuba and assumes that he is her father. She tells him that Malena died in 1959 while attempting to leave the country — having become disillusioned with Castro. When Bryan gets home, he sells the house (that he and his wife had raised three kids in) to raise money to get his Cuban daughter to the United States.

Although there is too much meditation on the nature of heroism, the book vividly depicts Cuban history and baseball. The doomed romance of the star-crossed lovers is presented without resorting to melodrama.

2000

Asinof, Eliot. *Off-Season.* Carbondale: Southern Illinois University Press, 2000.

Los Angeles Dodgers pitcher Black Jack Manning returns to his hometown, Gandee, Missouri, to celebrate the opening of Black Jack Field. The menacing-looking lefthander has a hundred-million-dollar contract and a wealthy girlfriend, Judith Pagonis, daughter of the owner of the Dodgers. Manning's agent, though, is turning what looks like an act of charity into another profit-making venture through television exposure and endorsements.

The visit to his hometown is marred for Manning when he discovers that his black high school mentor and batterymate has been murdered. Ruby Coles is in jail for the alleged killing of her husband Cyrus. Manning investigates the situation and realizes that racism is the motive. His father, the local sheriff, is a suspect as he does not want a black man to get any credit for his son's success. Manning and Hortense Foxx, a former schoolmate and now a journalist, expose the corruption. They fight for justice together, and the spoiled jock is transformed into a moral crusader.

On the plane trip back to LA, Manning meets Mike Kutner, and the old man tells the story of his sixteen-year minor league career and his great love of the game, which is the subject of Asinof's *Man on Spikes* (1955). The Dodgers pitcher, a changed person, appreciates Kutner's baseball tales. This should be no surprise, as the old man's fictional biography is vastly superior to the melodramatic mystery/thriller that features Manning.

Brock, Darryl. *Havana Heat.* New York: Total Sports/Sports Illustrated, 2000. (New York: Plume, 2001.)

Real major league pitcher Luther (Dummy) Taylor attempts a comeback with the Giants during a 1911 barnstorming tour in Cuba. During his tenure in the majors, Taylor posted a 116–106 record. He then pitched in the minors. Although his Cuban audition does not earn him a return to the Giants, he becomes a hero to the students from the Escuala del Orejas (School of the Ears). The deaf pitcher discovers a young pitching phenom, also deaf, and tries to recruit him for John McGraw's team. Taylor puts together a Cuban all-star team and beats the Giants. However, Taylor's plan is spoiled when the youth's grandfather shows up. He is black, and

McGraw backs off — not wanting the risk of signing a player with a Negro heritage. McGraw, who persists in calling Taylor "Dummy," also ridicules santeria, a Cuban folk religion that the ex-big leaguer is attracted to, by stating that it takes a bonehead to practice voodoo.

Luther Taylor turns to teaching and coaching at the Illinois School of the Deaf. In 1958, his alma mater, the Kansas School for the Deaf, honors him — shortly before his death.

In an Epilogue, reference is made of the Black Uprising in Cuba of 1912 that was defeated by the Cuban army and the United States marines. When the Giants later return to Havana, Christy Mathewson, on behalf of Taylor, asks about the pitching prospect. No trace of him is found, but the game in which he beat McGraw's team has become legendary.

The novel exposes American prejudices with John McGraw as the symbolic example. Despite the propagandistic tendency, *Havana Heat* approaches excellence in its portrait of a time and place — and is one of the forerunners in the field of fictional biographies.

Carver, John. *Hardball Fever.* Plano: Hard Times Cattle Company Publishing, 2000.

Rick Mason, a former Cleveland secondbaseman, tries to work his way back to the majors after a knee injury by accepting the job of managing the Tyler East Texans of the Big State League in 1951. Broke, alcoholic, and estranged from his wife, he is nevertheless hired by his father-in-law, Clyde Segars. With the help of Matilda, a ghost and/or guardian angel, the team gets off to a good start, and Mason's wife takes him back. Trouble arises, though, when the manager discovers that Segars is in debt to a New Orleans mob. Mason loses control of the team, and the new owners fire him. However, Leo Durocher of the Giants is looking for a way to overcome the Dodger's thirteen-game-lead in August, and he hires Mason as a coach.

The conclusion of the 1951 season, the Miracle of Coogan's Bluff, is embedded in baseball lore. The book, a strange blend of sci-fi and mystery, does not do justice, however, to the historical events of the era, as the plot is suspect throughout.

Crumbley, D. Larry, Douglas E. Ziegenfuss and John J. O'Shaughnessy. *The Big R.* Durham, NC: Carolina Academic Press, 2000.

Murders are being committed on the dates of perfect games in the majors. The Ballpark Killers threaten mass violence with the use of biological and chemical weapons if their demands for ransom are not met. Commissioner Bud Selig offers a million-dollar- reward for the detection of the criminals. Fleet Walker, internal auditor for the Yankees, Fred Campbell, member of the Society of American Baseball Research, and William Douglas, FBI agent, combine to track down Sandy Kojack, who is accosted at Yankee Stadium. He is killed, but the poison in his possession escapes, and many people die. Kojak's accomplice is still on the loose, and a threat is sent to the FBI on a Don Zimmer baseball card. Zimmer was managing the Padres in 1972 when Milt Pappas retired twenty-six straight before losing a perfect game on a questionable call. The book ends, then, with no solution to the Big R(isk).

Promoted as a teaching aide for an internal auditing class or graduate investment course, the novel is badly written. It has been proclaimed as one of the ten all-time worst baseball novels, but if the baseball romances are included, it will not be that low on the list.

Filicchia, Ralph. *The Ballplayers.* Baltimore: N.p., 2000: AmErica House, 2001.

Artie Fletcher and his three baseball-player friends finish their high school careers at Watertown, Massachusetts, in 1954. They all hope to turn pro, but it does not happen. When Fletcher's goal fails, he concentrates on training his son, Jeff, to be a ballplayer. Jeff is killed in a car accident, however, and his father eventually takes up softball in a pathetic attempt to find consolation.

Fletcher suffers from the ex-jock syndrome — an inability to adjust to life when the athletic phase is over (best exemplified by Tom Buchanan in *The Great Gatsby*). The obsession with a single dream and the inability to learn from experience tend to make Fletcher and his friends victims of their environment in the naturalistic tradition of James T. Farrell's Studs Lonigan. They also resemble Jack Keefe in their inability to learn from mistakes but are presented without the humor (or the skill) of Ring Lardner.

Fromm, Pete. *How All This Started.* New York: Picador, 2000. (New York: Picador, 2001.)

Abilene and Austin, sister and brother, live in a West Texas desert with their parents. Though female, Abilene can throw a baseball as fast as anyone on the high school team, but she is not allowed to play. Her mission then is to make a star pitcher out of Austin. They practice at the abandoned Rattlesnake Bomber Base, a relic of World War II. However, she blames the sexist society for eliminating her skill, and her obsession with transmitting it to her brother leads to manic depression. Austin goes on to pitch for the University of Texas, but he worships Abilene and is distraught with the change in her when she is put on medication. His epiphany is the break from Abilene's domination of him — the realization that he has to apply his talent and education to a higher level than their isolated desert domain.

The novel won the Pacific Northwest Booksellers' Association Award for the best work by a Montana-based author.

Holm, Stef Ann. *Honey.* New York: Pocket Books, 2000.

Alex Cordova quits baseball in 1898 when he accidentally injures the opposing catcher, Joe McGill. Three years later, Cordova is persuaded to play for the Harmony Keystones, a new American League franchise in Montana, because he needs money to help a friend. Camille Kennison manages the Keystones, her father's team. After a bad start, Cordova falls in love with the manager and pitches and bats the Keystones to a pennant, beating out Cy Young's team. Two days after the season, Alex and Camille get married. The recovered Joe McGill, the friend Cordova was helping, also ties the matrimonial knot that day.

The historical western setting and the female manager do not lift the book above the label of formula romance.

Hudson, Dennis F. *Royal Blue.* N.p.: Xlibris Corporation, 2000.

Brian Blazer grows up in a segregated Mississippi in the years 1955 to 1960. A Yankee fan, he plays for the Hartsville high school and American Legion teams coached by Jay Morris. As a boy, Brian is taught racial tolerance by his grandfather, and Coach Morris and his wife, a teacher, continue the ethical lessons. Brian responds by helping a black kid, Joshua Pitts, integrate the local Legion team. In his major moral moment, Brian argues for racial justice in a confrontation with the segregationist mayor of Hartsville. The integrated team goes on to a successful season — although after losing a playoff game, the protagonist burns his bats (with royal blue handles) when he realizes that his baseball career is over.

Years later, as a television anchorman, Brian Blazer still follows the game, but is unhappy with the changes which are symbolized by the 1998 home run race between McGwire and Sosa. The free agent market, the lowered pitching mound, the livelier ball, the new friendly-to-hitter ballparks, and the thinning of pitching talent caused by expansion are all signs of the decline in the sport. He looks back to the Yankee heroes of the past, especially Ruth and Mantle, as representatives of the golden years. When he receives word, however, of the death of Joshua Pitts, his former black teammate, Blazer realizes that baseball serves as a common denominator in pulling people together and in creating valuable lifetime memories.

Baseball's problems are common topics in the genre, but they are treated too sparsely here to be meaningful. The integration topic is the main issue, and Blazer's mentors prepare for its application. Blazer is taught to do the right thing, and he does it. The problem is that the book is too much a moral tract to be rated highly as literature.

Hutton, Jeff. *Perfect Silence.* New York: Breakaway Books, 2000. (New York: Breakaway Books, 2002.)

Joseph Tyler plays baseball with a neighbor and works on his father's farm in Virginia until Union troops approach in 1864. He joins the Confederate army and is wounded during the Battle of the Wilderness. Tyler consoles a dying enemy soldier and takes possession of a letter addressed to Sarah Kinsley of Rocker Falls, New York. Captured by the Yankees, he is sent to prison in Elmira, New York. Tyler recovers from his wound and plays baseball while a prisoner of war. He escapes during a ballgame and hides out until the Civil War ends.

Recruited by the Terryville Niners, Rebel Joe Tyler establishes himself as a pitcher and outfielder. He eventually delivers the dead soldier's letter to Sarah Kingsley, and a romance develops. Tyler gets married, turns down an offer to play pro baseball, and returns to his father's farm. His bride later joins him in Virginia on the farm that features a new house. Tyler enjoys the perfect silence of Nature in contrast to the commercialized North and its trend toward professional baseball.

The common theme of the pastoral game being changed by professionalism and economics is stressed, but purple patches crop up. The plot also tends toward the melodramatic, and although still a more than competent work, it falls short of *Play for a Kingdom,* Thomas Dyja's Civil War-baseball classic.

Leonard, Sam. *A Difficult Trade: The Baseball Mystery.* San Francisco: Robert D. Reed Publishers, 2000.

The Florida Manatees are the defending World Series champions, but owner Harry Hvide decides to unload the stars in order to cut the payroll. The biggest problem is how to deal with slugger Dick Johnson and his sixty-six-million-no-trade contract. Greg Barrett is given the assignment, and he attempts to murder Johnson but succeeds only in wounding him. Stanley Starfish investigates the disability claim for the insurance company. Just as he closes in on the solution, though, he accepts the job of vice president of security for Hvide Holdings. Barrett, meanwhile, resigns from Hvide's employ and tries to rectify his value system. Hvide gets tired of free-agency players and their ruthless agents and sells the team. The new owner moves to Salt Lake City, and the recovered Dick Johnson detests the location.

The main thrust of this unusual mystery is on revealing that spoiled athletes and amoral agents tend to victimize owners—an historical reversal of roles. There is a major concern for the characters' reactions to moral dilemmas, and the detection of the crime, therefore, is overshadowed—a concept that works only moderately well here.

Lynch, Chris. *Gold Dust.* New York: Harper Collins, 2000. (New York: Harper Trophy, 2002.)

A Young Adult novel that may transcend the label, it deals with a Catholic School of Boston in 1975. Napoleon Ellis of Dominica integrates the school and makes friends with Richard Moncrief, a seventh-grade classmate. Moncrief decides to make a baseball player out of the newcomer, who is proficient at cricket, and making them Gold Dust Twins—the term applied to Boston rookies Jim Rice and Fred Lynn. Moncrief, son of a laborer, and Ellis, son of a professor at Boston University, seem to bond while playing baseball. They are joined in friendship by Beverly, a girl who stands up to the school bullies and racists.

The relationship is threatened when Ellis, who has a great voice, is offered a chance to transfer to a more prestigious school. While the boys are at a game in Fenway Park, Moncrief realizes that the Dominican has other interests—that his obsession with baseball is not shared. With his Gold Dust dream shattered, Moncrief retaliates by beaning Ellis in a practice game at school. Later, Beverly informs him that Ellis has transferred. Moncrief tells her to wish her friend luck. He will be too busy trying to become another Fred Lynn.

Richard Moncrief is blinded by his obsession and does not understand the situation of Napoleon Ellis. There is no formula ending here, as they go their separate ways without a simplified resolution. Although aimed at a young audience, the book's well-handled racial situation makes it worthy of adult readers.

Mark, David. *One of the Boys.* Portland, OR: Xlibris, 2000.

Matty Johnson pitches in the majors from 1952 to 1970 and wins over 300 games before being unconditionally released. However, he refuses to accept the dismissal and plans to continue even if he has to be a switch-pitcher. In three off-season appearances as a speaker, much of Johnson's life is revealed. A perfectionist as a player, he cannot cope with life off the field. Johnson stubbornly continues his self-promotion as a folk hero. On the personal level, though, he refuses to make a connection with his son.

A victim of the ex-jock syndrome and his monstrous ego, Matty Johnson is doomed to have a devastating future. The complex non-sequential literary style makes for a tough 179-page read, but it may be worth the effort.

Platt, Randall Beth. *The 1898 Baseball Fe-As-Ko.* North Haven, CT: Catbird Press, 2000.

Royal Leckner, narrator and foreman of the Four Arrows Ranch near Idlehour, Oregon, tells how he becomes a co-owner of a baseball team. His wife, E. M., takes a trip to Portland and returns to the ranch accompanied by the Bowery Bulldogs, a pro team. The ranch owner, Levi, is retarded, but he is enamored with the game. The horsebarn becomes the site of winter training under the tutelage of Sully, the ranch blacksmith who was once a pitcher. E. M.'s father, the imprisoned Enrico Galluci, is talked into sponsoring the team, which becomes famous in the Northwest. The Boston Beaneaters are persuaded to come west for a contest, much to the interest of gamblers, and the Bulldogs emerge with a 10–9 win.

Levi, the owner of the Four Arrows who pitched for the team, decides to give up baseball, though, and Royal Leckner is glad to go back to ranching. The trainingbarn becomes the Horse Palace, and E. M. returns as a wife rather than a baseball aficionado. Told in Leckner's semi-literate western dialect, the book is a lighthearted glimpse of nineteenth-century life. The baseball aspect is significant in that it reveals the early influence of commercialism and gambling on the game.

Reid, Van. *Mollie Peer: Or the Underground Adventure of the Moosepath League.* New York: Viking, 1999. (New York: Penguin, 2000.)

Tobias Walton and his pals of the crime-solving Moosepath League combine with newspaper columnist Mollie Peer to rescue a child in Portland, Maine, in 1896. Joining in the adventure is Wyckford O'Hearn, the Hibernian Titan, a slugger for the semipro Portland Bantams. In the first of the two games presented, O"Hearn fans to end the event on a losing note. He gets a second chance, however, while filling in for an injured player on Louis Socakalexis' Penobscot team. This time he responds with a game-winning grandslam against the Brunswick Quibblings. Sockalexis is the famed Native American who played briefly for Cleveland and probably inspired the change of the name to Indians.

In the meantime, O'Hearn helps Mollie Peer and the Moosepathers track down the smugglers who are using Bird, a child, in their nefarious activities. The boy ends up in the safety of the farm of the O'Hearns, but the portrait of an unknown woman who the crime fighters suspect is his mother leaves the prospect of a new mystery in order. Mollie, a feminist who aspires to be a full-fledged journalist, writes the newspaper story of the case under the name of Peter Mall in order to be more convincing to the public — which is not likely to accept a female reporter.

The mediocre mystery is enhanced by the baseball element and the atmosphere of the Maine seacoast at the end of the nineteenth century.

Smith, April. *Be the One.* New York: Knopf, 2000. (New York: Pocket Books, 2001.)

Cassidy Sanderson, a thirty-five-year-old former member of the Colorado Silver Bullets (a female baseball team), is the only woman working as a major league scout. With the help of Pedro Pedrillo, a friend of her father, Sanderson signs Alberto Cruz, a Dominican, for the Los Angeles Dodgers. Cruz, though, becomes the victim of blackmail and death threats that are tied to a car accident in which the scout and her boyfriend, Joe Galinis, are also involved. Galinis is kidnapped, and Sanderson gets a letter from him. He confesses to being responsible for the accident that led to a woman's death. He also relates that he has evidence that may incriminate a Dominican criminal who is behind the blackmailing. Galinis is apparently murdered before completing his mission, however, and Sanderson has no solution for the crimes. She continues to scout while trying to pull her life together. She and Pedro Pedrillo decide to stay in baseball even though the game can sometimes be a dirty business.

There is no neat conclusion here — the criminals are not brought to justice. Baseball itself is victimized by opportunists who exploit the game for profit, and the people who care are helpless. The stark realism tends to make this one of the best baseball books featuring a female protagonist.

Spoerl, Steve. *Sut McCaslin: A Baseball Romance.* San Jose, CA: Writers Club Press, 2000.

A reserve outfielder for the Washington Senators in the 1950s, Sut McCaslin listens to the conversations on the philosophy of the game while riding the bench. He also observes the racism directed at teammate Cuban Kid Ebony. One night in St. Louis, McCasliln abandons the team and moves in with Ivy, a black woman. On the last day of the season, however, he reports back to the Senators. He is treated as if he has never been gone and is sent in to pinch-hit against the Yankees as the 156-page novella ends.

McCaslin is obsessed with the meaning of life during the era of the McCarthy witch-hunt. He tries to decide if baseball, with its rules and traditions, brings order to a chaotic existence. If not, it is merely another example of randomness that mirrors the meaningless universe. There is no easily discernible answer in this philosophical fantasy that is filled with baseball lore.

Weber, James A. *Pennants Ain't Peanuts.* Bloomington, IN: Authorhouse, 2000.

Joseph Ladislaus Kaslowski (Peanut Joe) sells peanuts at Friendly Field, home of the Chicago Chicks. A former major league pitcher, he lost a leg while saving a kid's life. Now the old man lives in an apartment overlooking the ballpark. Upset with the Chicks stand-pat front office, he leads a protest that demands the acquisition of quality players. It happens, and the Chicks win the division title. During the playoffs, Joe is hospitalized but is cheered when he discovers that the boy he rescued years ago is the father of the centerfielder of the Chicks. The team advances to the World Series as the centerfielder scores the decisive run.

In the Epilogue, a wake is held on the mound to honor Peanut Joe who died during the post-game celebration. Like the Steve Goodman song, it is apparently the last request of a dying Chick (Cub) fan. The joy of experiencing the miracle year of the Chicago Chicks, though, is thwarted by the melodrama and sentimentalism.

Whitlow, G. Artie. *Blue Bayou Days: The Summer of 61.* San Jose: Writers Club Press, 2000.

Skeeter Hayden, author, narrator and protagonist, is thirteen in 1961 and pitches for the youth baseball league in Monroe, Louisiana. He watches Dizzy Dean and Peewee Reese on television games and roots for Mantle and Maris of the Yankees— the team he hopes to pitch for. Since it is his book, Skeeter meets his heroes, including JFK and Elvis Presley. He falls for Elizabeth O'Neal, a summer visitor to Monroe, who plays for his team. She goes home at the end of the summer, and Skeeter becomes a high school star and eventually joins the Yankees. When Elizabeth attends a Yankee game, Skeeter uses his authorial powers and marries her at the stadium during the game.

The attempt at metafiction (a novel about writing a novel) produces instead an Horatio Alger success formula of self-indulgence.

Yankus, Tom. *Montana Summer.* Portland, OR: Xlibris, 2000.

A sixty-page section of *Montana Summer: The Boys in the Bus Leagues and a Mish-Mash of Other Things to Read* chronicles bits of the 1956 season of the Missoula Timberjacks of the Class C Pioneer League. The protagonist (Yankus) compiles a 5–4 record as a relief pitcher with a 4.56 ERA. He feels that he contributes more to the team as a bus driver. There are some amusing anecdotes of minor league life in the novella/memoir.

2001

Blue, Max. *God Is Alive and Well and Playing Third Base for the Appleton Papermakers.* San Jose: Writers Club Press, 2001.

This is a hodgepodge of loosely connected fictional anecdotes dating from the 1916 World Series to the 2001 Phillies. It includes a forty-page episode about a Teener State baseball tournament (for kids aged 13 to15), and a story in which a boy is informed by his grandfather that God is the thirdbaseman for Appleton because he can hit Lowell Grosskopf's curveball, a superhuman achievement.

While most of the book is in praise of the game, the 1916 Series, won by the Red Sox, presents a problem. The event is discussed by two boys who think that the Brooklyn Robins may have sold out. They realize that money can be more important than winning — that sportswriter Hugh Fullerton is right in saying that baseball is a commercial enterprise. Despite the negative aspects of the game, though, it prevails because a nation requires a pastime with the tradition, the folk lore, and the statistics of baseball-elements that are timeless and pervasive. Although not really a novel, it presents some interesting views of baseball.

Cochran, Mike. *Sport.* New York: Thomas Dunne Books, 2001.

Harlan (Sport) Hawkins is twelve in 1967 as he roots for the hometown Minnesota Twins, plays firstbase in a summer league, and collects baseball cards. He also lives in a dysfunctional family that his father has abandoned. Sport, his older brother Gerard, and his ailing mother live in urban poverty. George Walker, a neighbor and Sport's coach, tries to help by hiring the boy for odd jobs and getting him a scholarship at a prestigious private school. As the lives of his brother and mother disintegrate, Sport struggles to keep a positive attitude. Opposed to the chaotic domestic atmosphere is the stable world of baseball—the source of much of Sport Hawkins' consolation.

Aimed at both youngsters and adults, the novel is competently written. Its major weakness is the lack of psychological depth in the characters, as the fast-paced narrative floats on the surface of the troubled lives.

Friedman, Mark. *Columbus Slaughters Braves.* Boston: Houghton Mifflin, 2001. (Boston: Mariner Books, 2002.)

Sibling rivalry embitters Joe Columbus, the narrator and older brother of baseball star CJ. While Joe becomes an unenthusiastic science teacher, CJ excels in high school (Pasadena), college (UCLA), and pro baseball as the thirdbaseman of the Chicago Cubs. CJ becomes a national icon, but Joe's career and marriage flounder. Joe usually ignores his brother's accomplishments but finally consents to see him play. Shortly after, during the biggest season of his career, CJ is diagnosed with leukemia and rapidly declines. Joe spends time with him and tries to erase his jealousy, but the best he can do is to achieve a state of neutrality—a minor psychological victory in an attempt to change his life. CJ delivers a "Lou Gehrig speech" in his last public appearance, aptly at Wrigley Field, and soon dies.

In Mark Harris' *Bang the Drum Slowly* (1956), the death of Bruce Pearson, an average player is handled effectively. CJ Columbus' death, on the other hand, is presented in purple patches. Along with CJ's superhero status, the sentimentalizing in the last section of the book undermines the overall quality—leaving it in the mediocre range.

Grisham, John. *A Painted House.* Garden City, NY: Doubleday, 2001. (New York: Delta, 2004.)

Luke Watson is seven in the summer of 1952 as he listens to Harry Caray announce the Cardinal games. His grandfather had signed with the St Louis team before his career was interrupted by World War I, and it is Luke's ambition to be a Cardinal. Late in the season, the team is in third place, but Stan Musial is in the run for the batting title. Meanwhile, his family is hiring cotton pickers on the rented eighty acres in Arkansas. Pearl, his mother, had been raised in a painted house and is not happy living in a sharecropper's shack in the middle of a cotton field.

The laborers consist of hillbillies and Mexicans. In a sandlot baseball game, the Mexicans win behind the pitching of Cowboy, who shows Luke how to throw a curve. Violence erupts between Cowboy and Hank Spruill of the hillbillies, but Luke is more concerned with the pennant race, which is won by the Dodgers. He does manage, though, to please his mother by painting the house, with the help of some of the Mexicans, before a flood forces the family to move.

A departure from the legal thrillers of Grisham, the book is pervaded by baseball. The Cardinal broadcasts brighten Luke's world and give hope of an escape from the cotton patch that his mother detests. The subplot, however, involving the two groups of itinerant workers, borders on melodrama.

Hamilton, Steve. *The Hunting Wind.* New York: Thomas Dunne Books, 2001. (New York: St. Martin's Paperbacks, 2002.)

Alex McKnight of Prudell-McKnight Investigations is visited in his Upper Peninsula home by Randy Wilkins, a former teammate. McKnight was a catcher and Wilkins a left-handed pitcher for Toledo in 1971. The latter wants the former Detroit cop to help him find a girlfriend from that era, some thirty ears ago. McKnight finally tracks down the woman, but she turns out to be a crook. After retreating to the comforts of home and the Glasgow Inn, McKnight sends his old catcher's mitt to Terry Wilkins, Randy's estranged son, and convinces the ex-pitcher to call the boy.

A typical hard-boiled detective with a code of honor, Alec McKnight finds the unjust world a difficult place, but he does the best that he can.

Kinsella, W. P. *Magic Time.* Stillwater, MN: Voyageur Press, 2001.

Mike Houle, from a Chicago suburb, plays baseball at LSU and does well until his senior year. Undrafted by a major league organization, he accepts an offer to play in the semipro Iowa Cornbelt League. In Grand Mound, Iowa, he is assigned to a job and a room with a local family—just like the other members of the Greenshirts. The team practices in the morning, works in the afternoon, and plays intersquad games at night. It seems to be an ideal situation until Houle realizes that it is a trap—that the team is not part of a league. The community has engendered the plot to keep the players in town and to marry local girls in order to keep the town alive.

Houle's epiphany allows him to break the trance and rebel from the pastoral environment; he joins the AA Knoxville team as a secondbaseman. However, he discovers that the pressure of the pro game is more than he can handle—just like his last year in college. He returns to Grand Mound and yields to the Booster Committee and its scheme to actively recruit players that choke in the clutch as a means of stabilizing the community. Houle embraces the security of small-town mid–American culture. He has discovered that the competition of the outside world of baseball and business is too threatening. Mike Houle sacrifices his potential for the serenity of life that includes baseball but eliminates the economic and competitive pressures.

A cross between a pastoral romance and a horror story, the book confronts the common theme of the business of baseball in a unique manner. It is a return for Kinsella, almost, to the quality of *Shoeless Joe.*

Lebowitz, Paul. *Breaking Balls: A Novel of Baseball.* Jefferson, NC: McFarland, 2001.

Bret Samuels, a Jewish kid from Brooklyn, pitches for the Kingsboro Community College. He is medium-sized and has a mediocre fastball, but his breaking stuff is good. Passed over in the draft, he is invited to a Dodgers tryout camp. Samuels is assigned to a rookie team in Great Falls, Montana. Although he suffers from culture shock, he pitches well enough to work his way up to the San Antonio Missions in AA ball. When the Dodgers release a right-handed long-reliever, Samuels is called up to Los Angeles. In May, with the Dodgers in last place, he enters a game and realizes his ambition: the name of Bret Samuels will be in the *Baseball Encyclopedia.*

Narrated by the wisecracking pitcher, the book is filled with realistic game descriptions and ballplayer dialogues. Short of literary mastery, it is, though, a good read for baseball fans.

Polidoro, J. P. *Project Samuel.* Laconia, NH: Longtail, 2001.

Millionaire E. Royston MacDonald hires a biotech team to clone Ted Williams. Jack Danton, a fellow collector of baseball memorabilia, helps to put together a group of scientists and a surrogate mother. DNA is procured from hair clippings at Jack Rizzo's barbershop. In San Diego, the chosen woman is impregnated without knowledge of the source or the approval of the Hall-of-Fame ballplayer.

The project is successful, and MacDonald and two of the doctors win a Nobel Prize. The boy, Samuel, grows up in the San Diego neighborhood of young Williams. At the age of eight, he is excelling at baseball while playing at Ted Williams Field.

Published while Williams was alive, the book won some notoriety when the cryonic debate over the former baseball star became a news story. The writing, however, is amateurish, and the sensationalism is the only dominant factor.

Posner, Alan. *Base Hit.* New York: Vantage Press, 2001.

Yankee leftfielder Chris Donovan, a lifetime .362 hitter, is beaned by Don McGinniss in the playoffs. During the off-season, he announces his plan to get revenge on the Chicago pitcher. On next season's Opening Day, Donovan hits a liner that kills McGinniss. Noting the look of ecstasy on Donovan's face after the incident, Assistant D.A. Robert Kasoff decides to prosecute. He collects evidence of premeditation, including a corked bat and videos of the pitcher in action in Donovan's possession, and issues a warrant for the Yankee's arrest. A judge orders Donovan to be tried for first-degree murder. He plays the rest of the season under duress while waiting for a Court of Appeals to make a decision.

During the next off-season, the outfielder feels a need to atone for his deed. He visits the widow of the pitcher and makes promises to teach her son how to pitch. Donovan sets up a trust fund for the kid's college expenses, and he establishes a foundation for teaching "the techniques of nonviolent dispute resolution."

Kasoff is amazed at hearing of the good deeds. An expert on baseball trivia, he has grown disenchanted with the modern spoiled jock in a free-agent market. He now considers the possibility that the game is conducive to producing virtues that lead to moral action and redemption.

The author makes a strong effort to be convincing, but the events are too improbable to be valid, the propaganda too heavy-handed.

Rao, Ravi P. *Seven Lives, Seven Games.* San Francisco: Robert D. Read, 2001.

During a baseball strike, televangelist Josiah Hubert agrees to finance the teams of the major league North American Baseball Conference. In return, he is allowed to open a new franchise, the Midwest Miracles of rural Nebraska. With the hiring of the manager Brownie Jones, the team, led by Devon Jenkins, its only black player, becomes popular and competitive. It qualifies for the Double Day Cup, the conference's version of the World Series., but Nate Michaels, television Director of Sports Programming, decides that the Cup must go seven games in order to rejuvenate interest in baseball. He bribes players from both teams to try to make the plan work. However, a fan notices the strange play and confronts Michaels about "the fix." The television executive, who is in love with the Midwest owner's wife, argues that he is trying to save baseball — to bring back the fan enthusiasm that existed before its economic corruption. The widely-watched seventh game goes into extra innings — and supposedly revives interest in baseball.

The contradictory idea of restoring the game to national prominence by fixing a championship playoff is as illogical as the baseball strategy deployed in the book — which also features bad writing.

Rosen, R. D. *Dead Ball.* New York: Walker, 2001.

Moss Cooley, black outfielder for the Providence Jewels, is pursuing Joe DiMaggio's fifty-six-game hitting streak when he receives death threats. Ex-big leaguer Harvey Blissberg, after a stint as a motivational speaker, returns to private investigation at the request of a team executive. He traces the threats to Jewels announcer Snoot Coffman, who has a history of racist crimes.

Blissberg, of Jewish descent, first appeared in the Edgar Award winner *Strike Three You're Dead* (1984) when he was still a Jewels outfielder. He is in the hard-boiled tradition, but his witty, sarcastic persona hides his inability to settle comfortably into life after his baseball career is over. The ex-jock syndrome, or what girlfriend Mickey Slavin calls his "sad man-ism," is overly emphasized, but it is only a minor distraction from a mystery that is augmented by Rosen's accurate depiction of the type of racism that haunted Jackie Robinson and Henry Aaron, the forerunners of the fictional Moss Cooley. The author sometimes writes as Richard D. Rosen.

Rutkoff, Peter M. *Shadow Ball: A Novel of Baseball and Chicago.* Jefferson, NC: McFarland, 2001.

In 1919, Charles Comiskey decides to clinch a pennant for the White Sox by signing John Henry (Pop) Lloyd, fabled Negro League shortstop. He confers with Rube Foster, owner of Lloyd's team, the Chicago American Giants, in an attempt to make a legitimate deal. Fictional character Sam Weiss, a Jewish lawyer, serves as moderator. Observing the action is Comiskey's black maid Lizzie (Kid) Douglas, formerly known as Memphis Minnie during her career as a blues singer.

The historical background dominates in the beginning, including the 1919 Chicago race riot, the emerging dissatisfaction of Comiskey's players (culminating in the Black Sox Scandal), the change in baseball created by the slugging of Babe Ruth, and Foster's founding of the Negro National League. Comiskey's bold and greedy plan unfolds dramatically, however, as he talks Chicago's bigwigs and some of the other team owners into accepting integration as a prudent business deal.

Foster and Weiss make the arrangements for Lloyd, known as the black Honus Wagner, to play the last two months of the season in place of the weak-hitting Swede Risberg. The August race riot in the city, though, convinces Lloyd that it would be futile to try to enter the white world. He works in the underground freight network of Chicago, and the labor problems and racism that he encounters on the job help him to make a decision to reject the opportunity of integrating the national pastime. He may also have been aware of Risberg's mobilization of the South Side Faction of the White Sox to resist the move. Thus, Charles Comiskey's plot to break the color barrier is thwarted by events beyond his control — and the Black Sox Scandal lurks in the future.

Meanwhile, Sam Weiss, the moral arbiter of the novel, is disgusted by the business "ethics" and rampant racism that make a pawn of Pop Lloyd and that threaten his growing affection for Lizzie Douglas. The lawyer's judgments, though, have no effect on the acts of powerful men or the prejudices of society. The realistic rendering of the daring concept of the book makes it credible. The skillful blending of real and fictional characters and of stark realism and imaginative speculation (or alternate history) results in one of the touchstones of baseball fiction.

Standiford, Les. *Opening Day: Or the Return of Satchel Paige.* San Francisco: LiveREAD, 2001.

Leland (Buck) Wilson is an eighty-year-old batboy for the Vero Beach Grouper of the Double-A Florida League. He is promoted to thirdbase coach when the manager discovers that he was a star of the Negro Leagues and a teammate of Satchel Paige. Magic enters Wilson's arm, and he is assigned to pitch on Opening Day. Also featuring a female second baseman as part of a public relations scheme, the team hopes to boost attendance and save the franchise. Wilson conjures the ghost of Paige, and then stars by striking out eighteen and hitting a game-winning homer. His future plans include managing the club.

The short fantasy fails to evoke the atmosphere of the Satchel Paige era and is too frivolous to be more than mildly amusing. An essay of the Negro Leagues and bibliographies of books on early black baseball and Paige increase the length of the book to 143 pages.

Sturm, James. *The Golem's Mighty Swing.* Montreal: Drawn and Quarterly, 2001.

The 100-page graphic novel presents the adventures of the Stars of David barnstorming team in 1922. Narrated by Noah Strauss, manager and thirdbaseman, it relates the difficulties associated with economic survival and ethnic discrimination. In an effort to raise money, the team takes the advice of promoter Victor Paige and creates a Golem (a Jewish folkhero) out of a former Negro League player. The season is marred by a game against the Jewish-hating Putnam All-Americans that results in a riot. The Stars of David continue, though, and last another four seasons before disbanding.

Winegardner, Mark. *Crooked River Burning.* New York: Harcourt, 2001. (New York: Harvest Books, 2001.)

The decline of the city of Cleveland and its baseball team in the years 1948 to 1969 is featured with fictional characters David Zielinsky and Anne O'Connor interacting with historical figures. Eliot Ness, Alan Freed, and Carl Stokes are among the real people to appear, and the exploits of the Cleveland Indians are a part of the action.

Zielinsky is entranced by the 1948 season, especially when Bill Veeck signs the aged Satchel Paige. The Indians win the World Series from the Boston Braves — with over 86,000 fans attending Game Five. The 1954 season is also featured despite the disastrous four-game sweep by the Giants in the Series. The next setback for Cleveland baseball is the trade of Rocky Colavito to Detroit in 1960. Nothing can assuage the loss to Zielinsky, although the return of Paige, as a senior citizen, for a three-inning stint in 1965 is a diversion. As a local politician, Zielinsky continues to follow the team and attends a game in 1969 — a season in which the Indians post a losing record.

The city also reaches its nadir in '69 as the Cuyahoga River catches fire. In the 1948–1969 period, Cleveland drops from the sixth largest U.S. city to the twelfth — and becomes a national joke. The burning river symbolizes the plight of Cleveland–along with the declining fortunes of the Indians. However, people like David Zielinsky and journalist Anne O'Connor (the star-crossed lovers) endure and help keep Cleveland alive. Winegardner, author of *The Veracruz Blues,* reveals a vivid slice of social history in this book.

Wojciechowski, Gene. *About 80 Percent Luck.* Kingston, NY: Sports Illustrated Books, 2001. (Kingston, NY: Sport Classic Books, 2003.)

Joe Riley, an apathetic editor for a Chicago newspaper, is a victim of downsizing. He is offered the choice of unemployment or the role of a sportswriter. The result is a trip to Arizona to cover the Cubs in spring training. Riley learns the trade and makes contact with the equipment manager and a Hispanic catcher — moves that supply him with information. He impresses his rivals and Megan Donohue, an attractive employee of the paper. He also exposes the unfair tactics of a writer who continually gets scoops. Even though Riley gets fired, he returns to Chicago to find job offers and Megan waiting. He feels that he has something to live for again; he no longer has to depend on luck.

Baseball and work offer a redemption for Joe Riley, but he seems to be too lucky, the author too manipulative, to make the book credible.

2002

Amernic, Jerry. *Gift of the Bambino.* New York: Thomas Dunne Books, 2002.

In 1914, Lazo Slackowicz attends a game with his father at Hanlon's Point Stadium between the Toronto Maple leafs and the Providence Grays of the International League. Babe Ruth pitches a one-hit shutout and hits a three-run homer, the first of his career. The ball lands in the bay, and Lazo is entranced with the idea of recovering the submerged talisman hit by his hero. He goes on to become a pro outfielder under the name of Larry Slack, but in 1935 he realizes he will not make the majors, and he retires. However, he attends the game in Pittsburg at which the aging Ruth, now with the Boston Braves, hits three homers — the last of his career.

As an old man, Lazo tells the story of his baseball life to his grandson, Stephen Slack (the narrator). At eighty, he is dying, and he asks Stephen to bring him the ball that Babe Ruth hit into Lake Ontario. Lazo dies with a 'fake ball' in his hands. A year later, Stephen reflects on the lessons he had been taught by his grandfather. The baseball that he died with, though not the magical ball that Ruth hit, symbolizes the game that gives anyone with talent and desire a chance to participate — to pursue perfection. Stephen realizes that Lazo, in his hero worship, was blind to the debauchery of Babe Ruth, but by applying the quest for perfection to life as a whole, he is able to benefit from the positive aspect of his grandfather's story. He modifies the Bambino's carpe diem approach and finds an inner peace.

Although the bonding of Stephen and Lazo is somewhat maudlin, the baseball action is credible and occasionally humorous. The portrait of Babe Ruth, at his highest and lowest levels, is probably the best in fiction to this point.

Andre, Rae. *Cards: The Best and Only Novel about Baseball Card Collectors.* San Jose: Writers Club Press, 2002.

Will Finney is a collector of baseball memorabilia, and from his Card Room at Trader's Point on Long Island Sound, he sponsors shows for baseball card collectors. Because he tries to keep crooks, like the Cress Gang, from controlling the business, a consortium of international crime fighting agencies, SATIN, persuade Finney to work as an agent. Since the organization has evidence that he has cheated on taxes, Finny joins the team and is deployed to bait counterfeiters who are invading the card collecting area and are also considered threats to the world monetary system.

Finney's strange behavior in his new role alienates his girlfriend, but when he helps to capture the villains, she agrees to marry him. The ghosts of Babe Ruth and Lou Gehrig discuss the marriage, and Gehrig gives his approval. Other dead baseball legends also appear in the novel.

Featuring a winsome narrative style and five pages of Crib Notes that give baseball facts and correct errors that purposely appear in the text, the book maintains an amusing aura for much of the action. However, it eventually succumbs to sentimental heroism and romance. *The Bite of the Shark*, also about baseball card collectors, appears the same year.

Bennett, James W., and Donald Raycroft. *Old Hoss: A Fictional Baseball Biography of Charles Radbourn.* Jefferson, NC: McFarland, 2002.

Fictional journalist John Trapp of Chicago travels to Bloomington, Illinois, in 1914 for ceremonies in honor of Clark Griffith and the late Old Hoss Radbourn. Trapp meets Griffith on the train, and stories about Radbourn inspire the journalist to do some research into the pitcher's life. Old Hoss was 60–12 (some sources say only fifty-nine wins) for the Providence Grays in 1884 and also won all three games of the championship series against the New York Metropolitans. Pitching underhanded from fifty feet, he threw 678 2/3 innings that year. In a career that ran from 1880 to 1891, he posted a record of 309–195 and won a spot in the Hall of Fame. Trapp learns, though, that after the 1884 season Radbourn declared that baseball had become a dirty business with its contracts, reserve clauses, and greedy owners.

On further investigation, Trapp discovers that Radbourn's personal life was a disaster. He owned a tavern in Bloomington, but he was an alcoholic and suffered from syphilis. After a failed comeback attempt in 1894 with Von der Ahe's St Louis Browns, he tried to kill himself while hunting. He failed but died later in the year at the age of forty-two.

In interviewing Illinois residents, Trapp collects stories from Radbourn's career. One of the pitcher's friends was Baby Bliss, a 700-pounder, who once went to the aid of John L. Sullivan when the boxing champ was attacked by salesmen in Radbourn's bar. Another pal was Willie Larks, a black pitcher who learned how to throw the fadeaway pitch from Old Hoss. In a semi-pro game, Radbourn put Larks into pitch, and a riot ensued in which the ballplayers held off the racist crowd with their bats.

Including photographs of Bloomington people and places, most of the book is told in crudely phrased flashbacks of the protagonist's life from 1884 to 1894. John Trapp decides, however, that the story of the Hall-of-Famer's life should not be released to the public because America needed its heroes. The novel, with its debunking of a legend, contradicts the narrator's view. In the process, it creates a viable character who, like so many players in the early phases of the game, had trouble adjusting to celebrity status (on small salaries) — and perhaps even more trouble coping after the athletic phase was over, thus succumbing to the ex-jock syndrome. This book is indicative of the growing popularity of quality fictional biographies that emerged in the early twenty-first century.

Brock, Darryl. *Two in the Field.* New York: Plume, 2002.

In a sequel to *If I Never Get Back,* Sam Fowler is transported from the present back to 1875. He searches for Cait, his sweetheart from his 1869 time-trip. The Cincinnati Red Stockings have dissipated, and Cait's brother Andy is playing for Harry Wright in Boston. On his way to visit Andy, Fowler looks up Mark Twain, his friend from the first book. Cait's trail leads to O'Neill City, an Irish settlement in Nebraska, but he has to assure her that he did not willfully abandon her. Fowler hits a homer to help the Irish win a baseball game over Dyson's Party, a group of prospectors. Then he heads back East to claim the money that was swindled from O'Neill's Fenian organization. He succeeds, but on his return to Nebraska he learns that Cait's son, Tim, has been kidnapped. He, Cait, and Linc (a black Civil War hero now living in O'Neill City) follow the villains to the Dakota Territory. George Armstrong Custer refuses to join the search, but Goose, a Native American, guides the group to a hideout in the Black Hills. With the help of Goose's friend, Chief Crazy Horse, and the ghost of Colm, Cait's husband who was killed in the Civil War, Fowler rescues Tim and wins back the love of Cait — and hopes to settle in the Nebraska community.

More of a surreal historical romance than a baseball novel, it is weakened by the inclusion of the ghost — the time-travel aspect is easier to believe. Although a fast read with a lot of action, it rates lower than its predecessor (*If I Never Get Back*) and the author's *Havana Heat.*

Buro, John J. *Bite of the Shark.* Baltimore: PublishAmerica, 2002.

Andy Preneur (the narrator), Gus Tazio, and Donald Spahn, baseball card dealers, concoct a plan to rob Raymond Tremont of a 1909 T-206 Honus Wagner card that is worth over a million. The armed robbery at an auction succeeds, but Tazio is killed in the getaway. Preneur and Spahn decide to split the profit (a million and a quarter) of the sale with Tazio's son. Tremont suspects that Preneur is behind the robbery, but the card dealer considers the heist as a part of the business.

There is a plethora of rationalizing about economics and ethics in the card collecting field and little reference to the game of baseball. The book does not descend to the heroic action and romance of *Cards*, but its self-indulgent moralizing and lack of literary merit result in a low rating.

Chabon, Michael. *Summerland.* New York: Miramax, 2002. (New York: Miramax, 2004).

Ostensibly a children's book, it transcends the label. Coyote has a plot to destroy life, but he is challenged by Ethan Field, a mediocre little leaguer fo Ruth's Fluff 'n Fold Roosters of Clam Island, Washington. Along with teammate Jennifer T. Rideout, he is recruited by ferishers to oppose the evil Coyote. Accompanied by curious creatures, they enter alternate worlds. The quest ends with a baseball showdown between Ethan's Shadowtails and Coyote's Hobbledehoys. With the aid of Splinter, a magical bat made from the World Tree, the Shadowtails win the game and preserve life. Ethan and Jennifer return to the Roosters and resume a normal life.

The fantasy includes tall tales, Scandinavian and Native American myths, baseball lore, and an ecological motif. The children's story is merely the surface level.

Chastain, Bill. *The Streak.* Baltimore: PublishAmerica, 2002.

As a boy in Tampa, Florida, Dorsey McWhorter plays baseball under the tutelage of Walter Mobley, a former player of the Negro Leagues. Abandoned by his father, McWhorter (white) responds to the training and goes from high school directly to the majors. A star hitter for the Reds, he eventually grows complacent and seems to be at the end of his career as an out-of-shape designated hitter in Cleveland. However, he has an epiphany and changes his life-style and his approach to batting. McWhorter goes on to propel the team into a contender and to build a hitting streak that reaches fifty-five games at the end of the season — one short of the record.

Privately, McWhorter is in business with his old mentor, Mobley. As part of his changed attitude, he makes amends with his wife and son. To top off the run of success, he accepts the job of player-manager with the Texas Rangers for the next season. Unfortunately, the amazing heroics and transformation of the protagonist are not matched by literary merit.

Cook, Marshall J. *Off Season: A Novel of Love, Faith, and Minor League Baseball.* Superior, Wisconsin: Savage Press, 2002.

Casey Chastain, a female pitcher, arrives in Beymer, Wisconsin, to play for the Buffalo of the Great Northern Midwest League. A sequel to *The Year of the Buffalo*, the novel continues the story of the small town, its team, and the romance of Tommy Lee Smith and Billie Jo Ferkin — who are now married. They are the proprietors of the Dime-A-Cup Café, and Smith is now the manager of the baseball team.

The owner of the team has convinced the town council to build a new ballpark as part of an entertainment complex. Many townsmen are opposed to the concept, and when the complex burns down arson is suspected.

When the new season starts in the old stadium, Chastain and her female battery-mate, Heather Peterson, make the team. In the Big Game for the league pennant, the women star in a victory over the Baraboo Barons. During the victory celebration, a new owner announces that he plans to invest money in the old ballpark so that the spirit of the Buffalo will continue. Further, Billie Jo, who has been raped, and consequently impregnated, decides to accept the child with the blessings of Tommy Lee. Happiness and virtue prevail.

Creavy, Patrick. *Tyrus: An American Legend.* New York: A Tom Doherty Associates Book, 2002.

A fictional account of Cobb's 1905 season with Detroit and the trial of his mother in March of 1906, this is the period which forecasts the tumultuous career of one of baseball's greatest players. The death of his father, William Herschel Cobb, presumably the result of being shot while spying on his thirty-three-year- old wife, Amanda, haunts the teenager. Promoted from Augusta to the Tigers for the last forty games of the season, just after the fatal occurrence, Cobb refuses to accept the cruel treatment typically given to rookies of the era. He rejects the friendly advice of Wild Bill Donovan and Billy Armour and makes enemies of the rest of the team, especially fellow outfielders McIntyre and Crawford. Brooding alone in his unrelenting anger and fierce pride, Cobb finds relief with vicious play on the diamond. The mania associated with the legend is illustrated as he carries his father's pistol in the streets of the hostile northern cities whose fans taunt him for his arrogance and cruel aggressiveness. The 1905 season ends with Cobb displaying a hint of his future greatness.

Back home in Royston, Georgia, he has to deal with the trauma of his mother's impending trial for voluntary manslaughter. Amanda always supported his passion for baseball, but his father wanted him to be a scholar or soldier—and eventually a Southern Gentleman who would represent the tradition of the Pre-Civil War aristocracy. The trial exposes the tensions of the Cobb household, and the young ballplayer wrestles with the options of turning the pistol on Amanda and the intruding citizens of Royston or stifling his emotions and concentrating on baseball. Fortunately, he chose the latter course, but the price of his intensity may have cost his humanity. Like a mad scientist of Hawthorne, Cobb's obsession with perfection alienated him from almost everyone.

The novel gets to the heart of Ty Cobb's madness with its revelation of the negative influence of his strong-willed, bigoted father who opposed his son's vocation. The ignominy of William Cobb's death, and its ensuing notoriety, helped to create the controversial player of legend, but the book shows that the roots were formed when William married Amanda when she was a child and proceeded to ruthlessly formulate the type of son that he wanted Tyrus to be. This is the best of the fictional baseball biographies.

Dinger, Ed. *A Prince at First.* Jefferson, NC: McFarland, 2002.

Hal Chase (Prince Hal), legendary first baseman of the New York Highlanders, is the subject of this fictional biography. As a youth, he follows his brother John into townball of the 1890s in Alviso, California. Before John dies of polio, though, he begs Hal not to waste his life on baseball. Hal rejects the advice and plays at Santa Clara College. He becomes a pro in the Pacific Coast League and then makes it to the Highlanders, forerunners of the Yankees. Known as Prince Hal—a good hitter and a great fielder—he also earns the reputation as a troublemaker. He badgers managers, including Frank Chance and Christy Mathewson, and rails against the tight-fisted owners. Chase is convinced that Organized Baseball is in the hands of profit-seekers who maintain the image of morality at the cost of the truth: specifically the influences of gambling in the game and the exploitation of the players. He begins to throw games with the backing of gambler Fat Jack Delaney. During the infamous 1919 season, Chase talks to Chick Gandil (one of the eight men out) about fixing the World Series. Although he did not put up the money, the name of Hal Chase is usually associated with the Black Sox Scandal.

After his major league career, Chase returns to the Pacific Coast League, but he gets banned for fixing games. He ends up as a charity case in a California hospital. Irresponsible as a husband and father and immoral in his profession, Chase tells his story from the view of a victim of greedy ownership. He assumes the role as a potential savior of baseball by revealing its problems.

The irony is effective as Chase's prejudicial account of his participation in the historical events is credible. While not featuring the in-depth character analysis of *Tyrus*, it is a welcome addition to the field.

Ferris, Norman. *Yank.* Bloomington, IN: Authorhouse, 2002.

Loren (Yank) Temple moves with his family from Illinois to Tocqueville, Texas, in 1948. He joins the Southside Scorpions, a semipro baseball team, but he finds time to observe Mrs. Kaplan, a seductive neighbor, who may be a criminal. Yank also works with Buzz Howell as a member of Lyndon Johnson's senatorial campaign team. Howell educates the teenager in local politics, including the attempt of Texans to replace the liberal Harry Truman on the presidential ballot with segregationist Strom Thurmond. Yank impresses the scouts at a Yankee tryout camp, but his new-founded political views cost him his job with the Scorpions—who are essentially a group of rednecks. He later joins another semipro club.

In the fall, he becomes a high school football player, but athletic endeavors become secondary to the mystery involving Mrs. Kaplan. Yank realizes that Buzz Howell is an undercover cop on the trail of a New Orleans mob that may include the Kaplans.

The book stresses the education of Yank Temple, outsider, to the political, cultural, and athletic practices of East Texas. The baseball experiences and the historical lessons are vital in capturing the ambience of the time and place. The mundane mystery that monopolizes the second half, though, tends to reduce the overall quality.

Holland, Robert. *Things Got in the Way.* Oakton, VA: Ravens Yard Publishing, 2002.

Blake MacIntosh, a farm boy from Connecticut in the 1950s, matures into a superior being who may have been the greatest hitter in the history of baseball. Too many things get in the way, however, and he does not get a chance to prove himself in the major leagues. As an intellectual, he antagonizes coaches and managers of the jock culture who react by trying to sabotage his baseball career. MacIntosh is too interested in pursuing a Ph. D. in English to give himself totally to sports. He finally has a sensational year in the minors, but he is drafted into the army. Then he is injured in a car accident and is physically unfit for baseball. MacIntosh continues to farm, gets married and has a family, and develops into a successful novelist. Yet at the age of fifty, he participates in a Yankee fantasy camp and is so impressive as a hitter that Steinbrenner offers him a contract. The knowledge that he could have been another Babe Ruth is enough to satisfy MacIntosh, and he rejects the chance to gain fame and fortune as an athlete.

The book suffers by the emphasis on the superiority of Blake MacIntosh, who is an expert in just about everything. Also, the archetypal theme of nonconformity at odds with the norms of society is too didactic to be taken seriously.

Jenkins, Jerry B. *The Youngest Hero.* New York: Warner Faith, 2002.

This is a re-issue of the 1991 novel *Rookie* which depicts the incredible career of Elgin Woodall who starts his career with the Cubs at thirteen and goes on to break virtually every offensive record — presumably because he is a Christian.

Kaye, Farrell. *The New Paltz Outlaws: A Novel of Sex, Violence, and Baseball.* San Jose: Writers Club Press, 2002.

Lance Bangor is a pitcher for the Benedict Arnold High Turncoats and is taught by the coach to cheat whenever possible. As a pro, he is sent by the Yankees to the New Paltz Outlaws, a rowdy bunch that gets banned from Organized Baseball. The team continues to exist at the semipro level, and Bangor, a pitcher, is given a chance by the Yankees in the form of a one-year contract with a good-behavior clause. Known as the Iceman, he does some good work, but his riotous behavior results in banishment.

After brief careers as a stunt man, actor, stripper, and porn star, he returns to New Paltz and starts the team anew. With the big leagues on strike, the Outlaws challenge the Yankees to a game — with the proceeds going to charity. The unsanctioned game is played at Yankee Stadium, and the major league team wins in eleven innings, 3–2. The Iceman pitches the entire game for the Outlaws and ruins his arm in the process. As he and a teammate celebrate being the second best team in baseball, they discuss their encounters with comedian Alan Ackbar who has influenced all of the Outlaws to fight the Establishment — to turn their lives as losers around by challenging the hypocrisy and injustice of a corrupt society.

The problem is that Lance Bangor and his teammates have no code to back their rebellion against phoniness. The book presents tirades against immorality but counters with lectures supporting irresponsibility. The revolutionary text is further weakened by unfamiliarity with Standard English and proofreading.

Lupica, Mike. *Wild Pitch.* New York: Putnam Adult, 2002. (New York: Berkley, 2003.)

Showtime Charlie Stoddard, former star pitcher of the Mets, attempts a comeback at the age of forty. Chang, a physical therapist, has healed the back and shoulder problems that ended Stoddard's career five years earlier. The pitcher plays catch with Chang in Central Park and feels confident enough to join a semipro team. Before long, he draws the attention of Red Sox manager Tim Hartnett and becomes a teammate of his son, T-Mac Stoddard, on the Boston pitching staff as the team battles the Yankees in the pennant race.

Family problems exist, however, as T-Mac does not acknowledge his father — who is divorced from the youth's mother, Grace. Charlie persists in trying to make peace with T-Mac, though, and to win back Grace. At the same time, he makes a large contribution to the Red Sox by applying Chang's training methods: the therapist has been hired as a trainer by the team. The Stoddard family helps the Red

Sox to a first-place finish. In the Big Game, T-Mac holds the Yankees in check in relief after starting the day before. Charles admits that his son is a better pitcher, and T-Mac decides to accept Chang's training techniques—a way of acknowledging his father. Grace, meanwhile, attempts to resume a relationship with her ex-husband as the happily-ever-after formula unwinds. The pat conclusion, along with clichés and stereotypes, undermine the witty dialogue and fast-paced action. Lupica, who has also penned popular basketball and football novels (and made the best-seller lists with kid books), deserves more respect as a sportswriter than as a novelist.

McAllister, Troon. *The Kid Who Batted 1,000.* New York: Doubleday, 2002.

The Des Moines Majestyks of the American League are in last place after depleting the budget to acquire Juan-Tanamera Aires, superstar. A scout shows up with a kid, Marvin Kowalski, and tries to convince Zuke Johansen, manager, to put him on the team. Kowalski is just out of high school and looks more like a bookworm than an athlete, but he displays the ability to read pitches and to foul off every ball in the strikezone. When put into the lineup as a designated hitter, he walks every time. Kowalski also teaches teammates to study pitchers and umpires and to learn the fine points of the game. As a result, the Majestyks climb to first place. Johansen is delighted, and he goes to great efforts to protect the innocence of the kid in order to keep the parents happy.

In the play-offs against the Yankees, Kowalski changes the script. Knowing what pitch is coming, he decides to gamble by swinging for a hit rather than a foul. The ball sails over the fence for a homer that puts the team into the World Series. The kid, though, makes another big decision and opts to bypass the Series in favor of attending college. He explains to Johansen that he is tired of being a gimmick, a one-trick joke that does not really belong in baseball. The players, he thinks, have learned to win on their own. They no longer need him in order to compete with the best. Marvin Kowalski retires, then, with his on-base-percentage and batting average at 1.000.

Inspired by a children's book of the same title, the adult version is a blend of realism and fantasy with humorous touches. In the end, though, the credibility weakens, and the narrative gradually dissipates into a moralistic tract.

Owen, Howard. *The Rail.* Sag Harbor, NY: Permanent Press, 2002.

Neil Beauchamp, the Virginia Rail, is released from prison after serving time for manslaughter. The Hall-of-Famer had climaxed his alcoholic post-retirement life by driving a car that killed a state trooper. Beauchamp's son, David, escorts his father to Penns Castle. The house in which Beauchamp was born is now occupied by Blanchard, his demented half-sister and former lover. He tries to make amends for his past transgressions, including being a negligent father and husband, but his relatives and townspeople are not forgiving. Blanchard is the only one to accept him, and when she dies, he tries to reconcile with the long-neglected David—the son who is experiencing a mid-life crisis. The connection between Neil and David is tentative, but it is their only hope for contentment at the moment.

The author's fiction has been called Literate Southern Gothic (an implication of quality work) and this book fits that description.

Robinson, Patrick. *Slider.* New York: Harper Collins, 2002. (New York: Harper Paperbacks, 2004.)

Jack Faber, pitcher for St. Charles College in Louisiana, is invited to play in the prestigious Cape Marlin Summer League of Maine. His father, Ben, a poor farmer, accompanies Jack on the trip. In Chicago, they are joined by catcher Tony Garcia and Natalie, his mother. She is an impoverished music teacher who wants Tony to be a lawyer and is upset about the experiment with baseball. However, she falls in love with Ben Faber while their sons are starring for the Seapuit Seawolves.

In the fall, Jack Faber rejects a pro contract and returns to his college team. Despite a poor season that destroys his confidence, Jack is asked back to Cape Marlin for the summer. He regains his poise and defeats a major league team in an exhibition game. However, Jack decides to quit baseball and to concentrate on his education at Harvard. Meanwhile, Ben and Natalie pursue their romance — which is economically enhanced when natural gas is discovered on the Faber farm. The unlikely ending seals the fate of a badly written book.

Thomas, Trisha. *Roadrunner.* New York: Crown, 2002. (New York: Three Rivers Press, 2003.)

Dell Fletcher is known as the Roadrunner due to his base stealing exploits for Los Angeles, but his career is threatened by an injury. He then gets hooked on medication and physically abuses his wife, Leah, a successful screenwriter. Policeman Angel Lopez takes Fletcher into custody, but instead of booking his favorite ballplayer, he tries to teach him a lesson by turning him loose in the mean streets of Los Angeles. In the Roadrunner's absence, Lopez moves in on Leah and her two kids. In order to keep the family for himself, the cop arranges to frame Fletcher on drug charges. When the ballplayer returns to his home, Leah's prayers are answered as Lopez confesses, and the whole family is reunited.

The African American author was nominated for several awards for her first novel, but this is a sub par romantic thriller.

Wilson, M. R. *Protocol 9.* Portland, OR: Xlibris, 2002.

Photographer Rip Elytis makes the startling discovery that the Continental Federation of Baseball (CFB), a third major league, stages games that are fixed. They are the products of computer-generated scripts — or protocols. Team managers are programmed to direct the players to follow predestined instructions for each game as printed by the Old Man, a computer. The scripts provide exciting situations on the field in order to increase attendance.

The players are conditioned to accept their roles by sports psychiatrist Stuart J. Green. He also applies medication to deal with the disillusionment of many of the athletes. The financial rewards for submitting to the scripts help to suppress rebellion.

However, the photographic evidence of dishonesty garnered by Elytis is made public with the help of sportswriter Kathleen O'Casey. Commissioner Cyrus Hardy, in league with Dr. Green, works to discredit the charges, and a Senate subcommittee dismisses the evidence as being inconclusive. The seeds of revolution are planted, though, and one team, the Santa Fe Desperados, ignores the protocol and wins the CFB Super Series that is scripted for another team.

Although the future of the CFB is uncertain, it is assumed that the league will continue to try to control the actions of games. The dismissal of evidence by the Senate, which was aided by the apparent murder of a key witness, suggests that the power structure behind the program is firmly entrenched. Its symbol, Dr. Green, represents the technology that is geared for economic success at the cost of morality. The partnership of the computer and business is a threat to the integrity of baseball — a standard theme in the genre of sci-fi baseball fiction. The concept is presented reasonably well here.

2003

Ferrell, David. *Screwball.* New York: William Morrow, 2003.

Scout Stu Damato discovers Ron Kane in Texas, and four years later he joins the Boston Red Sox. With a 111 miles-per-hour fastball, Kane becomes a star as a pitcher, but he can also hit — and comparisons to Babe Ruth are inevitable. However, Neville Wulfmeyer, general manager, is troubled by the dissension Kane creates with his $186 million contract. Another problem is caused by the pressure of Barney Schacter, homicide investigator, who links a series of murders to the itinerary of the Red Sox. Wulfmeyer is threatened by tapes which cast suspicion on Kane as the probable murderer, but the GM tries to pin the blame on less valuable players.

The Red Sox make it to the World Series despite the turmoil. The Series goes to the seventh game, but Big Fish Sharkey, the manager, refuses to start Kane because he suspects that he may be the murderer. However, with the game on the line in extra innings, Sharkey uses Kane as a pinch-hitter, and his homer wins the Series and breaks the Red Sox jinx. Although Ron Kane is heralded as the greatest player of all-time after his one year in the majors, he is convicted of murder and given a life sentence.

The book is well-written, but that is not enough to save it from the absurd premise and the herculean heroics.

Latour, Jose. *Havana World Series.* New York: Grove Press, 2003.

President Batista is still in power in Cuba in 1958, and Meyer Lansky's casino is doing well. The owner of the Casino de Capri expects to make a fortune from the betting on the New York Yankees-Milwaukee Braves World Series. However, New York mobsters, Joe Bonanno and Joseph Profaci organize a gang of Cuban hoods with the purpose of robbing the casino on the day the Series ends. The crime takes place, but the aftermath, featuring the counterattack of Lansky, turns into a fiasco.

The Cuban noir novel concentrates on depicting criminals in a naturalistic style, and it succeeds on that level. The baseball action is secondary, but several of the games of the 1958 World Series are described in some detail. The Braves of Aaron, Mathews, Spahn, and Burdette are on the verge of beating the Yankees (like they did in 1957) with a three-to-one-game lead, but the Yanks, behind Hank Bauer and Bob Turley, rally to win the last three, including two in Milwaukee. The robbers have to wait until the Series is over to capitalize on all the betting that Lansky is covering in the Casino de Capri, and once the heist is made, baseball (in the second half of the book) is no longer a factor.

Looney, Mike. *Heroes Are Hard to Find.* Baltimore: PublishAmerica, 2004.

In a weak version of the Faust Legend (and a bad imitation of *The Year the Yankees Lost the Pennant*), Stormy Weather, retired Yankee Slugger, is given the chance to redeem a boyhood failure. Mac Swindell, the Mephistopheles figure, offers him a role in the Human Recycling Program. Weather becomes Cal Lucas, an eighteen-year-old Dallas resident who joins the Woodrow Wilson High baseball team coached by Cotton Parker.

Under Parker's Christian guidance, Lucas/Weather changes into a good guy in contrast to the egomania of his adult life. He wins the championship game for his team, makes up with his mother (who had abandoned him as a child), and wins the love of Susan, Cotton Parker's daughter. When he is changed back into an adult, he continues the altruistic trend. The new Stormy Weather leads a life dedicated to helping others and doing the right things.

Miller, John A. *Coyote Moon: A Novel of Love, Baseball, and the Heisenberg Uncertainty Principle.* New York: A Tom Doherty Associates Book, 2003.

Former MIT professor and perpetual Red Sox fan Benny Rhodes moves to a trailer in the Mojave Desert near Needles, California. His retirement follows the death of cohort Arthur Hodges, a brilliant mathematician. Accompanied by the much younger Becky Morgan, Rhodes blends in with the denizens of the desert as they search for inner peace and ecological harmony.

In the middle of the summer, Spencer, a star rookie catcher for the Oakland Athletics, appears at the trailer park. He has been amazing the baseball world with his stellar play. He has also been confusing people by the spouting of mathematical theories that seem unintelligible. Spencer has decided to quit the game. Gunter, one of the residents, argues that the young star, with no record of a baseball past, is the reincarnation of Rhodes' pal Arthur Hodges, as there is no logical explanation of the math and physics skills that the uneducated ex-ballplayer possesses. Rhodes and Gunter debate on whether life is as an ageless biological game of chance or the result of a divine purpose.

Spencer eventually returns to the Athletics and continues to apply his intuitive knowledge to the art of hitting a baseball. By predicting the position and speed of the baseball by its spin, he is able to transcend the uncertainty principle and thus make solid contact on the ball with regularity. In the meantime, Gunter has drowned in a flashflood, and Rhodes (in his sixties) is about to become a father.

The social and scientific aspects of the book are interesting, but the sci-fi/fantasy element seems unnecessary and detracts from the overall quality.

Mosher, Howard Frank. *The True Account of the Lewis & Clark & Kinneson Expeditions.* Boston: Houghton Mifflin, 2003. (Boston: Mariner Books, 2004.)

True Teague Kinneson, a Vermont school teacher, races Lewis and Clark to the Pacific. True's nephew, Ticonderoga, accompanies him and narrates the farcical episodes. One event of the trek involves a dispute between the Nez Perce and the members of the Lewis and Clark Expedition. True proposes that a ballgame could be used to settle the argument. True and Ti and twenty-eight of the Native Americans play against thirty of the expeditionists in the American game or

Kinneson-ball. True had (if it is "true") invented the game to entertain his students, and he stars as a pitcher and hitter in a 100–2 victory for his team. The Nez Perce make him a shaman and dub him "Noble Hurler and Striker in the Greatest Pastime Ever Invented" (a snide comment on the Doubleday fallacy).

At the conclusion of the journey, Ti becomes an artist of the flora and fauna of the American West, and True writes and produces his play about Ethan Allen. The book resembles *Muckaluck* (1980) in its comically exaggerated view of history, culture, and baseball.

Rowe, G. S. *Best Bet in Beantown.* Clifton, VA: Pocol Press, 2003.

In 1897, the owners of the Boston Beaneaters hire Will Beaman in a public relations role in order to increase attendance. However, when shortstop Germany Long is assaulted and bookkeeper Anne Anspach is found dead, his duties expand to detective work. Unfortunately, Beaman has been a failure in his father's Minneapolis detective agency, and he is merely looking for a chance to reform from his profligate past. With the help of landlady Claire Denihur and other friends, though, he discovers the source of the team's problems

Reserve player Billy Ewing has been paid by gambler Mike Muldine to injure Long in order to take his place in the lineup and then work to throw games. Muldine had also talked Anna Anspach into embezzling money from the Beaneaters. The gambler is, however, accidentally killed while arguing with Ewing, his associate. Beaman and Lieutenant O'Dwyer of the Boston police also uncover a plot to swindle Beaneater players by the Klondike Mining Syndicate after the discovery of gold in the Yukon. Beaman explains all this in the office of the owners with his father and Claire Denihur among the guests. He wins the respect of his father, the love of Claire, and a promotion with the team.

The emphasis on gambling and tight-fisted owners is typical of fiction dealing with the early years of baseball. The inclusion of real people in an historical setting that involves fictional characters and crimes, a pattern popularized by the Troy Soos mysteries, is less credible here. Nevertheless, the aura of nineteenth century baseball is presented with gusto.

Shawver, Brian. *The Cuban Prospect.* Woodstock, NY: Overlook, 2003. (Woodstock, NY: Overlook, 2004.)

Dennis Birch, a thirty-four-year-old former catcher turned scout, is assigned the task of smuggling Ramon Sagasta, left-handed pitcher, out of Cuba. The gargantuan Charlie Dance, who has sent glowing reports about Sagasta to America, is the Cuban contact who arranges for the escape attempt. However, a storm blows the boat back to the Cuban shore, and Birch and Sagasta become refugees in the wilderness with Castro's police in pursuit. When they are captured, Birch arranges for a baseball showdown between the pitcher and a cop who had once played against him. During the pitcher-batter contest, the scout's escape plan works. He arranges for Sagasta's trip to Florida, once again, but then Birch remains in Cuba and tries to save Rosa, the pitcher's girlfriend, from Charlie Dance, who has won the girl as part of the bargain that was made with Sagasta and his American sponsors. Birch rescues her from the man he considers a villain and platonically protects her while awaiting the return of her lover. He hears that the pitcher is with the Natchez Crayfish in Double A ball, but there is no word of an impending rescue of the girl.

Dennis Birch is doing what he thinks is right in the service of baseball — and romance. He thinks that the corrupted Dance is the epitome of talent gone bad when freed from restraint — a product of the business aspect of the game. Dance is further tarnished by the lack of ethics in a foreign setting in which normal rules of behavior are not applicable. Birch tries to stay clean by his idealistic views of Rosa's love for the athlete with such great potential — and by his own dedication to duty. Though on a lower level, the book nevertheless suggests comparisons with Conrad's classic *Heart of Darkness*.

Tooke, C. W. *Ballpark Blues.* New York: Doubleday, 2003.

Casey Fox makes a memorable debut with the Pawtucket Red Sox by slugging a teammate for being lackadaisical. Sportswriter Russ Bryant finds new interest in his job due to the intensity of the young catcher. Fox becomes a star, and Bryant is the only journalist that he talks to. When the catcher is called up to Boston, Bryant is assigned to do a feature story on him.

Both ballplayer and writer seem to be reaching the top of their professions, but Molly, Casey's foster sister, changes things. She inspires them to seek for higher responsibilities and challenges. Bryant plans to accompany her to Honduras as she puts her beliefs into practice by working in an orphanage. He realizes, though, that Fox is her true love, and he opts to give the ballplayer the privilege. Fox responds by hitting the homer that gives the Red Sox the division title over the Yankees and then shocks the baseball world by quitting the game with the playoffs and World Series coming up. He joins Molly in Honduras. Bryant, meanwhile, rejects a major offer in journalism and becomes a teacher.

Molly, then, has influenced them to discover grander purposes in life. Casey Fox realizes that business has exploited baseball and that he needs more than economic rewards and celebrity status to be fulfilled. He and Bryant put Molly's ideas of virtue into their daily routine and forsake the chances for personal aggrandizement. However, the concept is over-emphasized to the point of being preachy and melodramatic. Literary merit is thwarted in the process.

Weincek, Craig J. *The Perfect Game.* Baltimore: PublishAmerica, 2003.

Sportswriter Bob O'Toole narrates, in the near future, the amazing story of a thirty-two-year-old high school history teacher who develops a super pitch and catapults from obscurity to the limelight. Lou Malinski tries out his Butterfly Floater against college players in practice at Mt. Airy, Maryland. The manager of the AA Annapolis Pilots is notified, and when the team's left-handed relief pitcher is injured in August, Malinski is given a chance. He baffles the opponents with the magical pitch, and the Washington Commanders call him up to the majors. He stars in September as a relief pitcher, and when the team is down three to two in the World Series, Lefty Malinski starts and pitches back-to-back perfect games.

Then the trouble begins. In the off-season, most of the pitchers are traded as the new superstar is expected to pitch nearly every game. The Commanders get off to an 82–0 record, but the fans boycott games as no batter has been able to touch a Malinski pitch. Attendance drops drastically and after the All-Star break, the

Commissioner, at the urging of the owners, bans Malinski from baseball — the game cannot survive the imbalance created by an unhittable pitch.

Lefty Malinski's troubles increase as he is accused of making a deal with the devil. Although the Faust Legend is actually not applicable, the charge does not stop Malinski's pregnant wife from asking for a divorce. She claims that he has changed drastically since becoming a star. Finally, a fan murders the pitcher with the idea that he is acting for the benefit of baseball

The point is that the game depends on the balance between defense and offense — one player's perfection potentially ruins the game. The concept of a magical pitch goes back to *It Happens Every Spring* (1949), but this is not one of the better books on the subject. Also, the mistakes made in referring to real players detract even more from the quality.

2004

Cabral, R. A. *The Pitch: The Adventures of Luther Woundup and His Magical Ball.* Arlington, VA: Booksurge, 2004.

In 2007, Luther Woundup arrives on Earth from the planet Spalding. Zeltac, his father, had visited Earth in 1923. He became friends with Babe Ruth, and experimented on Ruth and Lou Gehrig with Spalding technology — which may have led to their early deaths. Luther's ambition is to play baseball, but he has unknowingly been sent to Earth as part of a plan to invade and conquer it.

Luther becomes a pitcher for the Sacramento Rider by using the magic of his planet. However, journalist Randy Bridger warns him that the aquatrilene experiments (that he has been tricked into using by Zeltac) are dangerous to humans. Luther realizes that his father is betraying him and decides to return to Spalding. His mission of becoming another Sandy Koufax in American baseball turns into the more important project of saving Earth.

A complicated subplot involves Rush Limbaugh, but it seems as irrelevant as the novel itself, which, unfortunately, is the first part of a projected trilogy.

Huston, Charlie. *Caught Stealing.* New York: Ballantine Books, 2004. (New York: Ballantine Books, 2005.)

Hank Thomson tends bar in New York City, but he once had a great future in baseball — before he broke his leg. He roots for the San Francisco Giants as they contend for a wildcard spot with the Mets. His life changes, though, when he accepts the job of cat-sitting for a neighbor. The cat's shelter contains a key to a locker that contains four-and-a half million dollars. Pursued by cops and crooks in a wild escapade of violence and betrayal, Thompson eventually escapes to Mexico with the loot. He peacefully watches the Giants and Mets vie for the playoffs. The fast-paced thriller uses baseball as a background that represents a sense of order in the chaos of the protagonist's life.

Irby, Lee. *7,000 Clams.* New York: Doubleday, 2004.

It is 1925, and Frank Hearn is a young bootlegger in New Jersey. He loses a shipment of booze but finds an IOU for seven thousand dollars signed by Babe Ruth.

The Yankee slugger owes money to a gambler, and he has not paid. In the meantime, he is on his way to St. Petersburg, Florida, for spring training. Singer Ginger De More, who is on the run from Al Capone's gang, accompanies Hearn to Florida in his attempt to collect from the Babe. Crooks and cops pursue the pair, and Irene Howard, a college student and ex-girlfriend of Hearn, also arrives in St. Pete. Irene's mother is trying to cure her daughter's depression, which is the result of Hearn's departure, with a Florida vacation. Through a miraculous series of events, the bootlegger and the college flapper end up together, and Ginger goes back to Chicago and her singing career.

Ruth is portrayed as the usual irresponsible profligate. Though his wife is with him, he persists in drinking and eating in excess—along with gambling and womanizing. She is prepared to leave him, but when he has a bellyache, she once again settles into a nursing role.

The book has the Troy Soos mixture of real and fictional characters in an historical setting—and it reads like an Elmore Leonard or Carl Hiaasen crime caper.

Maloney, Andrew. *End of a Dynasty.* Victoria, B.C: Trafford, 2004.

The Buffalo Pioneers prepare for the 2004 season after three straight World Series wins. However, the conflict between General Manager Trent Blair and Manager Jack Vaughan causes dissension on the team. Blair is a disciple of sabermetrics (computerized statistical evaluations), and Vaughan is a players' manager who knows how to motivate a team. After the Pioneers lose the World Series to Atlanta in 2004 and lose to Texas in the playoffs in 2005, Blair fires the manager and gains control of the team — which then sinks to last place in the next two seasons. Meanwhile, Vaughan wins a World Series as manager of the Yankees. The mess in Buffalo gets worse as Blair is arrested for income tax evasion and embezzlement. The new owner moves the team to Portland, Oregon.

The contrast between the general manager and the manager is the heart of the book. Jack Vaughan is the ultimate baseball man who sacrifices his domestic life in order to stay in touch with the players and promote a winning attitude. Trent Blair represents business and science — the ugly aspects of the game that are opposed by the humanitarianism and respect for the game exhibited by the manager. As the villain, Blair is justly punished, but the conflict is melodramatic and oversimplified.

Meeriken, E. Dee. *Dream Season.* New York: iUniverse, 2004.

This account of baseball in the 1890s focuses on a fictional view of Walter Settle, a real-life California pitcher. Scouts discover him at fourteen, but his mother and grandfather resent the foolish game and its vile participants. Their religious fundamentalism and prejudice tend to limit Settle's pitching to the Los Angeles area. Although he works diligently to perfect his art, he never plays in the majors. Ned Hanlon, manager, of the Baltimore Orioles, tries to break the resistance of the family to no avail. Settle's acme is a 1–0 victory in winter ball against a young Walter Johnson.

The story of the regional pitching phenom also includes incidents of California history and local color aspects, but the amateurish writing style is a big drawback.

Mitcham, Judson. *Sabbath Creek.* Athens: University of Georgia Press, 2004. (New York: Harvest Books, 2006.)

Lewis Pope, at thirteen, is riding with his mother in rural Georgia when the car breaks down. Mrs. Pope is trying to escape from her alcoholic husband, and she and her son take refuge for several days at the dilapidated Sabbath Creek Motor Court, run by a ninety-three-year-old black man, Truman Stroud. A former pitcher who was a friend of Satchel Paige, Stroud plays catch with Lewis and gives advice on baseball. He serves as a surrogate father for the bewildered boy — an aspiring pitcher with a good arm and a lack of control.

Mr. Pope gets killed in a car accident while searching for his wife and son, and Lewis attends the funeral on August 9, his fourteenth birthday. Haunted by the loss of a father he never knew and the story of Stroud's son, a war casualty, Lewis Pope has no clear direction for the future. He knows that it will be a struggle to gain control of his pitches — and his life. Baseball is equated with education and security in a coming-of-age novel of some merit.

Mosher, Howard Frank. *Waiting for Teddy Williams.* Boston: Houghton Mifflin, 2004. (Boston: Mariner, 2005).

E A. Allen grows up in Kingdom Common, Vermont, rabid Red Sox territory. He lives with his unwed mother (Gypsy Lee, a songwriter and entertainer) and Gran, a Sox fan who has been confined to a wheelchair since Bucky Dent's homer spoiled the team's bid for a championship in 1978. In lieu of a father, E. A. confides in a statue of his ancestor, Ethan Allen. The boy's two-part quest is to discover the identity of his father and to play for the Boston Red Sox.

A drifter shows up and starts giving E. A. advice about baseball. It helps him to become a star pitcher for the local Outlaws, a semipro team. The stranger is eventually identified as Teddy Williams, a former baseball player in the area and an ex-convict. He is also the father in question.

Meanwhile, Legendary Spence, manager of the Red Sox, has been informed that the team must win the World Series or be moved from Boston. Haunted by the Curse of the Bambino, Spence takes a chance on the seventeen-year-old E.A. Allen. The hunch pays off, as the kid picks up the team late in the season and then wins the seventh game of the World Series.

The eccentric characters and bizarre incidents are amusing, but the heroics are formulaic. The real-life deeds of the miracle 2004 Red Sox were just as amazing — but far less predictable.

Parker, Robert B. *Double Play.* New York: Putnam Adult, 2004. (New York: Berkley, 2005.)

Joe Burke, a veteran of World War II, accepts Branch Rickey's offer to serve as a bodyguard for Jackie Robinson during the 1947 season. Burke has grown callous as a means of protection from the trauma of his war wound and the betrayal of his wife. As an unfeeling hired gun, he ruthlessly faces mob leaders and their goons while protecting the famous Dodger. Burk befriends one of the hoods, Cash, and uses him to help keep Robinson safe. The two work in harmony much like Spenser and Hawk in the popular Parker mysteries. The relationship between Burke and Robinson also develops into friendship and mutual respect.

The mobster related threat to the Dodger first baseman is virtually erased, but Burke's work is complicated by his decision to help Lauren, an ex-girlfriend who is part of the underworld family. In the process, the hard-boiled exterior begins to disintegrate — revealing sentiment and the code of honor that is typical of the fictional tough-guy heroes.

A nice touch in the book is the inclusion of interchapters featuring Bobby, a boy who worships the Brooklyn Dodgers. Unaware of the racism directed at Robinson, he watches a game at Ebbets Field as a joyful fan — even though Warren Spahn and the Boston Braves defeat the beloved Bums of Brooklyn.

The novel differs from Honig's *The Plot to Kill Jackie Robinson* (1992) as Joe Tinker works from the outside to prevent a specific murder attempt while Joe Burke forms an intimate union with Robinson as a personal bodyguard through the season. Both of the gunmen, though, are rejuvenated by their experiences. Robinson, in both cases, remains more of a heroic stereotype than a developed character.

Rowe, G. S. *Squeeze Play in Beantown.* Clifton, VA: Pocol Press, 2004.

Will Beaman appears in his second Beantown mystery. It is still 1899, and Arthur Soden fires Beaman as a means of cutting expenses. However, when a new Beaneater is killed and veteran Jimmy Collins is beaten and his gold watch is stolen, Soden makes a bet that the amateur detective will not be able to recover the watch. Beaman's search brings him into the labor turmoil in Boston that is fueled by the speeches of Emma Goldman. The mystery also ties in with a missing manuscript — William Bradford's "Of Plymouth Plantation." Beaman befriends Eve Seilor, an enthusiast of social justice, and together they discover that the assault on Jimmy Collins was really a means of destroying the sketches of Sean Dennison, artist for a local newspaper and friend of the detective. The sketches were of the criminals who stole the valuable manuscript. Beaman recovers the gold watch and the manuscript, and Soden finds room for him on the payroll of the Boston Beaneaters

Much like Troy Soos, Rowe focuses on factual occurrences in baseball with actual events of the nation in the background. The fiction brings the historical era to life.

Sederburg, Arelo C. *The Girl Who Saved Baseball.* Lincoln: iUniverse, 2004.

Clay O'Farrell, long-time minor leaguer, manages the Bombers in a pro league not affiliated with the majors. A kid shows up, accompanied by a dog named Yaz, and requests a tryout. Making the team as a first baseman (with good speed but little power), the youngster eventually reveals herself to O'Farrell not only as a girl but as his daughter, Patricia, although she goes by the name of Pat Carrington. O'Farrell was briefly married to actress Ellen Carrington, but was not aware of a child. Pat continues to play disguised as a boy.

In the off-season, Pat, brothers Ty and Sean Quinn, and black outfielder Tim Offering train at O'Farrell's Arizona ranch. Pat's secret is kept — even when she makes it to the Boston Red Sox along with the Quinn brothers and her dad (as a coach). The new players star down the stretch, but Pat's cover is finally blown, and she becomes a sensation. Even Pat Carrington dolls are marketed as the Sox become the center of attention on and off the field. The team gets to the seventh game of the World Series before losing to the Giants.

Pat Carrington decides to retire, however, after her brief career as the first woman in the majors. She joins the injured Sean Quinn (who has confessed to using steroids) on a public relations campaign to save baseball. She plans to stress steroid testing, revenue sharing, salary caps, and absolute free agency. She also wants the union to adopt a plan in which high-paid players voluntarily take cuts after bad seasons. In the meantime, Pat enrolls in a music school.

Sean Quinn becomes an archeologist. His brother Ty is traded to the Dodgers and gives up part-time pitching to become a full-time outfielder. Tim Offering, another product of the Clay O'Farrell training camp, returns there following a good season as a Yankee. O'Farrell, now a Boston scout, continues to teach baseball at his Arizona retreat. He finds time to attend a Chopin concert (with Ellen Carrington) that features Patricia.

The book contains factual errors of baseball history, especially in regard to Ted Williams and Enos Slaughter. Then, of course, there is too much heroic action, plus an unlikely conclusion with its "campaign to save baseball." However, it is at least the equal to the other first-female-in-the-game novels: *A Grand Slam, The Sensuous Southpaw, Can't Miss,* and *Balls.*

Strachan, Don. *King of Diamonds.* Middletown, CA: Penthe Publishing, 2004.

The Megaglopoulis Mutants, a major league team in a parallel universe, are owned by Wellington P Sweetwater who for seventeen years has used his showman's tricks to keep his mediocre teams in business. He expects that the signing of Whizzo Mark Salot IV, just out of high school in Disfunction Junction, Arkansas, will greatly boost the chances for solvency. The owner convinces Manager Foo Foo McGonigle and veteran catcher Charlie Orange that the kid will have an immediate impact. He does, and the Mutants become contenders. The team catches the Lemon Sox on the last game of the season with Salot scheduled to pitch. The brash youngster with the exaggerated Southern dialect promises to stage a wedding extravaganza at the ballpark when the Mutants win the pennant. The bride descends from the sky in a hot air balloon after the victory, and a massive celebration occurs.

The Mutants go on to win the World Series, and Whizzo Salot has a sensational career until he is stopped by arm trouble (after posting 224 wins). Charlie Orange, revitalized by Clitorea Pearl's sexual therapy, buys an interest in a frog research lab and lives happily unmarried with a polyamorous tantrika parallel universalist physicist.

In a subplot, Ngaio, a rare type of frog, is rescued by a Mutant player and becomes an inhabitant of Professor Maxwell Veribushi's frog farm. He lives there (presumably) happily with other members of the preserved species.

The baseball heroics have the conventional events and players: the Monumental Season, The Big Game, the Old School Catcher, the Hotshot Rookie, and the Stengelese Manager. On the other hand, the parallel universe, the frog-eco-parable, and Clitorea Pearl's sexology are among the unique aspects. It adds up to an entertaining farce but not exactly great art.

2005

Boggs, Johnny D. *Camp Ford.* Farmington Hills, MI: Five Star First Edition Westerns, 2005. (paperback reprint New York: Dorchester, 2007.)

Win MacNaughton attends the 1946 World Series between the Cardinals and the Red Sox at the age of ninety-nine. His mind, however, is on his baseball experiences during the Civil War era. Between the games of the Series, he writes about his early years of baseball in Newport, Rhode Island.

He was introduced to the sport as a boy in the 1850s. When his father moved the family to Texas just before the war in order to argue against slavery, Win continued to play the game. Henry MacNaughton moved back to Rhode Island during the war in order to enlist in the Union army. He died at Gettysburg. Win, at seventeen, joined the Northern troops in an attempt to atone for his father's death. He was captured by the Confederates in Louisiana and sent to Camp Ford in Texas as a prisoner of war. He played ball in prison and participated in a challenge game between the Yanks and the Rebel guards—Mr. Lincoln's Hirelings (a racially integrated team) versus the Camp Ford Gallinippers. Even though the Southerners discovered that the game was part of a plan to escape, the contest was still played as a display of sectional pride. It ended when word arrived that the war was over.

Winner of the Spur Award in 2006 as the best western novel of the previous year, *Camp Ford* is the third fictional presentation of quality about baseball during the Civil War, joining Dyja's *Play for a Kingdom* (1997) and Hutton's *A Perfect Silence* (2000).

Booth, Robert. *The Perfect Pafko.* Seattle: Bugle Books, 2005.

Brady Greer of Midian, Georgia, has a mid-life crisis when his wife betrays him and his father dies. He decides to make amends for his past failures by engaging in a quest to save Major League Baseball from the greed of the players and their agents. He plans to restore the game to its glory days before free agency. A baseball card collector, a symbol of the era is a Topps 1952 Andy Pafko card in pristine condition, which he is able to purchase after receiving an inheritance. Pafko was the only Wisconsin native on the Milwaukee Braves when they arrived from Boston in 1953, and Greer, a Wisconsinite, feels a kinship with him.

In order to change baseball, Greer realizes that he has to confront the players' union. He kidnaps Kip Kapopka, an assistant to the baseball commissioner, and forces him to make a public reading of the demands of the Sandlot Liberation Army (consisting only of Greer, who feels that he is acting for the benefit of the fans who are being victimized by the multi-million dollar contracts of the players). The demands call for revenue sharing, a team salary cap, and a new drug policy. The union partially concedes to the deal, and Greer releases Kapopka and prepares to live his life on the run from the law—although planning to find a good place from which to watch the 2002 World Series.

Despite the bizarre incidents, the book deals with some of the problems that aggravate baseball fans. It is written skillfully enough to gain at least a respectable place in the genre.

Elias, Robert. *The Deadly Tools of Ignorance.* Cambridge, MA: Rounder Books, 2005.

Tom Licente, a Laurentian priest and chair of the Criminology Department of Fairmount University in San Francisco, is murdered. Graduate student Debs Kafka does not believe that the black man arrested for the crime is guilty, so he gives his criminology class the task of investigating the case. The students present a list of suspects, including the president of the school. They also discover that Licente's conservative views of religion and society made him unpopular on campus.

Meanwhile, Kafka practices with the Fairmount baseball team and is so impressive that he gets a contract from the minor league Sonoma Crushers. Near the end of the season, Clare LaFarge, female AVP of the San Francisco Giants, offers him a contract as a reserve catcher in the majors. Kafka discovers that a Giant relief pitcher is the victim of death threats and that the likely source is the person who killed Licente. He dramatically foils the murderer's plot and exposes him as an ex-con who is seeking revenge on LaFarge (and thus the Giants) because she had previously convicted him in her role as a prosecutor.

Although he does not make the post-season roster of the Giants, Kafka is content with fulfilling his boyhood dream of playing pro ball. For the immediate future his project is to return to Fairmount to put his progressive religious principles into action. With Licente's outmoded dogma no longer in effect, he feels that the university is now able to serve the public in a more humane manner.

Besides the unlikely events involving the mystery, the novel seems to be a series of lectures on the proper roles of academia, criminology, religion, and baseball in American life. It is still a surprisingly good read, but the excessive preaching and unlikely events keep the book from joining the elite in the genre.

Foley, Mick. *Scooter.* New York: Knopf, 2005. (New York: Vintage Contemporaries, 2006.)

Scooter Reilly grows up in the South Bronx in the 1960s and 70s as the area is changing from Irish to Puerto Rican. His father, Patrick, patrols a beat in Harlem; he is sympathetic to the victims of the environment but dysfunctional at home. He accidentally shoots his son and later hits his retarded daughter with a bat. The permanently limping Scooter retaliates by using his Willie McCovey bat on Patrick's leg. On the way to the hospital, a car accident further injures both father and daughter. Mrs. Reilly, convinced that she will never realize her ambition of moving to the suburbs, deserts the family.

Scooter suffers through adolescence as a crippled Irish kid in a Puerto Rican neighborhood, but his love for baseball, instilled by his father and grandfather, is symbolized by his McCovey bat and a ball signed by Joe DiMaggio. Taking his grandfather's advice, he builds up his forearms. He becomes a good hitter and makes the high school baseball team even though he has trouble running and fielding. Scooter also loses an eye, but he makes it as far as the Oneonta Yankees in class A ball before he quits the game when he realizes that he is essentially playing as a means of vengeance against his father and an unjust world. He decides to dedicate his life to his sister and to make up with his father.

Though at first showing promise as a naturalistic coming-of-age story (with a background permeated by pop culture), the book is too heavily dependent on melodramatic scenes involving the Excalibur-like baseball bat. Scooter's final atonement completes the melodrama.

Gervais, Marty. *Reno.* Niagara Falls, NY: Mosaic Press, 2005.

Henry "Reno" Armstrong is a polio-stricken twelve-year-old who observes the action of a small Canadian town from his attic window. He also collects celebrity photos, listens to the radio, and writes letters. His current hero is real Detroit Tiger infielder Reno Bertoia, who does not write back. In the meantime, the boy thinks that his new friend, Billy, has been specifically assigned the task of curing him and helping him pass the tests that will put him in the eighth grade in the fall. As Bertoia begins to fade in the batting race, Henry starts to take on new interests.

Thirty years later, Henry Armstrong is a medical doctor who finally meets Bertoia as a patient. The next day, the former Tiger responds with a letter and a photograph.

Reno Bertoia was a short-term mediocre big leaguer who apparently appealed to the fictional kid because of their shared Canadian backgrounds. The realization of the less-than-heroic stature of the ballplayer is a step in the maturation of the protagonist. A well-written but over-simplified novella (ninety-two pages), it is best suited for young adults.

King, Dave. *The Ha-Ha.* New York: Backbay Books/Little, Brown and Company, 2005.

Howard Kapostash, rendered mute by an injury in Vietnam thirty years earlier, relates the transformation he experiences through a relationship with a nine-year-old boy. Howie works for a convent that features a ha-ha — a walled ditch that creates an optical illusion of an uninterrupted pastoral scene. It symbolizes the unseen dangers that threaten Howie's quest to regain a satisfactory place in society.

Sylvia Mohr, an ex-girlfriend, enters a drug rehab facility and asks Howie to take temporary guardianship of Ryan, her racially mixed son. He and the boy are compatible, and the Vietnam vet finds a new enthusiasm for life — partly as the result of the boy's participation in Little League baseball. Howie's hope of renewing a romance with Sylvia is lost by her sexual betrayal, but Ryan's dependence on him provides a reason to confront the future optimistically.

This is not a typical novel of the beneficial aspects of Little League ball (such as *Flatland Fable* or *The Elements of Hitting*). There is not a neat resolution brought about by a ball-playing kid who brings a family together. Baseball is in the background however, and the stress is on more complex issues of personal turmoil that are not entirely solved. This is probably part of the reason that the book has been praised by the critics.

King, Kevin. *All the Stars Came Out That Night.* New York: Dutton, 2005.

After the Cardinals defeat the Tigers in the 1934 World Series, Satchel Paige challenges Dizzy Dean and his Gashouse Gang to a game against a black all-star team. Commissioner Kenesaw Mountain Landis will not allow the event. He claims that he is not a racist but that the owners of major league teams, the men he works for, are against any kind of integrated baseball contest. Clarence Darrow is retired from the practice of law, but he now takes the role as a champion of black baseball. He convinces Landis that a third major league that includes blacks is in the process of being formed. The Commissioner yields to Darrow's bluff and sanctions the game with the condition that it be held in secret and that the white team be limited to seven active major league players. He wants an excuse in case the white team is defeated. Henry Ford, who consents to sponsor the event, has the same worry, and he assigns his enforcer, Harry Bennett, the task of ensuring a win for Dean's group.

Bennett, with the help of Ford's unlimited slush fund, works with five members of the Gashouse Gang (Pepper Martin, Leo Durocher, Frankie Frisch, Ducky Medwick, and Dean) to choose the team of ten players. Lou Gehrig and Ernie Lombardi complete the big league roster. Babe Ruth is not currently under contract, so he is counted as an extra — along with a minor leaguer, Joe DiMaggio, and the aging Shoeless Joe Jackson, a semipro since being banned as a result of the Black Sox Scandal. Babe Didrikson Zaharias, famed female athlete, is given an audition as a pitcher, but she is considered to be of only Pacific Coast League quality.

In the meantime, Paige and catcher Josh Gibson put together a black team that includes Oscar Charleston, Cool Papa Bell, Ray Dandridge, Buck Leonard, and Martin Dihigo. Gibson and Charleston seethe over not getting a chance in the majors, but Paige keeps them under control. The game is set for October 20 in Fenway Park under improvised lights.

Before that date, there are several episodic adventures. Paige and Gibson narrowly escape from the Dominican Republic with Dihigo in tow after angering the dictator. Durocher looks up his minor league friend, actor George Raft, while on a scouting mission to check out DiMaggio. Along with two hoodlums, who serve as bodyguards and handymen, the Gashouse Gang attends a Hollywood party featuring Raft, Carole Lombard, Clark Gable, and columnists Walter Winchell and Louella Parsons. It is Winchell who posthumously relates the story of the secret game.

The night game in a virtually empty Fenway consists of seesaw scoring and continuous dialogue between the opposing players. In the ninth, a drunken Ruth pinch-hits a three-run single that puts the white team ahead. However, in the bottom of the inning Josh Gibson hit a blast that might have tied the game, but the lights go out with the ball in the air — and it is the conclusion of the game. Winchell reports that on the next day he discovers a ball five hundred feet from homeplate that may have been the one Gibson hit.

Humor, horseplay, and heroics tend to dominate the book. The game itself is anticlimactic and predictably ambiguous. It is an interesting concept, though, and the motives and actions assigned to the historical figures make it must-read for the baseball fan.

Pilek, Eugena. *Cooperstown.* New York: Simon & Schuster, 2005.

In 1979, Dr. Kerwin Chylak becomes a confidant of residents of Cooperstown, New York, in his role as a psychiatrist. A novice at baseball, he listens and observes as the community is torn between those in favor of the proposed theme park, Fielders' Dream, and some of the oldtimers who want to preserve the home of the Baseball Hall of Fame in its present condition. The mayor, alcoholic Amos Fusselback, and the former high school coach, Duke Cartwright, lead the battle to keep the theme park out.

Along with two dead comrades, Chuck Daulton and Frank Paquette, Amos and Duke have also been the guardians of a seemingly terrible secret. In a copy of James Fennimore Cooper's *The Last of the Mohicans,* they have hidden an 1816 newspaper account that banned the playing of Ball within the village limits. Their discovery of the ordinance in 1957 was witnessed by Manny Barrett, a kid baseball phenom. The gang of four coerces the teenager into keeping the secret, but he loses his enthusiasm for baseball in the process.

The mayor concocts the plan of determining the future of the theme park by having a contest — a baseball game between the Town and the State — with the idea that if the Town team wins Fielders' Dream will be nullified. The State wins, though, and the theme park soon becomes a reality.

Chylak objectively surveys the action between the myths and realities of Cooperstown residents, which include the origins of baseball itself. The roles of the town and Abner Doubleday in founding the game are challenged by the reference to Ball in an 1816 newspaper (and by a mention of a Ball game in Cooper's 1838 novel *Home as Found*), thus exposing the error of the mythical invention of baseball by Doubleday in 1839. Chylak gets drawn into the drama and eventually begins to make connections with patients and family that he could not do previously. He also makes the discovery that the ordinance supposedly banning baseball in 1816 had really only limited the game to certain sections of the town. Chylak decides that it is too late to reveal the truth.

The book presents the threat of commercialism to the tradition of a fabled community that clings to the imaginary idealism of the past. The effects on the townspeople are varied and are presented with humor and skill. The premise regarding the Gang's Big Secret, though, is too flimsy to be the dominant factor of the plot.

Rowe, G. S. *Double Play in Beantown.* Clifton, VA: Pocol Press, 2005.

In his third mystery, Will Beaman decides to leave the Beaneaters and join the new Boston team of the American League as an assistant business manager. The year is 1901, and Charles Somers hopes to make the Boston Americans a viable franchise despite the crosstown rivalry of Arthur Soden's established team. In the meantime, Beaman is drawn into the search of a missing girl, Maggie Denihur, the cousin of his longtime sweetheart. The quest takes him into the political furor over Irish independence and the rallies inspired by the arrival in town of Maud Gonne, "the Irish Joan of Arc." Maggie, it turns out, has run away with a ballplayer in order to work for the Free Ireland Movement. Beaman finds her, but in the process, he loses Claire Denihur and gains a new girlfriend, Libby, who helps him in the chase. The Boston Americans, meanwhile, get off to a good start in the baseball season, along with several other teams of the fledgling league.

Again, the combination of history and fiction produces a success. Baseball is depicted in its professional infancy against a realistic background of actual events that are spiced by an imaginative plot.

Wuerfel, Jason. *Pray for Rain: A College Baseball Story.* N.p.: Lulu Press, 2005.

R.J. "Squat" Hansen, a reserve catcher, narrates the story of his senior year at the University of Michigan. A new coaching staff under Tom Nichols is installed and Squat hopes to improve his status as a bench-warmer who is seen as an asset because of his character. Most of the book describes the off-season antics of the jocks— stressing parties and the initiation of the freshman recruits.

When the season starts, Squat still languishes on the bench as the Wolverines struggle — finally losing out for title contention but qualifying for the conference tournament. Squat gets a pinch-hit that helps win a game but sees little action and loses his girlfriend, Beth. However, outfielder Benjamin Marker intervenes to save the romance and also teaches the catcher the special joy the love of baseball can bring — contradictory to the idea of some of the players that it is a job in which one prays for rain. Although the Wolverines lose in the tournament, Marker makes a miraculous catch that saves a game; in the process, he is injured and later dies in a hospital.

A former player visits Coach Nichols and explains that Marker is a martyr as both a spiritual and an athletic hero. Thirty years later, Squat Hansen also uses his former friend as an example while morally instructing his son. The plot works better as a Christian novel rather than as commendable art.

2006

Angell, Kate. *Squeeze Play.* New York: Dorchester, Love Spell/Contemporary Romances, 2006.

Risk Kincaid, hero of the major league Richmond Rogues in the World Series, returns to his hometown of Frostproof, Florida, with a few of his teammates to take part in a charity event. Romance blooms as he reunites with Jacy Grayson, his high school girlfriend. Her brother Aaron, pitcher for the Tampa Bay Bombers, falls for Natalie Llewellen, and Kincaid's fellow Rogue, Zen Driscoll, connects with Stephanie Cole, who had been in love with Aaron. True love, interspersed with pornography, prevails.

Bain, Donald. *Murder, She Wrote: Three Strikes and You're Dead.* New York: New American Library, 2006. (New York: Obsidian, 2007.)

Jessica Fletcher, amateur detective of the television series and the fictional author of mystery novels, appears at a baseball game in Mesa, Arizona, as the guest of Jack and Mary Duffy. Ty Ramos, from the Dominican Republic, is a foster son of the Duffys and a shortstop for the Mesa Rattlers, a Class A team. When Junior Bennett, son of the team's owner, is found dead, Ramos is accused of murder. Jessica attempts to prove that he is innocent.

H.B. Bennett had ordered the manager to play Junior at shortstop even though Ramos is a vastly superior player. The animosity between the two shortstops was evident, but Jessica is sure that Ramos is too ethical to kill his rival. She uncovers a gambling problem involving the Ramblers that implicates the owner, who has been betting against his own team. The trail leads, though, to a sports agent who is trying to sign Ramos as a means of clearing his gambling debts.

The baseball aspect of the book is sparse and contrived, and the detective work of Jessica Fletcher goes according to formula. The heroine outsmarts the law on her way to solving the case.

Bauer, Brad. *Hitting in the Clutch.* Lincoln: iUniverse, 2006.

Jack "Clutch" Thompson plays for the Arizona Diamondbacks in the 2003 season and hits only .198 but with twenty-one pinch-hit homers. He records his exploits during the 2004 campaign with the idea of being a writer. After a great first-half as a starter, Thompson makes the all-Star team and gets a contract extension with a raise — plus, his agent says that he can get him a book deal.

In July, however, Thompson is traded to the Boston Red Sox. He proceeds to injure his knee and to break two fingers by hitting a wall in frustration. When life is at its worst, he meets Alexis, a porn star, who inspires him to prevail. In the sixth game of the World Series against his former Diamondback team, Clutch is sent in to pinch-hit. He faces a hated rival pitcher with the chance to win the Series for the Sox; he gets the pitch he expects and swings — as the book ends, presumably on a happy occasion.

Thompson is depicted as the vulgar, spoiled jock of the free-agent era, but under the guidance of a "good woman," he matures, like Henry Wiggen of Mark Harris' *The Southpaw*, into a responsible person. The book reads, to a large extent, like a weak parody of the Harris works.

Feldman, Jay. *Suitcase Sefton and the American Dream.* Chicago: Triumph Books, 2006.

In 1942, Mac "Suitcase" Sefton, a scout for the Yankees, takes the wrong turn in Arizona and arrives at the site of a game played by Japanese in an internment camp. Pitcher Jerry Yamada is so impressive that Sefton approaches him with the idea of playing pro ball by passing as an Apache. Yamada is too proud to accept the offer, but Sefton hangs around the camp until he falls in love with Annie, the pitcher's sister.

The scout talks his boss, an old minor league teammate, into transferring him to Arizona. Sefton finds other prospects, but his secret mission is to sign Yamada. In the process, he befriends many of the Japanese prisoners, coaches their baseball team, and helps to build a new ballpark at the camp. Meanwhile, Yamada comes up with the idea that he can apply to the American Friends Service Committee and possibly play baseball in college somewhere away from the West Coast.

During the spring of 1943, while Sefton is off at spring training, the Yamada family is relocated to Tule Lake, California, due to the Asian Exclusion Act. Sefton loses touch with them until after the war, but the estrangement from Annie finally goads him into taking action. He rushes to California to confess his love. Before long, he quits his job, becomes an expectant father, and enters a farming partnership with the Yamadas. Sefton also manages an amateur baseball team featuring Jerry Yamada.

The book stresses the ethnic prejudice that is part of the history of World War II. The taboos against non-white baseball players and racially integrated romance highlight the cultural conflict. While slightly far-fetched and melodramatic, it is nevertheless a competent historical novel.

Ferguson, Marvin P. *The Unknown Baseball Player.* Island Lake, IL: Parker Publishing, 2006.

Orville Hodge emerges from a farm near Cedar Lane, Indiana, to mysteriously become a member of a major league team. He apparently represents the ordinary guy who succeeds through hard work and virtuous living. Without the special privileges of the wealthy or the training of the athletically gifted, he endures hardships and deprivation in gaining fame and fortune in the tradition of the Horatio Alger stories.

Hodge receives an invitation to join the Boys from the Gold Coast, an amateur team in Chicago, and from there he is somehow catapulted to the Big Red Machine of Cincinnati. An outsider who is unknown to the manager, he nevertheless gets a chance to pinch-hit in a big game, and with his eyes closed hits a walk-off grandslam.

The social realism established through much of the narrative is overshadowed by the shift to magical realism. Naturalism yields to fantasy, and the rags to riches theme becomes a fanciful moral tale with most of its message lost.

Nemo, John. *The King's Game.* N.p.: johnnemobooks.com, 2006.

As an abandoned baby, Cody King was rescued by a stranger. At the age of thirty-six, he is pitching for the Warriors against the Cardinals in the seventh game of the World Series. He reminisces about his life as the game is being played. Cody was raised by Aunt Judy and a series of foster families and continually wonders about his real parents. Cody is having an affair with Janet, who is pregnant. He also sees a psychiatrist at the request of the team.

The game, meanwhile, is interrupted periodically by rain. King has a chance to score the lead run in the seventh inning, but he is thrown out at the plate, and the game is halted with a tie score. It matters little to King, though, as he has miraculously accepted the Lord and, in his heart, has "arrived home safely."

The author explains that baseball is a submerged metaphor for life — by which he means Christianity, and the book presumably qualifies as Christian literature. It is patterned after Shaara's *For Love of the Game*, a mediocre novel at best, and there is no improvement here.

Rowe, G.S. *Foul Ball in Beantown.* Clifton, VA: Pocol Press, 2006.

In the fourth Will Beaman Beantown mystery, the nation is troubled by war and a flu epidemic in 1918. The Boston Red Sox are battling for a pennant amidst rumors of a shortened season and a possible cancellation of the World Series. The presence of gamblers at Fenway Park add to the problem, and when a derelict is found dead after talking about fixed games, John Haggerty, former head groundskeeper for the old Boston Beaneaters, calls on Beaman to investigate the death and look into the possibility of a gambling conspiracy.

Beaman, down on his luck and recovering from a serious malady, recovers enough to go into action. He encounters Wobblies who are trying to unionize ballplayers and also confronts bullies from the American Protective League in their zealous search for pro–German activities. The private eye also consorts with real Red Sox players Carl Mays and Harry Hooper and talks to historical figures Harry Frazee (Red Sox owner) and Honey Fitz Fitzgerald (former Boston mayor). The large figure of pitcher Babe Ruth looms in the background.

When the players threaten to strike, Beaman intervenes and persuades them, with the help of Hooper, that it would be a disservice to the game and a setback to their careers. He helps to save the Series, then, and Ruth stars in the Sox defeat of the Cubs. Besides his baseball mediation, Beaman writes for a magazine that promotes fair labor practices and aids the Red Cross in its attempt to control the flu epidemic. He also courts two beautiful women and, at the end, chooses the most compatible mate. He accepts a job with a Boston newspaper and decides to keep his detective agency open. Will Beaman is back!

The protagonist is too lucky to be completely credible, and the book does not quite match the quality of its three predecessors. However, Rowe still blends history, baseball, and fiction (in the Troy Soos tradition) into an entertaining and informative novel.

Starr, Jason. *Lights Out.* New York: St. Martin's Minotaur Mysteries, 2006.

Jake Thomas, egotistical star of the Pittsburgh Pirates, visits his parents' home in Brooklyn during the off-season in an attempt to escape the pressure of a pending statutory rape charge. The black outfielder also feels that a marriage to his hometown sweetheart, Christina, will improve his image as a marketable product. However, his white teammate from a Canarsie high school, Ryan Rossetti, is currently dating Christina. The competition for her hand sets the stage for some amazing events.

Rossetti is a former minor league pitcher whose career was ended with arm trouble. He now paints houses and lives with his parents in Brooklyn. He and Christina plan to break her engagement with Thomas, but she is tempted by the wealth of the big leaguer. Full of doubts and self-pity, Rossetti goes on a drunken spree in the black ghetto—an act that leads to complications. He talks two hoods into mugging Thomas—which results in the accidental death of one of them while struggling with the pro athlete. Rossetti also has a one-night encounter with a black woman and thus becomes a target for her irate husband who, after missing him with gunshots, seriously injures the house painter with his car.

Detective Noll tries to find the connection between the incidents, but in the meantime Thomas flees from Brooklyn after his lawyer persuades him that the rape charge will be dismissed. The Pirate outfielder has persuaded the vacillating Christina to marry him—figuring that he can dump her in a year or two (not realizing that she has the idea of doing the same to him and collecting a large divorce settlement in the process).

A naturalistic crime novel in the tradition of James M. Cain, the plot races along in the urban jungle with no moral compromises. The racial element is subsumed by class differences as the bleak lives of the ghetto inhabitants and Ryan Rossetti are contrasted to the successful commercial enterprise of Jake Thomas—with assists from his lawyer and his agent. Although somewhat slight and slick, the novel features fast-paced action mixed with social commentary.

2007

Angell, Kate. *Curveball.* New York: Dorchester, 2007.

The Richmond Rogues, first introduced in *Squeeze Play*, return to action—most of it off the field. Psycho, Romeo, and Chaser dominate the narrative here, with Risk and Jacy Kincaid, now married, in the background. The three sluggers, the Bat Pack, get suspended for fighting and spend their time successfully courting attractive women. There is much less emphasis on sex than in the previous novel, but true love triumphs as before. The suspended players return to baseball in time to lead the Rogues to another World Series win, as the stock characters and incidents of formulaic romance prevail.

Bauer, Brad. *Homering in the Clutch.* Lincoln: iUniverse, Inc., 2007.

Author of a baseball memoir *Hitting in the Clutch* (actually a 2006 novel), Jack "Clutch" Thompson returns as a Texas Ranger in the 2007 season. A baseball outcast since the publication of his book, he hit fifty-eight homers with Toronto and helped the team win the World Series in 2006. Although his maturity is a major theme here, Thompson still practices his carousing, which leads to a separation from Alexis—the porn queen from the first novel. He also retains his gift for alienating teammates and opposing players.

Rival Stephen Fischer, the pitcher who fanned Thompson at a strategic time in the 2004 World Series at the conclusion of *Hitting in the Clutch* (although the reader is not informed of the strikeout until the second book), appears as a member of the Oakland Athletic and serves as the antagonist. Ranger teammate, Matt Terry, a longball threat like Thompson, competes with Clutch for top billing on the team. In the meantime, Clutch Thompson continues with his numerous sexual affairs that drive Alexis away—eventually into the clutches of Fischer. Thompson gets some revenge against the pitcher with a timely hit that hurts Oakland's postseason chances. The Rangers fail to make the playoffs, but Clutch has adapted somewhat to being a team player. He also enters a relationship with Heidi, a respectable girl who inspires him to perform good deeds.

In September, a car accident supposedly ends Thompson's baseball career. Hopefully, his tenure in baseball books as a protagonist/writer/ narrator in the tradition of Henry Wiggen (from the Mark Harris novels) is also terminated.

Carrington, Tori. *Foul Play: A Sofie Metropolis Novel.* New York: Tom Doherty/Forge, 2007.

A private investigator in her uncle's detective agency, Sofie is hired by the wife of a New York Mets pitcher to investigate the strange behavior of her husband. Sofie's professional career, like her love life, has been a disaster, but she works diligently to succeed in her first big case. She somehow gets to the heart of the matter.

Reni Valenzuela is a switch-pitcher who works as a closer for the Mets. Gisela insists that he has changed dramatically since a trip to Pittsburgh, and she wants the attractive detective to follow her husband in order to discover the reason. Sofie finds that the pitcher engages in extramarital affairs while on the road, but Gisela accepts that as part of the game of being married to a handsome star athlete. The problem, she feels, is more complex. An obvious sign of the change in Reni is that he has been pitching with only his left arm in recent appearances.

Sofie finally realizes that the man is an impostor. Reni has been replaced by a look-alike brother, Santos Bastardo, who has held Reni captive while trying for his own glory as a big league pitcher. The participants, however, decide to keep the matter a secret, and Reni returns to the Mets in time to help them compete for a playoff spot. Sofie Metropolis emerges from the case with no fanfare but with the knowledge that she has done a good job and learned a lot about the profession.

The "Greek Nancy Drew" narrates a fast-paced story with gusto from the team of Lori and Tony Karayianni. The baseball action and the mystery are far-fetched and detract from a novel that, however, still manages to be mildly entertaining.

Deford, Frank. *The Entitled.* Napierville, IL: Sourcebooks, 2007.

Howie Traveler is hired as the manager of the Cleveland Indians after forty years in the minors. The star of the mediocre team is outfielder Jay Alcazar, born in Cuba but raised in Miami. The tenuous relationship between the master of strategy and the gifted athlete is strained when Alcazar is accused of rape. Struggling to keep his job, the manager does not tell the police that he saw a woman apparently trying to escape from the ballplayer's room on the night of the alleged crime. If he reveals the truth, he thinks that he might lose the services of the outfielder and the chance to make the playoffs. Traveler's moral dilemma is compared to the attitude of Alcazar, the entitled commercial product who makes millions from baseball and advertising.

A failure as a player and a husband, Traveler wants success enough to keep Alcazar on the field, and his hot hitting gives the Indians a chance for postseason action. Shortly before the season ends, Patricia Richmond, the accuser of Alcazar, warns the manager that failing to report the truth will be another crime against women, the victims of a sexist society and the special privileges granted to the entitled male athletes. Feeling guilty, Traveler confesses to his daughter Lindsay, a lawyer, that he plans to confront Alcazar and then tell the police what he saw. Lindsay, though, talks her father out of the plan and secretly makes a deal with Alcazar. In exchange for her father's silence, she requests that the outfielder persuade the Cleveland front office to hire Traveler for the next season. Alcazar agrees and also tries to convince the lawyer that a rape never occurred; it was just a misunderstanding.

The rape charge is dismissed, the Indians make it to the playoffs, and Traveler keeps his job. Although the much-traveled manager is aware that he has failed his moral test, his daughter and Alcazar take a more pragmatic view. Their decisions are based on practical matters—primarily economics. Lindsay saves her dad's job, and Alcazar maintains his commercial enterprise. Morality, to them, is an obsolete term.

Deford, prominent sportswriter and commentator (also the author of *Casey on the Loose*), presents a commendable study of modern values in *The Entitled*. The characters act in their own self-interest as business ethics overshadow old-fashioned morality. This seems to be the way of the world, and of professional baseball, in the early twenty-first century.

Farrell, James T. *Dreaming Baseball.* Ohio: Kent State University Press, 2007

The Black Sox Scandal is a major event in a novel fashioned by editors Ron Briley, Margaret Davidson, and James Barbour from the unpublished papers of Farrell (1904–79). Protagonist Mickey Donovan was a fictional member of the infamous 1919 Chicago White Sox. Currently a scout for the Sox, he reveals, in a series of flashbacks, the events that led to the alleged fix of the 1919 World Series.

Although the eight players, including Donovan's boyhood hero Buck Weaver, were acquitted in court, they were banned from the majors. Donovan feels betrayed by his teammates, and the trauma of the scandal permanently haunts him.

Farrell is less sympathetic to the "eight men out" than the other fictional accounts. The portraits of Ty Cobb and Babe Ruth are an added attraction, but the overall quality of the writing is inferior to the author's famous books of Studs Lonigan and Danny O'Neill. However, Mickey Dondovan's view of the era, plus his dream of a trouble-free game, is a welcome addition to baseball literature.

Golenbock, Peter. *7: The Mickey Mantle Novel.* Guilford, CT: The Lyons Press, 2007.

After dying in 1995, Mantle emerges in a playboy version of heaven in which he confesses his misbehavior to sportswriter Lenny Shecter. From Toots Shor's bar, the ex-Yankee talks about his favorite activities: baseball, drinking, and womanizing. The major regrets of his life are the mistreatment of his fans and his family; he admits to sometimes cursing at autograph seekers and of "not being there" for his wife and four sons. In what the author calls an imaginative memoir, Mantle attempts to expiate his guilt and to explain why he became an alcoholic and a sex addict.

The baseball legend blames his behavioral pattern on his roots in Commerce, Oklahoma, where his dad demanded that he become a pro ballplayer and an older sister sexually abused him. As an adult, Mantle was haunted by the fear of failing his father and of death. Drinking and copulating developed into escapes, and Billy Martin, Yankee teammate, helped Mantle on his journey to dissipation.

In relating his experiences, Mantle's bigotry and pettiness are exposed. His dislike of Joe DiMaggio, a rival on and off the field, resulted in revenge consisting of a one-night stand with Marilyn Monroe. Mantle ridicules major models of decorum, Lou Gehrig and Cal Ripken, for their fidelity to fans, family, and teams. He scorns the opponents who beat the Yankees in the World Series in his era (the '55 Dodgers, '60 Pirates, and '64 Cardinals), considering them lucky rather than skilled. Only a few of his Yankee teammates (particularly Whitey Ford and Joe Pepitone) are thought to be worthy of the standard of behavior that he and Martin have established.

Mantle's confession, then, is undermined by his pride in irresponsible acts. Success as a ballplayer and the pursuit of fun — even at the expense of hurting people — are seemingly more important to him than being a decent person. The book poses the question as to whether it is a debunking of Mantle or an apology for the vagaries of a hero. The ambiguity contributes to the quality.

Howe, LeAnne. *Miko Kings: An Indian Baseball Story.* San Francisco: Aunt Lute Books, 2007.

Lena Coulter, a Native American writer living in Ada, Oklahoma, in 2006, finds a mail pouch containing newspaper clippings and the journal of Ezol Day, her grandmother's cousin who died in a fire in 1907. The ghost of the former postal worker visits Coulter and helps her reconstruct the past involving the Day family and the Miko Kings baseball team, owned by Henri Day, Ezol's uncle. According to Ezol, baseball was played by Native Americans long before the arrival of Europeans and was a central part of their culture.

The Miko Kings won the Indian Territory League championship in 1907. Much of the team's story is related by Hope Little Leader from the confines of a nursing home in 1969. Once a pitcher with magical deliveries, but now handless and near death, Little Leader talks and dreams about the past, especially his part in the 1907 Twin Territories Series, a nine-game playoff with the white soldiers from Fort Sill's Seventh Cavalry. In one version of the legendary Series, gamblers bribe him to throw the final game, and his teammates retaliate for the fix by chopping off his hands.

Woven into the plot is the movie that the real-life Carl Laemmle makes. He employs the Miko Kings to portray the Choctaw Indians that take on the fictional Jimtown Bar, a team of local whites. Little Leader is cast as Choctaw Bill, a pitcher who is kidnapped by gamblers when he refuses to accept a bribe. In the movie, *His Last Game*, which is an actual fourteen-minute film released in 1909, Bill pitches his team to victory but meets with a bad end.

Another aspect of Hope Little Leader's life is his love affair with Justina Maurepas that begins at Hampton Normal School for Blacks and Indians and continues in Indian Territory in 1907. Maurepas, a mixture of Indian and African American, known as Black Juice, leaves her lover and becomes famous as a militant black leader in New Orleans. Her protest against injustice is also evident in the Four Mothers Society, a group augmented by the Day family, which focuses primarily on resisting the allotment of Indian land in the Territory to white settlers.

As Lena Coulter and the spirit of Ezol Day turn back time, they try to justify Choctaw culture in its conflict with its Anglo counterpart. Baseball is a metaphor of the struggle. The mystical Indian game of no limitations is overwhelmed by the new rules of the dominant society — including measures to eliminate or limit participation by minority groups. A common bugaboo in both cases, however, is the influence of gambling in the early years of the sport. The author, a member of the Choctaw Nation in Oklahoma, makes a valiant effort to merge baseball, history, and art into a memorable novel. The magical realism is reminiscent of Kinsella's fiction, and the historical evocation of Native American baseball is unique.

Hudgens, Dallas. *Season of Gene.* New York: Scribner, 2007.

Joe Rice is the manager and catcher of the Whip Spa Yankees of the Metro D.C. Men's Recreational Baseball League. In the fall season, Gene Dellorso, Rice's best friend and business partner, dies of a heart attack during a game. Among other shady secrets, Dellorso had in his possession a baseball bat reputedly used by Babe Ruth in the 1932 World Series. The bat may be worth millions, and hoods are after it. Rice is involved in the quest for the bat and also gets involved with Joy, his friend's widow. Although the madcap adventures result in chaos, Joe Rice tries to do the right thing. He eventually makes a deal with the "bad guys" and gives his share of the loot to Joy Dellorso — perhaps the first step in atoning for the errors of the past.

Narrated in Rice's spicy vernacular, the crime caper is fast-paced and humorous although not in the same league as the fiction of Elmore Leonard, Carl Hiaasen, or George V. Higgins.

Jansen, George. *The Fade-away.* Clifton, VA: Pocol Press, 2007.

Port Newton, California, is a small coastal town that once had a good semi-pro baseball team. In 1900, however, the members of the Athletic Club are unhappy about the ten-year slump of the local nine. Then one night Constable Long John Sheets rescues a Native American from the Carquinez Strait, and fate intervenes. The "big fish" is revived at Foghorn Murphy's Railroad Exchange Saloon and reveals that he is Jack Dobbs, former star pitcher for the Boston Beaneaters. Although he has been banned from major league ball for allegedly throwing games, Foghorn, the manager, persuades him to pitch for Port Newton. The team becomes an instant winner, and townspeople are filled with civic pride — although some are concerned about the new commercialism and the introduction of dirty ball.

"Chief" Dobbs, the target of racism during his time in the National League, becomes a local savior and is followed through the streets by hero-worshipping boys. His fade-aways and curves baffle opposing hitters and result in victories. Foghorn soon hires the two McDowell brothers of Oakland and Juan Cabalerro, the black "Cuban," to help keep the winning streak going. The four new players advocate dirty play and insist that covert cheating is an acceptable part of the game. Foghorn cashes in on the new fan interest by charging admission to the games and selling beer at the park. He also bets heavily on the team. The morality of the enterprise is finally challenged by player Charlie Meyers, journalist Riley Towne, and physician Sam Fuller.

Although Meyers leads a revolt that ends in the dismissal of the four newcomers, his motives are suspect. He wants to replace Dobbs as pitcher. His supporters on the team state that they do not want to play with "coons," a reference to the Indian and the Cuban. With a scratch lineup of locals, Port Newton loses in a Fourth of July tournament. Meanwhile, Dobbs fades away from the town; years later he is seen selling peanuts in an Oakland ballpark.

Dr. Fuller, one of the moral arbiters, feels guilty over allowing the antics of Foghorn Murphy to occur. He feels that the world is falling apart at the dawn of a new century of industrialism and technology. He and the townspeople have traded their souls for temporary glory. Greed and hooliganism, he feels, have triumphed over ethics, and baseball has been turned into a business. The return to local ball at the end is not likely to improve the status of the game given the nature of the egotistical and intolerant players.

Variously narrated by Sam Fuller, his teenage daughter, Sophie, and Cal Elwell, bartender for Foghorn and blood brother to Dobbs, the book is also spiced by the newspaper commentary of Riley Towne. The battle between economics and integrity is colorfully portrayed without resorting to slick solutions. The depiction of baseball in 1900 reflects the turmoil in society, and the result is a first-rate novel.

Lewis, Hal. *The Marinolli Treasure.* N.p.: Lulu Press, 2007.

The discovery of a set of 1909 T-206 Honus Wagner baseball cards, almost a century after printing, is the occasion for an unprecedented bidding war. The owner, in the expectation of raising money to pay the mortgage on a park used by orphans, presents the cards to a dealer. Offers of millions of dollars soon follow. Subtitled "A Malenglish Novel," the narrative is replete with "male English," which stresses references to pop culture trivia, sports facts, and quotes from movies, songs, and television.

Joey Marinolli was an orphan who in 1909 did janitorial work for a factory that produced baseball cards for the American Tobacco Company. When Honus Wagner objects to being portrayed on the cards, they are destined for destruction. Marinolli, however, saves a box from the furnace. He dies in World War I, and his son inherits the collection. As an old man, he tries to save Stratton Park for the orphanage his father had inhabited. The card dealer, Barry Stone, offers them to Chuck Evans, a sports agent who is trying to buy a Wagner card for his egotistical big league client, Jerry Johns. The news gets out, though, and soon Duke University, the Baseball Hall of Fame, and a wealthy German are making bids. The card set is finally sold for thirty-five million dollars, and Marinolli is able to pay the mortgage for the park and to cover operating expenses for the orphanage well into the future.

The melodramatic plot, augmented by malenglish, is presumably entertaining for the nonliterary. Antecedents in the subgenre of card novels include *The Burglar Who Traded Ted Williams, Diminished Capacity, Cards, Bite of the Shark,* and *The Perfect Pafko.*

Moffie, Sam. *Swap.* N.p.: UEL Enterprises, 2007.

Former major leaguers Sheldon Marsh and Tom Easterbrook pitch for the Youngstown Monsters in the minors. Marsh, half-Jewish and deaf in one ear, is unhappily married to Eleanor and unduly attracted to Lucy, Tom's wife. He devises the plan of swapping mates, and it is accepted.

Presumably inspired by the real-life swap of two New York Yankee players and their wives, the novel focuses primarily on sexual exploits and movie trivia rather than on baseball. The rambling narrative includes seemingly irrelevant activity such as an argument against the political motives of religious fundamentalists and a plea for the banning of parents from Little League ball. The humorous tone keeps the book from being a disaster.

Perry, Thomas K. *Just Joe: Baseballs Natural, as told by his wife.* Clifton, VA: Pocol Press.

Shoeless Joe Jackson is presented as a baseball legend, an all-around great guy, and an innocent victim of the Black Sox Scandal in this fictional biography. Katie, Mrs. Jackson, narrates the story through the imaginary perception of the author. From a boyhood in the South Carolina cotton mills in the 1890s to his death in 1951, Jackson maintains the moral and athletic qualities of a hero. An illiterate who was banned from major league ball while still in his prime, he never lost his love for the game or the qualities of a gentleman.

The man who hit .408 in his first full season and posted a lifetime batting average of .356 (topped only by Ty Cobb and Rogers Hornsby) was reluctantly drawn into the 1919 World Series fix, according to Katie. He gave the money, left in his hotel room as a bribe, to White Sox owner Charles Comiskey and asked Kid Gleason, manager, not to play him in a Series that was tainted. (He did play and hit .375.) His illiteracy is cited as the reason for his "signed confession" of guilt in the matter. He is seen as the victim of the owners who wanted to keep the poorly paid players under control and to cover up the widespread gambling in the game.

Shoeless Joe comes to the realization that the sport has become a business and that his status as a player is similar to working in the textile mills as a youth. He loves baseball and is one of its biggest stars, but Commissioner Landis and the team owners, despite the acquittal of the eight White Sox players in court, take the professional game away from him for their own purposes.

The problem with the book is the obsession with apologizing for Jackson's part in the Black Sox Scandal through the glorification of his character. The testimonials to his great natural prowess as a hitter (by Ty Cobb, Babe Ruth, and Ted Williams) are paralleled by tributes to his ethical attributes. There is no objectivity in Katie's view of her husband.

Rychlik, Michael. *Journeymen.* Clifton, VA: Pocol Press, 2007.

Cub reporter Jersey Paige of Gainesville, Florida, composes obituaries for a local paper, but he wants to be a sportswriter. The son of a United States senator, Paige watches the hometown G-Men of Class D baseball in 1948. The journeymen of note on the team are Myril Hoag and Jake Powell, former New York Yankees (real players who both hit .271 in their major league careers). Hoag is the playing manager who has converted to a pitcher, and Powell has been assigned to Gainesville in the hope that he will be a drawing card. Both men have dreams of returning to the majors. Jersey Paige, meanwhile, dreams of making a name for himself as a journalist. He also pursues Katina, but her over-protective Greek father makes it difficult.

Powell, one of the journeymen, has a drinking problem and never gets into shape in Gainesville. He is released by the G-Men before the end of the season. Hoag pitches well and even hurls a no-hitter, but all it gets him is a job in Class B ball in St. Petersburg. Paige has trouble in trying to convince Katina's father that he is a qualified suitor. The youth gets a big opportunity, though, when he is assigned to write the obituary for Jake Powell — who has committed suicide.

While the two journeymen are struggling to recapture the prowess of the past — the ghosts of the boys inside the men — Jersey Paige is maturing into adulthood. His major discovery is that his father's political popularity is based on pandering to the financial interests of the populace. He learns that the economic motif carries into the realm of pro baseball as well — and that the world offers no promises of success or happiness. Paige's experiences and observations result in a more than competent coming-of-age novel.

Valenti, Chris. *Innings Through Time: The Greatest Baseball Story Ever Told.* Mustang, OK: Tate Publishing, 2007.

The novel, which does not live up to the claim of its subtitle, features an alternate history. In the first version of the story, an aging Joe King relates his biography to a nephew, Richard Russell. In 1943, as a member of the Atlanta All Stars, a Class A team in the Southern Association, he was shocked by a bus accident that claimed the life of Maria, his fiancée. Also killed in the crash were the opponents in the league championship series, the players of the Memphis Maulers. The only survivor was Bobby Reed, a Mauler catcher. The All Stars were declared the league champs by default. Joe King, however, lived the next sixty years brooding over the loss of Maria.

The important event in King's early life is his introduction to Babe Ruth in 1931. As the winner of a local contest, the boy is sent to Yankee Stadium. He sees a game and participates with Ruth and other prize-winning kids in a film. He also gets Ruth's autograph on a baseball card. The Babe Ruth card plays an important role in the alternate version of the plot.

At the age of seventy-nine, King is in a nursing home while recovering from a stroke. He is joined there by Ray Ramsey, a former teammate from the All Stars. Ramsey, apparently a guardian angel, teaches King to see the 1943 tragedy from a larger perspective rather than just as a personal loss and a reason for a traumatizing self-pity. Presumably as a reward for King's new awareness of a big picture, a new world view, the events of his life are changed. The accident of 1943 never happened. Maria and the Maulers are still alive. In the series between the teams, King stars as Atlanta wins in seven games. He also achieves a moral victory by presenting his rival, Bobby Reed, with the Babe Ruth baseball card. King realizes that a lucky charm is irrelevant in the game of life. He marries Maria and enjoys sixty years of marital bliss. After his death, his son (rather than the nephew, who does not exist in this version) discovers the manuscript of *Joseph King, King of the All Stars*, which becomes a bestseller.

In a form of fantasy or magical realism, the religious motif dominates to the detriment of the overall quality. The melodramatic baseball content is relevant only for the purpose of illustrating the obvious message.

2008

Mitchell, Bob. *Once Upon a Fastball.* NY: Kensington Publishing Corporation, 2008.

Seth Stein, Harvard historian, engages in a series of time travels in a quest for his grandfather, Papa Sol, who has recently disappeared. His first trip into the past is to New York City for the Miracle of Coogan's Bluff in 1951—the Shot Heard Round the World. Sol catches the Bobby Thomson homerun ball. Later trips are to the pivotal World Series games of 1962, 1986, and 2004. Papa Sol has left cryptic messages about baseball's importance as a learning tool that his grandson tries to decode.

Schilling, Peter, Jr. *The End of Baseball.* Chicago: Ivan R. Dee, 2008.

Bill Veeck buys the Philadelphia Athletics and stocks the team with Negro League stars for the 1944 major league season. Satchel Paige, Josh Gibson, Buck Leonard, Cool Papa Bell, and Martin Dihigo are the big names on a club that contends for a pennant despite the racist reaction of much of the country. The nobel experiment, predating the actual integration of baseball in 1947, lacks credibility, but the book is nevertheless gutsy and entertaining.

Appendix A
Mystery Novels

The baseball detective appears in juvenile dime novels in the 1890s and in the Stratemeyer syndicate books of the early twentieth century, but the adult version does not arrive until 1934. *Death on the Diamond* by Cortland Fitzsimmons features a reporter who tracks down gamblers who, unlikely as it seems, murder ballplayers—some of them while they are on the field. This incredulous method of protecting bets is doomed to failure, as is the book.

In 1947 Aaron Marc Stein (a pseudonym for George Bagby, a reputable mystery writer) finally produces the second entry in the field. *The Twin Killing* involves a murder in which two New York rookies are the prime suspects. Inspector Baggy Schmidt, though, is able to clear Whitey Roos and Blackie Crawford, and they respond by breaking out of their slumps. The quality is questionable here, too, and the baseball mystery languishes for another long period.

John Ball, famous as the creator of black detective Virgil Tibbs, snaps the drought in 1969 with *Johnny Get Your Gun*. Tibbs follows the flight of a youth to Anaheim and corrals him at the home of the California Angels with the help of Gene Autry. The Angels owner dons his cowboy regalia and rides a horse onto the field to distract the kid so that the detective can make the capture. Tibbs then confronts a black gang with the evidence that the boy did not kill one of its members. This is the first competent novel of the subgenre; it was reissued as *Death for a Playmate* in 1972.

Starting in 1973, mysteries appear with regularity, but the glory years do not arrive until the 1990s. The most notable book of the seventies is Robert B. Parker's *Mortal Stakes* (1975). The legendary Spenser accepts a job with the Boston Red Sox in order to check on the reputed gambling activities of a star pitcher. The sleuth gets to the core of the problem but kills two men in the process. He feels that he may have violated his Hemingwayesque code of honor, and a friend, Susan Silverman, has to convince him that the end justifies the means.

The other mysteries of the decade and in the early eighties are nondescript with the possible exceptions of A.B. Guthrie's *Wild Pitch* (1973) and James Magnuson's *The Rundown* (1977). In 1984 Richard D. Rosen introduces Harvey Blissberg, a Jewish ballplayer who emerges as the first series detective. In his first appearance, the ex–Red Sox outfielder is playing with the expansion team in Providence. When a teammate is murdered, Blissberg, known as the Professor, takes the responsibility of finding the solution. He is later featured in *Saturday Night Dead* (1988) and *Dead Ball* (2001) as he continues sleuthing after his playing days are done.

Gordon DeMarco's *Frisco Blues* is published in England in 1985 and is set in San Francisco shortly after World War II. Riley Kovach, a series detective making his only appearance in baseball, delves into a murder of a Negro League player and the possible involvement of the Pacific Coast Purity League, a racist group. It is 1947, the year of Jackie Robinson's Dodger debut, and an exhibition game between segregated all-star teams led by Satchel Paige and Bob Feller stresses the racial tension of the era. The novel was revised for its 1995 American edition.

At the end of the eighties, the series detective becomes a fixture. Slots Resnick, Bull Cochran, Kate Henry, and the team of Tom and Scot join Harvey Blissberg as reappearing characters. In the nineties, they are joined by Gun Pedersen, Duffy House, Joe Tinker, and Mickey Rawlings. Will Beaman shows up for the first time in 2003. Alison Gordon's female sportswriter makes her entry in *Dead Pull Hitter* (1988). Duffy House, also a sportswriter and amateur sleuth, shows up in Crabbe Evers' trio of 1991 publications, including *Murder in Wrigley Field*. A utility infielder for a number of major league teams in the early twentieth century, Mickey Rawlings first appears in *Murder at Fenway Park*—a Troy Soos creation of 1994. Beaman is another amateur detective, and he begins his career while working for the Boston Beaneaters in 1897 (as a product of G.S. Rowe) in *Best Bet in Beantown*. Gordon, Evers, Soos, and Rowe are the best of the series writers so far. The historical fiction of Soos and Rowe is especially well done as they both realistically incorporate factual events and people into their novels.

In *Hanging Curve* (1999), Soos depicts the 1922 season of the St. Louis Browns. Rawlings is a reserve who gets little playing time, so he moonlights with a semipro team in East St. Louis, Illinois. The town, which experienced the race riot of 1917, is still a hotbed of racism, and Rawlings checks out the murder of a black pitcher. His investigation leads to a confrontation with the KKK and to meetings with Cool Papa Bell and Oscar Charleston of the Negro National League.

Rowe's *Double Play in Beantown* (2005) sees Will Beaman leave the Beaneaters of the National League for Boston's new American League team in 1901. However, he gets sidetracked into searching for a missing girl—a quest that brings him into contact with Maud Gonne, the Irish Joan of Arc, who arrives in the city to promote Irish independence.

The socio-historical topics of Soos and Rowe are also present in novels by Donald Honig and Robert B. Parker. Honig's *The Plot to Kill Jackie Robinson* (1992) and Parker's *Double Play* (2005) focus on the 1947 season and the danger that Robinson faces in his integration of major league baseball. Joe Tinker and Joseph Burke, embittered veterans of World War II, have humanizing experiences as they deal with the problems of protecting the Dodger player and finding those responsible for death threats. Both authors reveal the tumultuous temper of the times in postwar America.

Van Reid's *Mollie Peer* (2000) is another historical mystery. Set in Portland, Maine, in 1896, it features the amateur detectives of the Moosepath League, female journalist Mollie Peer, and baseball player Wyckford O'Hearn. They confront smugglers amidst the eerie ambience of the seacoast in their pursuit of a boy named Bird. Louis Sockalexis, the real-life former major leaguer (*the* Cleveland Indian), appears with a Penobscot team that hires O'Hearn to take the place of an injured player.

About eighty baseball mysteries have been published from 1934 through 2007 — although the category can be somewhat uncertain. Most of the better literary works are in the series mysteries, which begin in 1984. The outstanding feature is the tendency to place the element of detection into a cultural milieu that evokes the flavor of a specific time and place — a method that Troy Soos popularized in the Mickey Rawlings books.

The Best Mysteries by Year

1969	*Johnny Get Your Gun*	John Ball
1975	*Mortal Stakes*	Robert B. Parker
1984	*Strike Three You're Dead*	Richard D. Rosen
1985	*Frisco Blues*	Gordon DeMarco
1988	*The Dead Pull Hitter*	Alison Gordon
1990	*Safe at Home*	Alison Gordon
1992	*Night Game*	Alison Gordon
	The Plot to Kill Jackie Robinson	Donald Honig
1994	*Tigers Burning*	Crabbe Evers
	Murder at Fenway Park	Troy Soos
1995	*Striking Out*	Alison Gordon
1996	*Murder at Wrigley Field*	Troy Soos
1997	*Prairie Hardball*	Alison Gordon
	Hunting a Detroit Tiger	Troy Soos
1998	*The Cincinnati Red Stalkings*	Troy Soos
1999	*Hanging Curve*	Troy Soos
2000	*Mollie Peer*	Van Reid
2003	*Best Bet in Beantown*	G.S. Rowe
2004	*Double Play*	Robert B. Parker

	Squeeze Play in Beantown	G.S. Rowe
2005	Double Play in Beantown	G.S. Rowe

A Chronological List of All Baseball Mysteries

1934	Death on the Diamond	Cortland Fitzsimmons
1947	The Twin Killing	George Bagby (Aaron Marc Stein)
1969	Johnny Get Your Gun	John Ball
1973	A Handy Death	Robert L. Fish
	Wild Pitch	A.B. Guthrie
1974	The Devil to Play	Leonard Holton
1975	The Pro #3: Strike Zone	Richard Curtis
	Mortal Stakes	Robert B. Parker
1977	The 7th Game	Don Kowett
	The Rundown	James Magnuson
1978	The Cocaine Caper	Vincent A. Paradis
	The Screwball King Murder	Kin Platt
1979	Seven Games in October	Charles Brady
1980	Gamemaker	David Keith Cohler
	The Stranger City Caper	Ross H. Spencer
1982	Five O'Clock Lightning	William DeAndrea
	Strictly Amateur	Tom McCormack
1983	Dead in Centerfield	Paul Engleman
1984	Strike Three You're Dead	Richard D. Rosen
	Squeeze Play	Paul Benjamin
1985	Frisco Blues	Gordon DeMarco
	Follow the Sharks	William G. Tapply
1987	Kirby's Last Circus	Ross H. Spencer
1988	Major League Murder	Michael Geller
	The Dead Pull Hitter	Alison Gordon
	Saturday Night Dead	Richard D. Rosen
1989	Strikezone	David F. Nighbert
	Beanball: Murder at the World Series	Tom Seaver and Herb Rescinow
	A Simple Suburban Murder	Mark Richard Zubro
1990	Comeback	L.L. Enger
	Safe at Home	Alison Gordon
	Gone to Glory	Robert Irvine
1991	Fielder's Choice	Michael Bowen
	Swing	L.L. Enger
	Bleeding Dodger Blue	Crabbe Evers
	Murderer's Row	Crabbe Evers
	Murder in Wrigley Field	Crabbe Evers
	Suicide Squeeze	David Everson
1992	Strike	L.L. Enger
	Three Strikes, You're Dead	Michael Geller

Appendix A: Mystery Novels

1992	Night Game	Alison Gordon
	The Plot to Kill Jackie Robinson	Donald Honig
	Squeezeplay	David F. Nighbert
	Caught Looking	Randy Russell
	All the Dead Heroes	Stephen F. Wilcox
1993	Sacrifice	L.L. Enger
	Fear in Fenway	Crabbe Evers
	Last Man Out	Donald Honig
1994	The Burglar Who Traded Ted Williams	Lawrence Block
	The Sinner's League	L.L. Enger
	Tigers Burning	Crabbe Evers
	Drover and the Designated Hitter	Bill Granger
	Dead End Game	Christopher Newman
	Murder at Fenway Park	Troy Soos
1995	Striking Out	Alison Gordon
	Shutout	David F. Nighbert
	Murder at Ebbets Field	Troy Soos
1996	Murder at the Baseball Hall of Fame	David Daniel and Chris Carpenter
	Murder at Wrigley Field	Troy Soos
	Rust on the Razor	Mark Richard Zubro
1997	Baseball Cat	Garrison Allen
	Prairie Hardball	Alison Gordon
	Caught in a Rundown	Lisa Saxon
	Hunting a Detroit Tiger	Troy Soos
1998	Brushback	K.C. Constantine
	The Cincinnati Red Stalkings	Troy Soos
1999	The Final Detail	Harlan Coben
	Hanging Curve	Troy Soos
2000	A Difficult Trade	Sam Leonard
	Mollie Peer: Or the Underground Adventure of the Moosepath League	Van Reid
2001	The Hunting Wind	Steve Hamilton
	Dead Ball	Richard D. Rosen
2003	Best Bet in Beantown	G.S. Rowe
	Screwball	David Farrell
2004	Double Play	Robert B. Parker
	Squeeze Play in Beantown	G. S. Rowe
2005	The Deadly Tools of Ignorance	Robert Elias
	Double Play in Beantown	G. S. Rowe
2006	Murder She Wrote: Three Strikes and You're Dead	Donald Bain
	Foul Ball in Beantown	G.S. Rowe
	Lights Out	Jason Starr
2007	Foul Play	Tori Carrington

A Chronological List of Series Mysteries

Protagonist	Year	Title	Author
Harvey Blissberg	1984	*Strike Three You're Dead*	Rosen
	1988	*Saturday Night Dead*	
	2001	*Dead Ball*	
Slots Resnick	1988	*Major League Murder*	Geller
	1992	*Three Strikes, You're Dead*	
Kate Henry	1988	*Dead Pull Hitter*	Gordon
	1990	*Safe at Home*	
	1992	*Night Game*	
	1995	*Striking Out*	
	1997	*Prairie Hardball*	
Bull Cochran	1989	*Strikezone*	Nighbert
	1992	*Squeezeplay*	
	1995	*Shutout*	
Tom and Scott	1989	*A Simple Suburban Murder*	Zubro
	1996	*Rust on the Razor*	
Duffy House	1991	*Murder in Wrigley Field*	Evers
		Murderer's Row	
		Bleeding Dodger Blue	
	1993	*Fear in Fenway*	
	1994	*Tigers Burning*	
Gun Pedersen	1990	*Comeback*	Enger
	1991	*Swing*	
	1992	*Strike*	
	1993	*Sacrifice*	
	1994	*The Sinner's League*	
Mickey Rawlings	1994	*Murder at Fenway Park*	Soos
	1995	*Murder at Ebbets Field*	
	1996	*Murder at Wrigley Field*	
	1997	*Hunting a Detroit Tiger*	
	1998	*The Cincinnati Red Stalkings*	
	1999	*Hanging Curve*	
Joe Tinker	1992	*The Plot to Kill Jackie Robinson*	Honig
	1993	*Last Man Out*	
Will Beaman	2003	*Best Bet in Beantown*	Rowe
	2004	*Squeeze Play in Beantown*	
	2005	*Double Play in Beantown*	
	2006	*Foul Ball in Beantown*	

Appendix B
Science Fiction and Fantasy Novels

Fantasy has a long history in baseball fiction, while science fiction is a relatively recent creation. Definitions are due, though, in order to verify the statement. Fantasy in baseball is closer to magical realism, a twentieth-century phenomenon which depicts a realistic framework that is contrasted with supernatural occurrences, as in *Shoeless Joe*. Sci-fi is identified by plots in which advanced technology, often applied to the future, dominates the action. Marvin Karlins' *The Last Man Is Out* (1969) is the first full-fledged novel of the subgenre.

Old-fashioned fantasy, which is essentially an obvious break from reality in an unusual environment, can be traced back to Mark Twain's short interlude of baseball in *A Connecticut Yankee in King Arthur's Court* (1889) and to Whiting's tall tales of *The Fat Mascot* (1902). Smith's *Rhubarb* of 1946, in which a cat inherits a major league team, is a borderline case that edges toward magical realism — although farce may be the better term.

The first major novel in the field is Malamud's *The Natural* in 1952, a blend of realistic ball, folklore, and mythology. King Arthur and the Knights of the Round Table provide the mythological background as Roy Hobbs with his bat, Wonder Boy (like Arthur's sword, Excalibur), sets out on a belated quest to win a pennant for the New York Knights. Hobbs' ego overcomes his morality, however, and he fails. Instead of claiming the grail, he becomes associated with the Black Sox scandal.

The Year the Yankees Lost the Pennant (1954) is the next big book, as Wallop's use of the Faust legend to turn an aging Senator fan into a super ballplayer who leads Washington to first place in the American League has been immortalized as *Damn Yankees*. The magical bargain with a Mephistopheles figure, featuring Joe Boyd's change into the heroic Joe Hardy by Mr. Applegate, is a part of American folklore.

Nye's *Stay Loose* (1959) and Molloy's *A Pennant for the Kremlin* (1964) are of some note in fantasy, but Coover's *The Universal Baseball Association, Inc., J. Henry Waugh, Prop* (1968) is one of the great ones. Waugh's obsession dominates most of the action, but the protagonist disappears in the last chapter. The players, created in the accountant's imagination, develop lives of their own in the Universal Baseball Association — a game consisting of dice and a probability chart — as magical realism replaces psychological realism.

Roth's *The Great American Novel* (1973) deals with the Patriot League during World War II that is erased from the record books due to a suspected communist infiltration. Word Smith, writing from a retirement home, attempts to tell the truth about the government intervention that destroys history. His narration includes the story of the Rupert Mundys, a homeless team whose field is taken over by the War Department. The unlikely events are the author's means of commenting on the dangerous reactionary political climate of the era that mushroomed into the communist witch hunt led by Senator McCarthy.

In 1982, *Shoeless Joe* appears, and Kinsella's realistic economic picture of an Iowa farmer struggling to survive is offset by the magical appearance of Joe Jackson and other banned members of the 1919 Black Sox. The ghosts of the past play in the former cornfield that the protagonist converts into a ballpark — the field of dreams that the movie version of the book helped to popularize. Baseball is presented as a positive symbol that counters the ugly reality of business, thus providing hope and a renewed faith in humanity.

Home Game (1983), *Joy in Mudville* (1989), and *The Year I Owned the Yankees* (1990) are interesting entries in the realm of fantasy, along with Brock's time-travel tales (*If I Never Get Back*, and *Two in the Field*), but Bishop's *Brittle Innings* (1994) is on the list of the best baseball novels. Featuring Mary Shelley's *Frankenstein* (the "monster"), the book nevertheless manages to give a stirring account of life in the minor leagues. The three outcasts (the monster, the mute, and the mulatto), work out their unique destinies against a realistic baseball background.

The technology associated with science fiction, meanwhile, is first seen in Davies' *It Happens Every Spring*, in which the accidental discovery of a chemical that avoids wood leads to baseball magic. The professor applies the stuff to baseballs and becomes a major league star. In Grantham's *Baseball's Darkest Days* (1965), a form of remote control is used on doctored baseballs so that games can be manipulated. The perpetrators make money by betting on the Cubs, who win the pennant, but their crime is eventually discovered. *The Last Man Is Out*, a 1969 novel by Karlins, takes scientific knowledge to a higher level as a mad scientist uses a computer to build a domed stadium (on the ocean floor), to cause an accident to eliminate the toughest competition, and to manipulate the players on his team. Professor Norbert emerges from the fiction of Poe and Hawthorne to take a place as an evil genius whose head outweighs his heart. The mad scientist figure appears in such later works as *The*

New AToms Bombshell (a 1980 rewriting of the Karlins novel by Robert Browne in 1980), *Child's Play* (1986), *Open Season* (1993), and *Special Treatment* (1996). Further misuse of computer technology (in which games and players are unduly influenced) occurs in *The Batting Machine* (1981), *Ballpark Numbers* (1992), and *Protocol 9* (2002).

Baseball on other planets or in alternate universes is a topic for the first time in 1987 with Lupoff's *Countersolar*. Titles included in the category are: *They Still Play Baseball on the Moon* (1994), *The Aliens of Summer* (1995), *If Wishes Were Horses* (1996), *Summerland* (2002), *The Pitch* (2004), and *King of Diamonds* (2004). Another science fiction subject, genetic engineering, meanwhile, is featured in *Superbaby* (1969) and *Project Samuel* (2001). While the unique concepts offered in hardcore sci/fi are often interesting, the literary quality of the books is often ambiguous.

In contrast, the novels more aptly falling into the fantasy-magical realism realm are generally on a higher artistic level. *The Natural, The Universal Baseball Association, Shoeless Joe,* and *Brittle Innings* rate as the best. Along with the other aforementioned books, the list can be extended to include Beckham's *Runner Mack* (1969), an African American militant protest novel. Kinsella's *The Iowa Baseball Confederacy* (1986) features a forty-day game set against a mythological background. Plimpton's *The Curious Case of Sidd Finch* (1987) is about a Buddhist scholar with an unhittable fastball. McAllister's *The Kid Who Batted 1.000* (2002) depicts another scholar who can draw walks by fouling off pitches endlessly — even on a major league level. Miller's *Coyote Moon* (2003) applies the Heisenberg Uncertainty Principle to baseball. These books, and more, attest to the happy union of fictional baseball and surrealism — a combination that is as valid as realistic novels of the game.

Baseball Science Fiction and Fantasy: A Chronological List

1889	*A Connecticut Yankee in King Arthur's Court*	Mark Twain
1902	*The Fat Mascot*	Robert Rudd Whiting
1946	*Rhubarb*	H. Allen Smith
1949	*It Happens Every Spring*	Valentine Davies
1952	*The Natural*	Bernard Malamud
1954	*The Year the Yankees Lost the Pennant*	Douglas Wallop
1959	*Stay Loose*	Bud Nye
1964	*A Pennant for the Kremlin*	Paul Molloy
1965	*Baseball's Darkest Days*	Kenneth L. Grantham
1968	*The Universal Baseball Association*	Robert Coover
1969	*The Last Man Is Out*	Marvin Karlins
	Superbaby	Felix Mendelsohn
1972	*Runner Mack*	Barry Beckham

1973	The Great American Novel	Phillip Roth
1974	Flawless Play Restored: The Masque of Fungo	Gilbert Sorrentino
1975	All G.O.D's Children	John Craig
1977	Spitballs and Holy Water	James F. Donohue
1978	Noonan	Leonard Everett Fisher
1980	The New AToms Bombshell	Robert Brown
1981	The Batting Machine	Mel Knopf
1982	Andy, the First Switch-Pitcher	Al Carmona
	Shoeless Joe	W.P. Kinsella
1983	Home Game	Paul Quarrington
1984	Wier & Pouce	Steve Katz
	Things Invisible to See	Nancy Willard
1985	Chin Music	James McManus
1986	Child's Play	Sal Conte
1986	The Iowa Baseball Confederacy	W.P. Kinsella
1987	The Boozer Challenge	Charles Gill
	Countersolar	Richard Lupoff
	The Curious Case of Sidd Finch	George Plimpton
1988	Southpaw	Frank King
1989	Joy in Mudville	Gordon McAlpine
	If I Never Get Back	Darryl Brock
1990	The Year I Owned the Yankees	Sparky Lyle and David Fisher
1991	Rookie	Jerry G. Jenkins
1992	Ball Park Numbers	David P. Hullinger
1993	Spirit of the Season	Heather Graham
	Open Season	Scot Moon
	Baseball and Benevolence	Mark Allen Valenza
1994	Brittle Innings	Michael Bishop
	They Still Play Baseball on the Moon	James Garrett La Femina
1995	Out at the Old Ballgame	Bernie Bookbinder
	The December Rose	Robert Grant
	The Aliens of Summer	Calvin Ross
	The Final Game	Rob Shoemaker
	The 30 Hit Season	D. Michael Tomkins
1996	Special Treatment	Nancy Fisher
	If Wishes Were Horses	W.P. Kinsella
1997	Snow in August	Pete Hamill
1999	Our Lady of the Outfield	David Craig
	Gifts of the Gods	Robert J. Kelly
	One More Time	Ed Orzula
2000	Hardball Fever	John Carver
	The Big R	D. Larry Crumbly, et. al.
	Sut McCaslin	Steve Spoerl
2001	Project Samuel	J.P. Polidoro
	Opening Day	Lee Standiford
2002	Two in the Field	Darryl Brock

Appendix B: Science Fiction and Fantasy Novels

	Summerland	Michael Chabon
	The Kid Who Batted 1.000	Troon McAllister
	Protocol 9	M.R. Wilson
2003	*Coyote Moon*	John A. Miller
2004	*The Pitch*	R.A. Cabral
	King of Diamonds	Don Strachan
2007	*Innings Through Time*	Chris Valenti

Appendix C

Novels That Explore Race, Ethnicity, Gender and Class

Race

1895	The Plated City	Bliss Perry
1950	The Long Discovery	John Burgan
	Behold, Thy Brother	Murrell Edmunds
1953	The Southpaw	Mark Harris
1955	Man on Spikes	Eliot Asinof
1967	The Bed Fellow	Eliot Asinof
1969	Johnny Get Your Gun	John Ball
1972	Runner Mack	Barry Beckham
1973	The Bingo Long Traveling All-Stars and Motor Kings	William Brashler
	Sam's Legacy	Jay Neugeboren
1974	The Last Western	Thomas Klise
1976	Luke	Peter Wharton
1979	The Seventh Babe	Jerome Charyn
	Chappie and Me	John Craig
1981	The Original Colored House of David	Martin Quigley
1983	Suder	Percival Everett
1985	Frisco Blues	Gordon DeMarco
1987	Getting Blue	Peter Gethers
	Countersolar	Richard Lupoff
1989	The Comeback Kids	Bob Cairns
	Prospect	Bill Littlefield
1992	All the Dead Heroes	Stephen Wilcox
	The Plot to Kill Jackie Robinson	Donald Honig
	White Heat	C.C. Risenhoover
1994	Brittle Innings	Michael Bishop
	Tigers Burning	Crabbe Evers

Appendix C: Race, Ethnicity, Gender and Class

1995	I Never Played Catch with My Father	Gene Cartwright
1996	The Last Hotel for Women	Vicki Covington
	The Veracruz Blues	Mark Winegardner
1997	The Way Home Is Longer	Christopher Renino
	Caught in a Rundown	Lisa Saxon
1998	Strikeout at Hell Gate	Robert David Jaffee
1999	In the Fall	Roy Minor
	Hanging Curve	Troy Soos
2000	Off Season	Eliot Asinof
	Havana Heat	Darryl Brock
	Royal Blue	Dennis F. Hudson
	Gold Dust	Chris Lynch
2001	Dead Ball	Richard D. Rosen
	Shadow Ball	Peter M. Rutkoff
	Opening Day	Les Standiford
2002	Roadrunner	Trisha R. Thomas
2004	Sabbath Creek	Judson Mitcham
	Double Play	Robert B. Parker
2005	Camp Ford	Johnny D. Boggs
	All the Stars Came Out That Night	Kevin King
2008	The End of Baseball	Peter Schilling, Jr.

Ethnicity

LATINO CHARACTERS OR CULTURE

1895	The Plated City	Bliss Perry
1952	The Old Man and the Sea	Ernest Hemingway
1969	Knave of Eagles	Robert Wade
1977	The Rio Loja Ringmaster	Lamar Herrin
1984	The Greatest Slump of All Time	David Carkeet
1988	Short Season and Other Stories	Jerry Klinkowitz
1995	The New York Yanquis	Bill Granger
1996	The Veracruz Blues	Mark Winegardner
1999	Castro's Curveball	Tim Wendell
2000	Havana Heat	Darryl Brock
	Be the One	April Smith
2001	A Painted House	John Grisham
2003	The Cuban Prospect	Brian Shawver
2005	All the Stars Came Out That Night	Kevin King

JEWISH CHARACTERS OR CULTURE

1965	Voices of a Summer Day	Irwin Shaw
1973	Sam's Legacy	Jay Neugeboren

1973	The Great American Novel	Philip Roth
1978	Rachel, The Rabbi's Wife	Silvia Tennenbaum
1983	The Celebrant	Eric Rolfe Greenberg
1984	The Grace of Shortstops	Robert Mayer
	Strike Three You're Dead	Richard D. Rosen
1987	Florry of Washington Heights	Steve Katz
1988	Saturday Night Dead	Richard D. Rosen
1990	Brooklyn Boy	Alan Lelchuk
1991	This Is Next Year	Philip Goldberg
	In Days of Awe	Eric Goodman
1995	The Spy in a Catcher's Mask	Kurt Willinger
1997	Snow in August	Pete Hamill
	Big League Dreams	Allen Hoffman
1998	Last Days of Summer	Steve Kluger
1999	Battle Creek	Scott Lasser
	The Rabbi of Swat	Peter Levine
2001	Breaking Balls	Paul Lebowitz
	Dead Ball	Richard D. Rosen
	The Golem's Mighty Swing	James Sturm
2007	Swap	Sam Moffie

NATIVE AMERICAN CHARACTERS OR CULTURE

1980	Muckaluck	Richard Anderson
1982	The Seventh Game	Roger Kahn
1984	The Dixie Association	Donald Hays
1986	The Iowa Baseball Confederacy	W.P. Kinsella
1992	The Cleveland Indian	Luke Salisbury
2003	The True Account	Howard Frank Mosher
2007	Miko Kings: An Indian Baseball Story	LeAnne Howe
2007	The Fade-away	George Jansen

JAPANESE AND JAPANESE AMERICAN CHARACTERS OR CULTURE

1991	Fielder's Choice	Rick Norman
1995	Japanese Game	Richard Hoyt
2006	Suitcase Sefton and the American Dream	Jay Feldman

Gender

These novels have women characters in major roles with baseball teams

1959	Stay Loose	Bud Nye
1973	A Grand Slam	Ray Puechner
1976	The Sensuous Southpaw	Paul B. Rothweiler

Appendix C: Race, Ethnicity, Gender and Class

1977	*Spitballs and Holy Water*	James F. Donahue
1978	*A Baseball Classic*	Merritt Clifton
1981	*Toot-Toot-Tootsie, Good-bye*	Ron Powers
	The Man Who Brought the Dodgers Back to Brooklyn	David Ritz
1983	*Summer Season*	Vella Munn
	Wild Roses	Sheila Paulos
	Double Play	Natalie Stone
	Home Game	Paul Quarrington
1984	*The Dixie Association*	Donald Hays
1985	*Partners*	Ken Beardslee
1987	*Can't Miss*	Michael Bowen
	She's on First	Barbara Gregorich
	Fun and Games	Anna Hudson
	Countersolar	Richard Luplof
1988	*The Dead Pull Hitter*	Alison Gordon
1989	*A Season to Remember*	Lynda Stowe Landers
1990	*Safe at Home*	Alison Gordon
	Squeeze Play	Jane Leavy
	The Year I Owned the Yankees	Sparky Lyle and David Fisher
1992	*A League of Their Own*	Sarah Gilbert
	Three Strikes, You're Dead	Michael Geller
	Night Game	Alison Gordon
	The Woman in the Dugout	Gary Lovisi and Terry Arnone
1994	*Smokey O*	Celia Cohen
1995	*Balls*	Gorman Bechard
	The Cranberry Trail	Kent Cowgill
	Striking Out	Alison Gordon
1996	*The Sweetheart Season*	Karen Joy Fowler
1997	*Prairie Hardball*	Alison Gordon
2000	*Honey*	Stef Ann Holm
	Mollie Peer: Or the Underground Adventure of the Moosepath League	Van Reid
	Be the One	April Smith
2002	*Off Season*	Marshall J. Cook
2004	*The Girl Who Saved Baseball*	Arelo C. Sederberg

Class

1838	*Home as Found*	James Fenimore Cooper
1868	*Changing Base*	William Everett
1895	*The Plated City*	Bliss Perry

1948	*The Great Blizzard*	Albert Idell
1950	*The Long Discovery*	John Burgan
1953	*Win — Or Else!*	D.J. Michaels (pseudonym of Charles Einstein)
1955	*Man on Spikes*	Eliot Asinof
1967	*The Bedfellow*	Eliot Asinof
1973	*The Bingo Long Traveling All-Stars and Motor Kings*	William Brashler
1977	*The Rio Loja Ringmaster*	Lamar Herrin
1980	*Take Me Out to the Ballgame*	Gary Morgenstein
1991	*Blue Rain*	Brendan Boyd
1992	*The Brothers K*	David James Duncan
1995	*The Aliens of Summer*	Calvin Ross
2001	*A Painted House*	John Grisham
2006	*Lights Out*	Jason Starr

Appendix D

Best Baseball Novels by Year

1916	*You Know Me Al*	Ring Lardner
1950	*The Sunlit Field*	Lucy Kennedy
1952	*The Natural*	Bernard Malamud
1968	*The Universal Baseball Association*	Robert Coover
1979	*The Seventh Babe*	Jerome Charyn
1981	*Toot-Toot-Tootsie, Good-bye*	Ron Powers
1982	*Shoeless Joe*	W. P. Kinsella
1983	*The Celebrant*	Eric Rolfe Goldberg
1984	*The Dixie Association*	Donald Hays
1991	*Blue Ruin*	Brendan Boyd
1992	*The Brothers K*	David James Duncan
	The Cleveland Indian	Luke Salisbury
1994	*Brittle Innings*	Michael Bishop
1996	*The Veracruz Blues*	Mark Winegardner
1997	*Play for a Kingdom*	Thomas Dyja
1999	*Castro's Curveball*	Tim Wendell
2000	*Havana Heat*	Darryl Brock
2001	*Shadow Ball*	Peter M. Rutkoff
2002	*Tyrus*	Patrick Creavy
2003	*The Cuban Prospect*	Brian Shawver

Second Place Novels

1923	*The Sun Field*	Heywood Broun
1953	*The Southpaw*	Mark Harris
1954	*The Year the Yankees Lost the Pennant*	Douglas Wallop
1955	*Man on Spikes*	Eliot Asinof
1973	*The Bingo Long Traveling All-Stars and Motor Kings*	William Brashler

1973	*The Great American Novel*	Phillip Roth
1977	*The Rio Loja Ringmaster*	Lamar Herrin
1983	*Hoopla*	Harry Stein
1987	*Veteran's Park*	Don J. Snyder
1999	*Hanging Curve*	Troy Soos
2005	*All the Stars Came Out That Night*	Kevin King
2006	*Suitcase Sefton and the American Dream*	Jay Feldman
2007	*The Entitled*	Frank Deford
	The Fade-away	George Jansen

Appendix E
Chronological List of Titles

1838	*Home as Found*	James Fenimore Cooper
1868	*Changing Base*	William Everett
1884	*Our Baseball Club and How It Won the Championship*	Noah Brooks
1888	*"Casey at the Bat"*	Ernest L. Thayer
1889	*A Connecticut Yankee in King Arthur's Court*	Mark Twain
1895	*The Plated City*	Bliss Perry
1902	*The Fat Mascot*	Robert Rudd Whiting
1914	*Coming Back with the Spitball*	James Hopper
1915	*The Ladder*	Philip Curtiss
	A Man's Code	W.B.M. Ferguson
1916	*You Know Me Al*	Ring Lardner
1918	*Treat 'em Rough*	Ring Lardner
1919	*The Real Dope*	Ring Lardner
	From Baseball to Boches	H.C. Witwer
	A Smile a Minute	H.C. Witwer
1920	*There's No Base Like Home*	H.C. Witwer
1923	*The Sun Field*	Heywood Broun
1925	*The Great Gatsby*	F. Scott Fitzgerald
1926	*The New Klondike*	Peggy Griffith
1929	*The Sound and the Fury*	William Faulkner
1933	*Lose with a Smile*	Ring Lardner
1934	*Death on the Diamond*	Cortland Fitzsimmons
1932–40	(novels of Farrell and Wolfe)	
1940	*Dust in the Afternoon*	Holmes Alexander
1940–70	(juvenile novels of Tunis and Scholz)	
1946	*Rhubarb*	H. Allen Smith
1947	*The Twin Killing*	George Bagby (Aaron Marc Stein)
1948	*The Turning Point*	Ed Fitzgerald
	The Great Blizzard	Albert Idell

	Flashing Spikes	Frank O'Rourke
1949	*It Happens Every Spring*	Valentine Davies
	The Team	Frank O'Rourke
1950	*The Long Discovery*	John Burgan
	Behold, Thy Brother	Murrell Edmunds
	College Slugger	Ed Fitzgerald
	The Sunlit Field	Lucy Kennedy
	Bonus Rookie	Frank O'Rourke
1951	*The Big Out*	Arnold Hano
1952	*The Old Man and the Sea*	Ernest Hemingway
	Yankee Rookie	Ed Fitzgerald
	The Natural	Bernard Malamud
	Never Come Back	Frank O'Rourke
	Nine Good Men	Frank O'Rourke
1953	*The Southpaw*	Mark Harris
	The Catcher and the Manager	Frank O'Rourke
	The Hard Way	Jack Weeks
1954	*Win — or Else!*	D.J. Michaels (Charles Einstein)
	The Year the Yankees Lost the Pennant	Douglas Wallop
1955	*Man on Spikes*	Eliot Asinof
	The Only Game in Town	Charles Einstein
	The Take-Charge Guy	Jack Weeks
1956	*Autumn Comes Early*	Howard Breslin
	Bang the Drum Slowly	Mark Harris
	A Ticket for a Seamstitch	Mark Harris
	Strictly from Brooklyn	William Heuman
1957	*The Ballplayer*	Ed Fitzgerald
1958	*Casey's Redemption*	Burgess Fitzpatrick
1959	*Stay Loose*	Bud Nye
1961	*The Orange Air*	Roy Doliner
	Squeeze Play	Walter Feldspar
1964	*A Pennant for the Kremlin*	Paul Molloy
1965	*Baseball's Darkest Days*	Kenneth L. Grantham
	Today's Game	Martin Quigley
	Voices of a Summer Day	Irwin Shaw
1966	*Letters from Lefty*	Mickey Herskowitz
1967	*The Bedfellow*	Eliot Asinof
	To Brooklyn with Love	Gerald Green
	The Chosen	Chaim Potok
1968	*The Universal Baseball Association*	Robert Coover
1969	*Johnny Get Your Gun*	John Ball
	The Last Man Is Out	Marvin Karlins
	Superbaby	Felix Mendelsohn, Jr.
	Knave of Eagles	Robert Wade
1972	*Death of a Playmate (Johnny Get Your Gun)*	John Ball
	Runner Mack	Barry Beckham

Appendix E: Chronological List of Titles

1973	*The Bingo Long Traveling All-Stars and Motor Kings*	William Brashler
	A Great Day for a Ballgame	Fielding Dawson
	A Handy Death	Fish and Rothblatt
	Babe Ruth Caught in a Snowstorm	Alexander Graham
	Wild Pitch	A.B. Guthrie
	The Idolaters	William E. Hegner
	Sam's Legacy	Jay Neugeboren
	A Grand Slam	Ray Puechner
	The Great American Novel	Philip Roth
1974	*The Devil to Play*	Leonard Holton
	The Last Western	Thomas Klise
	Flawless Play Restored	Gilbert Sorrentino
1975	*All G.O.D.'s Children*	John Craig
	The Pro# 3: Strike Zone	Richard Curtis
	The Sensation	Norman Keifitz
	Mortal Stakes	Robert B. Parker
1976	*The Journal of Leo Smith*	Randolph Linthurst
	Season's Past	Damon Rice
	The Sensuous Southpaw	Paul B. Rothweiler
	Luke	Peter Winston
1977	*Two Penny Lane*	Fielding Dawson
	Spitballs and Holy Water	James F. Donohue
	The Rio Loja Ringmaster	Lamar Herrin
	The Morning Light	Curt Johnson
	The 7th Game	Don Kowet
	The Rundown	James Magnuson
	Whichaway?	Trebor Swed
	Grandstand Rookie	Irwin Zacharia
1978	*A Baseball Classic*	Merritt Clifton
	Noonan	Leonard Everett Fisher
	The Cocaine Caper	Vincent A. Paradis
	The Screwball King Murder	Kin Platt
	Rachel, the Rabbi's Wife	Silvia Tennenbaum
1979	*Breaking Balls*	Marty Bell
	Seven Games in October	Charles Brady
	The Seventh Babe	Jerome Charyn
	Chappie and Me	John Craig
	It Looked Like Forever	Mark Harris
	Long Gone	Paul Hemphill
	The Last Great Season	Donald Honig
	It Had to Be a Woman	Paul Newlin
	Stealing Home	Philip O'Connor
	Mulligan Stew	Gilbert Sorrentino (inclusion of *Flawless Play Restored*)
1980	*Muckaluck*	Richard Anderson
	The New AToms Bombshell	Robert Browne

	Gamemaker	David Keith Cohler
	Screwballs	Jay Cronley
	Letters from Lefty (reissued)	Mickey Herskowitz
	Take Me Out to the Ballgame	Gary Morgenstein
	The Stranger City Caper	Ross H. Spencer
	Season of the Owl	Miles Wolff
1981	The Batting Machine	Mel Knopf
	Toot-Toot-Tootsie, Good-bye	Ron Powers
	The Original Colored House of David	Martin Quigley
	The Man Who Brought the Dodgers Back to Brooklyn	David Ritz
	Surfaces of a Diamond	Louis D. Rubin, Jr.
1982	Andy, the First Switch-Pitcher	Al Carmona
	Five O'Clock Lightning	William DeAndrea
	The Seventh Game	Roger Kahn
	Shoeless Joe	W.P. Kinsella
	Hit and Run	Dave Klein
	Jock and Jill	Robert Lipsyte
	Strictly Amateur	Tom McCormack
	Ballpark	Michael Schiffer
	Almost Famous	David Small
1983	Dead in Centerfield	Paul Engelman
	Suder	Percival Everett
	The Celebrant	Eric Rolfe Greenberg
	Ironweed	William Kennedy
	The Man Who Wanted to Play Center Field for the New York Yankees	Gary Morgenstein
	Summer Season	Vella Munn
	Wild Roses	Sheila Paulos
	Home Game	Paul Quarrington
	Hoopla	Harry Stein
	Double Play	Natalie Stone
1984	Squeeze Play	Paul Benjamin
	The Greatest Slump of All Time	David Carkeet
	Every Young Man's Dream	Morry Frank
	The Dixie Association	Donald Hays
	The Cheat	Pat Jordan
	Wier & Pouce	Steve Katz
	Changing Pitches	Steve Kluger
	The Grace of Shortstops	Robert Mayer
	Strike Three You're Dead	Richard D. Rosen
	Things Invisible to See	Nancy Willard
1985	Partners	Ken Beardslee
	Frisco Blues	Gordon DeMarco
	Second Brother	David Guy
	Chin Music	James McManus
	Out at Home	Gary Pomeranz

Appendix E: Chronological List of Titles

	Follow the Sharks	William G. Tapply
1986	*The Heart of the Order*	Tony Ardizzone
	Road Game	Mark H. Burch
	Child's Play	Sal Conte
	A Flatland Fable	Joe Coomer
	Largo	Bob Dews, Jr.
	The Conduct of the Game	John Hough
	The Iowa Baseball Confederacy	W.P. Kinsella
	Fever Pitch	Pamela Toth
1987	*Can't Miss*	Michael Bowen
	Getting Blue	Peter Gethers
	The Boozer Challenge	Charles Gill
	She's on First	Barbara Gregorich
	Fun and Games	Anna Hudson
	Florry of Washington Heights	Steve Katz
	Countersolar	Richard Lupoff
	The Curious Case of Sidd Finch	George Plimpton
	Veteran's Park	Don J. Snyder
	Kirby's Last Circus	Ross H. Spencer
	The Spoiler	Domenic Stansberry
1988	*Major League Murder*	Michael Geller
	The Dead Pull Hitter	Alison Gordon
	Southpaw	Frank King
	Short Season and Other Baseball Stories	Jerry Klinkowitz
	Saturday Night Dead	Richard D. Rosen
	The Eight Corners of the World	Gordon Weaver
1989	*The Comeback Kids*	Bob Cairns
	Casey on the Loose	Frank Deford
	Graves' Retreat	Ed Gorman
	A Season to Remember	Lynda Stowe Landers
	Prospect	Bill Littlefield
	Joy in Mudville	Gordon McAlpine
	Strikezone	David F. Nighbert
	Beanball	Tom Seaver and Herb Rescinow
	A Simple Suburban Murder	Mark Richard Zubro
1990	*If I Never Get Back*	Darryl Brock
	A Short History of the Long Ball	Justin Cronin
	Comeback	L.L. Enger
	Safe at Home	Alison Gordon
	A Stone of the Heart	Tom Grimes
	The Fabulous Fifty	Morton Grosser
	Gone to Glory	Robert Irvine
	California Rush	Sherwood Kiraly
	Squeeze Play	Jane Leavy
	Brooklyn Boy	Alan Lelchuk
	The Year I Owned the Yankees	Sparky Lyle and David Fisher

	No Fun on Sunday	Frederick Manfred
	Diamonds Are Trumps	Marty Slattery
1991	Fielder's Choice	Michael Bowen
	Blue Ruin	Brendan Boyd
	Swing	L.L. Enger
	Bleeding Dodger Blue	Crabbe Evers
	Murder in Wrigley Field	Crabbe Evers
	Murderer's Row	Crabbe Evers
	Suicide Squeeze	David Everson
	This Is Next Year	Philip Goldberg
	In Days of Awe	Eric Goodman
	Rookie	Jerry B. Jenkins
	Box Socials	W.P. Kinsella
	Pledge of Allegiance	Mark Lapin
	Fielder's Choice	Rick Norman
	For Love of the Game	Michael Shaara
1992	Past the Bleachers	Christopher A. Bohjalian
	What Hearts	Bruce Brooks
	The Brothers K	David James Duncan
	Strike	L.L. Enger
	Three Strikes, You're Dead	Michael Geller
	A League of Their Own	Sarah Gilbert
	Night Game	Alison Gordon
	Season's End	Tom Grimes
	Rat Palms	David Homel
	The Plot to Kill Jackie Robinson	Donald Honig
	Ball Park Numbers	David P. Hullinger
	The Dreyfus Affair	Peter Lefcourt
	The Woman in the Dugout	Gary Lovisi and Terry Arnone
	White Heat	C.C. Risenhoover
	Caught Looking	Randy Russell
	The Cleveland Indian	Luke Salisbury
	All the Dead Heroes	Stephen F. Wilcox
1993	Sometimes You See It Coming	Kevin Baker
	Yankee Belle	Richard Bennett
	The Liberty Campaign	Jonathan Dee
	Sacrifice	L.L. Enger
	Fear in Fenway	Crabbe Evers
	Spirit of the Season	Heather Graham
	Last Man Out	Donald Honig
	Open Season	Scot Moon
	Done Deal	Les Standiford
	Baseball and Benevolence	Mark Allen Valenza
	Line Drive	Bob Wake
1994	The Burglar Who Traded Ted Williams	Lawrence Block
	Brittle Innings	Michael Bishop

Appendix E: Chronological List of Titles

	Strike Zone	Jim Bouton and Eliot Asinof
	Smokey O	Celia Cohen
	The Sinner's League	L.L. Enger
	Tigers Burning	Crabbe Evers
	Drover and the Designated Hitter	Bill Granger
	The Elements of Hitting	Matthew F. Jones
	They Still Play Baseball on the Moon	James Garrett LaFemina
	Dead End Game	Christopher Newman
	Mob Power Plays	William F. Roemer, Jr.
	Murder at Fenway Park	Troy Soos
1995	The Fan	Peter Abrahams
	Balls	Gorman Bechard
	Out at the Old Ball Game	Bernie Bookbinder
	I Never Played Catch with My Father	Gene Cartwright
	The Cranberry Trail	Kent Cowgill
	Fugitive Moon	Ron Faust
	Independence Day	Richard Ford
	64 Intruder	Gregory T. Glading
	Striking Out	Alison Gordon
	The New York Yanquis	Bill Granger
	The December Rose	Robert Grant
	Japanese Game	Richard Hoyt
	A Diminished Capacity	Sherwood Kiraly
	Basepaths	Jerry Klinkowitz
	Shutout	David F. Nighbert
	The Aliens of Summer	Calvin Ross
	The Final Game	Rob Shoemaker
	Murder at Ebbets Field	Troy Soos
	The 30 Hit Season	D. Michael Tomkins
	The Spy in a Catcher's Mask	Kurt Willinger
1996	The Last Hotel for Women	Vicki Covington
	Murder in the Baseball Hall of Fame	David Daniel and Chris Carpenter
	Special Treatment	Nancy Fisher
	The Sweetheart Season	Karen Joy Fowler
	Another Jackie Robinson	M.L. Hester
	If Wishes Were Horses	W.P. Kinsella
	Diamonds	Shari MacDonald
	Chance	Steve Shilstone
	Murder at Wrigley Field	Troy Soos
	The Veracruz Blues	Mark Winegardner
	Rust on the Razor	Mark Zubro
1997	Baseball Cat	Garrison Allen
	A Double Play of Underground Baseball Novellas	Merritt Clifton (*A Baseball Classic*) and John Sandman (*Praying for Rain*)
	The Year of the Buffalo	Marshall J. Cook

	Pafko at the Wall	Don Delillo
	Underworld	Don DeLillo
	Play for a Kingdom	Thomas Dyja
	Prairie Hardball	Alison Gordon
	Snow in August	Pete Hamill
	Diamond Sutra	Colin Hester
	Big League Dreams	Allen Hoffman
	The Way Home Is Longer	Christopher Renino
	Caught in a Rundown	Lisa Saxon
	Hunting a Detroit Tiger	Troy Soos
	Isabelle's Inning	Donna Winters
1998	Brushback	K.C. Constantine
	Strikeout at Hell Gate	Robert David Jaffee
	Last Days of Summer	Steve Kluger
	The Man Who Once Played Catch with Nellie Fox	John Manderino
	Caught Stealing	Ben J. Martin
	Early Dreams	David Nemec
	The Cincinnati Red Stalkings	Troy Soos
1999	The Migration of Willie Mackerels	Mike Clarke
	The Final Detail	Harlan Coben
	Our Lady of the Outfield	David Craig
	Hardball	T. Hitman
	Taking Lottie Home	Terry Kay
	Gifts of the Gods	Robert J. Kelly
	The Girl Who Loved Tom Gordon	Stephen King
	Battle Creek	Scott Lasser
	The Rabbi of Swat	Peter Levine
	In the Fall	Roy Minor
	One More Time	Ed Orszula
	A Diamond in Spring	Donald T. Phillips
	The Bush League	Jon Sharpe
	Hanging Curve	Troy Soos
	Castro's Curveball	Tim Wendell
2000	Off-Season	Eliot Asinof
	Havana Heat	Darryl Brock
	Hardball Fever	John Carver
	The Big R	Crumbley, Ziegenfuss, and O'Shaughnessy
	The Ballplayers	Pete Filicchia
	How All This Started	Pete Fromm
	Honey	Stef Ann Holm
	Royal Blue	Dennis F. Hudson
	Perfect Silence	Jeff Hutton
	A Difficult Trade	Sam Leonard
	Gold Dust	Chris Lynch
	One of the Boys	David Mark

Appendix E: Chronological List of Titles

	The 1898 Base-Ball Fe-As-Ko	Randall Beth Platt
	Be the One	April Smith
	Sut McCaslin	Steve Spoerl
	Mollie Peer	Van Reid
	Pennants Ain't Peanuts	James A. Weber
	Blue Bayou Days	G. Artie Whitlow
	Montana Summer	Tom Yankus
2001	*God Is Alive and Well and Playing Third Base for the Appleton Papermakers*	Max Blue
	Sport	Mike Cochran
	Columbus Slaughters Braves	Mark Friedman
	A Painted House	John Grisham
	The Hunting Wind	Steve Hamilton
	Magic Time	W.P. Kinsella
	Breaking Balls	Paul Lebowitz
	Project Samuel	J.P. Polidoro
	Base Hit	Alan Posner
	Seven Lives, Seven Games	Ravi P. Rao
	Dead Ball	Richard D. Rosen
	Shadow Ball	Peter M. Rutkoff
	Opening Day	Les Standiford
	The Golem's Mighty Swing	James Sturm
	Crooked River Burning	Mark Winegardner
	About 80 Percent Luck	Gene Wojciechowski
2002	*Gift of the Bambino*	Jerry Amernic
	Cards	Rae Andre
	Old Hoss	James W. Bennett and Donald Raycraft
	Two in the Field	Darryl Brock
	Bite of the Shark	John J. Buro
	The Streak	Bill Chastain
	Summerland	Michael Chabon
	Tyrus	Patrick Creavy
	A Prince at First	Ed Dinger
	Yank	Norman Ferris
	Things Got in the Way	Robert Holland
	The Youngest Hero	Jerry Jenkins (reissue of *Rookie*)
	The New Paltz Outlaws	Farrell Kaye
	Wild Pitch	Mike Lupica
	The Kid Who Batted 1.000	Troon McAllister
	The Rail	Howard Owen
	Slider	Patrick Robinson
	Roadrunner	Trish R. Thomas
	Protocol 9	M.R. Wilson
2003	*Screwball*	David Ferrell
	Havana World Series	Jose Latour

	Heroes Are Hard to Find	Mike Looney
	Coyote Moon	John A. Miller
	The True Account	Howard Frank Mosher
	Best Bet in Beantown	G.S. Rowe
	The Cuban Prospect	Brian Shawver
	Ballpark Blues	C.W. Tooke
	The Perfect Game	Craig J. Weincek
2004	*The Pitch*	R.A. Cabral
	Caught Stealing	Charlie Huston
	7,000 Clams	Lee Irby
	End of a Dynasty	Andrew Maloney
	Dream Season	E. Dee Meeriken
	Sabbath Creek	Judson Mitcham
	Waiting for Teddy Williams	Howard Frank Mosher
	Double Play	Robert B. Parker
	Squeeze Play in Beantown	G.S. Rowe
	The Girl Who Saved Baseball	Arelo C. Sederberg
	King of Diamonds	Don Strachan
2005	*Camp Ford*	Johnny D. Boggs
	The Perfect Pafko	Robert Booth
	The Deadly Tools of Ignorance	Robert Elias
	Scooter	Mick Foley
	Reno	Marty Gervais
	The Ha-Ha	Dave King
	All the Stars Came Out That Night	Kevin King
	Cooperstown	Eugena Pilek
	Double Play in Beantown	G.S. Rowe
	Pray for Rain	Jason Wuerfel
2006	*Squeeze Play*	Kate Angell
	Murder, She Wrote: Three Strikes and You're Dead	Donald Bain
	Hitting in the Clutch	Brad Bauer
	Dreaming Baseball	James T. Farrell
	Suitcase Sefton and the American Dream	Jay Feldman
	The Unknown Baseball Player	Marvin P. Ferguson
	The King's Game	John Nemo
	Foul Ball in Beantown	G.S. Rowe
	Lights Out	Jason Starr
2007	*Curveball*	Kate Angell
	Homering in the Clutch	Brad Bauer
	Foul Play	Tori Carrington
	The Entitled	Frank Deford
	Dreaming Baseball	James T. Farrell
	7: The Mickey Mantle Novel	Peter Golenbock
	Miko Kings: An Indian Baseball Story	LeAnne Howe
	Season of Gene	Dallas Hudgens

	The Fade-away	George Jansen
	The Marinolli Treasure	Hal Lewis
	Swap	Sam Moffie
	Just Joe	Thomas K. Perry
	Journeymen	Michael Rychlik
	Innings Through Time	Christopher Valenti
2008	*Once Upon a Fastball*	Bob Mitchell
	End of Baseball	Peter Schilling

Index

About 80 Percent Luck 174
Abrahams, Peter 135
African American novelists 11, 16, 21, 65, 90, 152, 182
Alexander, Holmes 7, 45
The Aliens of Summer 19, 140–41
All G.O.D.'s Children 12, 71
All the Dead Heroes 127
All the Stars Came Out That Night 30, 194–95
Allen, Garrison 21, 147–48
Almost Famous 89–90
Amernic, Jerry 28, 174–75
Anderson, Richard 81–82
Andre, Rae 25, 175
Andy, the First Switch-Pitcher 86
Angell, Kate 197, 200–1
Another Jackie Robinson 144–45
Ardizzone, Tony 99
Arnone, Terry 21, 125–26
Asinof, Eliot 7, 9, 30, 34, 55–56, 62, 132, 161
Autumn Comes Early 8, 56–57

Babe Ruth Caught in a Snowstorm 10, 66–67
Bagby, George (Aaron Marc Stein) 6, 47
Bain, Donald 197
Baker, Kevin 127–28
Ball, John 9, 63, 65
Ball Park Numbers 125
Ballpark 15, 89
Ballpark Blues 186
The Ballplayer 58
The Ballplayers 163
Balls 21, 136
Bang the Drum Slowly 57

Base Hit 171
Baseball and Benevolence 130–31
Baseball cards 25, 113–14, 176–77, 191–92, 205
Baseball Cat 21, 147–48
A Baseball Classic 76–77
Baseball Joe, Home-run King 4
Baseball Joe of the Silver Stars 4, 39
Baseball Joe on the School Nine 4, 39
Baseball's Darkest Days 8, 60–61
Basepaths 26, 140
The Batting Machine 13, 84–85
Battle Creek 26, 158
Bauer, Brad 197–98, 201
Be the One 27, 166–67
Beanball 110–11
Beardslee, Ken 97
Beaumont, Gerald 42
Bechard, Gorman 21, 136
Beckham, Barry 11, 65
The Bedfellow 9, 62
Behold, Thy Brother 7, 49–50
Bell, Marty 12, 78
Benjamin, Paul 93–94
Bennett, James W. 28
Bennett, Richard 128
Berg, Moe 17, 24, 127–28, 142–43
Best Bet in Beantown 29, 185
Big League Dreams 23, 150–51
The Big Out 57
The Big R 162–63
The Bingo Long Traveling All-Stars and Motor Kings 10, 66
Bishop, Michael 20, 34, 131–32
Bite of the Shark 25, 176–77
Black Sox Scandal 16, 34, 93, 116–17, 172, 178, 202–3, 206

239

Bleeding Dodger Blue 18, 117
Block, Lawrence 25, 132
Blue, Max 168
Blue Bayou Days 168
Blue Ruin 16, 34, 116–17
Boggs, Johnny D. 34, 191–92
Bohjalian, Christopher 25, 121
Bonus Rookie 6, 51
Bookbinder, Bernie 22, 136
Booth, Robert 25, 192
The Boozer Challenge 103
Bouton, Jim 132
Bowen, Michael 14, 102, 116
Box Socials 119–20
Boyd, Brendan 16, 34, 116
Bradley, Matt 60
Brady, Charles 78
Brashler, William 10, 66
Breaking Balls (Bell) 12, 78
Breaking Balls (Lebowitz) 33, 170–71
Breslin, Howard 56–57
The Bride and the Pennant 4
Brittle Innings 20, 26, 34, 131–32
Brock, Darry 19, 27, 31, 111–12, 161–62, 176
Brooklyn Boy 114
Brooks, Bruce 25, 121
Brooks, Noah 3, 36
The Brothers K 23, 34, 121–22
Broun, Heywood 5, 42
Browne, Robert 82
Brushback 153
Burch, Mark H. 99–100
Burgan, John 7, 49
The Burglar Who Traded Ted Wiliams 25, 132
Buro, John J. 25, 176–77
The Bush League 160

Cabral, R.A. 31, 187
Cairns, Bob 16, 108
California Rush 113–14
Camp Ford 34, 191–92
Can't Miss 14, 102
Cards 25, 175
Carkeet, David 94
Carmona, Al 86
Carpenter, Chris 143
Carrington, Tori 201–2
Cartwright, Gene 25, 136–37
Carver, John 162
"Casey at the Bat" 3, 36
Casey on the Loose 14, 108–9
Casey's Redemption 8, 58
Castro's Curveball 27, 34, 160–1
The Catcher and the Manager 54
Caught in a Rundown 21, 152

Caught Looking 126
Caught Stealing (Huston) 187
Caught Stealing (Martin) 27, 154–55
The Celebrant 16, 17, 24, 34, 90–91
Chabon, Michael 25, 31, 177
Chadwick, Lester 4, 39
Chance 145–46
Chance, Frank 4, 178–79
Changing Base 3, 35
Changing Pitches 15, 22, 96
Chappie and Me 10, 79
Charyn, Jerome 10, 26, 34, 78–79
Chastain, Bill 30, 177
The Cheat 95
Child's Play 13, 100
Chin Music 98
The Chosen 62
The Cincinnati Red Stalkings 18, 155
Civil War in fiction 23, 34, 149, 164, 191–92
Clarke, Mike 155–56
Class 223–24
The Cleveland Indian 24, 127
Clifton, Merritt 76–77
Cobb, Ty 28, 34, 93, 135, 150–51, 152, 178
Coben, Harlan 156
The Cocaine Caper 12, 77
Cochran, Mike 168–69
Cohen, Celia 20, 132–33
Cohler, David Keith 82
College novels 4, 37, 50, 152–53, 181–82, 196–97
College Slugger 50
Columbus Slaughters Braves 169
Comeback 98, 112
The Comeback Kids 16, 108
Coming Back with the Spitball 39
Comiskey, Charles 93, 116–17, 172–73, 206
The Conduct of the Game 15, 101
A Connecticut Yankee in King Arthur's Court 4, 36
Constantine, K.C. 153
Conte, Sal 13, 100
Cook, Marshall J. 26, 148, 177
Coomer, Jay 25, 100
Cooper, James Fenimore 3, 35
Cooperstown 33, 195–96
Coover, Robert 9, 34, 62–63
Countersolar 13, 104
Covington, Vicki 26, 143
Cowgill, Kent 21, 137
Coyote Moon 31, 184
Craig, David 156–57
Craig, John 10, 12, 26, 71, 79
The Cranberry Trail 21, 137
Creavy, Patrick 28, 34, 178

Cronin, Justin 112
Cronley, Jay 12, 82–83
Crooked River Burning 13, 173–74
Crumbley, Larry 162–63
The Cuban Prospect 27, 34, 185–86
The Curious Case of Sidd Finch 13, 31, 104–5
Curtis, Philip 4, 39
Curtis, Richard 71
Curveball 200–1

Damn Yankees 8, 20, 34, 55
Daniel, David 143
Davies, Valentine 6, 48
Dawson, Fielding 66, 73–74
Dead Ball 15, 30, 172
Dead End Game 134
Dead in Centerfield 90
The Dead Pull Hitter 15, 106, 172
The Deadly Tools of Ignorance 192–93
De Andrea, William 86–87
Death of a Playmate 65
Death on the Diamond 6, 44
The December Rose 139
Dee, Jonathan 128–29
DeFord, Frank 14, 108–9, 202
DeLillo, Don 25, 148–49
DeMarco, Gordon 16, 97–98
The Devil to Play 12, 69–70
Dews, Bob, Jr. 100–1
A Diamond in Spring 159–60
Diamond Sutra 25, 150
Diamonds 143
Diamonds Are Trumps 115–16
A Difficult Trade 164–65
DiMaggio, Joe 67, 172, 194–95
A Diminished Capacity 25, 139–40
Dinger, Ed 28, 178–79
The Dixie Association 17, 25, 34, 94–95
Doliner, Ray 9, 59
Done Deal 130
Donohue, James F. 11, 74
Double Play (Parker) 189–90
Double Play (Stone) 93
Double Play in Beantown 29, 196
The Double Squeeze 40
Dream Season 28, 188
Dreaming Baseball 202–3
The Dreyfus Affair 22, 125
Drover and the Designated Hitter 133
Duncan, David James 23, 34, 121–22
Durocher, Leo 45, 162, 194–95
Dust in the Afternoon 7, 45
Dyja, Thomas 22, 34, 149

Early Dreams 22, 155
Edmunds, Murrell 7, 49–50

The Eight Corners of the World 17, 24, 107–8
The 1898 Baseball Fe-As-Ko 29, 166
Einstein, Charles 8, 55, 56
The Elements of Hitting 25, 133–34
Elias, Robert 192–93
End of a Dynasty 188
The End of Baseball 208
Enger, L.L. 18, 112, 117, 122, 129, 133
Engleman, Paul 90
The Entitled 202
Everett, Percival L. 16, 90
Everett, William 3, 35
Evers, Crabbe 18, 117–18, 129, 133
Everson, David 118
Every Young Man's Dream 26, 94

The Fabulous Fifty 113
The Fade-away 204–5
The Fan 135
Farrell, James T. 6, 44–45, 202–3
The Fat Mascot 4, 37
Father and Son 44
Faulkner, William 6, 43
Faust, Ron 25, 137
Fear in Fenway 18, 129
Feldman, Jay 31, 198
Feldspar, Walter 9, 59
Ferguson, Marvin P. 198–99
Ferguson, W.B.M. 5, 40
Ferrell, David 32, 183
Ferris, Norman 179
Fever Pitch 102
Field of Dreams 87–88
Fielder's Choice (Bowen) 116
Fielder's Choice (Norman) 23, 120
Filicchia, Ralph 163
The Final Detail 156
The Final Game 141
Fish, Robert L. 66
Fisher, David 20, 115
Fisher, Leonard 11, 77
Fisher, Nancy 143–44
Fitzgerald, Ed 6, 47, 50, 51, 58
Fitzgerald, F. Scott 6, 42
Fitzpatrick, Burgess 8, 58
Fitzsimmons, Cortland 6, 44
Five O'Clock Lightning 86–87
Flashing Spikes 6, 48
A Flatland Fable 25, 100
Flawless Play Restored 70–71
Florry of Washington Heights 104
Foley, Mick 193
Follow the Sharks 99
For Love of the Game 120–21
Ford, Richard 137–38

Foul Ball in Beantown 29, 199–200
Foul Play 201
Fowler, Karen J. 20, 144
Frank, Morry 26, 94
Frank Merriwell's Danger 4, 37
Frank Merriwell's Double Shot 37
Friedman, Mark 169
Frisco Blues 16, 97–98
From Baseball to Boches 5, 41
Fromm, Pete 32, 163
Fugitive Moon 25, 137
Fun and Games 104

Gamemaker 82
Gehrig, Lou 107–8, 194–95
Geller, Michael 15, 19, 106, 122–23
Gender 222–23
Gervais, Marty 193–94
Gethers, Pete 16, 102–3
Getting Blue 16, 102–3
Gibson, Josh 104, 175, 194–95, 208
Gift of the Bambino 28, 174–75
Gifts of the Gods 157–58
Gilbert, Sarah 20, 123
Gill, Charles 103
The Girl Who Loved Tom Gordon 21, 158
The Girl Who Saved Baseball 32, 190–91
Glading, Gregory T. 138
God Is Alive and Well and Playing Third Base for the Appleton Papermakers 168
Gold Dust 25, 165
Goldberg, Philip 24, 118
The Golem's Mighty Swing 173
Golenbock, Peter 203
Gone to Glory 113
Goodman, Eric 24, 119
Gordon, Alison 15, 18, 106, 112, 123, 138, 149–50
Gorman, Ed 109
The Grace of Shortstops 96
Graham, Alexander 10, 66–67
Graham, Heather 129
A Grand Slam 9, 32, 68
Grandstand Rookie 76
Granger, Bill 19, 26, 133, 138–39
Grant, Robert 139
Grantham, Kenneth L. 8, 60–61
Graves' Retreat 109
The Great American Novel 9, 34, 69
The Great Blizzard 7, 47
A Great Day for a Ballgame 66
The Great Gatsby 6, 42
The Greatest Slump of All Time 94
Green, Gerald 62
Greenberg, Eric Rolfe 16, 34, 90–91
Gregorich, Barbara 14, 103

Grey, Zane 4, 38
Griffith, Peggy 5, 43
Grimes, Tom 24, 113, 123–24
Grisham, John 33, 169
Grosser, Morton 113
Guthrie, A.B. 12, 67
Guy, David 98

The Ha-Ha 194
Hamill, Pete 20, 150
Hamilton, Steve 169–70
A Handy Death 12, 66
Hanging Curve 18, 160
Hano, Arnold 6, 51
The Hard Way 54–55
Hardball 22, 157
Hardball Fever 162
Harris, Mark 7, 34, 53–54, 57, 79–80
Havana Heat 27, 34, 161–62
Havana World Series 27, 183
Hays, Donald 17, 34, 94–95
The Heart of the Order 99
Hearts and the Diamond 42
Hegner, William E. 67
Hemingway, Ernest 7, 52
Hemphill, Paul 11, 26, 80
Heroes Are Hard to Find 184
Herrin, Lamar 10, 34, 74–75
Herskowitz, Mickey 61–62, 83
Hester, Colin 25, 150
Hester, M.L. 144–45
Heuman, William 57–58
Hit and Run 88
Hitman, T. 22, 157
Hitting in the Clutch 197–98
Hoffman, Allen 23, 150–51
Holland, Robert 179
Holm, Stef Ann 163
Holton, Leonard 69–70
Home as Found 3, 35
Home Game 13, 92–93
Homel, David 124
Homering in the Clutch 201
Homosexuals 96, 101, 125, 132–33, 136, 147, 149–50
Honey 163
Honig, Donald 12, 19, 80–81, 124–25, 129–30
Hoopla 16, 34, 93
Hopper, James 39
Hot Curves 9, 60
Hough, John 15, 101
How All This Started 32, 163
Howe, LeAnne 203–4
Hoyt, Richard 139
Hudgens, Dallas 204

Hudson, Anna 104
Hudson, Dennis F. 163–64
Hullinger, David P. 125
Hunting a Detroit Tiger 18, 152
The Hunting Wind 169–70
Huston, Charlie 187
Hutton, Jeff 23, 34, 164

I Never Played Catch with My Father 25, 136–37
Idell, Albert E. 7, 47–48
The Idolaters 67
If I Never Get Back 19, 31, 111–12
If Wishes Were Horses 20, 143
In Days of Awe 24, 119
In the Fall 26, 159
Independence Day 137–38
Innings Through Time 207–8
Iowa Baseball Confederacy 13, 101–2
Irby, Lee 29, 187–88
Ironweed 91
Irvine, Robert 113
Isabelle's Innings 21, 152–53
It Had to Be a Woman 81
It Happens Every Spring 6, 31, 48
It Looked Like Forever 79–80

Jackson, Shoeless Joe 87–88, 194–95, 206
Jaffe, Robert David 26, 153
Jansen, George 204–5
Japanese Game 139
Jenkins, Jerry B. 119, 180
Jock and Jill 88–89
Johnny Get Your Gun 9, 63
Johnson, Curt 75
Johnson, Nunnally 32
Jones, Matthew F. 25, 133–34
Jordan, Pat 95
The Journal of Leo Smith 72
Journeymen 208
Joy in Mudville 14, 110
Just Joe 206

Kahn, Roger 15, 87
Karlins, Marvin 8, 64
Katz, Steve 95–96, 104
Kay, Terry 26, 157
Kaye, Farrell 157, 180
Keifitz, Norman 71–72
Kelly, Robert J. 157–58
Kennedy, Lucy 7, 34, 50–51
Kennedy, William 91
The Kid Who Batted 1.000 31, 181
King, Dave 194
King, Frank 106–7
King, Kevin 30, 194–95

King, Stephen 21, 158
King of Diamonds 31, 191
The King's Game 199
Kinsella, W.P. 13, 20, 31, 34, 87–88, 98, 101–2, 107, 119–20, 145, 170
Kiraly, Sherwood 25, 113–14, 139–40
Kirby's Last Circus 105
Klein, Dave 88, 139–40
Klinkowitz, Jerry 26, 107, 140
Klise, Thomas 11, 70
Kluger, Steve 15, 23, 96, 153–54
Knave of Eagles 9, 65
Knopf, Mel 13, 84–85
Kowet, Don 75

The Ladder 4, 39
LaFemina, James Garrett 19, 134
Landers, Lynda Stowe 109
Landis, Kenesaw Mountain 93, 116–17, 172–73, 194–95, 206–07
Lapin, Mark 120
Lardner, Ring 5, 40, 41, 44
Largo 100–1
Lasser, Scott 158
Last Days of Summer 23, 153–54
The Last Great Season 80–81
The Last Hotel for Women 26, 143
The Last Man Is Out 8, 12, 64
Last Man Out 19, 129–30
The Last Western 11, 70
Latour, Jose 27, 183
A League of Their Own 20, 123
Leavy, Jane 21, 114
Lebowitz, Paul 33, 170–71
Lefcourt, Peter 22, 125
Lelchuk, Alan 114
Leonard, Sam 164–65
Letters from Lefty 9, 61–62, 83
Levine, Peter 23, 158–59
Lewis, Hal 25, 205–6
The Liberty Campaign 128–29
Lights Out 200
Line Drive 131
Linthurst, Randolph 72
Lipsyte, Robert 88–89
Littlefield, Bill 109–10
The Long Discovery 7, 49
Long Gone 11, 26, 80
Looney, Mike 184
Lose with a Smile 5, 44
Lovisi, Gary 21, 125–26
Luke 73
Lupica, Mike 180–81
Lupoff, Richard 13, 104
Lyle, Sparky 20, 115
Lynch, Chris 25, 165

MacDonald, Shari 145
Magic Time 31, 170
Magnuson, James 12, 75
Major League Murder 15, 106
Malamud, Bernard 7, 34, 52–53
Maloney, Andrew 188
Man on Spikes 7, 34, 55–56
The Man Who Brought the Dodgers Back to Brooklyn 14, 85–86
The Man Who Once Played Catch with Nellie Fox 26, 154
The Man Who Wanted to Play Center Field for the New York Yankees 13, 91–92
Manderino, John 26, 91–92
Manfred, Frederick 22, 115
Mantle, Mickey 164, 168, 202–3
The Marinolli Treasure 25, 205–6
Maris, Roger 90, 113, 136, 168
Mark, David 165–66
Marlowe, Dan J. 98
Martin, Ben J. 27, 154–55
Mathewson, Christy 4, 16, 17, 24, 34, 38, 90–91, 161–62, 178–79
Mayer, Robert 96
McAllister, Troon 31, 181
McAlpine, Gordon 14, 110
McCormack, Tom 89
McGraw, John 91, 142, 161–62
McManus, James 98
Meerikens, E. Dee 28, 188
Mendolsohn, Felix, Jr. 8, 64–65
The Migration of Willie Mackerels 155–56
Miko Kings 203–4
Miller, John A. 32, 184
Minor, Roy 26, 159
"Miss Gulp" 32
Mitcham, Judson 31, 189
Mitchell, Bob 208
Mob Power Plays 134
Moffie, Sam 206
Mollie Peer 29, 166
Molloy, Paul 8, 60
Montana Summer 168
Moon, Scot 19, 130
Morgenstein, Gary 12, 13, 83, 91–92
The Morning Light 75
Mortal Stakes 12, 29, 72
Mosher, Howard Frank 29, 32, 184–85, 189
Muckaluck 81–82
Munn, Vella 92
Murder at Ebbets Field 18, 142
Murder at Fenway Park 18, 135
Murder at the Baseball Hall of Fame 143
Murder at Wrigley Field 18, 146
Murder in Wrigley Field 18, 117–18

Murder, She Wrote: Three Strikes and You're Dead 197
Mystery novels 209–14

The Natural 7, 34, 52–53
Needham, Henry 40
Nemec, David 22, 155
Nemo, John 199
Neugeboren, Jay 10, 66
Never Come Back 53
New AToms Bombshell 12, 82
The New Klondike 5, 43
The New Paltz Outlaws 180
The New York Yanquis 27, 138–39
Newlin, Paul 81
Newman, Christopher 134
Nighbert, David F. 134
Night Game 123
Nine Good Men 53
No Fun on Sunday 22, 115
No Star Is Lost 44
Noonan 11, 77
Norman, Rick 23, 120, 126
Nye, Bud 8, 58–59

O'Connor, Philip 81
Of Time and the River 45
Off Season (Cook) 177
Off-Season (Asinof) 161
Old Hoss 28, 175–76
The Old Man and the Sea 7, 52
The Old West 81–82, 109, 160, 163, 166, 184–85
Once Upon a Fastball 208
One More Time 159
One of the Boys 165–66
The Only Game in Town 8, 55–56
Open Season 19, 130
Opening Day 31, 173
The Orange Air 9, 59
The Original Colored House of David 10, 85
O'Rourke, Frank 6, 48, 49, 51, 53, 54
Orszula, Ed 159
O'Shaughnessy, John J. 162–63
Our Baseball Club and How It Won the Championship 3, 36
Our Lady of the Outfield 156–57
Out at Home 98–99
Out at the Old Ballgame 136
Owen, Howard 33, 181

Pafko at the Wall 25, 148
Paige, Satchel 66, 173, 174, 194–95, 208
A Painted House 33, 169
Paradis, Vincent A. 77

Parker, Robert B. 12, 29, 72, 189–90
Partners 97
Past the Bleachers 25, 121
Paulos, Sheila 92
A Pennant for the Kremlin 8, 60
Pennants Ain't Peanuts 167
The Perfect Game 31, 186–87
The Perfect Pafko 25, 191–92
Perfect Silence 23, 34, 164
Perry, Bliss 4, 36–37
Perry, Thomas K. 206
Phillips, Donald T. 159–60
Pilek, Eugena 33, 195–96
The Pitch 31, 187
The Plated City 4, 36–37
Platt, Kin 77
Platt, Randall Beth 29, 166
Play for a Kingdom 22, 34, 149
Pledge of Allegiance 120
Plimpton, George 13, 104–5
The Plot to Kill Jackie Robinson 124–25
Polidoro, J.P. 31, 171
Pomeranz, Gary 98–99
Posner, Alan 171
Potok, Chaim 62
Powers, Ron 14, 34, 84
Prairie Hardball 18, 149–50
Pray for Rain 196–97
Praying for Rain 151–52
A Prince at First 28, 178–79
The Pro #3: Strikezone 12, 71
Project Samuel 31, 171
Prospect 16, 109–10
Protocol 9 31, 182–83
Puechner, Ray 9, 32, 68

Quarrington, Paul 13, 92–93
Quigley, Martin 8, 10, 26, 61, 85

The Rabbi of Swat 23, 158–59
Race 220–21
The Rachel Rabbi's Wife 77–78
Radbourn, Charles 28, 72, 175–76
The Rail 33, 181
Rao, Ravi P. 171–72
Rat Palms 124
Raycraft, Donald 28, 175–76
The Real Dope 41
The Red Headed Outfield and Other Baseball Stories 4, 36
Reid, Van 29, 166
Renino, Christopher 26, 151
Reno 193–94
Rescinow, Herb 110, 11
Rhubarb 6, 47
Rice, Damon 10, 72–73

The Rio Loja Ringmaster 10, 34, 74–75
Risenhoover, C.C. 26, 126
Ritz, David 14, 85–86
Road Game 99–100
Roadrunner 182
Robinson, Jackie 19, 29, 118, 124–25, 150, 189–90
Robinson, Patrick 182
Roemer, William F., Jr. 134
Rookie 119
Rosen, Richard D. 15, 30, 96–97, 107, 172
Ross, Calvin 19, 140–41
Roth, Philip 9, 34, 69
Rothblatt, Henry 12, 66
Rothweiler, Paul B. 9, 73
Rowe, G.S. 22, 29, 190, 196, 199–200
Royal Blue 163–64
Rubin, Louis D., Jr. 86
The Rundown 12, 85
Russell, Randy 126
Rust on the Razor 19, 22, 147
Ruth, Babe 4, 10, 28, 29, 66–67, 68, 74, 90, 107–8, 110, 118, 129, 142–43, 146–47, 164, 184–85, 187–88, 194–95
Rutkoff, Peter M. 30, 34, 172–73
Rychlik, Michael 208

Sabbath Creek 31, 189
Sacrifice 129
Safe at Home 18, 112
Salisbury, Luke 24, 127
Sam's Legacy 10, 68
Sandman, John 151–52
Saturday Night Dead 107
Saxon, Lisa 21, 152
Schiffer, Michael 15, 89
Schilling, Peter, Jr. 208
Scholz, Jackson 6, 46
Scooter 193
Screwball 32, 183
The Screwball King Murder 12, 71
Screwballs 12, 82–83
Season of Gene 204
Season of the Owl 83–84
A Season to Remember 109
Season's End 24, 123–24
Seasons Past 10, 72–73
Seaver, Tom 110–11
Second Brother 98
Sederberg, Arelo C. 32, 190–91
The Sensation 71–72
The Sensuous Southpaw 9, 73
7: The Mickey Mantle Novel 203
Seven Games in October 12, 78
Seven Lives, Seven Games 171–72
7,000 Clams 29, 187–88

The Seventh Babe 10, 34, 78–79
The 7th Game 12, 75
The Seventh Game 15, 87
Shaara, Michael 120–21
Shadow Ball 30, 34, 172–73
Sharpe, Jon, 160
Shaw, Irwin 9, 61
Shawver, Brian 27, 34, 185–86
Shelstone, Steve 145–46
She's on First 14, 103
Shoeless Joe 13, 34, 87–88
Shoemaker, Rob 141
A Short History of the Long Ball 112
Short Season and Other Baseball Stories 26, 107
The Shortstop 4, 38
Shot heard round the world (Miracle of Coogan's Bluff) 84, 148–49, 208
Shutout 140
A Simple Suburban Murder 15, 111
The Sinner's League 133
64 Intruder 138
Slattery Marty 115–16
Slider 182
Small, David 89–90
A Smile a Minute 42
Smith, April 27, 166–67
Smith, H. Allen 6, 47
Smokey O 20, 22, 132–33
Snow in August 20 150
Snyder, Don J. 105
Sometimes You See It Coming 127–28
Soos, Troy 17, 18, 22, 29, 135, 146, 155, 160
Sorrentino, Gilbert 70–71, 81, 141–42, 152
The Sound and the Fury 6, 43
Southpaw 106–7
The Southpaw 7, 34, 53–54
Special Treatment 143–44
Spencer, Ross 83, 105
Spirit of the Season 129
Spitballs and Holy Water 11, 74
Spoerl, Steve 169
Sport 168–69
The Spy in a Catcher's Mask 24, 142–43
Squeeze Play (Angell) 197
Squeeze Play (Benjamin) 93–94
Squeeze Play (Feldspar) 9, 59
Squeeze Play (Leavy) 21, 114
Squeeze Play in Beantown 29, 190
Squeezeplay (Nighbert) 126
Standiford, Les 31, 130, 173
Standish, Burt L. 4, 37, 38
Stansberry, Domenic 105–6
Starr, Jason 200
Stay Loose 81
Stealing Home 181

Stein, Harry 16, 34, 93
Stengel, Casey 44, 142, 152
Stone, Natalie 93
A Stone of the Heart 113
Strachan, Don 31, 191
Stranger City Caper 83
The Streak 30, 177
Strictly Amateur 89
Strictly from Brooklyn 57–58
Strike 122
Strike Three You're Dead 15, 96–97
Strike Zone 132
Strikeout at Hell Gate 26, 153
Strikezone 110
Striking Out 138
Studs Lonigan Trilogy 44, 203
Sturm, James 173
Suder, 16, 90
Suicide Squeeze 118–19
Suitcase Sefton and the American Dream 31, 198
Summer Season 92
Summerland 25, 31, 177
The Sun Field 5, 42
The Sunlit Field 7, 34, 50–51
Superbaby 8, 64–65
Surfaces of a Diamond 86
Sut McCaslin 167
Swap 206
Swed, Trebor 75–76
The Sweetheart Season 20, 144
Swing 117

The Take-Charge Guy 56
Take Me Out to the Ballgame 12, 83
Taking Lottie Home 26, 157
Tapply, William G. 99
The Team 49
Tennenbaum, Silvia 77–78
Thayer, Ernest L. 3, 36
There's No Base Like Home 5, 42
They Still Play Baseball on the Moon 19, 134
Things Got in the Way 179
Things Invisible to See 97
The 30 Hit Season 20, 142
This Is Next Year 24, 118
Thomas, Trisha R. 182
Three Strikes, You're Dead 122–23
The Thrill of the Grass 98
A Ticket for a Seamstitch 57
Tigers Burning 18, 133
To Brooklyn with Love 62
Today's Game 8, 61
Tomkins, D. Michael 20, 142
Tooke, C.W. 186
Toot-Toot-Tootsie, Good-bye 14, 34, 84

Toth, Pamela 102
Treat 'Em Rough 41
The True Account 29, 184–85
Tunis, John R. 6, 46
The Turning Point 6, 47
Twain, Mark 4, 36
The Twin Killing 6, 47
Two in the Field 19, 31, 176
Two Penny Lane 73–74
Tyrus 28, 34, 178

Underworld, 148–49
Universal Baseball Association, Inc,. J. Henry Waugh, Prop. 9, 34, 62–63
The Unknown Baseball Player 198–99

Valenti, Christopher 207–8
Valenza, Mark 130–31
The Veracruz Blues 27, 33, 34, 146–47
Veterans Park 105
Voices of a Summer Day 9, 61

Wade, Robert 65, 131
Waiting for Teddy Williams 32, 189
Wake, Bob 131
Wallop, Douglas 8, 34, 55, 107–8
The Way Home Is Longer 26, 151
Weaver, Buck 87–88, 93, 116–17, 202, 206
Weaver, Gordon 17, 24, 107–8
Weber, James A. 167
Weeks, Jack 6, 54–55, 56
Weincek, Craig J. 31, 186–87
Wendell, Tim 27, 34, 160–61
What Hearts 25, 121
Wheeler, John 38
Whichaway? 75–76
White Heat 26, 126
Whiting, Robert Rudd 4, 37
Whitlow, G. Artie 168

Wier & Pouce 95–96
Wilcox, Stephen F. 127
Wild Pitch (Guthrie) 12, 67
Wild Pitch (Lupica) 180–81
Wild Roses 92
Willard, Nancy 97
Williams, Ted 31, 171, 206
Willinger, Kurt 24, 142
Wilson, M.R. 31, 182–83
Win — or Else! 8, 55
Winegardner, Mark 27, 33, 34, 146–47, 173–74
Winston, Peter 73
Winters, Donna 21, 152–53
Witwer, H.C. 5, 41–42
Wojciechowski, Gene 174
Wolfe, Thomas 6, 45
Wolff, Miles 83–84
Woman in the Dugout 21, 125–26
Won in the Ninth 4, 39
Wuerfel, Jason 168

Yank 179
Yankee Belle 128
Yankus, Tom 168
The Year I Owned the Yankees 20, 115
The Year of the Buffalo 26, 148
The Year the Yankees Lost the Pennant 8, 20, 34, 55
You Can't Go Home Again 45
You Know Me Al 5, 34, 40
The Young Pitcher 4, 38
The Youngest Hero 180

Zacharia, Irwin 76
Ziegenfuss, Douglas E. 162–63
Zubro, Mark Richard 15, 19, 111, 147

www.ingramcontent.com/pod-product-compliance
Ingram Content Group UK Ltd.
Pitfield, Milton Keynes, MK11 3LW, UK
UKHW041938140426
5217IPUK00014B/540